BOOK REVIEWS

The main characters' faith and perseverance throughout their trials are inspiring and engaging. The adventures in this novel are reminiscent of Lewis' Chronicles of Narnia.

Lovers of Christian fantasy might find the author's book fits the bill.

Her perspective is the most interesting and hints at more to come.

—The US Review of Books

THE VISION OF THE QUEST

KIMBERLY COLE

Copyright © 2024 Kimberly Cole.
www.kcstories4life.com

All rights reserved. No part of this book may be reproduced, stored, or transmitted by any means—whether auditory, graphic, mechanical, or electronic—without written permission of both publisher and author, except in the case of brief excerpts used in critical articles and reviews. Unauthorized reproduction of any part of this work is illegal and is punishable by law.

ISBN: 979-8-89419-176-8 (sc)
ISBN: 979-8-89419-177-5 (hc)
ISBN: 979-8-89419-178-2 (e)

Because of the dynamic nature of the Internet, any web addresses or links contained in this book may have changed since publication and may no longer be valid. The views expressed in this work are solely those of the author and do not necessarily reflect the views of the publisher, and the publisher hereby disclaims any responsibility for them.

DEDICATION

Special recognition to my husband while I was writing The Vision of the Quest *for giving me the confidence to run the race and not give up. I could not have completed this book without you.*

To my mother, Anna Louise, for recognizing my writing skills with-in me when I was unsure of myself. Thank you for cheering me on. Continue to stand firm as a lighthouse to bring hope to others.

To my beautiful daughter, Meghan, you were the spark that united the fire in me to the starting point of the incredible adventure of the Quest. I am grateful for my special son, Jay, who is always there until the last dance. My son Isaac, from a frog to a prince, has become my knight in shining armor.

As a child living in a world of fantasy and dreams, my creative daughter, Kimberly, tipped the iceberg to adventuring into the unknown, a blessing in disguise in fulfilling this book. Nathanael, my son, and my daughter, Cassidy, are my eager beavers and inspiration in supporting my stories. My kindred spirit, my sister Debbie, is a friend that sticks closer than any other.

In appreciative memory of my mother-in-law, Ruth, who is now in the arms of the King of Glory. She has stood in the gap, a woman that knew how to wield the sword of life. Her prayers will not return void.

CONTENTS

Prologue ix

Chapter 1   The Darkness of Bronze 1
Chapter 2   Entering Abethar 21
Chapter 3   In Uncertain Times 45
Chapter 4   The New Discovery 61
Chapter 5   Trust 71
Chapter 6   Lead the Blind 77
Chapter 7   An Escape 93
Chapter 8   The Ice Legend 105
Chapter 9   Faith of a Mustard Seed 125
Chapter 10   Hope in Dire Times 149
Chapter 11   Are You Worthy? 155
Chapter 12   Deliverance 165
Chapter 13   The Sound of Wisdom 179
Chapter 14   Reunited 191
Chapter 15   With Hope There is a Way 199
Chapter 16   Many Faces of Stone 211
Chapter 17   Friends of the Kingdom 225
Chapter 18   Know the Scripture or Perish 251
Chapter 19   Dark Shadows 267
Chapter 20   Light in the Darkness 283
Chapter 21   Perfect Sacrifice 297

PROLOGUE

During the late hours of the night, Roger woke up abruptly. He thought he was dreaming; an evil presence drew him out of his bed and into the hallway. He walked through all kinds of twists and turns and stopped suddenly in front of a door needing a repainting.

Roger felt strange, as if pulled into the room. Once inside, he realized where he was. *This is Sir Bronze's museum, which the butler spoke of!* He saw swords and shields from medieval times. He also saw an antique table with old war relics; small, standing, handcrafted men fighting battles along with terrifying and peculiar-looking beasts.

"Cool," Roger said quietly. He found himself being drawn unwillingly to a red oak door that bore carved symbols. Roger was stunned to hear voices speaking to him behind the mysterious door.

"Open the door. Just look in and see." The voices spoke.

In the center was a narrow slide with a small opening. "Look and see! Look and see!" the voices called him out and urged him on.

Bit-by-bit, Roger looked into the slot...

Chapter One

THE DARKNESS OF BRONZE

THE VISION OF THE QUEST

Liana, a mother of two girls and a mother figure to a young man named Roger was in a desperate situation. Worry etched into her face as dark clouds partially covered the moon, shadowing a fragment of its light. The pervading grimness of the surroundings made it difficult to see. The trees looked like they would reach out and grab her, as a chilly breeze blew through the air.

Her car broke down, far from civilization where cellphone services were nonexistent. She and her kids got out of the car as Liana cried softly, tears of stress cascading into her smooth, ivory skin. *These past two years had been a struggle, then now this happens. More importantly, I'm worried about my kids' safety on this pitch-black, lonely road.*

She began introspecting. *Well, at least I have Roger with me, built more robust and taller than most sixteen-year-olds. If someone did stop to bring harm, they might think of Roger as a man and go on, but how strange... it's been over two hours, and still, no sign of a vehicle, not even an eighteen-wheeler, which are usually present during the late hours.*

"Mom, my hands are going numb. I can barely feel them," complained Emily, her spunky nine-year-old daughter.

Liana reached for Emily's cold hands and rubbed them as she turned toward Alicia and Roger. "I'm amazed by the sudden change of weather. Storms are to be expected during the summer, but this sudden drop in temperature is unusual. I wonder if I took a wrong turn." Liana gently touched Emily's cold cheeks.

"Get back in the car, dear. I don't need you catching a bad cold and have your asthma act up again. I will be there in a few minutes."

Liana brushed her long blonde hair out of her face, displaying her high cheekbones and dazzling blue eyes. She saw lights flickering about a mile ahead, thinking it might be a hotel—or anything, for that matter. She was nervous but kept her voice calm for her children's sake. "We need to walk toward the lights. I feel it's our only option."

Alicia, her fifteen-year-old, quickly affirmed but was cut off by her little sister.

"Mom, I am turning into an ice pop, my nose feels like it's falling off." Emily cuddled her mom. "Mom, I want to go home, please, I want to go home," she repeated.

Liana ran her fingers through Emily's loose blonde curls and had Roger get their suitcase out of the trunk. She wrapped a bath towel around her petite body. While Emily continued to whine, Alicia asked, worried. "Mom, what happened and where are we?"

Liana answered uneasily. "I am not sure, but I would never have thought to bring a blanket this time of year. That weird storm hit while I was driving. Lightning struck completely around our car from all directions. I panicked, thinking all of us would be fried like eggs in a pan. I stopped in the middle of the street, unable to see but fortunate that you, Emily, and Roger were sound asleep, for the light was extremely bright. I was forced to shut my eyes. After what seemed like an eternity—the lightning ceased, that's when I remembered not seeing another vehicle or road sign for two hours. Then my car suddenly conked out."

Liana became quiet, dazedly thinking what could have happened. She was jolted back from her thoughts by Emily, now whining she was scared. Her mother spoke softly to calm her fears. "Emily, everything will be okay. Did you forget our secret? Look up toward the sky and see who is watching over us." Her mother pointed upward in the direction of the gloomy, dark sky.

"Mom, that's not the sky. That's heaven, Father's waving to us in the clouds." Emily, cold and frightened, managed a smile as she remembered her father tucking her into bed at night.

"Yes, honey, you're right. Your father is waving from heaven, and he sees what a beautiful girl you have become. Now we must be brave and walk toward what I believe are flickering candles. It's getting colder by the minute and perhaps may even rain. Father would want us to go forward and find a safe place for tonight—and quickly." Liana still saw fear in her daughter's big, blue eyes. "Baby, you are safe and have nothing to worry about." She cupped Emily's chin gently in the palm of her hand.

Liana, from the corner of her eye saw Roger zip the suitcase back up having a head full of brown hair tinged with blonde highlights smiled at Emily in an attempt to console her. "Yeah, your mom's right, short fry. Because whoever messes with you will have to contend with my massive biceps."

Roger flexed his arm muscles, seemingly confident in his portrayal of the Incredible Hulk. Emily giggled, letting go of her mother's hand. She smacked Roger playfully, ready to please her father and find somewhere safe to stay.

Liana, too, aimed her longing for her husband towards the vast expanse of the skies; the winds bearing witness to her cries. "I pray you were still with me. I drove to another state out of my comfort zone to see a house for sale and check what jobs are available in that area, but my car broke down. Now, I worry about paying the towing bill and getting the car fixed." She sighed lightly, taking Emily by her hand. At Liana's heels, Alicia and Roger walked for about fifteen minutes when Roger spoke, sounding surprised. "Miss Liana, look, you're right. The flickering lights are candles—hundreds of them. What hotel could be that big and have that many windows?"

Before Liana could answer, the kids yelled with immense excitement. "Wow! It's huge!"

They walked, wide-eyed, up to a set of enormous, black metal gates. The moon finally peeked out from behind the dark clouds, revealing beyond the peculiar gates a seemingly endless and old, rocky trail.

"Mom, the fence is bigger than our house." Emily declared.

Liana was just as surprised by the gate's massive size. "It's not bigger than our house, but maybe close to it."

Alicia perked up. "What house?" she asked. "Have you forgotten? We lost our home to those snobby people."

Alicia's words was flushed with palpable anger. "We're leaving our memories of father in the home the banks forced you to sell. The bank should have given you enough time to come up with the money—father had always been faithful in paying on time." Liana, too felt the bank should have considered that, but she held on to her courage and faith regardless.

Liana's heart broke hearing the hurt in her daughter's voice, "Alicia, this will be a new beginning for all of us. We will go on and continue to carry your father in our hearts. It will be hard, but we will stick together and be strong," she reassured her, but inside she wasn't sure herself anymore.

Liana returned her focus to Roger. She saw he was utterly obsessed with the gates; forgetting to set down the heavy suitcase, he finally dropped the heavy luggage and placed his hand on Alicia's shoulder. "I gave up my summer to be a help. I am here for you with this big change, friends forever, right?" a phrase they used since elementary school.

"Roger, we've known each other as far back as I can remember, yes, friends forever," Alicia smiled, her mother drawing her attention.

Liana was surprised when the gates opened slowly. She discreetly said, "It's as if someone's expecting us—welcoming us with open arms, but into what? And, where are we? It's definitely no yellow brick road, but a paved road with round, historic stones, which seemed to have no end."

Liana was in doubt at their surroundings but laughed when Emily giggled, shouting, "Open, sesame!" and hammered Roger with questions.

"Roger, how did you make that big gate open? This is the biggest trick you have done! It's better than your quarter disappearing behind your ear. How did you do it? Tell me! Tell me! I won't snitch to anyone about your magic trick. Please? I promise!"

Emily noticed everyone staring speechlessly. "Hey, are you listening?"

Liana stood silent as a mouse. It was startling why the gates had opened, but even more startling was the sudden appearance of a thick patch of heavy fog which took the form of a tall, cloaked man.

"Wow, another magic trick?" Emily bobbed up and down, seemingly forgetting her earlier dilemma.

Liana remained still as the mysterious fog moved toward the flickering lights and then disappeared. All remained speechless except for Emily, still babbling about Roger's new fog trick. Liana looked at Alicia, baffled by what she had witnessed when out of the blue a memory of being held by someone etched itself into her mind. She thought, *"What is this uncanny emotion I cannot shake? I'm about to enter this unfamiliar place which I know nothing of. I may be putting my kids at risk, but as cold as it is, I have no other choice under the circumstances. Turning back is out of the question."*

Alicia broke the silence. "Mom, it's going to storm again. We need to get Emily out of these freezing winds before she gets badly sick again." Liana realized Alicia was correct—they needed shelter immediately before it got any colder and it started to rain. Everything within her resisted walking through the gates. Every particle in her body tingled with just the thought of it.

Alicia looked into her mother's face and noticed she looked worried as she brushed long strands of hair out of her eyes. Alicia tried to make sense of something that had bothered her ever since she was a little girl. She speculated. *Mom still managed to stay beautiful even on her worse days. I'm the oddball in the family, having straight black hair, not thick curls like Emily's or wavy like mothers.* She looked down at her arm. *My skin is even shades darker.* Alicia glanced up, seeing Roger walk through the gate.

Liana noticed that things were too quiet as they made their entry. Nothing out of the ordinary happened, though bats fluttered above their heads as if they were dancing and the screeching of owls that scared Emily. Liana felt slightly more comfortable having the moon's light.

The ancient road led them toward the flickering candles. Liana's eyes were able to adjust quickly to the darkness, and just in time when the fog cleared. Liana spotted an enormous rock building. She slowly edged closer until they stood, in awe, twenty-five feet from an out-of-this-world, historic mansion. They haven't seen anything like this before except possibly in movies about the medieval times.

"Maybe we're in Hollywood," Roger jested as a means of diffusing the tense atmosphere.

Liana found herself at the bottom of a sloped hill in front of a large flight of marble steps, leading up to a set of doors to this unusual place out in the middle of no-man's-land. Alicia and Roger were tense, not knowing what to expect, a subtle sense of excitement perforating through their veins.

Liana became more nervous as she felt light drops of rainfall upon her. Drums rang deep sounds of doom, warning her the heavens were about to open.

"Let's hurry, kids, before we get caught outside in this mess."

Liana removed the bath towel from Emily's shoulders and placed it around her head draping down her back. "Let's keep your hair dry, dear. I don't need you back in the hospital."

Liana lightly touched Emily's nose, comforting her. She thought of her husband Ken, wishing he was with them, sheltering and protecting them from this terrible situation.

Liana and her kids rushed up the marbled steps, making their way closer to the extraordinary front entrance. Liana detected another odd wave of emotions come over her; she sensed an unknown presence. She didn't like it and couldn't explain it but was relieved that the clouds held back the rain, not opening their faucets on them.

Alicia and Roger noticed carved markings along the exterior of the mansion.

"That's odd-looking." Roger side-glanced at Alicia while placing his index finger into a groove of an ancient carving.

Alicia slapped his hand away from the wall. Her dark, pretty eyes sparkled in the gleam of the moon's light.

"Don't do that," she whispered. "You might set off a booby trap."

"A booby trap?" Roger questioned.

Alicia half-heartedly teased. "Roger, you're a good friend with intelligence beyond your years, but at times, you lack wisdom." As Roger laughed, she couldn't help but notice his smile with his pearly white teeth and handsome babyface.

"You forgot to mention I am also kind and thoughtful. The list goes on," Roger beamed. "But getting back to your booby trap, the only booby trap here is Emily's feet bouncing to wake me up in the morning, and that's enough for me, especially when it involves my family jewels being smashed."

"I don't need the details, ugh... You have to get over what happened a year ago. It was an accident. Be satisfied she didn't have shoes on."

"Yeah, I guess. What more damage could she have done? It wasn't your family jewels." Roger lightly punched Alicia's arm good-naturedly while Emily tugged at the hem of her mother's blouse.

Emily stared up into her mother's eyes. Liana knocked on the door more than once but there was no answer.

Liana looked at Emily's drowsy face illuminated by the moonlight. She, also, felt exhausted and was desperate to find clean, warm beds to rest from this long, dreary night.

Liana knocked again. She, also, noticed the attractive carvings with fancy designs which was unlike anything she had seen before. She gave Emily a reassuring hug, praying someone friendly would greet them, but still, no one answered.

"Mom, no one is home. What are we going to do?" Emily quietly asked. Liana wrapped the towel more snugly around Emily's head and kissed her. "Someone has to be inside; candles are burning in the windows," she reassured her.

Roger spotted a big, historic bell hanging above their heads and pointed to it. Liana looked up and saw a lengthy chain dangling inside. She hesitated after seeing too many cobwebs. She mustered enough courage to reach for it, wondering whether spiders would spring out of it.

"Be careful, Miss Liana," Roger teased, looking at Alicia. "It might be a booby trap."

Alicia smacked him across his back.

"Ouch, call the medivac. A gnat has struck me."

Liana blocked out the kids with shaky hands and a firm grip on the rusted chain. She yanked it, praying a tarantula wouldn't jump into her hair. She wondered what lingered behind those closed doors. With a few strong pulls, the bell pierced through the cold, crisp air.

Alicia complained. "I just hope no flying bats come out of that bell, or you'll see me run like a bolt of light…" she stopped as the heavy doors slowly opened, perpetrating a dreadful, ear-piercing sound. Liana wished someone would just fling the doors open and get it over with, else her fear will consume her.

Roger complained, pressing his hands against his ears. "I'd rather hear fingernails running down a chalkboard then this god-forsaken sound. As rich as these people are, I'm sure they can afford some WD-40 to lubricate the bolts on that thing."

At last, the dreadful torture ended, a tall, bald headed butler appeared, wearing a white suit jacket, coattails running down to the back of his knees with white gloves to match.

Alicia pulled Roger aside and whispered. "What are the white gloves for? Is it for killing us without leaving any fingerprints? Should we all run?"

Roger leaned into her ear and boldly ascertained, "I'll take him on any day of the week. He'll be picking the day of his disappointment." He stood up straight and flexed his muscles. Liana overheard him and hoped Roger wasn't getting a big head on his shoulders.

"Good evening." The butler's voice carried a deep, bottomless tone. He sternly glanced at Roger as if aware of what Roger had just said.

"He's freaky," Alicia barely breathed. Liana wasn't sure what to think of him. She half-heartedly agreed.

Roger became quiet, eyeing the man that resembled Mr. Clean, seeing if they could trust him. Emily took hold of the hem of Liana's blouse and buried herself behind her mother's back. The butler's voice boomed. "I have informed my master of your arrival. He will be here shortly to greet you. He's a busy man, attending to an emergency."

Suddenly, the sky let loose. Luckily, the roof's overhang protected them from the heavy downpour. Liana reflected on his peculiar words. She gave the man a distorted look. "Master? Our arrival?" She asked, still standing outside. "We did not plan this, but if your master ..." Liana felt a little uneasy. "Well, if you would be kind enough to allow me to use your cell phone, I would appreciate it so much. For some odd reason our cellular phones had stopped working." Liana paused to see the butler's reaction, but he remained silent. "I need to get ahold of a truck company to tow my car to the nearest mechanical shop. I also have to call for a cab." However, she still thought about how she would pay for such expenses. She smiled politely, waiting for the man's reaction. Again, he remained silent. Liana felt like she was speaking to a wall, her words just getting absorbed into the dry, rough surface. She emphasized herself once more. "My cellular phone is out of service in this place; I need to get hold of a mechanic and a cab company. Will you be able to help me?" Finally, the butler nodded and answered, "Are you speaking of communicating with the outside world?" Liana is not sure how to answer. "Outside world? Well, if that's what you call it." The butler replied emotionlessly, "Unfortunately, we have no service in this location for miles. Please follow me; my master loves to help those in need." He motioned with his long, stout arms, directing the family to come inside.

Liana thought that she had no other choice. They had to get out of the bad weather. She cautiously followed the eerie man inside, the kids following behind their mother. Liana had stepped inside the mansion and felt she had entered a different timeline. She observed old relics on top of unique historical tables and large historical pictures hanging along the tall walls. The butler led them through a spacious lobby with elegant benches on both sides of the wall. They came in front of a set of wide doors. Standing in awe, she eyed the room and was speechless, soaking in the beauty of bright, white marble floors, with stones of different shapes and sizes fitting together flawlessly like a puzzle. She slowly walked inside as the kids followed behind her. Liana saw spectacular artistry thinking whoever had designed this divine hall had done an outstanding job. Her lovely blue eyes fastened upon the elegant ceiling and floor trims, excellent creative artworks with beautiful designs too overwhelming to look upon.

Liana became fascinated by the dimensions of eight pure gold chandeliers hanging tall from a twenty-five-foot ceiling supported by three-foot-round gold columns embedded with a thousand diamonds. She thought the chandeliers supported at least fifty candles. As the heat melted the hot wax, it sent the gold fixtures lightly swaying back and forth and sending four hundred lights swirling gracefully around the grandiose room. The reflection of the countless fiery flames danced upon the white marble floor. Liana found herself walking toward the middle of the room, feeling somehow entranced and reminiscent as if she had danced in this great hall before. "Mother, are you coming?" Alicia asked. Liana was startled awake from her trance and turned around. She did not want to leave this majestic scene, but she still reluctantly walked out with her girls and Roger, wondering why she sensed a strong love in her heart. But for who? She shook herself free of that weird feeling as she followed the butler up a long spiral stairwell, listening to Emily complaining about the number of steps. Roger swung her onto his back. Liana, becoming increasingly exhausted, was grateful Roger took the initiative to help Emily. The butler turned his head towards Liana. "This is the west wing of my master's dwelling."

"How nice." Liana, worn out, managed a weak smile, thinking logically to herself. *I am beginning to believe the butler's leading a shipwrecked crew to God only knows where. I feel lost and divorced from reality, with waves high above my head and a crew of children to keep me from drowning in the dangers of this unfortunate situation.*

Liana reached the top of the stairs. The butler led them with long strides down a lengthy, narrow hallway. He turned his head towards Liana again. "My master is a generous man, and his families are pleasant people; feel free to ask for anything you require." The butler's deep voice carried through the dim hallway. Liana recognized the elegant lanterns hanging on both sides of the walls. She spotted Alicia and Roger whispering back and forth.

Liana asked the butler kindly, "How many are fortunate to live in this lovely place? To be honest, I seek the manor of people who live here, ensuring my family is safe."

The butler's long arms hung straight down, stiff as boards. "Well, ma'am, twenty-two, to be exact, my master's brothers, aunts, uncles, cousins, and young nieces and nephews share this mansion."

Liana walked alongside the strange man. She said, "It must feel good to hear the children in the mansion laughing and playing, running throughout this huge place. I am sure that tickles your caregiver's heart knowing he is able to bless others and especially children."

Liana felt more at ease to hear other children lived in the mansion. Maybe now she can lay her head down to sleep and not wake up at every noise she hears.

The tall man skimmed past Liana. He glanced down at Alicia. "Melanie, my master's niece, is about your age; she lives in the north wing near my master's special room—his museum, where he stores old artifacts for safekeeping…." He stopped walking, staring firmly at everyone. "He allows no one in that room without his permission; only certain servants may enter that domain to tidy up, but be aware and keep your distance." He starts walking again. Roger couldn't help but stare at him weirdly.

Liana expressed. "I have no concern with my kids venturing into the north wing of the mansion. I plan to get them to bed and leave at a decent time in the morning, allowing them no time to wander off."

Roger came up beside the man. He interrupted, asking him boldly. "Why do you use funny phrases like being aware today we say, 'watch your back?' I'll tell you what you need to do." he voiced. "Get out of your chicken coop and explore the outside world." Liana's face became a shade of red, embarrassed at how Roger's mouth at times, unwittingly, gets him into trouble, and this was one of those times.

Liana shot him a look, but Roger didn't notice her correction.

He smiled, "I bet you don't even have a cell phone." The teenager looked intently at the bald man, "Do you even know what a television is or an Xbox 360, or Bluetooth for that matter?" He questioned.

The butler looked puzzled. Roger said to the unknowledgeable Mr. Clean, "I didn't think so."

"*What dimension does this guy come from?*" he asked himself.

Alicia elbowed Roger seeing her mother's lips curl up, but it was too late.

"Oh, you're in trouble, now." Emily blurted out. "Do a magic trick, Roger, and disappear."

Liana protested bluntly. "The butler has been kind enough to take us in for the night, giving us shelter from the storm; mind your manners." Her expression and tone said it all. Roger bit his tongue. Liana thought to say more but tried not to be too hard on him. She considered that his life had not been an easy path, feeling how his mother left him at the age of three, with his father the neighborhood drunk. Since he was a young boy, his father went missing from his life week after week until he remembered he had a son and would come back, only to leave again. At those times, Roger was tucked into bed by her husband, whom Roger also loved and missed. Liana looked from Roger to the butler. "I am sorry for Roger's rudeness. I assure you it will not happen again. Maybe tomorrow morning, before we leave, we will have the opportunity to meet this Melanie you spoke highly of earlier." Liana smiled at Alicia, knowing she would be happy to meet someone her age.

The butler remained quiet and lifted his right arm, pointing his finger down the hallway. "Your room is around this corner."

They rounded a narrow turn. Liana was brought to a halt in front of a door. She observed the area was dimmer than the other hallways, with fewer lanterns hanging from the walls. Liana turned toward the butler and politely asked, "Excuse me, I know I asked to use a cell phone earlier, but may I use your caregiver's house phone? It would be quite helpful to me."

"House phone?" Roger snickered, this time to himself.

The butler stared at Liana, dumbfounded; she wondered if she had said something wrong. He spoke slowly. "I am sorry, madam, my memory sometimes comes and goes; our phone lines are not working due to the storm that came through not long ago. Hopefully, soon someone will be arriving to fix the problem. Unfortunately, the storm was caused by the different kingdom we are living in."

Liana recanted in thought. *I certainly disapproved of Roger's rudeness, but I agree with him, the Different kingdom? The man is definitely off his rocker though I do not feel threatened by him, which is good.*

The butler removed a large key from his pocket, unlocked the door, and swung it open. Alicia and Roger gazed into the luxurious room, forgot their manners, and ran inside like a bunch of wild boars' satisfaction was written across their faces admiring the elegant furniture, including two enormous beds, and exploring the room. Things were tidy and clean—all but one place. Emily tugged the hem of her mother's blouse and cried out her name. Liana heard an urgent tone in Emily's voice.

Softly she asked, "Yes, dear?"

Emily pleaded with her legs crossed, "I have to pee really bad. I can't hold it any longer."

The butler pointed to a door inside the room. "Necessary needs are through that door."

Alicia was ecstatic, "Oh, wow, I can't wait to take a nice hot shower." She smiled at the butler then glanced at Roger, "See, they have electricity." Alicia strung open the bathroom door, and a large jawbreaker could fit into her opened mouth, finding some kind of portal pot and no shower but a big basin of water inside a wooden stand.

Alicia whispered under her breath, disappointed. *Roger's right. What age do these people live in?*

The butler spoke with no emotion: "Plumbing problems." He briskly turned and walked out and closed the door behind him.

Emily's urgent needs diminished as something caught her attention. "Oh, Mom, look at the pretty blackbird inside that cage. May I pet it?" She couldn't wait to touch it.

Liana looked in the direction of her daughter's finger and observed a crow, her head spinning in contemplation why someone would keep a wild bird as a pet, especially one that's known to be aggressive. Liana remained calm and firmly glanced at Emily that she had no notion of disobeying her. Liana answered. "No, do not go near it. That's a crow; they are mean and dirty. Now use the bathroom, wash up, and get to bed. It's late, dear, about two in the morning." Emily griped, looking over her shoulder. She hesitantly went into the bathroom and shut the door behind her. Everything was quiet until Emily screamed.

"Aww! This funny toilet doesn't flush. Roger, did you make this stinky mess?"

Liana, too tired to laugh, managed a smile. Emily exited the indoor outhouse giggling, jumping up and down on her feathered mattress. Her curls engulfed her pretty face, and her blue eyes, tinted with a hint of gray, shone with mischief, ready to explore the mansion. "Come on, Roger, let's bounce!" the spunky nine-year-old child shouted. Roger ignored her, keeping a distance between him and her wild bouncing feet.

Liana saw playfulness in her daughter's eyes. "Not tonight, Emily." She handed Emily her pajamas.

She protested. "Ah, it's not fair that I must go to bed." She stared into her mother's eyes and figured this battle she would not win; upset, she slipped into her pajamas and crawled up under her warm blanket. Her body sunk into the feathered mattress; she snuggled into her wool blanket and fastly dozed off peacefully to sleep as the black crow stared its red eyes at Alicia. "Mom, look at the crow's eyes. Aren't they freaky?

Crows' eyes are supposed to be black; it's eyes are red and hideous. I don't like its looks; the ugly thing keeps gawking at me."

Liana stretched out her arms and yawned. "I agree, the crow is not on my 'good' list, but as long as it's in a cage not hurting anyone, we're fine. It's late, Alicia; let's get some shut-eye morning will be here soon enough." She objected. "Mom, the bird gives me the creeps. Let me at least throw a blanket over its ugly head. I can't sleep with that nasty thing staring at me."

Roger heard Alicia babbling about the crow. He came out of the indoor outhouse and laughed with his toothbrush in his mouth. There was pleading in her voice. "Then, mom, let's set it outside the door, then you won't have to worry about the blanket suffocating it."

Liana, too drained to argue, gave Alicia a kiss good-night on her forehead. "Go get ready for bed, dear. I agree, the bird is unpleasant to look upon, but crows are God's creation too …" Her sentence was cut short as a faint knock was heard on the door. "I'll answer it," Roger mumbled, his toothbrush still in his mouth. He fast swallowed his toothpaste. "Who is it?" he asked with alarm but firm.

Behind the door, a masculine voice answered, "I am the master of this mansion. May I come in?" His voice seemed pleasant and didn't sound like a threat. Roger glanced toward Liana for her approval. She gently nodded her head, yes. Roger cautiously opened the door. A tall, good-looking man entered with coal-black hair and dark eyes, handsome in every aspect, a man of steel, similar to Superman, with a solid frame and broad shoulders to match his entire body structure. The man spoke friendly to Liana. "I heard about your misfortune. Luckily my brother is a mechanic it will be no problem for him to look at your car in the morning. I hope your stay will be most pleasant."

"Mr. …" Liana searched for the polite gentleman's name.

The tall, dashing man walked refined toward Liana. He gently bent forward and kissed her hand. "I am sorry. I have not properly introduced myself. My name is Sir Bronze Pierce, but you may call me Bronze, my lady." Liana slowly withdrew her hand, feeling uncomfortable, and again found herself thinking, *where are these uncertain feelings coming from? This man is unknown to me. However, an inner urging draws me into his presence.*

THE VISION OF THE QUEST

I feel a part of his life in some way, but how, oddly, I am beginning to think there is more to this man than meets the eye, and this is not just a mansion. I sense something unique about this place but am unable to pinpoint what it is. Inside this place, somehow, I feel like royalty, unique, set apart from the unknown.

Liana brought her thoughts back to the man, thinking he seemed a little off though kind. "Well, Sir Bronze, I am grateful for your hospitality. You have been mighty generous in sharing this beautiful mansion with my family after such a hard night. I am much obliged my girls and Roger have a warm bed and roof over their heads protecting them from the awkward weather outside."

Bronze stared at Liana with great desire but hid his emotions, "Thank you for your gentle words. I agree the weather has been quite different. However, tomorrow morning, the sun shall shine again, and maybe I will have the honor of showing you and your kids around my mansion; I have a lovely pond outside that is gorgeous to look upon." Liana said with a soft yawn. "It sounds wonderful, but first thing in the morning, right after my daughter meets Melanie, your butler mentioned her name to me, then we must be on our way, but that is thoughtful of you." The man persisted. "Besides that, pond, there's another pond hidden that goes back many generations. It is said it's a doorway to many kingdoms and a portal to different dimensions with three special keys, but unfortunately, I have not found it. Now, may I have the honor of all of your names?"

Liana politely answered. "Yes, of course, my name is Liana, and this is my daughter Alicia, and our good friend Roger, and my youngest daughter Emily, who is finally sleeping." Liana glanced over and saw Emily sitting up in bed, wondering who the foreign man was telling an extraordinary Magic Kingdom story. Alicia looked at her mother. "Mom, the knock must have awakened her."

"That's okay. I'll lay down with her in a few minutes." Liana's face looked utterly weary as she yawned again, striving not to appear rude, in front of the man who came to their rescue.

Liana turned back and faced Bronze. He again took her hand into his. "I see you are tired. It was nice meeting you and your family. May we continue our conversation tomorrow morning?" Liana politely withdrew her hand from his. Bronze cringed as he turned to leave, closing the door behind him.

Liana was too tired to think as she climbed into the high bed and cuddled up beside Emily, hoping for a good night's sleep, knowing she would be busy in the morning making arrangements to leave. Emily again fell fast to sleep.

Liana's eyes half shut looked at Alicia. "Get to bed, sweetheart. The morning will be here before you know it." Alicia listened and laid down beside her mother, pulling the covers up to her chin, appreciating the warmth of the thick blankets. The heat was coming from the fireplace, but the room still carried a cold chill. Alicia was glad her mother allowed one candle to burn to give them a sense of comfort as they slept.

She wasn't in bed for more than a minute when she started to complain again. "Mom, that crow. I am telling you; it is staring at us."

Liana's voice cracked. "I believe that's what crows do close your eyes and get some sleep in the morning. You will not have to worry about the bird again."

Alicia rolled over onto the side of her head, facing the crow. She searched the layout of the room and reasoned *that whoever lived in this mansion was expecting us to show up, the fireplace had been burning, and the candles had been lit for hours, being short with much-melted wax.* She took one last look at the hideous crow and soon enough fell asleep.

Unknown to the family, the mysterious crow was the seeing eyes of Bronze, observing Liana's every move. Bronze stared at her as if looking through a crystal ball.

Roger clueless to it. Liana and the girls had fallen asleep, knocked out completely. He poured himself a glass of water from a pitcher inside the room, gulped it down, and jumped into his oversize feathered mattress. Roger exclaimed, pleased. "No one to share this with. This is the life!" He, too, eventually fell into a deep sleep. During the late hours of the night, Roger woke up abruptly. He thought he was dreaming; an evil presence drew him out of his bed and into the hallway. He walked through all kinds of twists and turns and stopped suddenly in front of a door needing a repainting.

THE VISION OF THE QUEST

Roger felt strange, as if pulled into the room. Once inside, he realized where he was. *This is Sir Bronze's museum, which the butler spoke of!* He saw swords and shields from medieval times. He also saw an antique table with old relics of war; small, standing, handcrafted men fighting battles along with terrifying and peculiar-looking beasts fighting...

"Cool," Roger said quietly. He found himself being drawn unwillingly to a red oak door that bore carved symbols. Roger was stunned to hear voices speaking to him behind the mysterious door.

"Open the door. Just look in and see." The voices spoke.

In the center was a narrow slide with a small opening. "Look and see! Look and see!" the voices called him out and urged him on.

Bit-by-bit, Roger looked into the slot, now hearing one single voice, "The eyes are the light of the body." Immediately, the door opened slightly. Roger wasn't aware. The light of his eyes caused it to happen. With the curiosity of a cat, he cautiously opened the door completely. He was stunned to see a horrific war. The terrorizing forces of darkness was conquering different kingdoms. Roger, frozen in fear at what he was seeing and the evil presence he felt somehow, knew these overpowering forces of demonic activity were winning because the kingdoms would not stand together and unite as one to rally against the forces of wickedness.

Suddenly, out of nowhere, a large terrifying, jet-black horse jumped up in front of Roger, standing inside the doorway, rearing powerfully on its hind legs. Roger was amazed at the muscles the horse displayed, and, as the rider yanked back its reins, the beast gave a frightful, thunderous grunt, mouth wide open, exposed a set of sharp teeth. Its dark black eyes penetrated Roger's eyes, sending a quick chill throughout his body. Mysteriously out of the brutal horse's mouth, Roger breathed in the odor of burning coals into his nostrils, feeling the breath of the ferocious beast in his face. Too scared to run, terror took his breath away. The horse made a horrific noise, a sound of defeat as it lowered its legs. Roger's eyes widened as his body almost crashed to the floor: the man sitting upon its back was Sir Bronze Pierce. Bronze's pants and cloak were every bit black; even his buttons, as their faces locked the light from Roger's eyes, caused a glare in Bronze's pitch-black marble eyes, stunned Roger somehow knew he was the light standing in the man's way.

"But standing in the way of what?" Roger questioned over the noise of the battle cries, hearing savage outrage brewing thunderously behind Sir Bronze. Roger felt covered in goosebumps and the hair on his arms standing straight up as his flesh shouted, "Get out of there!"

Bronze leaned over into Roger's petrified face. The man exclaimed in a harsh tone. "Give me the keys!" His marble eyes pierced every fiber in the boy's body.

Roger staggered and fell backward out of the doorway, not understanding what keys Bronze was talking about nor the evil presence that hovered over him. The dark-headed man poked his head into the museum and glared wildly at the boy. Roger knew to move fast, jumping up as quickly as his body would allow him. Frightened, he forcefully slammed the door shut, hearing a loud thump as the door smacked hard up against Sir Bronze's head. Roger hoped he knocked the creep out cold. His body trembling, he rushed out of the room.

Somehow, he found his way back to the bedroom, still shaken, confused about whether it was a nightmare or reality. After quite some time, Roger slowly fell asleep, hoping the horrendous, hellish incident did not happen.

Chapter Two
Entering Abethar

Morning came too quickly. Liana and Alicia were awake, listening to Emily bellyaching about her stomach growling. "Mom, I need food before I pass out. I'm literally about to faint." She complained.

"Yeah, but you're not dying either." Alicia made fun as she headed to the so-called bathroom.

"Not yet anyway.'" Emily became sidetracked and hopped onto Roger's bed. "Get up, lazybones." She demanded.

Roger jumping out of bed, grabbed Emily, "I'm awake, little livewire." He tossed her onto the soft feathered mattress when suddenly, he remembered his nightmare. He thought. *It seemed so natural, like I was in another world or dimension.* He shook his head and shrugged it off. Emily repeatedly yelled, hyped-up. "Again, again, throw me one more time but higher!"

Her mother scolded her while making her bed. "Emily, you must calm down this is not our place to be making that kind of noise, now, go into the bathroom with Alicia and get dressed. We have a busy day."

"Huh, I was having fun. Why are adults party poopers?" She jumped off the bed full of pep and skipped to the bathroom.

Liana finished making her bed when she heard a knock on the door.

"Please come in," She turned and faced the door to see the dashing Sir Bronze Pierce enter the room.

Roger's mind again flashed back to his dream. *But was it a dream?* He murmured under his breath, "Well, either way, I don't trust him, no matter how rich he is."

"Oh, Sir Bronze," Liana said, placing her hands on her hips. "I am tidying up a bit, and we will be on our way, that is, as soon as Alicia meets Melanie. I sincerely thank you for your hospitality." Liana reached into her shirt pocket, retrieving the little cash she had. As she walked toward Bronze, the man found himself enjoying the sweet, swaying motion of her hips. Liana handed him forty dollars. "I am sorry I am unable to pay more. My finances have been slim since I lost my husband."

Roger caught the man admiring Liana. He wondered what was up his sleeve.

Sir Bronze waved his hand, not accepting the money. "Liana, I am sorry for your loss. I hope you don't mind me calling you by your first name. Miss is formal for a beautiful woman like you." Bronze delighted in watching Liana's high cheekbones blush as he moved closer, standing a few feet away and searching deep into her sweet blue eyes. He reached over, taking her hand into his, gently caressing it. Liana thought he was making it a habit and tried politely, withdrawing her hand. Bronze would not allow it, clutching it more strongly. He saw Liana becoming nervous. He loosened his grip and reluctantly let go but stared more deeply into her face, thought her to be in her mid-thirties but admired the fact she didn't look over a quarter-century old seeing her young-looking. She was pleasing to his eyes. Bronze desired to hold, kiss, and caress her in his arms. Stronger feelings overrode him as his heart pumped wildly. He knew it was not the time and stepped backward, containing himself before he spoke again.

From the corner of his eye, Alicia walked out of the bathroom as Emily followed behind her.

Bronze's focus was entirely on Liana. "It's been my pleasure to be a help to someone who truly needs it, but I do have bad tidings. I am sad to say my brother has taken a look at your car, and it's on its last leg. You're welcome to stay a few more days until you get things worked out. As you can well see, we have plenty of rooms." Bronze, full of himself, threw up his arms, expressing the magnitude of his mansion.

Liana answered respectfully, "It's very thoughtful of you, but the storm has passed, and we really must be on our way. Sir Bronze, your butler mentioned your phone line is down. Has it been fixed yet?"

The man acted friendly. "Please. Again, call me Bronze. Concerning my phone, the company is busy first getting the school's emergency lines functioning. Hopefully, by Thursday, it might be in service."

"That's four days from today," Liana answered, and suddenly, she felt the walls spin slowly around her.

Bronze observed Liana. He noticed the patch of medicine he had cunningly pressed upon her delicate hand he had shaken a few minutes ago was taking effect. His black shadowing eyes looked into hers. She did not feel like herself. Bronze gazed mysteriously into Liana's eyes. His voice was alluring. "How about your family joins me for breakfast, and we shall talk things over." In a trance-like state of agreeing, Liana motioned for the children to come along.

"Miss Liana, we really must be going to find help outside of this place," Roger said firmly.

Bronze turned and faced the boy. Roger was appalled and stepped backward, spotting a massive knot on the man's forehead. His heart skipped a beat. He wondered whether it was a reality after all.

Bronze took Liana by her arm and walked her out into the hallway. Roger and Alicia followed, unsure of things, while Emily bounced down the hallway singing, "I have a rumbling in my tummy to be filled with something yummy."

Bronze led Liana toward the dining area. Within five minutes, she and the kids stood before two massive doors, making them feel small. Two butlers stood straight and rigid near the entry, dressed like the butler they met the previous night. With the snap of his fingers, Bronze motioned them to open the doors. The men moved as one, obeying their master's wishes.

Emily skipped inside the dining area and raved. "Mom, this room is bigger than my school cafeteria." She pulled on her mother's arm, and she received no answer. Her mother seemed overcome with unsureness, and she pulled harder. Liana smiled to a certain degree, coming out of her confusion, "I am blown away myself, Emily. It's spacious."

Bronze's dark shadow, a second time, stared into Liana's eyes, the windows of her soul. Quietly he whispered words of untruth and brought her back into a state of disarray with locked elbows. He walked her to a large table.

Alicia perceived her mother was again in a complete daze, for Liana paid no mind to Emily, full of energy and running past her. She didn't even see how her little sister's mouth expanded to the size of a grapefruit discovering all sorts of dishes, including food she had never seen before.

Bronze politely pulled out Liana's chair, and the kids sat close by at the table. Emily couldn't contain herself any longer, her lungs ready to burst. She exclaimed, "There are so many chairs, and look at all the food, Mom, he must think we are pigs!"

Her voice shook her mother somewhat awake, at a slow pace. Liana shook her head in disapproval. "Shhh, let's be polite, Emily." Her mind felt cloudy with a slight headache. She looked toward Bronze. Liana said quietly, for she felt fatigued. "Everything is beautifully arranged and smells delicious. You must give my compliments to the chef."

Bronze looked with pleasure, waiting impatiently to steal the heart of Liana to be his. He tolerated her children without complaining, desiring the brats out of the picture as soon as he got the chance. Bronze briefly touched Liana's soft hand, but again she withdrew it quickly, Bronze thought. *In time I will have my way with her.* He smiled at Liana, "Well, what are you waiting for? Go ahead and make yourselves at home. We have plenty more where this came from."

Roger whispered to Alicia, "The food looks tempting, but do you think it's safe to eat? It may be poisoned." Roger looked at Bronze to see if he was eavesdropping.

Alicia answered in a hushed tone, "His lid isn't screwed on tight, but besides that, eat your food, corny, it looks too good to pass up, but if you're that worried, wait until Bronze eats first, then we'll know whether it's safe."

Alicia and Roger waited patiently, as Emily was impatient. She hurried and reminded her mother, "We have to say grace. Your head is in the clouds again." Emily, with all her strength, shook her mother free. "We have to say grace," she repeated. Liana's mind, still somewhat cloudy, looked across the table and nodded at Bronze, giving him the honor of saying the blessing.

Bronze cringed. "I am not a holy man, but I respect your faith. Please proceed." He stared into her enticing eyes once more and touched her arm. He admired Liana's beauty and strong character, observing her gentle and kind spirit. His dark marble eyes still fixed upon Liana's until he was disturbed by Alicia's voice.

"Mom, are you okay?" she asked.

THE VISION OF THE QUEST

Liana jolted back to reality. She answered motionless. "I am fine, honey. I believe I am tired." She placed her head in her hands for a few moments, not even hearing Emily as she took the initiative to say grace.

Alicia was like a jackrabbit. She heard her little sister say amen and jumped up. "Bronze, you've been a big help to my family. It's my honor to make your plate, and you to take the first bite."

"Young lady, proceed. You have won my favor," the liar answered. Alicia filled Bronze's plate high. Roger watched intently, satisfied witnessing the man eating. He cried out, "Well, chow down, kiddies. The man did say he has plenty more where this came from." Roger looked toward Liana. He knew something was wrong when she didn't scold him. He couldn't believe he was beginning to miss that side of her.

Roger watched Emily squirm in her seat; exultant he had said the magic words. "Let's eat!"

Emily shouted out. "About time! I am so hungry I could eat a horse."

Bronze looked perplexed at the child. "Horse? I ensure you horses would not be tasty." Emily snickered at the goofy man, and as seconds turned into minutes. They filled their plates with various foods. Alicia worried their mother had not said a word. She noticed Emily desired her full attention. "Mom, I ate every bite, not missing a crumb. My stomach could pop. Look!" She raised her shirt slightly, and Liana continued to stare. "Why do I have to keep pulling on you to listen to me?" Emily again tugged on her arm, bewildered by her mother's behavior. "Mom, wake up; why are you asleep with your eyes open? Mom! Mom!" Liana popped to her senses with a few loud yells and another tug.

Bronze watched, frustrated, having to place her in the same state of mind again. He ground his teeth, breathing silently under his hot breath, *"The brats are becoming a nuisance. When the time is right, and my plans are completed, I will do away with them and get the annoying ticks out of my hair, once and for all."*

Liana glanced over at Bronze. She felt drained. "It was delicious, but all good things must end, my children, and I must be on our way." She spoke with a slur.

"It was my pleasure," Bronze replied, again taking her hand into his pressing a patch of potent medicine against her palm and going into her skin like wildfire. He once more latched his devious eyes fixed into hers, bringing her under his influence as he heard Emily becoming restless, fiddling with things on the table, wiggling nonstop in her seat.

"Mom, may Roger and I take Emily outside to play for a short while?" Alicia asked only to speak with Roger alone for her mother's sake. All three shot up out of their seats.

Bronze countenance brightens, thrilled to get rid of her whining pups allowing him suitable time to bring his stunning prized possession into a deeper turmoil, one difficult to shake out of. He said, "That's a brilliant idea the pond I had mentioned before is to the right of the mansion. Take some bread for your little sister to feed the ducks." He walked over toward the kids. They were already heading fast toward the door. Their backs faced Bronze. Bronze glanced over at Liana for her approval. "That is, of course, if it would be okay with your mother." Liana did not answer.

Alicia and Roger turned around. Emily too faced the space cadent. "Is it the Walt Disney pond to the Magical Kingdom? Is it, is it?" Emily asked.

Bronze looked at her, puzzled, "Walt Disney?"

"Yeah, silly goose, haven't you ever heard of Walt Disney?" Emily chimed.

Alicia and Roger locked eyes, thinking, who doesn't know of Walt Disney?

Bronze for once became quiet until Emily broke the silence. "Well, Mom, may we go to the pond? Please, I'll listen and will not go near the edge. I promise."

Liana's head felt like a three-ring circus. She wondered why she felt numb. Alicia looked in the direction of her mother. She begins to worry even more as her mother's face looked pale.

Bronze impatiently noticed a part of an exquisite necklace dangling around Alicia's neck that emerged from her shirt. With eagerness, he rudely reached over and grasped the necklace and examined it, causing the chain to tighten around Alicia's throat. He asked. "May I have this

THE VISION OF THE QUEST

to hold to view the gems more closely?" Alicia, with the innocence of a young girl, removed it and handed it to Bronze. He had it within his grasp, viewing every little detail, sensing power radiating from it. He lusted for that power. He realized this was one key to the kingdoms, with two more to be discovered, becoming anxious, and knew he had to be patient reluctantly. He handed the fine piece of jewelry back to Alicia, ecstatic after many years, and finally found one key to his freedom. Bronze schemed. *"Luring this family to me is starting to pay off."*

He hated handing it back. He stared vacantly at the gems as Alicia placed them safely back onto her neck. He desired it with each second that passed. "This necklace is but one of three." Alicia felt his breath upon her face. She slowly retreated backward as the man again stepped toward her.

Bronze bent over, and he fiddled with it. Alicia thought she was off the hook when he finally released her necklace. Standing tall with a firm look, he asked with a demanding tone, "Where did you find this?"

Alicia cast her eyes toward her mother, seeing her completely zoned out, not even blinking her eyes. Anger stirred within her as she lashed out, "What are you doing to our mother. At times she acts like we don't exist. Look at her. She hasn't been herself since this morning, and she doesn't respond to us at all. Each minute she is in your presence, she becomes worse and worse! What did you do to her?"

Roger listened, keeping a sturdy hold on Emily's hand. Alicia became aware Roger had observed her brave stance. He quietly staged-whispered. *"Bronze is a psycho, but wow, what a lady."*

Alicia held her ground. Bronze grew impatient and ignored her. He spoke harshly. "I am not concerned with your petty whining. Now, where did you get this necklace?"

"Why are you so concerned about it?" Alicia asked, troubled. "All I know, my mother does not remember anyone placing it into her hands; she has always had it but feels it's been passed down through her lineage."

Bronze grew doubly impatient, irritated that the time wasn't right, desiring it badly with another lie. He asked boldly. "May I have it to hold to keep in my possession for a short time? I will return it to you soon. I give you my word." Bronze raged inside as he tried to think straight. *I will not accept no for an answer. Eventually, I will have it in the palm of my hands, going to any length to get it, including murder.*

Alicia gripped her necklace tightly, protecting it. She spoke headstrong. "No, this necklace has not left my sight since my mother gave it to me. I will not part with it."

The man hid his disgust for the girl and thought of vengeance. *Its mine! For my destructive purposes, my oh my, but how I feel the power radiating from the fine gems. I will have that power, but this is not the time to end the girl's life.* Bronze found himself contemplating his next chess move. *I will use that loudmouth as a worm on my hook to see the other two missing keys, then do away with her and the other two brats. My plans for murder will go into effect.* He couldn't hide his anger any longer and looked at Alicia with disgust. He thought. *But as for their mother, I have peachy plans in mind.* Bronze, with a clenched mouth, forced a grin.

He operated with craftiness. "This is such a rare necklace. Maybe you will change your mind later and let me examine it more closely." He searched into Alicia's face and became aware her eyes were not glazed like her mother's. He knew for sure he had placed a drug into the pesty kid's pitcher and had watched Roger and Emily fill their cups. The manipulator again searched into Alicia's innocent eyes, hoping to bring her into the same state of disorder as her mother. He simmered with displeasure. The deceiver spoke. "Be careful and hang tight to this precious jewel. It's ancient, of days, very old." His words were full of malice.

Bronze running against the clock anxiously he became overjoyed as her treasure sent waves of colorful lights throughout the room. It wasn't Alicia and Emily's first time seeing their gems light up like the northern skies. Bronze struggled to hide his secret volcano from erupting. *I waited a thousand years for the three that hold the keys to life to rule over the three kingdoms with a tyrant and unyielding hand*—being *that a thousand years is like a day in Liana's time. I had waited long enough!* Bronze paid no mine as a butler cleaned the breakfast table and overheard pieces of his conversation. The butler couldn't count the times it sent Bronze into a stormy turbulent like a spoiled child. He pushed a cart full of dishes into the kitchen, where another butler waited for him. Mr. Clean asked. "Did you throw out the pitcher that was filled with Bronze's drug and replace it with fresh tea?" With long brown hair, Caleb pulled it back into a ponytail with hush puppy eyes and answered. "Yes, everything was taken care of."

"Good." Mr. Clean answered. "Bronze isn't the only one with something up his alley. In time things will unfold, but that's another story. Let's get busy, Caleb. We got work to do." The two blended in with the concrete kitchen wall and disappeared.

Bronze did not know what was happening right under his nose inside his domain. He was too concerned with finding the keys to his freedom. He stood annoyed, with another look of disgust as he contemplated. *If Liana has the other two necklaces, I will soon find them. It will be like taking candy from a baby; I will have her unknowingly place them into my hands.* The stubborn man eventually took his eyes off the scattered animated lights. He invented another wild lie. "Young lady, I know about the history of that fine piece. I spend extra time studying rare things such as this. I am sort of an archeologist. It is truly a remarkable piece, one of a kind, no doubt about it. I will..."

Bronze is interrupted by Emily's sudden outburst. "I am bored." She complained. Alicia felt saved by the bell.

She remarked, "Sir Bronze, my mother would have permitted me to take Emily to the pond if she was in her right mind. Please excuse us." Bronze tried not to freak out that she was let off his shark hook. "In time." He breathed.

Alicia grabbed Roger's arm and pulled him toward a door. She whispered. "I noticed that same butler earlier that poured our drinks. The one with a long ponytail ventured outside with a shovel, but who was that man—and bury what?" Emily held on to Roger's hand and tagged along beside him as she followed Alicia outside.

Emily's soft curls flew in every direction as she speeded out the door. She couldn't wait until the door slammed shut. She saw they were in the clear. She proudly paraded, "I didn't tell that nosey man about Mom's and my necklace. I kept a good secret, didn't I?"

"Emily, you almost spilled every bean there was if I didn't keep you entertained with my magic tricks…." Roger's words dropped as Alicia winked at him. She smiled at her little sister. "Yes, I can't believe you kept a secret. I also thought you would have spilled the beans, but good job, there's hope for you after all." Alicia teased.

Not having a care in the world, Emily changed the subject, "Look, the sun is out, it's summertime again, hip hip hooray!" She danced joyfully in circles around the two worried teenagers and said, "I can't wait to tell Mom. She will feel so much better."

Alicia blocked her out as she bombarded Roger with what on earth was going on, "Why did that nut want my necklace so bad? He's too intrigued with it and with my mother. He couldn't take his eyes off of her. I am worried about her. She's not acting like herself. We must devise a plan to get her out of that crazy man's grasp and get all of us out of here before something dreadful may happen."

Roger made sense. "Hey, slow down; we must remain calm to work out a plan, and remember, Alicia, we are in the middle of nowhere. We must think of every option to keep safe, when, and what game piece to move, because our lives may depend on it. I am sure he is good at his game; whatever Bronze is up to. It's like he lured us here, for I am sure we will soon find out."

Alicia took in a deep breath and exhaled to calm her nerves. She asked, upset. "What do you feel is going on? Roger, please, hold nothing back from me. This is serious."

Emily stopped dancing and singing, sensing tension in her sister's voice, "Alicia, are we in trouble?" she asked, afraid.

Alicia searched for the right words without scaring her little sister. Roger pole-vaulted in with his quick thinking. "Emily, we will throw your mom a surprise birthday party."

Emily looked up and giggled. "We already did, goofball. Remember two weeks ago? Are you teasing me?"

Roger sighed, "Oh, yeah, we did throw her a birthday party, but this party will be a moving party, since she's moving us into a new home."

Emily was thrilled. "I won't tell Mom, I promise, pinky swear." She extended her hand toward Roger.

THE VISION OF THE QUEST

He was, enjoying Emily's spunkiness. "Whoa, wait a minute, short fry, first you must promise not to tell Bronze or anyone in the mansion; we must sneak your mom out for her surprise because Bronze might tell her our top secret."

Emily saw stars in her eyes. "I promise! I promise!"

Roger gently shook her pinky. "Okay, it's a done deal, little munchkin."

Alicia was taken back by watching Roger. She found herself aware of his charisma, drawing her closer like a magnet finding herself pleased with his kind heart. For the first time, she saw Roger as more than just a friend. "Thank you," Alicia whispered, somewhat embarrassed, hoping he didn't sense her passion for him at that moment.

Emily returned dancing. Alicia and Roger walked further away from the mansion. She twirled around them, "Mom's having a surprise party. Mom's having a surprise party!"

Roger begins where he left off concerning the tall, tanned, handsome Bronze. "I don't have the answers to all your questions, but this I do know. Bronze is no archeologist. He seems too much of a ladies' man, and I agree with you: he has some hold on your mother."

Alicia stressed. "My mother needs deliverance soon, and what if …" Her words trailed off. Emily suddenly stopped dancing. Roger remained silent, all staring as if half-conscious, speechless, gazing at a pond they stumbled upon. A pin drop could be heard. As they wondered where it had come from, seeing it wasn't there before, they marveled at its breathtaking beauty. Magnificent historic rocks circled the fountain of dreams—dreams the kids were unaware of—they looked upon many gorgeous flowers beyond any they had ever seen before dancing in accord, in rare colors. The three listened as the wind blew lightly, hearing each flower chime a musical sound of humming pleasing to their ears. A mist—a white fog- lingered over the suburb splendor. Alicia and Roger still stood in awe.

Emily broke the silence. "Are we in heaven?" she whispered. Roger and Alicia shift their eyes toward one another, and, for a split second, they wonder the same thing.

Alicia looked back at the pond. Her eyes stayed peeled, marveling at its glory. She breathed to her little sister in a hushed tone, thinking if she were too loud, everything might fade into nothing. "No, silly goose, but maybe close to it," she answered.

Emily innocently declared with adventure in her eyes, "This is Walt Disney's the Magical Kingdom. Bronze told Mom about it last night that he needs three special keys to find the kingdoms. Don't you remember?"

"Yeah, I remember," Roger answered, "and I think he's a nut case. There are no keys to different kingdoms and dimensions. The man talks crazy, no, scratch that, he is crazy." Roger suddenly remembered the door inside Bronze's museum. "But what baffles me is how this pond appeared out of nowhere on the green earth? This is not the pond where we could feed the ducks. This water is pure and sparkles. It's captivating beyond any words I can even attempt to explain. Who knows, maybe it is the hidden pond." Roger immediately threw his arms up, frustrated. "What am I talking about? I'm starting to sound like the kook. It's impossible." He didn't know what to think.

Alicia walked closer to the picture-perfect paradise, with Roger and Emily tagging close behind. With each step, the pond became more breathtaking; they stopped as Alicia remembered to breathe. She inhaled in life abundantly and with vibrancy. As adrenaline rushed through her veins, having a sense of heaven with every step, the pond became clear as crystal. Roger came beside Alicia, both drawn closer to it. They stood in disbelief a foot from the edge, and they stared within, seeing into the depths of the bottomless fountain a reflection of something extraordinary that caught their attention and wondered whether the pond might be of another world.

Both stunned Alicia and Roger, searching closer into the depths of clear, glass water, saw their reflections. Alicia timidly swallowed. Roger rubbed his eyes, startled as they looked into the eyes of warriors. The teenagers seemed puzzled as the water called out to the depths of their souls, giving insight into who they were and who they could become. They have seen into the depths of their potential through an open mirror.

THE VISION OF THE QUEST

"Is this a fountain of dreams of some sort?" Roger asked, still in unbelief.

Alicia heard Roger, but she remained silent as her vision opened up, leading her closer to the entrance of a fantastic kingdom. She felt drawn more powerfully than before, and, as she nervously took a step of faith, staring non-stop into the mystic pond, she sensed mighty arms that could reach out and just pulled her into it. She wondered if this divine place even existed in time.

Alicia heard a mighty, captivating voice telling her to come closer, and she obeyed. Somehow, she trusted the voice. She inched even closer. The tip of her shoes emerged in the water as she stood at the edge of the bank, wondering, if she fell into the unknown pond, would it be to the point of no return. Directedly, her necklace pulled her into the fountain of dreams; somehow, she sensed inside her heart this was the only way to save her family from Bronze's games he played. Roger shouted for Alicia to get away, and everything happened so fast. She allowed her necklace to pull her off the edge, placed her foot into the mystic water, and as it touched, it became even more abundantly alive. Within Alicia's vision, steps emerged. She wondered whether it was reality or her mind playing tricks on her.

Roger and Emily stood close to Alicia and witnessed the departure of the water and steps appearing out of nowhere. "What is going on?!" Roger yelled, skeptical of what was real and what wasn't. Emily squeezed Roger's hand with a fearful grip, and his blood flowed to his fingertips. Alicia stood at the entrance to a new kingdom that was not of this world. Roger and Emily knew to follow her.

Alicia, with extreme caution, proceeded down the smooth rock steps, perplexed by how the water stood tall and erect on both sides and above her head. She felt shielded by an unknown force, not comprehending the water was an illusion, along with the pond—a trick to hide the entrance of the first kingdom from Bronze and all others. Instead, it would only be exposed to the chosen ones, a domain the kids did not know of, and, as Alicia looked fixedly upon the walls of water, a servant of Bronze's entered his master's museum to dust. He heard voices in his mind. "Come see, come now! Come and behold the light!" the teller of lies repeatedly echoed. The abyss of the unknown led the servant to the portal door curiosity killed the cat as he looked into the peek hole. The light of his eyes opened an unknown gateway he was clueless too.

The man felt a dark fog and an icy chill slip out through the small slot and blow strongly into his face, raising the hair on his back. He continued to peek through the opening. He thought it was haunting. All he could see was darkness. Greedily, he longs to know what lay behind the mystery, unsure of his decision. Suddenly, the old worn-out door flung open violently he fell backward, so frightened he moved in slow motion. He lost time to slam it shut. Within a second, a sizeable hairy paw of a wolverine displaying merciless sharp claws dragged him by the leg into its domain. The man screamed in terror, sensing a dark presence. He detected warm blood gushing from his leg. He screamed in agony as the beast had a secure hold on him, digging deeper into his flesh.

Wolf Fang, the leader of fierce hunchback wolverines, screams, "Meat is on the table tonight, boys!" The ferocious black beasts licked up the thick drool around their mouths, driving their large, pointed fangs into the man's flesh. He heard the sound of bones breaking as his body ripped apart until the only thing left was chewed-up bones. As the pack feasted on his leftovers, the broad hunchback wolverines jerked up their heads with a fast impulse. They smelled kids from far off, with a taste of blood in their mouths. They desired their flesh. As they ran full force into the mansion, other deadly creatures escaped. They, too, sensed the presence of sweetmeat, searching the place seeking the chosen ones out foretold in a prophecy the hands of children would the kingdoms be saved and that peace would reign throughout the realms, but they must be found worthy, or death would be their reward.

Because of this, another beast the leader of the Snaken, Sorelle, went to work. The sixteen-foot creature slithered to his master's window inside his museum, lifting his upper torso packed solid every inch of muscle from his waist in the form of a man. Using his strapping arms, he gripped onto the outskirts of the high window and uncurled his lower body, as round as a tree trunk, onto the floor, alert, his keen eyesight seeing something going on in his master's garden. A man peered out the window with beady, piercing snake eyes on his stern, cruel face. He located the last child entering the pond below. "I wonder if master Bronze is aware of this secret pond the children had entered." Sorelle hissed with his long, slithering tongue, "No escape, children! I will wrap myself around you and feast on your flesh! My, what a nice delicacy buffet all of you will become. The sad thing is I might have to share you with the others."

Sorelle became disturbed, reminding himself. *"But of course, Sir Bronze makes that call, and I must obey what he first commands me to do."* The Snaken slithered from the tall window, wondering why Sir Bronze let the children out of his sight. "Fool!" The word slipped out, and he feared his overpowering master might have heard him.

Sorelle begins to justify, hoping what he sensed was accurate. He reasoned. *The hidden door to my master's freedom had finally opened, which he hungered for so long, desperately, to reenter his past, a burning desire to recover and regain what was lost, a longing in the pit of my master's black soul.*

Sorelle, after witnessing where the chosen ones were going, his tribe remained unyielding ready to fight for Bronze's freedom. The other repulsive creatures had plans of their own and returned to Bronze's museum to reenter the portal and found it shut. Upset their time expired, the creatures shrieked backward, angry, now, are at the mercy of their master, locked outside their portal.

The creepy things wanted nothing more but to retaliate as the Snakens' hissed with tongues of cobras, waiting for Sorelle to communicate to Sir Bronze through the open gate of his portal, allowing him to speak to his mind. Sorelle exclaimed. "My lord, we know where the chosen ones are! Do you desire us to follow them?"

Bronze shouted out, livid. "Alicia's necklace had drawn her into the pond too quickly—at last, the portal had been discovered. Soon, the kingdom of King James, my archenemy, shall be within my reach. Yes, follow them, but quickly, the brats have a head start. Chase them to the pits of hell, if you must, but get them! Sorelle, do not let the pests enter that second door, overpower them, and bring them to me. I will make use of them for my plans and purposes." Bronze took in a deep breath to stop from ventilating and continued mad as a hornet's nest. "Alicia will be mine to torture endlessly until she tells me where the other two keys are. She will look like a torn-up pin cushion when I am through with her! I will keep her alive to go through life deformed and maimed, wishing she had never been born." Bronze clanged his hands into a tight fist. "Now, what are you waiting for? The clock is ticking the longer I remain in this dimension. I will start withering old like the others. Finding those brats will lead me to the keys, to control all the kingdoms, and with that kind of power, I would have access to the pool of life and live forever. I must control all or nothing!"

Sorelle, even though he couldn't see his master, he bowed his head in reverence. He heard Bronze's black crow fly into his master's presence, cawing with an ear-piercing noise. Sorelle thought how he would love to strike his tail of poison venom through the crow's heart, but knowing he would be dead when Bronze got through with him. "Yes, my lord, at your command." Sorelle answered. He glanced over his broad shoulders, giving his Snaken's a stern look, "Let's go!" he hissed noisily. Sorelle sent word to all the different revolting creatures trapped inside Bronze's domain. "Meet me near the garden. Do not delay. The chosen ones have opened a portal; we must reach them before they open the door to King James' kingdom. Sir Bronze desires them returned to him at the drop of a hat and in one piece!"

The different sizes and shapes of creatures departed to do their master's bidding, left in haste. A few of them had no intention of bringing the chosen ones back. Their taste buds shouted out for a tasty treat, scheming plains once inside the Kingdom of Abethar, killing them off. And after their blood bath, the repugnant things would flee into the wildness of King James's domain, safe and out of their master's reach, thinking the man would be a fool to reenter Abethar.

Bronze's hateful forces arrived. Sorelle placed them in position following behind him—with six kinds of deadly creatures and six groups of each kind—departing the garden, making their way down the steps into the pond, in order and rank, as a sinister presence encamped around them.

THE VISION OF THE QUEST

This evil presence could be felt within the first kingdom of Abethar, the city of King James, instantly… Graven, a robust and mighty griffin, a genuinely brave knight of the king, sensed the presence of evil nearing. His faithful comrades discerned the same darkness lingering heavily in the air.

Their king, King James, stood erected though weak within his castle. He felt the prophecy of old unfolding causing hope to rise within him, but it was evident he, too, discerned an evilness. Something was off balance. The King was unaware Sorelle led his hordes down a long, narrow path to reach the three of the foretold prophecy before they entered another world they knew nothing about. Sorelle's tribe in the front line slithered across the rock floor, not known for tremendous speed but paralyzing venom striking into their enemies with pointy, arrowhead-shaped tails, a sure victory of death.

Sorelle felt Wolf Fang's pack breathing down his neck. Wolf Fang and his furious pack of wolverines, glaring their jagged teeth, with thick piles of drool splashing everywhere, thunderous growls penetrated the air, the beasts' razor-knife claws scraped firmly against the rock floor, embedding deep scratches into the stone. The Snaken gloated over the fact the wolverines rips meat off the bones of their enemies, separating their flesh into threads of yarn.

Sorelle's face cringed up distorted as he heard the dreadful spider's long legs make annoying shuffling sounds. He lost his stomach catching a whiff of the spider's thick, coarse hair smelling like dead rats. He would do anything to wrap his coils around their fowl three-foot vast body, squeezing their insides out to hear them pop like a huge pimple. Sorelle was displeased that Bronze needed their expertise being able to jump through the air at a distance of fourteen feet to catch and slay their prey, spitting out venom paralyzing, using two horns upon their heads, trapping innocent victims inside their steel webs, to nibble on them, bite after bite, day after day, making a gruesome, unspeakable noise devouring their victims' flesh in a slow, torturous death.

He glanced behind him, spotting Bronze ten-foot bats, known to sense movement at a great distance, even a pin drop, they slacked behind like crippled men, with twisted legs shaped as roots of a tree, walking at a slow pace due to their deformity. Sorelle was amused with their cruelty with thin, long, fish hook claws, sharper than a double-edged blade, plunging into their victims' stomachs, ripping out their guts, leaving them for dead. Sorelle kept an eye on the bats realizing their mighty wings and powerful talons were strong enough to carry the chosen ones away with ease. He began hearing shuffling different hordes fighting who would reach them first. Sorelle demanded with a shout. "Stay in order and rank. I am the first to receive the children and place them into our master's hands alive! I am taking no chance in them being slaughtered! I will not reap the consequences of receiving a harsh punishment at the hands of Sir Bronze."

With his wide scaly trunk, Sorelle began to slide up and down the ranks, satisfied that the hordes had become calmer as his pea-sized eyes skimmed past the bats onto six hellish scorpions which he also despised. Hearing them pitter-pattered across the floor, the size of a raccoon, with flying wings, he found himself entertained with the fierce face of a lion and a nasty, brutal sting that killed instantly, sending burning flames of fire throughout its victim's body.

The Snaken slimed his way closer to the back, making sure the gruesome porcupines kept up with his tribe, which moved sluggishly, dragging slowly behind the end of the line, with tiny eyes and pocket-knife teeth displaying sharp needles which shoot poison into all directions, paralyzing their victims. Sorelle entertained the thought of how the porcupines loved to eat and enjoyed watching their prey suffer. He slithered his way back to the front of the line. The creatures under his command searched to and fro as a dark fog hovered over the fearless beasts. The wolverines sniffed to the left and the right, smelling and detecting the chosen ones. He overheard Wolf Fang speak to his clan. "Not too much longer to go. We are gaining ground." Wolf Fang snarled. "I can smell their stench.""

Sorelle hissed, creating the sound of a thousand annoying mosquitoes. "I shall determine that! Bronze put me in command over all of you. Everyone harkens to my voice, and it's my voice and no other! Am I understood?"

THE VISION OF THE QUEST

Wolf Fang waxed hot. He snarled his mouth upward and exposed his teeth. "Back down, slime bucket! I am the leader of my pack!"

Sorelle's head hit the ceiling but, in this case, walls of water. He and Wolf Fang stared eye-to-eye, desiring complete control. The bell rang the match was on with no afterthoughts. Both tore into each other's throats, striking and biting, clawing and ripping; blood flowed. Wolf Fang scurried, bringing his razorback teeth into Sorelle's back, not relenting, shaking him violently within his great jaws. Without mercy, viciously, he sank his teeth farther into him. Sorelle retaliated. Settling the score, he smoothly coiled himself around the hot-headed wolverine, sucking the life out of him, squeezing him with all his might. Wolf Fang was forced to let go of his nasty bite, gasping for air. He used all his strength with a tremendous powerful thrust of his body, and Wolf Fang broke free from his deathtrap squeeze. He aimed for the slimeball's throat, but missed.

Wolf Fang's mouth dropped significant piles of drool mixed with blood. The fight rammed on intensely. Both were furious. Sorelle grew impatient with a terrible hiss. He aimed his arrow-shaped tail toward the wolverine, striking him with his deadly poison, erasing him from the equation. Wolf Fang saw it coming, jumping full force through the air, exhibiting his bulging muscles, and landing behind the Snaken. He violently used his mighty powerful jaws, biting and digging brutally again into Sorelle's lower back, swishing his flesh back and forth inside his mouth. The Snaken's back went limp with no power to strike but not giving in to a hard blow, turning swiftly, he gripped Wolf Fang forcefully into his bulky, rippled arms, squeezing the ambitious beast hearing his ribs crack. Wolf Fang fought back, clawing and biting, breaking loose a second time with another confrontation both rumbled. In the end, sternly growling and hissing for more wasted minutes, equal powerhouses, at long last, both ended in a draw. Their joust for power, however, allowed Alicia, Roger, and Emily enough time to get away and safely reach the portal door to the kingdom of Abethar.

"As I said, I shall lead!" Sorelle hissed, infuriated. Wolf Fang growled, showing off his sharp iceberg teeth. He was a hot torpedo with flames of fire in his eyes. The Wolverine snarled toward Sorelle, spatting blood everywhere with venom in his voice. "Watch your back, slime bucket. There will be a day you will be all mine!" Sorelle spit wildly. "Now, remember, I am also under my master's firm hand. With that being said, enough time has been wasted. If the chosen ones get away, we are both done for." Wolf Fang stepped down, and his blood boiled, his back arched full of bitter scorn. He reluctantly followed Sorelle and his Snakens.

Sorelle slithered painfully back into the front of his cohorts blazing mad, lost in thoughts planning Wolf Fang's doom day… as Alicia, Roger, and Emily reached a dead-end standing bewildered in front of an odd-looking door made of old rock, having no knob or keyhole but all sorts of engravings.

Roger talked over the loud walls of water. "What is it with all these engravings we keep coming across?"

Alicia noticed an area on the door identical to the shape of her necklace. She slipped it off her neck and placed it inside the groves of the door. Unexpectedly, it matched up. She noticed an area she could put her fingers into that circled her jewelry. She turned it into a complete circle. She and Roger were flabbergasted as a crystal glass knob appeared. They stood back watching the door open, seeing bright green grass on the other side without having a hint it was the same portal when they first entered the pond.

Alicia moved forward to enter into the unknown, not knowing what they would encounter. Roger gripped her arm and drew her back. "Like you said when we first arrived at Bronze's mansion it could be a booby trap. It may not be safe," he said.

"Roger, what other choice do we have? We must go inside, please trust me?" she asked.

Emily stayed quiet, debating who would win.

"Trust you?" Roger expressed. "Do you remember the bee that landed on me, and you said, 'Stay still, and it will fly away'—yeah, of course, after stinging me three times, my face swelled up twice its size—yeah, I trust you, alright."

"Roger, that's a thing of the past. It happened how many years ago, so hurry and stop your squawking. We must go through this door quickly, especially before Bronze catches wind that we are missing. Who knows what that insane man will do to us?" This time she pulled on his arm. "What are you waiting for? Come on, Roger, it may be our only hope of saving my mother. He may try to kill her."

Roger rolled his eyes teasingly. "Bronze is infatuated with your mother. You don't have that to worry about. But now that I'm on a roll, I held a flimsy pipe for you. Bees flew up through it and zapped me all over my body. Every time you want me to trust you, I am the one getting stung, but to be honest, Alicia, we don't know what's behind that door." Roger said, anxiously.

"And we never will if you keep procrastinating. Let's go, Roger. It could be our only chance." Alicia became sidetracked as she watched her necklace drop to the cold floor, the door slammed shut, and then the knob disappeared. Alicia placed her hands on her tiny hips, upset.

Emily sensed the tension. She exclaimed. "Movie time, hey guys, make the battle worth my wild, oh and I hope it has a happy ending! I love tear jerkers." She snickered. "If only I had popcorn."

Roger turned a deaf ear to Emily. He acted maturely. "I guess we waited too long." He looked into his friend's tan face. "Alicia, you must know I would do about anything for you. We don't know the dangers behind that door. Honestly, I am not sure if I will be able to protect you or Emily. As much as I hate to admit this, that scares me."

Emily couldn't believe what she was hearing. She smirked, pretending to throw popcorn into her mouth. "Come on, Roger. Make it more smoochy; just kiss the girl. I know that you like her."

Roger ignored Emily. He looked into Alicia's dark chocolate eyes and saw something different. The beginning of a spark of true love. He didn't know what to think when Emily screamed, pulling on Alicia's shirt. "Alicia! What is that noise? It's a scary sound closing in behind us!" Roger and Alicia looked over their shoulders and witnessed frightful-looking snakes-like men moving in their direction, fifty feet away, and other terrifying creatures behind them.

Alicia screamed in fear. "Roger, what could be worse behind that door than what is coming at us now!" Her heart jumped into her throat. She snatched up her necklace with trembling hands, placing it into the key-shaped groove. The odd-looking door seemed to take an eternity to open. "What are they?" Roger shouted as he grabbed petrified Emily's hand to run into the portal. "Come on, Alicia!" he screamed as the door opened completely. His only thought was to keep Alicia and Emily out of their spine-chilling path.

"You won't need to ask me twice!" Alicia cried out, scared stiff. Her legs felt like spaghetti noodles as she followed Roger inside the new territory. She attempted to pull herself together, watching Roger try and slam the door shut as a wolverine's ruthless paws wedged in the crack. With all her strength, Alicia helped Roger push on it, but the beast was overpowering. They pushed harder. Their faces turned beet red. The wolverine's bloody paw finally fell to the earth before their eyes as the other paw remained slightly wiggling within the heavy door. Emily screamed fearfully. The door sheltered her from seeing the hordes near the back of the line breaking order and rank, smelling the taste of blood as carnivores with no sense of loyalty. Wolf Fang's and Sorelle's tribes attempted to fight off the spiders and scorpions while the bats and possums turned on one another. Many foolish creatures died. Alicia and Roger listened to the cutthroats growing louder and louder. Emily was too afraid to move with the awful, earsplitting noise. Immediately without warning, a strong wind brushed past them, slamming the door completely shut. The wolverine's paw went limp.

Alicia, Roger, and Emily were startled as the door disappeared. Green grass and a clear blue sky appeared in its place. The pond was gone. Bronze mansion nowhere in sight, in wonderment, they didn't know what to think or what to believe as they searched around, exploring and thinking wherein the dickens are they, straightway they had to do a double-take, surprised as a bright light shined upon them. "Wow! I told you we were in heaven! Who's the silly goose now?" Emily squealed.

Alicia, too much in shock, didn't have an answer, she slowly turned to Roger. "Where do you think we are? Could we really be in another dimension?"

"Heaven—I told you!" Emily waved her arms on cloud nine. "Alicia, we got to find Mom because we might be able to find Father here too."

Roger reassured Emily. "Half-pint, this is not heaven, but frankly, I'm not sure anymore," he stood baffled, not knowing what to do. No sooner had he spoken than the brilliant light around them dimmed, a great cloud lowered in their presence, and two unicorns with gorgeous white wings appeared. All three were astonished. "Okay, if this is a dream, do not wake me up," Roger spoke up, pleased.

Alicia grabbed her little sister's hand, who could not remain still. "Then if we're not in heaven, maybe we are inside a game," Emily bubbled with joy as the white unicorns knelt peacefully and tossed their heads to the side, directing them to get onto their backs.

"Well, what are we waiting for? We can't stand here all day." Emily bellowed as she ran to pet the unicorns, with a sparkle in her big blue eyes. Roger noticed they looked harmless and tossed Emily onto her ride, *but a ride where?* he thought. Alicia ran and picked up her necklace from the grass where the door once stood. Roger helped her onto the same unicorn with Emily, and as he touched Alicia's arm, he sensed a warm sensation come over him. Alicia experienced butterflies in the pit of her stomach. She looked down from where she sat. Roger gazed up into Alicia's face noticing more and more how beautiful she was, before jumping upon his unicorn next to them.

Chapter Three

In Uncertain Times

THE VISION OF THE QUEST

The unicorns flew gracefully, their wings outstretched with a powerful thrust that winds blew cool breezes into the chosen ones' faces. Emily held tight around Alicia's waist as they flew with remarkable speed. "This is fun!" Emily shouted. Alicia and Roger searched below and were speechless, witnessing all the wonders like a painting without flaws, the mountains, fields, and waterfalls unique and colorful.

They swiftly arrived at an eye-appealing castle and watched a draw gate slowly lower. The unicorns descended from the air, not wasting time, and smoothly landed. They gaited across a sturdy wooden bridge that led toward the castle. They stopped. Alicia jumped off, helping Emily down. Roger leaped off and surveyed the region, wondering where in the universe they could be.

Alicia whispered, "It's beautiful, Roger."

"Yeah, it's too beautiful, almost overwhelming. Its hair raising." Roger responded, still looking all around.

"Pinch me. I can see if I am dreaming." She spoke in a hushed tone.

Emily overheard and didn't hesitate to give her sister one good pinch.

"Ouch! What was that for?" she asked, surprised.

"Didn't you want to be pinched?" Emily snickered.

"Not really, and you didn't have to pinch that hard," Alicia said upset, turning her focus back to Roger. "Well, then, I guess I am not dreaming. Where do you think we are?" Before Roger could answer, one of the unicorns spoke. Alicia and Roger's mouths dropped open.

Emily was ecstatic. "You can talk! Wow! You can fly, and you can talk!" She beamed at Alicia with questions in her eyes. "Do you think Mom will let me bring her home? Maybe I can keep her as a pet? I'll potty-train her. I promise!"

The unicorn replied, "I am not a female, and I'm quite potty-trained." He turned toward Alicia and Roger. "My name is Acorn. You will be greeting Princess Lilly. Please follow me; it's not safe for you to be seen."

The chosen ones listened respectfully and quickly followed Acorn. The other unicorn went its separate way. Alicia noticed the carvings outside the castle embedded into the rocks, similar to Bronze's mansion. They ventured inside the court, taken into a great room inside the castle. Acorn brought them before a young princess dressed elegantly, her blonde hair flying in long waves down her back. The unicorn bowed. Alicia, Roger, and Emily followed suit and kneeled on the cold marble floor. Alicia thought about how the princess looked close to her age. Emily blurted out. "What are we praying for?"

"Shhh," Alicia lifted her eyes slightly. She recognized the creative floor trim similar to what Bronze had in his mansion.

The young princess spoke. "You may rise."

Emily noticed the princess dress and cried out, full of joy, "You are dressed like my fairy tale stories my Mom used to read to me when I was younger. I know we are not inside a game, so are we inside a book?"

Alicia shot Emily a stern look.

The princess smiled with kindness. "You are fine little one, and the answer to your question is no. You're not inside a book, but a kingdom where all things are possible."

Princess Lilly brought her attention to Alicia. "There is supposed to be someone else with you. Where is she?"

Alicia wondered if she meant her mother. But remained quiet. Princess Lilly continued. "All of you have been chosen for this appointed time. Destiny has brought you through our kingdom's portal, we have been waiting for your arrival, but where is she, where is the other?" the Princess asked once more.

"Our arrival?" Alicia answered, confused, "It's just us three. Besides our mother who is not with us."

The young princess still standing looked unsettled but went on to speak. "My name is Princess Lilly. This is my father's kingdom. With the expression on each of your faces, I know you have many questions and desire answers. It's only fair that you should know the truth. Abethar, which you have entered, is the first kingdom out of three but two of the kingdoms had been snatched from the King. However, there are other kingdoms."

Princess Lilly focused her eyes deeply on Alicia. "The power within your necklace that I see around your neck has drawn you to our kingdom. However, there was a time your necklace was fashioned into one complete key, which kept the three kingdoms standing strong. We were as one until the key was broken into three separate pieces that unlocked the answers to each of the three kingdoms, but the keys had been lost until now because of lust, greed, and the desire for power."

"Now, in the time when we were as three kingdoms, the king was brave and robust, and his lands flourished. Sadly, the king was deceived by his closest friend and bravest knight, Sir Bronze Pierce."

Roger interrupted. He spoke up, disturbed. "Excuse me, Princess Lilly, we met a man named Sir Bronze Pierce. Is it possible that he's the same man we met, and if so, why did he want Alicia's necklace so badly?"

Princess Lilly replied, "Most likely, he is the same man we speak of today. He is an evil man. Bronze will go to any length to receive your necklace or the one I sense hanging around your little sister's neck hidden inside her shirt." Princess Lilly smiled at Emily.

Alicia cried out, "What must we do? Our mother may be in grave danger. She is under Bronze's influence."

Princess Lilly spoke with a concerned heart. She realized the chosen ones sought help, but, on the contrary, King James and his kingdom sought the aid of the chosen ones. "I will speak with my father, the King of Abethar." Alicia and Roger became thrilled, hearing the mention of a true king.

Princess Lilly said straightforward. "But for now, I must explain a story from long ago that all three of you will need to know." Alicia glanced at Roger, wondering what they had to do with the story of this unusual but marvelous place and its history. Alicia took a tomboyish stance and listened to what the lovely princess had to say.

The princess went to sit on her throne. A guard dressed head to toe in armor again ordered everyone to kneel, and as she sat down, the guard called all to stand. Princess Lilly spoke. "The story of our kingdom is there was a time a beautiful woman named Leah was torn between two men, Bronze who lusted for power and domain, and my father who desired righteousness and liberty for his people; both men were in love with my mother. My mother chose my father, King James, and married him. I am their only child, and because of her decision, and though my father and Bronze were friends, Bronze became highly jealous that Leah chose my father over him. He began to despise the king and reluctantly half-heartedly served him."

"Bronze figured the only way to get my mother was to kidnap her, probably thinking if he can't have her, then my father can't have her either, but all the while, he still lusted for power and desired my father's kingdom, a great battle came. Bronze knew this was his opportunity for victory, and as the battle raged, he retreated, leaving the king's side. He returned to the castle, hoping to find Queen Leah, but found out my father's enemies had set the castle on fire. Bronze fought hard against his enemies as he diligently searched for the woman he loved. With regret, he lost Leah, which was never his in the first place. A servant spotted Bronze looking back at the castle in flames and watched him flee, managing to take several of my father's men with him. Bronze was pursued into the dark forest, drove him into the rocks at Mount Horeb, the last I had heard of him, he fell into a portal."

Princess Lilly's countenance became sad. "My father returned from battle with victory in his hands. He defeated his enemy, but sadly, on his return home, he beheld his castle on fire from far off. He rode his horse hard to the court to find half of it up in flames. His men worked long hours throughout the night to put out the fire; unfortunately, a few did not survive the heat. During this time, my father would not stop frantically searching the castle for his wife, though his body was mangled and burned, screaming and crying out her name all night until morning, but to no avail. He then searched desperately throughout the entire kingdom of Abethar for days, weeks, and months but never found her. He concluded that she died inside the castle my father grieved and mourned her absence."

"Painfully, he had won the battle but lost his beloved wife in the process. He would rather have felt the agony of his burned body than the brokenness he felt from losing his true love. The only thing he was able to save was her beautiful portrait, and with this great tragedy, even though my father's heart was filled with grief, he had to remain strong to rebuild his kingdom for his people, and so he did." Princess

Lily tried to hide her frown. "When the battle took place, I was at my aunt's and uncle's house; I was kept safe. I was very young, and I also miss the warmth of my mother's arms she would have given me if she were alive today."

The king remained behind a curtain of lattice glass. Princess Lilly was only aware of his presence. Alicia, Roger, and Emily could not see the tears that sprang from the king's eyes as he heard the mention of Queen Leah's name.

Princess Lilly has seen Emily becoming restless and decided enough was said. She spoke with authority. "I extend my hand to the three of you to indulge in a gratifying meal. However, I will not be able to take part. I have affairs that need attending too. However, I invite you to be my guest at my breakfast table in the morning." Alicia, Roger, and Emily were fired up to be asked such an honor. The princess right away had them follow her through a wide hallway showing them toward the dining hall. Alicia and Emily stopped in their tracks as they saw a portrait of Queen Leah hanging on a wall. They cried out, "Mother!"

The princess was taken by surprise. "You know this person?"

"Princess Lilly, this is our mother!" Alicia exclaimed. Emily began to cry as she saw the portrait. She began to worry about her, missing her soft touches and warm embrace.

The princess asked, startled, "How can this be? This portrait is of my mother, Queen Leah. This is the portrait I had spoken of that my father had saved from the fire."

The girls, including Roger, became speechless, wondering, "How …?"

Alicia said with respect. "I don't understand, but she looks so much like our mother. Please forgive us?"

"There is nothing you need to be forgiven for." Princess Lilly has seen it was having an impact on Emily. She changed the subject. "After you eat, please feel free to retire to your rooms. My butlers shall show you the way. We will discuss much tomorrow morning. I hope you will feel most welcome."

The princess was true to her word, for on a wide table the butlers brought out superb food dishes They ate until their stomachs became full, weary from the long day; they called it a night. Emily giggled as she rang a gold bell next to her. Immediately butlers came from the corners of the dining hall and began to lead them to their rooms.

Roger pointed in the direction of the king's butlers, who walked only an ear drop away. "These men are dressed like Bronze's servants, wearing those funny-looking white outfits. I wouldn't be caught dead in them because …."

Alicia softly elbowed him. Roger grinned. "I think you need to be more careful with your elbow and stop making it a habit."

Alicia calmly whispered. "Bronze's servants were beyond eerie, but these people are kind and trying to help us. I'm starting to see why my mother was always correcting you."

Roger complained. "Man, now I understand what your father meant, not to argue with a woman when they think they're always right, to keep peace in the family, but you are right, I should show appreciation for what the king and his daughter are doing for us."

Roger noticed the butler pointing to a door. "This is where you will be dwelling for tonight."

Roger, slipped out a yawn nodding his head. He entered his bedroom and flopped onto his bed. Alicia and Emily also felt zonked out. They entered their room which joined Roger's bedroom. It wasn't long before the three fell fast asleep, and, as morning quickly arrived, the sun shined through the castle window. The three felt the warmth on their faces waking up out of pleasant sleep, exceedingly peaceful and tranquility until a butler knocked on both their doors. Alicia swung her door open. The servant spoke. "Breakfast shall be served in the dining hall. Please join the princess."

Alicia's mind went blank. She suddenly remembered. *He's the man with the shovel at Bronze's mansion. But how?*

"It's a small world, isn't it?" The butler's mouth did not budge. She heard him speak within her mind. Alicia stepped backward, worried for Emily's safety.

The man saw Alicia was nervous. "Don't worry; I bring you no harm. I am Caleb, your guardian."

"You can read my thoughts?" she asked, staggered, coming to grips that her lips, too, did not budge. She didn't know if she should grab Emily to make a run for Roger's room.

Her guardian answered. "No, I cannot read your thoughts. I can communicate to you and you to me through our minds. Again, I bring no harm but to warn you that this is not just a battle to bring the three kingdoms together but a battle to be prepared for the end times."

Alicia was quiet. She didn't know what to think of the man standing before her. She sensed his friendlessness and looked at his sweet face. She wasn't sure what to believe. Instantaneously, she had a flashback as a little girl saved by this man but saved from what? The man's face shined toward her and then turned to walk away. Alicia watched him disappear into thin air as if through an open door; her mouth dropped to the floor. Roger and Emily were now standing behind her. Emily beamed. "Alicia, you've been standing at that door like a stature saying nothing, just staring. It looks like you've seen a ghost."

Alicia looked past Emily. She was tongue-tied but finally managed to speak. "Roger, didn't you see that man? He was the man I had seen at Bronze's mansion with the long brown hair and ponytail. Didn't you see him? Did you?" She repeated.

Roger snickered. "Huh, Alicia, you must have been sleepwalking. The only man I see is a butler setting food on that king-size table. I'm starving."

Emily peeped in. "Yeah, me too. You were just seeing things, Alicia. Let's go eat."

Alicia wondered herself was she daydreaming. Her head felt like it was spinning on wheels. She suddenly had another flashback of the same brown-headed ponytailed man picking her up from her father's car and sitting her on the cold, wet grass before the car went up into flames with her father inside the vehicle. Tears slipped down her cheek as she recalled screaming and crying for him on that painful night, the darkest hour of her life. Alicia felt the touch of her guardian's hand gently touch her shoulder. She remembered the words he had spoken to her mind. "Run the race, keep the faith to the prize of His calling. You are never alone." That lonely night as Alicia had sobbed with her face in her hands. She felt strengthened by his words. She had looked up and watched her guardian disappear as he did a minute ago. She shook her head, being too much to comprehend at that time.

Alicia wiped tears from her eyes with the back of her shirt sleeve. She searched from Roger's eyes to Emily's and saw they were dumbfounded about what she had shared. She realized she was on her own. "Let's go. The princess is waiting for us." She quickly placed her guardian onto a shelf in the back of her mind, and he quickly faded from her thoughts.

The three entered the dining hall. Princess Lilly was already seated. The immense room caught Alicia and Roger's attention, too tired to notice last night. It reminded them exactly of Bronze's dining hall, but smelling something delicious, they brought their focus to the royal spread, a grander breakfast spread than what Bronze had offered; fit for a king.

"Thank you," Alicia said, bowing her head toward the princess. Roger and Emily did the same.

Princess Lilly spoke warmly. "Please be seated and enjoy your meal."

The king remained nearby, hiding his scars and frail body behind the lattice glass.

Princess Lilly, after a half-hour, ranged a silver bell. Butlers came and cleared the table and brought out desserts of all kinds. Emily and Roger's eyes widened.

The princess addressed Alicia. "Last night I shared with you concerning my father's kingdom but now I would like to know where do you come from and how may the king be a help to you?"

Roger and Emily both spoke with deserts piled in their mouths. "I believe Princess Lilly has asked me," Alicia softly corrected. Roger and Emily became quiet. Alicia turned her attention toward the kind princess and spoke. "Somehow, during a frightful storm, we have traveled far from home. Bronze had horrifying creatures of some sort which I feel came from the pits of hell. They chased us to the portal of your kingdom. Thank God. Roger slammed it shut in time. Bronze desired us for his use, trying to take my necklace from me, given to me by my mother. This immoral man has a stronghold on my mother, and as Roger mentioned last night, she is in his care. Somehow, since I entered the kingdom of Abethar, I know we need to save her by discovering the mystery of our necklaces, but you have done so much for us. I should be asking how we may help you."

The princess smiled sweetly, delighted by Alicia's wisdom. "Ask, and you shall receive. There is something of prominent value that all three of you can do for my king, for it is said there is a tree of enlightenment that stands near the waters of life. The person who controls the keys of the kingdom may receive a 'divine pitcher of water', including healing leaves from the tree. Please, bring these gifts back to my king so he may receive strength back. In return, he will have the strength to deliver you and your family from the evil one and know this. You must travel hard and be swift because my king grows weaker with every passing season. Will you accept this quest?"

Princess Lilly glanced at Emily. Her cheeks puffed out like a gerbil. She was pleased to hear Alicia and Roger, without hesitating, said yes, and agreed to take on the quest. The two did not realize the dangers each would face, but Alicia feared her mother's life would be jeopardized if they did nothing. Roger felt the same, feeling Bronze's infatuation would wear off after the jerk sees Miss Liana would rather die than allow him to have his way with her.

"Good," the princess said. "Please follow me to the grand hall where you will meet my king's royal knights for your safety and well-being. They will protect you in getting to the third kingdom."

"Royal knights?" Alicia and Roger look at each other flabbergasted as all three follow the princess through many twists and turns similar to Bronze's mansion and enter the great hall once more. The princess sat down on her father's throne. She smiled at the chosen ones. "Graven, the griffin will show---" her words cut off.

"A, a, Griffin?" Alicia stuttered.

"Yes, a griffin. What world do you kids come from?" Princess Lilly questioned. Alicia bluntly answered. "A world that has trucks, cars, and motorcycles." Princess Lilly seemed baffled. "I would love to hear more about your stimulating world, but for now, I must continue, for we are pressed for time. Graven knows the location of the Second and Third

Kingdom. With his strong, mighty wings, the griffin will not have a problem leading you, but most likely you will come across adversaries for there are those that try to rob, kill, and destroy good men, women, and children that stand and fight for the truth, in saying this there will be battles to be fought. Now, about the king's knights, there is also Granite, half-man, half rock, an ultimate powerhouse, and of course Chip, a chipmunk, who will be protecting all of you at all cost."

Alicia snickered. "I apologize, but how is a chipmunk for our protection. I would hate to see him get hurt."

Emily shook vibrantly, full of life. "I bet he is adorable. I'll carry the little fellow in my pocket. I will keep him safe."

Princess Lilly laughed. "Don't let little Chip fool you. He changes form at will. That little fellow can get you out of some really tough spots."

Princess Lilly witnessed amazement upon all three faces, their eyes the size of quarters, having trouble believing what they were hearing. She looked toward Alicia and spoke pleased. "Acorn, whom you have met, is a unicorn beautiful beyond words and wonderful in stature. You, Alicia, will have the honor of traveling on the back of this gorgeous beast." Princess Lilly looked toward Roger. "You will venture on White Lightning, a wolf and white as the pure driven snow, with a broad back and powerful muscular legs, and a unique black stripe from his head to his tail with wings greater than those of a Pegasus."

"Wow." was the only word Roger could think to say.

Princess Lily looked at Emily and smiled. "And you, little one, will ride on a Cheetah called Spot. I named him when I was your age because he's covered in numerous black dots." Emily jumped up and down over the wall with excitement. "Does he have wings, like Alicia's and Roger's?"

"Yes," Princess Lilly answered, enjoying Emily's rambunctious personality. Emily reminded her of herself when she was her age. She thought weird even somewhat resembled her but regardless, she continued. "This Cheetah is known for its profound speed on the ground as well in flight."

THE VISION OF THE QUEST

The kids were beside themselves as the princess sent word for the king's knights, the protectors of the chosen ones, to come quickly. With haste, the knights arrived outside the castle and waited patiently as the king's soldiers flew open the two gigantic doors. Alicia and Roger were certain the doors looked like Bronze's doors inside his domain, even the carved markings. Graven landed abruptly before them. His large wings caused heavy wind to blow in their faces. They smelled Graven's thick fur, similar to smelling a dog after getting a bath. Granite the rock man, entirely huge and bulky, jumped off Graven's back. Alicia, Roger, and Emily were speechless. The rock man looked toward the three kids. He teased, asking boldly. "What is it my big brainy rock head?" The three remained lost for words as they watched a chipmunk hidden in the Griffin's fur, and jumping off Graven's back. Chip jested. "Granite, I assure you, your head's as empty as it gets." Granite flexed his rock arms. He pushed out his boulder chest.

"What, little punk? I will smush you like a mosquito." Chip transformed into an enormous jackhammer that breaks rocks into tiny pieces. Granite backed down and teased. "You're scaring the little ones, if one of them wet their pants I am not cleaning it up." Chip transformed back into a chipmunk. "Listen, big boulder. I am not cleaning up no one's mess…," Chip's words faded as Emily cried out. "Hey, We don't wet our pants!" Everyone laughed except Emily, as Acorn, Spot, and White Lightning, entered through the king-size doors, and once their magnificent wings had settled, White Lightning cried out. "What did we miss the party?" Roger could not hold his tongue any longer, overwhelmed with their many talents. "Whelp, it's like this everyone." he determined. "I am thinking of this as a wild, crazy, dream but, somehow, my gut is telling me its reality."

Granite chuckled. "Well, kid your gut will be telling you, soon enough airborne with White Lighting would make even a fly's wings barf." Chip complained toward his friend. "Fly's barf, your airhead."

Emily, less afraid, squealed laughing, tilting her head to the side. "He's right silly fly's wings do not barf the fly's do! I learned it in school." Emily caught the princess's attention. She pondered how Emily tilts her head the same way she does when she laughs. She shook herself as she heard Granite beam with a rebuttal. "Chip and you say I am the one without the brain? Anyone smart would know that the fly's wings do barf."

Emily held her hands over her ears and laughed. "Huh! Fly's silly, not wings?"

Chip smirked. "Little girl, it's way over the rock head's empty eggshell."

Alicia finally chimed in. "I agree with Roger. I don't know if this is a dream or reality but what I do know is, my mother needs us. What are we waiting for? We have a mission to complete, and it's not getting done with all of you flapping your jaws."

"I like this one!" Granite exclaimed with a deep, booming voice. "She's a bossy one and straight to the point. My kind of lady."

"Yeah, I bet she's potty-trained too." Acorn winked at Emily as Roger helped the ball of energy onto Spot. He jumped onto White Lightning and surprisingly found himself again admiring Alicia. Acorn lowered onto the white marbled floor, allowing Alicia to slip gracefully onto his back. Quickly, they departed in good spirit toward the Second Kingdom. Graven hoped to find allies on the way to find the precious gifts for King James before reaching the third kingdom. Each hour Alicia and Emily traveled, their hearts longed for their mother, though they carried the confidence to prevail. After a long flight, the king's knights decided to land and walk a short way, giving the chosen ones, time to stretch their legs. Chip spoke out. "Let's take a shortcut through the woods to find food and clean water to strengthen us." Graven agreed and touched down into a tropical jungle. The others followed suit, smelled the fragrance of bananas and honey, and heard the nearby water flow. They immediately looked up into the trees and spotted tons of thousands of bananas with gigantic beehives of honey right under their noses, hidden and covered with branches. Alicia, Roger, and the others happily ate and were surprised how easily their stomachs became full-on bananas. Graven said. "We must move quickly to find water and make haste to the second Kingdom." The Quest listened and followed Graven and the sound of the water's melody. They came upon a stream leading to a lake, discovering bright, colorful lights dancing upon the

THE VISION OF THE QUEST

clear water, reflected by the many rainbows above them. Alicia and Roger stood mesmerized, witnessing a lake of that magnitude. Graven knew the territory. Suddenly, an extraordinary buzzing noise sounded like numerous bees storming and heading their way.

"Let's go!" Graven shouted, though before anyone could do anything, an ape-like creature hovered over their heads with fluttering wings. Swiftly, Granite, and Graven, were lifted into the air and held there like a feather, both tied up like a box with a ribbon. Chip disguised himself, transforming into one of the apes while the others were surrounded and going nowhere. Emily exclaimed, "They are the color of grapes!"

"What is the meaning of this?" Alicia yelled out, upset toward them, causing her to lose time helping her mother. She thought after seeing Bronze's terrifying creatures. The apes weren't half as scary besides being funny-looking and big and smelly. Congo, the leader of the Conchidas—a mighty ape with the strength of an ox and a vast robust frame—flew swiftly and stared face-to-face with Alicia. His cream-colored wings fluttered non-stop as he hovered in mid-air.

Congo answered with a strong voice. "I will ask the questions here. Why have you trespassed through our jungles? Who gave you the right to partake of our food and water, and most importantly, who are you?"

Alicia's spirit rose within her. She declared boldly. "We are on a quest for the second kingdom to unlock the mysteries leading to the third kingdom to behold the tree of living waters for the healing of King James of Abethar. He grows weak each day, and every minute counts into finding what he seeks. Will you stand with him in this hour of his need? Can we count on your help for the strengthening of the king, which will enable him to save the kingdoms from such a brut, selfish man named Sir Bronze Pierce and help save my mother from his mischievous hands."

The powerful Congo ordered loudly. "Soldiers release the captives. Look, a king's friend is like a banana to us." Congo grinned like a Cheshire cat. The Conchidas released Graven and Granite. Graven swooped down and caught Granite before he slammed onto the hard earth. Congo slowly touched the ground. He stood tall on his feet and banged his chest. He skimmed past the others and onto the great griffin and nodded his head in respect toward him. He recognized Graven, a friend from long ago. Without hesitating, Congo turned and spoke firmly to Alicia. "You may continue on your journey, but know this; there is a horde of black winged wolverines close on your tail. You must move quickly! We will slow them down, but there are too many for us to handle. We will do what we can. God Speed!"

"Why are you helping us?" Alicia asked, curious.

Congo looked her way. "When I beheld the key of the kingdom around your neck and saw virtue in your eyes. I knew you could be trusted, now away, promptly, before the enemy overtakes you."

Like a conductor in an Orchestra, Congo waved his hand for his troops to follow him. They took off like a plane toward the open sky. Congo searched across the horizon. The brute ape a few miles ahead spotted the sky darkened with black-winged wolverines. He eyed the ground, and white wolverines caught his attention, with no wings but running fast like a cougar. Congo yelled out in a loud booming voice, "It's now or never!"

Congo allowed the Quest a lead way. The king's knights soared speedily, with their wings beating explosively against the warm air, moving fast out of the wolverines' grasp toward their destination.

Chapter Four

THE NEW DISCOVERY

THE VISION OF THE QUEST

Graven and the entire Quest flew with great haste through the sky for a considerable amount of time, right into Crystal Mountain's frozen territories. Despite the concerted efforts of Congo and his troops' in holding the enemies at bay, the spawns of Bronze were still gaining ground. Too close, even, that some of the king's knights with keen hearing could clearly hear the sounds of grinding teeth. Graven could already spot Wolf Fang and his clan over the horizon, dotting the sky like a dark cloud. He observed the beasts' laborious efforts despite their need to land after their initial bursts of flight. Graven bellowed out, "The callous beasts are hot and heavy on our trail!"

Graven immediately motioned to the others. "Get the chosen ones to safety!" he demanded. Acorn, White Lightning, and Spot soared ahead. Graven turned around swiftly, flying toward his opponents with an acute aim, shooting red hot lasers from his eyes. He destroyed four of Wolf Fang's scouts, watching them disintegrate with each blast. Far off, he spotted Zoroc, the second in command of Bronze's monstrous regiment chasing after them. Zoroc, with his clan of white wolverines, was speeding over hurdles like thick waves of icing on a cake. Graven glimpsed down onto the boundless mountain coved in layers of ice slowing down Zoroc's wolverines. He returned swiftly to the Quest and was pleased to find no one was hurt. His warriors looked ready to drop after flying for countless hours. Graven knew it was too cold for Alicia, Roger, and Emily. They had to seek shelter soon.

The chosen ones shivered, snuggling within Acorn and Spot's mounts in hope for warmth. Their hands numb, making it more difficult to hold on tight. Roger decided earlier to ride with Emily on Spot. She was fearful of the wolverines. He held onto her tightly, keeping her from falling off. Emily was too cold to complain. She felt like an ice pop inside a freezer.

The Quest neared a high, towering mountain covered in glittering snow. Alicia and Roger watched the skies as if they would swallow the mountain up along with them. Emily closed her eyes after seeing trees as tall as the Eiffel tower covered with ice drops. The sun hit them just right, sending lights in all directions. One, however, stood out among the rest an extremely ambient light in the shape of a finger. Graven was confident it was pointing toward a single mountain. Graven hoped for a lighthouse, leading them to safety from the dark clouds of bloodthirsty wolverines.

Graven shouted. "Follow the light ahead!" The Quest did as commanded, raced toward the bright light leading to a path near a gigantic cave, high up on the mountain, covered by lofty trees and completely out of sight. After a hasty landing, mid-way up the mountain, Graven spoke, "We need to go on foot. The trees will keep us hidden from the enemy. Be careful. The ice will make it difficult, but it can be done with each other's help." They hurried up a narrow, steep, zigzag path. With Emily on Roger's back, many of their legs felt like boulders reaching the mouth of the immense cave. Graven yelled out with gratitude. "Thank the heavens for the guiding light. If it hadn't been for the lighthouse, we never would have found this haven." The Quest entered the wintry cave, glad to be out of the shivery wind camouflaged from the enemy. It was dark, and they could barely see their hands in front of their faces. Graven spoke strongly. "Mighty warriors, we need to rest and wait until the winds calm down before leaving this place. We will sleep through the night and leave at the break of dawn."

"Sounds good to me." Granite said as he plopped his heavy body down onto the cave floor. The walls trembled. Chip complained. "Granite, that better be the walls vibrating, and not your bottom."

"Chip, if that were my bottom, you would have been blown away, but boy, am I beat! That was a long haul."

"You, big airhead. Graven carried your wide load up here. How is it that a rock man has any feeling in his body?" Chip questioned.

"Listen, you little pipsqueak. I may be a rock, but I can still feel. Don't talk trash …!"

Alicia fumbled in the darkness. "Hey, guys, calm down a notch. We have shelter, and we're safe. Let's rest a little."

"I don't feel safe. It's scary in here." Emily quietly spoke up.

Chip transformed into a ball of light to calm Emily's fears, and as the winds raged outside like a madman, the Quest settled down inside the damp cave. Spot, Acorn, and White Lightning huddled around the chosen ones, sheltering them in their warm fur.

"Thank you," Emily whispered, curled up against Spot like a big throw rug falling into a deep sleep, dreaming she was curled up beside her mother. The cave floor was cold and complex—the warriors were wiped out and managed to sleep through the chilly night. Graven, awoken at the crack of dawn, found himself looking into the faces of solid ice. Icemen encircled the king's knights, barricading them from escaping. Graven did not put up a fight, for they were numerous and large in stature. He recognized the men were not a threat, or they would have already demolished them. Graven hoped their King would remember him from long ago. He awakened everyone; the kids were startled seeing the tall Icemen, which looked powerful and outstanding with no default or chips. For a split second, Alicia and Roger were scared witless but chose to be unmoved.

Graven spoke calmly. "We are going with these icemen to be taken to their ruler. Remain brave. Keep your backbone strong. Do not lose hope." King James's knights were ready and willing to defend them at all costs.

Emily held onto her cheetah, afraid. "I will protect you, my little one," Spot whispered. She felt comfort in his words and clanged firmly to his neck.

The big overpowering icemen flung Alicia and Roger under their freezing arms and carried them. The two still showed no fear. Their only concern was seeing the Ice King soon before they froze to death. The icemen used their fingertips to shoot paths of ice ahead of them. Their big ice feet slid upon the smoothness of it at accelerating speeds. In a short time, the well-built ice men dropped the warriors at their ruler's feet inside a large mountain, a complete ice glacier. Chip transformed into a gigantic wool blanket and wrapped himself around the kids, keeping them from freezing. Alicia and Roger thought the room looked like one colossal fantastic crystal inside a diamond rock but cold as anything. Graven and his comrades stood in front of the chosen ones protecting them. Alicia nudged Roger. Her lips quivered as she whispered. "These icemen look smooth like glass, but so thick we

THE NEW DISCOVERY

can't see through them. Roger, I bet they put your muscles to shame." Alicia became silent as she observed the appearance of the Ice King's firm expression change. He raised his scepter in midair. "Who are these, brought to me and placed at my feet?" he asked boldly.

Quickly, his commander firmly replied, "They had come from the skies and were resting in a cave before we brought them to you. They did not put up a fight and came with us in peace."

The Ice King's eyes rested on Graven. He remembered some connection with the griffin. He forcibly questioned Graven. "What is your name, and are you friends or foes?" He asked with direct authority, not bending until he heard the griffin's reply as he stood elevated and powerful.

"Graven is my name. I am a knight of King James, protector of the realm. We had an acquaintance many years ago. With that said, if you are a friend of King James's of Abethar, then friends, but if you are a foe to our king, then enemies."

The King spoke firmly. "I am ruler of Crystal mountain, and if you are wondering. I and my soldiers are made up of rock-hard ice and as the sun rays hits just right it looks as if we are crystal. That is how we received the name of Crystal mountain, from ones that dared to be so brave to enter into our domain. Now, all I know of you and your company, besides you being a knight of King James of Abethar, is that you came from the skies and are being pursued by a large force of wolverines. Why does this force seek you out?"

Graven, too, spoke with the authority of a superior leader. "We are on a quest for our King, and the dark forces will stop at nothing to keep us from our vision."

"What is the vision of your quest?" the Ice King asked, waiting patiently for an answer.

"I cannot answer unless I know whether you are with us or against us." Graven was unyielding.

The Ice King, too, was unwavering. His scepter was still held firmly in his hand. "We are not your enemies, nor are we your allies. For so long, my people have remained neutral. We have protected our own, and our only hope is to survive—protect ourselves—and we shall now know what is the vision of your quest?" he asked.

"We are seeking the water of life and the tree of healing for our noble king, for his body is growing weak," Graven answered.

"I hope the best for your King; now my company of soldiers will lead you through this vast land of ours but know this: any act of aggression toward my ice men is an act of war. We shall not tolerate any aggressors. You may go in peace." The Quest watched the Ice King lower his scepter.

Graven bowed his head. "As you have spoken," he said reverently and stepped back. The Quest with the King's Icemen turned toward the mouth of the cave, alert and preparing to take off. Alicia whirled around and dashed toward the King of Crystal Mountain.

"Alicia, what are you doing?" Roger asked alarmingly.

Alicia ignored Roger and proceeded courageously toward the king. She knelt and bowed her head. "Your Majesty, please forgive me for my intrusion, but I need to share my heart with you."

"Arise, my child, and continue," replied the valor Ice King.

Alicia courageously stood looking solemnly into his glass eyes. "Your Majesty, war may be upon the kingdoms. I would hope all of us would stand together against Bronze; he is a wicked man full of wrong motives and evil desires. He is the head of a strong army of men and wild beasts who will rage against King James's kingdom and possibly yours."

"You have seen this army?" he asked.

"Well, not I, but my good friend." Alicia glanced over at Roger and caught him admiring her. Her cheeks flushed. She brought her attention back to the Ice King. Alicia spoke dauntlessly.

"Roger, my friend, had a glimpse of Bronze's army after accidentally opening a mysterious portal of his realm. He had a vision, well…, that is or reality but either way, he witnessed that vulgar man preparing to take over all the kingdoms and eventually your vast land, as well."

The Ice King answered apathetically. "He was foolish to have done such a thing, but no, I will not help you in this battle. It is yours and yours alone; now depart and make haste to help your king."

Alicia stood strong and unmovable, not allowing fear to override her. She made up her mind and stood gallant with the boldness of a mighty warrior—a gift stirred up inside her, preparing and directing her for a mighty battle to come. Somehow, she knew it would come, and on that day, she would stand still and witness the salvation of her God. She proclaimed valiantly. "Oh, King, all things are possible to them that believe!"

The Ice King gave Alicia a look of approval. He values her passion and bravery. She touched his heart this day. "Bow before my throne, honorable one." Alicia obeyed. He touched her shoulder with his scepter. "Go in the boldness that you display and continue to give hope to others that it may be possible to come against all obstacles with the faith that you hold."

"Yes, Your Majesty," Alicia replied. She stood to her feet and bowed her head, departing his presence. She made her way toward Acorn.

The Quest followed the King's soldiers through the limitless glaciers. At last, they reached the peak of another mountain. They stopped to rest for a few moments. The commander cautiously spoke to Graven. "You and your party can make no sound from here on out. It would be wise to place something over your eyes, as the sun reaches the peak of the mountains, its total blindness to look upon this place, stay close to my soldiers until further notice is given."

Graven nodded his head and had Acorn, White Lightening, and Spot take off with the powerful thrust of their wings as the Ice soldiers glided over the mountains in paths of ice again created with the lifting and pointing of their hands. They came near the opposite side of the hill. The climate became warmer as they landed in what they thought was safe. "This is as far as we can take you," said the commander. "The further the travel, the hotter it gets and besides, we won't be any good to you if we are melted." The Ice commander grinned for the first time. Graven approved. "This climate will be better for the chosen ones." No sooner did Graven speak than fireballs of thick, hot lava swirled through the air, catching everyone off guard. Molten men came marching off a high peak from the left and right side of a mountain like a herd of cattle.

THE VISION OF THE QUEST

Graven yelled at the top of his voice, and he frightened Emily. "White Lightning, fly the chosen ones to safety! Guard them with your life!" Roger moved fast and lifted Emily onto White Lightning's long back. Emily edged her way onto his broad shoulders, waiting for Roger and Alicia.

"I can fight, too." Roger called to Graven, "Princess Lilly had given me a sword for moments like these." Roger drew a man's sword, ready for battle. "And so, can I," Alicia reaffirmed, prepared for action. "We are not children and can help."

Graven half-heartedly agreed. "Yes, you shall have your time—perhaps a battle to come, but not at this time!" Alicia and Roger heard the urgency in Graven's voice. The two obeyed and, with the help of Granite, leaped up onto White Lightning's back. "Depart!" Graven shouted. The daring knight took off like a bolt of lightning; in a flash, he blended in with the sky. Acorn and Spot followed them at a certain distance, and once they were in the clear, the two returned to help the others clean house.

The molten men were composed of fire; red-hot flames, all but their eyes, noses, and mouths. They were black holes of dark shadows. The mountain now completely covered in a blaze of fiery red, the ambushed attack was strong, as fast fireballs devastated two of the commander's icemen. They were like two large melted cubes of ice baked in the hot blazing sun.

The icemen were a proud generation. "We have this!' the commander asked the Quest to stand aside. He had his men stand at a far-off distance inside a somewhat cooler climate. They thrust titanic balls of firm, bulky ice with robust arms, aiming directly at their enemies. They demolished countless molten men. However, the mountain was still covered with red hot molten lava."

The captain of the molten men rumbled in laughter, "Oh, look, the blocks of ice are throwing snowballs our way. Take this!" He swirled a boulder of lava in his fiery hands and threw it. The icemen together formed a barricaded broad wall of ice that didn't last long. The heated boulder broke through their division with a terrible force, destroying two more of the Ice King's soldiers. "Two strikes, I won!" The molten

THE NEW DISCOVERY

men threw balls like a batting machine. The ice soldiers fought hard. Unfortunately, three more were destroyed. Everything was a game to the hot heads until Graven stepped into the picture. Granite received his command to do his thing. The rock man displayed a big grin. He said with fun, "Light my rocks on fire, big boys, today you are going down!" The molten men were no threat to him.

Granite began smashing them left and right as he dodged their rocks. Graven joined in shooting his dynamite red laser beams, striking and destroying many walking firebombs. Chip transformed into a hurricane of water shaped into a thirty-foot surpassing man as to the image of the days of old. He could only do so often for it robbed him of his strength. "Do you want a piece of me!"

Chip yelled out. He moved aggressively and brought his excessive hurricane of water down upon them, putting out their flames from top to bottom. "Take that, you hot lava heads!" Chip hollowed. He transformed back into himself and climbed onto Graven's back. He laid back, stretching out his tiny body, sinking into piles of thick ashes, his hands behind his small head. He grinned from ear to ear. "Welp, big boys, now that's done, all I need is a toothpick to chew on a bit. Granite, will you do me the honor of finding me a toothpick or two?" Chip asked tauntingly, with sarcasm.

Granite answered gladly. "Yeah, I will find a nice size toothpick and stick it straight up your little...," Chip stood to his paws, his hands on his hips. "Now, that's not the way to be." Chip was side-tracked. He took in a big sniff. "Oh, Graven, you definitely need a bath. Rats couldn't even take this kind of odor." He shook Chip off like an unwanted flea. Graven's throat was dry, but he managed to laugh quietly. Everyone's energy was depleted from the heat. Graven spoke. "I hate to be the party pooper. We slowed down the hot lava men for now, but they will come back like locust. We have to get out of here and move fast."

The commander saluted Graven with honor. "I did not realize the Quest was very multitalented."

Graven replied. "I never did get your name."

THE VISION OF THE QUEST

The commander and his ice men leaped with giant steps making ice paths, and as they slid away, he shouted. "My name is Commander David." Quickly, without looking back, he returned to Crystal mountain and stood in his Ice King's presence. He bowed his head in respect to his father. "My faithful King, we lost a few good men due to the molten men. If it wasn't for the Quest's determination and true grit, I might not have been standing here before you this day." His King spoke pleasingly that the Quest could be trusted. "Know this today: we have allied ourselves with King James. We are no longer neutral. His enemies are our enemies. We shall prepare for the future!"

Graven thought of the Ice King as he soared through the sky, hoping they would stand with them in the great battle to come. Graven and his knights returned to White Lightning, and the chosen one's, finding Alicia on her knees. "What are you doing?" Graven asked. Alicia looked up into their weary faces. "I was praying for all of you for your safe return, and he had answered my prayer, but now, knights I speak on behalf of myself, and my little sister, and Roger, that enemies from all sides tried to destroy us, but we have endured trials and tribulations. We must not stop but press on to the finished line and move with haste to find the water of life and the tree of enlightenment. King James needs his healing to rule as a strong king to find our mother that Roger, Emily, and I hold dear to our hearts is lost." Alicia spoke firmly. Graven smiled at the young girl with honor, proud of the young warrior. She was already becoming. Alicia thought, stunned herself. *Is this me that had spoken? Ever since I entered Bronze's domain and the kingdom of Abethar... I feel different. Gifts stirred up within me. I didn't know I possessed a strength I was not aware of before.* She pondered on it when she heard Graven boomed loudly. "For the cause!"

"For the cause!" the Quest shouted.

Alicia was ready and jumped up onto Acorn. Roger was pumped up. He quickly placed Emily onto Spot, then hopped onto White Lightning. Chip climbed up and leaped onto Graven. Granite followed suit. The Quest left again in pursuit of the Second Kingdom. Graven boomed. "For the cause!"

"For the cause!" the Quest shouted again and again.

Chapter Five

TRUST

THE VISION OF THE QUEST

The Quest entered the Valley of Shadows even though the sun shined. They soared through a heavy presence. The king's knights and the chosen ones heard voices of hopelessness and felt the weight of a heavy depression bringing fear to their hearts. They began to lack confidence, and fear began to overtake them, ruling their emotions.

The Quest became careless of the things around them and distracted. Within a few hours, they exited the Valley of Shadows and entered the Valley of Woe. The farther the Quest ventured, the more they experienced overwhelming despair, with a sense they would never make it to the Second Kingdom, second-guessing one another, feeling weaker as if their strength were being zapped out of them. They continued to stay the course, not looking to the left or the right but their high calling. The Quest began viewing each other differently, thinking negatively toward one another, blaring words of hurt, piercing one another's hearts, and weighing down their souls. The only one not affected by this negative, gloomy presence was Emily. She was free from it because of her childlike faith but became fearful, seeing the others tearing one another apart.

Granite on Graven's back had enough as he threw his rock arms up into the air. "Graven, why are you leading us? You don't even know where you are going. I doubt if you are even going to get us there. You're wasting our time. Maybe we should go our own separate ways!" He hollered.

Emily sat quietly holding onto Spot, listening to them bickering back and forth, as they doubted one another's honor, and, as the Quest flew farther, the more their faith failed, falling into dismay. Still, regardless they pressed on for hours, nothing but strife surrounded them, leaving them with lost hope. Alicia and Roger remained respectfully quiet, though their faces displayed anger and fear.

"Stop it! Stop fighting!" Emily cried out desperately, looking down at Spot, biting down his tongue, not to make a rude remark toward Emily. Acorn did it for him. "What's she whining for? Keep the child quiet. Her rude behavior is getting under my skin," Spot thought to himself, *I am a cheetah from a proud, strong race. Acorn is right. Why should I allow a snot-nosed child to rule me?* He growled under his hot breath.

White Lightning inflamed the cheetah's fire even more. "Do you know what your problem is, Spot? You're a softy."

"Shut up! Emily's on my back and not yours, unless you desire the badly behaved child on your back and listen to her whining, be my guest!"

Emily was crushed. "Let me down, you are rude!" she screamed.

Emily's piercing scream could have awakened the dead, but instead, she had awakened something worse. Without warning, they saw two big yellow eyes approaching them extremely fast. A threatening, black dragon shot out fire, aiming in their direction, his coat of armor of many diamonds, making it difficult to look upon. Chip sprang into action, sheltering the Quest as he placed a force field around all of them. The dragon flew back and forth, blasting out fire with each encounter. Unexpectedly, the climate changed, with the feeling of fall becoming cooler and damper. The king's knights strived to outsmart the beast.

Graven spotted a body of water in the air with precise vision. He hollered. "White Lightning, Spot, and Acorn, fly the chosen ones further from here! Protect them at all cause! I will lead the dragon away." Graven turned his head and looked at Granite and Chip. Chip had transformed back into himself sitting upon his broad back. "Trust me, my two warriors. About a mile from here is a sea we will plunge into together. It may be our only chance to keep the chosen ones out of harm's way." Graven soared, with the savage beast heavy upon them.

White Lightning, Spot, and Acorn listened to Graven's command. They beat their wings with full force to fly the chosen ones to a safe haven. In a heartbeat, dreadful winds with the strength of a twister came out of nowhere, forcing White Lightning, Acorn, and Spot toward a cliff. The same cliff and body of water Graven soared toward. The chosen ones held on for dear life. Alicia held tight onto her little sister. She felt her fingers slowly slipping, and with everything in her. She gripped on tighter, not realizing she was pinching the life out of Spot's skin. Graven dodged the dragon's long, fiery flames, reaching the sea.

THE VISION OF THE QUEST

He plunged over the cliff, with the dragon of death still in hot pursuit on their tails, chasing them headlong into a downward spin.

Graven shouted out. "For the cause!" before he was covered in water over his head. Granite and Chip still on Graven's back plunged into the depths of the sea. Graven quickly shot up out of the water. Granite waited, standing on Graven's back. He slowly counted one, two, three. The dangerous beast shot full force out of the deep sea. Granite grinned ear-to-ear. He leaped off Graven's back and onto the dragon, pounding him relentlessly upon its head. The unruly beast flung him off like a light paper clip. Granite fell hard into the water and with his ton of weight. He sinks fast, unable to swim back to the surface.

Chip raced in a blank of an eye and transformed into a gigantic marlin, diving into the deep. He snatched Granite's head tightly into the grip of his mouth with jet speed. He broke through the surface of the cold water, transforming into a humongous eagle, shooting straight up into the air. He brought his friend to the top of the cliff and plopped him down onto the hard ground.

Granite was hilarious. "Oh, boy! Good thing you got me out of there quick enough. I had barnacles growing on my rear end inside that smelly fish bowl!"

Chip said before swinging back into the action, "I wish I had a nut every time I saved your big barrel. I was crazy going to the bottom of the sea to bring your wide caboose back up. Anyway, I would love to shoot the breeze but we have a big problem on our hands."

Back on the scene, Chip and Granite watched the beast aim toward Graven's head. Graven, not a bit frightened with high speed, daringly moved toward the fiery creature shooting his laser beams repeatedly into his armor of diamonds. The angry cannon shot scorching fire from his mouth and just skimmed the griffin's back. He charged forward and swatted Graven backward with his enormous tail, knocking him into the water.

With Emily fifty feet from the cliff mustered up enough courage and screamed. Every limb in her body shook. "Leave my friends alone, you big bully!" Her big, blonde curls were soaked, dangling in her fiery, round face. The diamond beast turned and headed toward Emily with hostility. Acorn stood in front of the chosen ones. White Lightning and Spot flew to the side of the kids. Still an eagle, Chip flew hastily to the rescue and transformed into an enormous, sharp, double-edged sword. He placed himself into Alicia's and Roger's hands, and the two held tightly onto the blade. The dragon hurtled forward in a head-on collision to destroy Acorn to reach the three who had the prophecy of old to keep from bringing the kingdoms together as one. He went berserk with wrath. He charged full blast. Alicia and Roger screamed out, "Now!" Acorn dove to the side. The dragon, caught off guard, did not see the sizeable double-edged sword that stabbed deep through his heart. Chip felt the rhythm of it, little by little, scarcely beating.

He became a sword knowing the dragon of death would have killed them all. The vehement beast screeched out in severe pain, taking many giant leaps backward, throwing itself hard into the depths of the sea with Chip still wedged into his heart. The dragon flipped and turned in a downward spin, landing heavily into the bottomless pit. The sea swallowed him up into a lonesome grave. The dragon's fall created such an impact, large amounts of water splashed up in all directions.

The chosen ones ran to the end of the cliff with the king's knights searching for Chip. Everyone found themselves holding their breath, waiting as seconds turned in minutes and minutes into a half-hour. Graven concluded… the dragon had plunged to his death. Sadly, Chip died with him. It grieved him terribly. He turned toward the others.

"We must leave now. There may be another dragon coming." Granite reluctantly jumped onto Graven's back. His heart was heavy with grief for his friend. "Follow me!" Graven yelled.

Alicia shouted. She couldn't believe Graven was giving up. "We can't leave Chip! What about Chip? We cannot leave him!" she repeated.

Facing Alicia, Graven looked devastated with brokenness. He tried to remain strong for everyone, through his hurt went deep. He spoke softly, encouraging Alicia. "Chip gave his life that we may live. We must go on. That's what our friend would have wanted."

The Quest, without realizing it, we're no longer in their doubtful state of mind for perfect love cast out fear and conquered the Valley of

Woe. For greater love, no man than this, that he's willing to lay down his life for a friend.

"Chip," the chosen ones cried out sadly. No one could believe that the life of the party, with all his wit and wisecracks, was gone. With devastation in their hearts, everyone stayed the course, but the hurt was evident. Emily cried a long downpour of tears. Alicia, on the back of Spot with her little sister, wrapped her arms around her for comfort. She, too, secretly cried. The Quest had to proceed for the cause. They pressed on no matter how hard it was and as time slowly passed, a few accepted the reality that Chip was no longer with them and, as they grieved, the Quest could see the sun rising.

Graven yelled out loudly, "Shield your eyes or lose your sight! We must fly toward the sun in order to locate the door to the Second Kingdom!" Everyone shielded their eyes, and, as the Quest soared toward the sun, each repented for all of the negative comments spoken towards one another, especially the comments aimed toward Chip.

Chapter Six

Lead the Blind

THE VISION OF THE QUEST

Bronze returned to his museum, finding Liana staring sadly out the window into open fields, her fingers clutching a children's book.

"Liana, I have been worried for you. I went to your room and could not find you." he lied, watching her every move through his subjects. Bronze sat down beside Liana on the sofa and was quiet. He stared into her face and admired her beauty. Liana felt her strength zapped from her, replaced with a mind-boggling weariness, not knowing where her girls and Roger were.

Liana spoke softly. "This is one of Emily's favorite stories when she was younger about a handsome prince who sweeps a beautiful princess off her feet." She turned toward Bronze with hurt imprinted on her face. Moist tears ran down her cheeks. "I need to know where my babies are. I am sick with worry. You keep telling me they are safe, but my faith in you has subsided."

Her teary eyes searched Bronze's face. His heart was darker than ever, and he was trapped inside the mansion for such a long time as if a wild beast had overtaken him, but at this moment, he was gazing into Liana's eyes. He sensed a fire rekindling in the depths of his soul. He desired her with a rush of passion but again knew he must contain himself. Liana's medicine was wearing off. His hold fading from her mind. Bronze hid his anger. He acknowledged that the medicine he now practically hand-fed Liana into cups of warm tea only lasted a short while. He had a servant bring her in another cup. "Please," Liana pleaded. "Bring my children safely to me, please."

Bronze continued to stare into her lovely face. He sat quietly beside her for about five minutes. He watched Liana slowly drink her tea. As he patiently waited, he began to see the drug had taken effect, gaining control over her mind again. Bronze found a small amount of hope in his soul, how Liana's strong, loving character reminded him of his past feelings for Queen Leah. As one pleases, he placed his hand through her hair of thick, blonde waves. He caressed her warm cheek, brushing away her moist tears. Bronze sensed a touch of happiness sparking within the depths of his cold heart.

Slowly, he leaned into her lips. She fought him and weakly pulled away. Bronze reluctantly pulled back, not needing Liana frightened of him, but in the same breath, every part of him screamed out for her, desiring her comfort, her love, and beauty. He couldn't help but continue feeling the warmth of her face and caressed the smoothness of her ivory skin. It pleased him, bringing his fingers across her moist, tender lips.

Liana jerked her face back from his hand. This time he ignored her pleas freely, running his fingers back and forth rapidly across her desiring mouth, removing her hair back from her face. Bronze bent forward and whispered to her, "I need you." He brought his focus back to Liana. He searched cunningly into her frightened eyes. He spoke his lies, bringing her back into a deeper state of confusion.

"Why are you doing this to me? Why?" Liana asked. He leaned into her once more. She jerked her head back from him. It caused her head to spin. She rested her head on the back of the couch and closed her eyes, hoping that the lustful man would get the hint and stop. She tried to free her mind from the turmoil of not understanding what was happening. She felt the warmth of his fingers, now pressed more firmly against her lips. Anger rose within her shattered soul with a weak voice. She cried out desperately, "My God, help me!"

Bronze was startled as he removed his hand from her lips, a fast train putting on his breaks within his cold heart. There was a piece of him that hated to see her suffering. It brought him discomfort. "Liana, you know how kids are always busy playing, especially in this large mansion with so much here for them to do, using their active imaginations." Bronze gently took her hands into his. "My dear, to ease your mind—I saw them not too long ago, playing with my niece Melanie. Have you forgotten I brought your children in earlier?" he manipulated.

Bronze releasing her hands, gently slid his arm around Liana's shoulders and embraced her. He spoke softly. "Open your eyes, Liana." She obeyed like a puppet on his string. He stared deep into her soul to brainwash her, further taking control of her thoughts. "I will send Alicia to you in a short while. Let me help you to your bedroom where

THE VISION OF THE QUEST

you can lay down and relax comfortably." Bronze wrapped his arm around Liana's waist. She tried to resist his help but was too weak. Reaching her bedroom, he sat her down on her bed.

Bronze held his breath as he caught a glimpse of a gold chain on Liana's neck—ecstatic, thinking another key out of his cage right before his eyes. Sitting down next to Liana, feeling at liberty to lift it out of her blouse, marveling, he fumbled his victory back and forth in his hands, profoundly admiring the fine gems. He asked himself, *"How was I so blinded not to realize Liana's would be around her neck? Emily's as well."* He begins to scheme. *She's smart as a whip. I will steal this necklace without Liana having any knowledge of it. But first, I need to win her heart. Keep her as my jewel, for as much as I desire the three kingdoms in the palm of my hands, I desire her even more.*

Bronze reasoned. *I will remove it from her after she falls deep asleep.* He cringed his hands into a tight fist, his knuckles turning a deep shade of red. *But for now, I am growing impatient to hear from Sorelle and his hordes. It's been weeks since those brats have been missing. Something must have gone wrong if I could get into the Kingdom of Abethar. I would finish the brats off myself and have the honor of ripping the necklace right off Alicia's bloody neck! And most likely Emily's too! But first, I must wait to hear from Sorelle.* Bronze returned to his private quarters to spy on Liana through the seeing eyes of his despicable crow.

He had a servant retrieve Melanie for him, but a few hours beforehand, Bronze was cruel toward the young girl. Melanie slowly made her way inside his museum. She felt she would wet herself. Bronze stood near a bookshelf piled high with historical books. The threatening man looked toward Melanie. He scraped a shiny sharp knife across the palm of his hand. Drops of blood hit the floor. He spoke treacherously to frighten the young girl even more. "I can't think of nothing better to do than kill your family, held captive inside my prison, one false move. I promise you my violent beasts will rip them to shreds. The last time I checked, they were pretty hungry. I hope you do what I had called you to, continue tricking Liana concerning her little imps. Do you get my drift?" Melanie could barely breathe. She answered in a faint whisper. "Yes, master." She left his evil presence shaking head to toe.

The young girl shortly stood in Liana's opened doorway. She looked at Liana in a daze clutching a baby book. Liana could barely see, upset that Bronze had placed drops of something warm that felt like a bee sting into each of her eyes. She turned to face a blurry figure the size of Alicia. Liana softly asked. "Alicia, is that you?"

Melanie cried out within herself. *One slip up, his ugly crow will snitch and will place my family's lives in terrible jeopardy. What should I do? What should I do?* she thought, disturbed as she walked over and stood at the side of Liana's bed. "Alicia, is that you?" Liana asked again.

"Yes, Mama, it's me." Melanie hated to lie.

Liana smiled. "Your voice sounds different and I never heard you call me 'Mama' before. It's always been 'Mom,' but my mind is in so much shambles. I am just so happy you are here. Where have you been? Where are Roger and your little sister? Is everybody okay?" Liana had many questions. Bronze watched through his crow. He was pleased to see her smile.

Liana was in high spirits as she talked. "I have been worried sick about all of you. Come, Alicia, and give me a hug. I feel I have not touched you for weeks. I don't understand. My heart longs for all of you, even though you are here with me, inside this, this dreadful place." Tears spilled from Liana's eyes. "I'm sorry. I have not been feeling like myself lately." Grief-stricken, she broke down. Melanie quickly wrapped her arms around her, and she, too, cried, dreaming of being in her own mother's arms, hearing her mama whispering in her lonely ear, "Everything will be all right." She desired desperately to be back in her dimension.

Melanie eventually left. Liana remained sitting up, waiting for Bronze's aggravating routine visit. She knew she would repeatedly demand the idiotic man, like a broken record, to bring her children to her so they could leave at once. It wasn't long. Liana heard Bronze make his way into the bedroom. The annoying man sat down in a wooden chair across from her. He had a servant bring his prize possession, another hot cup of tea. Bronze delighted in watching Liana take small sips. She was naïve about how the control freak slipped in a strong sleeping drug. Liana, ten minutes later, was a little woozy and slumped back onto the bed to rest her head. Bronze waited for the drug to take its full effect as it gave him time again to stare into her gorgeous face.

He asked deceitfully, "Would you like me to find Alicia again? She is in the dining hall with the others, enjoying a great lunch."

She mustered a hateful stare and shot straight up in bed, again her head pounded. She cried, "No, I want my daughters and Roger with me right now! Now, I said!"

Bronze acted fast as he witnessed pure anger on Liana's face. He tried a different approach, tired of her nagging about her no-good-for-nothing children. He lied. "Liana, you are not feeling well, poor thing. Don't you remember your children died in the car accident with your husband two years ago?"

"Liar!" the frantic mother angrily managed to stand to her feet, although she was weak and her head felt like it would pop. She slapped Bronze hard across his face leaving an imprint of her hand on his cheek.

"My children are alive! Now bring them to me!" she strongly demanded.

Bronze was firm. He forced Liana into his arms. She fought him like a ticked-off mother bear protecting her cubs. "I am sorry, Liana, that you do not believe me." His head was towering over her head, his chest close to hers. Bronze leaned his face into her hair, smelling the sweet fragrance of her perfume. She continued to fight to get out of his tight embrace. The drug finally kicked in full blast. Bronze stared into Liana's vexed eyes. He calmly talked to her and slowly zapped her back into a state of bewilderment. Liana had no more strength left to fight. She began to sob, "I do not believe you. Please, Bronze, I beg of you, tell me where my girls and Roger are." Her words were soft and pleading. Bronze still held her close to his chest. He caressed her soft cheeks and gently kissed her forehead. Once more passionate memories of his love for Queen Leah began to bombard his mind. "I am sorry, Liana, your children are gone. I would do anything to bring them back, but it's impossible."

Liana groaned in sorrow. Her spirit was broken along with her heart, sobbing until she finally fell asleep in Bronze's receptive arms. He looked at her, again admiring her high cheekbones and tender-shaped lips with a gentle spirit. "You are the spitting image of your great ancestor, so many centuries ago, but you will not slip from me as she did," Bronze whispered close to her ear. He gently laid her back onto her feather mattress, sound asleep. "I have work to do, my love, but I will be back." He pulled back Liana's hair and slipped her necklace off her swan neck. He quietly left, this time locking her bedroom door behind him. If she believes her children are no longer with her, she may attempt to escape. Having the necklace in his hands caused adrenaline to run through his veins. His heart pounded rapidly, ecstatic.

Bronze made haste to the other side of the mansion to a worn out, black door to a dungeon that eventually leads to a portal door. For many years, he could not enter without the missing key; now, he was psyched up. Bronze hastily reached into his pocket to retrieve the fine piece of art. He beamed with a sense of freedom, marveling at the unique designs intertwined with different colors of gems and stones, giving him a sense of security. He blared with anticipation. "I will finally overcome King James and rip his Kingdom out of his hands, conquering whoever stands in my way!" Bronze walked through the dungeon. Reaching the portal door, he found himself clutching the key.

He placed the necklace inside the carving of the portal door. It did not budge. Bronze was infuriated. He attempted again and again. Finally, he kicked and punched the door with all his might, madly throwing his body weight up against it, but to no avail.

Liana's mystical gems begin radiating rainbow colors, but nothing happened, ticked off, he reached out to retrieve the jewelry. He quickly shrank back, hot to the touch, and burned his hand. "Why can I not open this door?!" he shouted, then a light bulb went off. He shouted even louder. "You fool! It has to be her! Yes, as I had planned. I shall rule the kingdoms with Liana at my side." Bronze slipped on a pair of gloves out of his pocket. He was a man that didn't like getting his hands dirty unless it was with blood. He retrieved the necklace in his greedy grip and paced out of the dungeon through a different secret passage leading back to Liana's bedroom. He stood reluctantly at her side, knowing he had failed.

THE VISION OF THE QUEST

Liana was still asleep, weary from the trauma, thinking her children might no longer be with her. Bronze touched the necklace with his bare fingers feeling it had cooled, and softly placed it back around her elegant swan neck. He departed, walking with long strides to his historical museum, scheming once more how he would get his beautiful future queen to open the door to his throne of ultimate power and authority.

Liana slept for hours. She woke up crying and sorrowfully. She sat up in bed and wept. Suddenly, she was caught up in a vision, a glorious white cloud engulfing her trembling body, bringing with it a smell of a pleasant fragrance. She felt a peace beyond her own understanding. Softly, a sweet voice spoke to her spirit: "I have never left you or forsaken you." Still drugged from whatever Bronze had given her. She cried a prayer of hope before falling back to sleep.

As Liana slept, Melanie was deep in thought, dwelling on the love Alicia's mother had shown her—a love that she missed and desired from her mother. A boldness overcame her lightly freckled face. She was worked up and cried out. "I have to help her and save her from Bronze's hollow lies, even if it means jeopardizing my family. Something in me is telling me it's the right thing to do!"

Melanie ran through the many hallways, trying not to be seen. Her adrenaline caused her heart to beat fast as she dashed fearfully to Liana's room, hoping to avoid the red, piercing eyes of the black silence of the night. Fortunately, and unbeknownst to Melanie, the black crow was on another assignment for his master. But she worried as well about Bronze's hideous bats with black pitch wings he uses to spy. She finally reached Liana's door, pushing her straight, brown hair out of her eyes. She went to turn the doorknob and found it locked. She tapped softly, waiting for a reply. After numerous tries, she knocked a little louder. Tempted to give up, she suddenly heard the noise of blankets being ruffled and the movement of rusty springs on an old bed. Melanie was comforted hearing soft steps approach the door. Liana asked faintly, "Who is it?"

"My name is Melanie, my lady," the girl whispered in low tones, looking back and forth down the dim hallway. She asked nervously,

"Please, may I come in?" realizing every second outside Liana's door could mean death for her, "Please hurry, my lady, it's important that I have words with you."

Liana tried turning the knob. She answered softly, "Yes, yes, but my door is locked. I am unable to open it."

Melanie, afraid for a second, forgot she had a key. "No worry, Miss Liana, I have a spare that I have kept hidden until now." She removed the key from her apron pocket, and, with trembling hands, she unlocked the door. She surveyed the hallway one last time that the coast was clear, no one lurking nearby watching her. Fearfully, she quietly slipped inside Liana's bedroom.

Melanie hurriedly spoke. "Please sit down, my lady." She took hold of Liana's shaking hands and noticed Liana's swollen teary eyes. She said, "I have to be quick for Bronze, the man who has locked you in here, is an evil man. He has a stranglehold over you, feeding you with lies." She was petrified as she talked, looking over her shoulder, afraid Bronze would enter any moment.

Liana stared at the girl with disbelief and confusion.

Melanie was aware of the key outside of Liana's blouse. "My lady, I can help you find your children, but you must trust me. The special key you have around your neck will help you find them, but we must hurry."

Liana covered her mouth to keep from crying. "My babies, please take me to wherever you are talking about." she moaned quietly. "I have been deceived so much that I question what the truth is."

Melanie whispered, frightened. "But we must hurry before Bronze returns, for the eyes of his black crow go to and fro. If Sir Bronze finds out where I am, I will surely be punished." Not wasting a second, she grabbed Liana's arm and pulled her toward the hidden door inside her room and fast led her through it. Liana was slow-moving from the drugs but pushed forward, dragging herself beside Melanie throughout many long and short narrow turns. It reminded Liana of a corn maze. Finally, the two arrived in front of a big, dark wooden door. Liana's hope had faded weeks ago. She doubted everything around her, what was real and what was not. She pondered. *Everything here is so strange, but where is here? Is this a nightmare? What am I to do? Wake up! Wake up!*

she told herself. She softly cried until she remembered the vision of a compassionate voice saying, 'I have never left you or forsaken you.' She managed to pull herself together.

Melanie nervously spoke. "This is the door that leads us through a dreary tunnel. But first, there is something you should know, the necklace around your neck is a key to a kingdom—another place, another time—and again, that is where you will find your children, but we must enter through this sunless dungeon to find the portal. It's scary and won't be easy, but it beats just standing out here. Bronze's crow cannot see us once we enter through this door."

Liana held onto her necklace. "Everything sounds far-fetched and crazy to me, but being in the state I am in right now, I will do anything to get out of this hell-hole and find my girls and Roger."

The drug was wearing off, and for the first time, Liana noticed Melanie's freckled nose. Her skin was as fresh as a baby's bottom, and she had glazing cat-like eyes. She admired Melanie for giving her hope. Liana somehow heard Melanie's voice before but could not remember when. She noticed the young girl losing color in her face. Liana thought maybe an anxiety attack. Melanie spoke in a shaken voice. "My lady, I need to remain calm and keep my emotions under control to get you to the door that matches your necklace and find your children."

Liana desired answers. "I see you are terrified of Bronze. Why are you helping me?"

"Miss Liana, I will explain it to you, but for now, we must enter through this door. Please make your decision before it's too late, or I will have no choice but to take you back to your room and pray to your God that Bronze does not have me hanging from a long rope."

Liana answered. "There was never any decision to be made. Let's get my children. But I would love for you to enter this so-called kingdom with me. It will keep you out of the grasp of that, of that… monster!"

Melanie was touched by her thoughtfulness. "I thought if I stayed, maybe Bronze would not destroy my family, but I know surely that if I followed through with that decision. I would not be here, and most likely, and sadly, he would destroy my family anyway. I will help you find your children, but afterward, I will find my loved ones and somehow set them free. I will explain the dimensions and portals inside the tunnel, but for now, we are pressed for time."

Liana softly grabbed Melanie's arm. "Lead me, and I will follow you." Melanie quietly opened the large, wooden door, causing loud creaking noises making the young girl more frightened. Liana saw Melanie was a bag of nerves. She took the first step and ventured through the door and found herself inside a gloomy dungeon, cold drafts of damp air smacking her face. Melanie followed and, with nervous hands, took a torch off the wall and lit it with matches from her apron. Liana looked around and saw the place was dingy and dirty, with rock walls and a dirt floor. She tried focusing her eyes in the darkness and with the help of Melanie's torch. She could see somewhat ahead. The dungeon seemed straight and narrow.

"How did you know of this tunnel?" Liana asked as she stared out into the darkness.

Melanie slipped her hand into Liana's. She opened up as they walked together. She spoke in a hushed tone. "I have been kept hidden in this mansion for a while now. Time after time, I have witnessed Bronze handling his wicked affairs. He threatened me to do his biddings or he would cause my family a great deal of harm. Because of that, I know what goes on concerning him and what he is after. He is up to no good, so we must continue to move as quickly as we can."

Liana replied. "I can't express my appreciation of you risking your life for mine? But you still haven't told me why you are helping me?" Her head hurt from the medicine, but her mind was no longer cloudy.

Melanie responded softly. "In the weeks Bronze has imprisoned you here, I have seen truth and love in your eyes and witnessed the authentic touch of your tenderness toward your children, my lady. That's why we must find the portal door that holds your key. Bronze does not miss much. He will be onto us shortly."

"The door is at the end of the tunnel, which I was told by a trusted servant who works inside Bronze's mansion. He escorted you to your room when you first arrived. I was always too afraid to venture in here. I kept my distance from this place until now." Something ran across Liana's feet. She screamed. Melanie cried. "Please, don't scream sometimes. I think Bronze has the ears of a bat." Melanie quickly tilted the torch toward the filthy floor, revealing hundreds of rats. Both were now trembling, squeezing hands more tightly, terrified. They continued to walk, trying their best not to lose it. Suddenly, a few more daring rats ran across their feet and tried crawling up their legs. They quickly shook them off.

Melanie whispered, hoping to redirect their minds off the dirty rats. "I will finish where I left off concerning the portals and dimensions, after escaping your bedroom." Her voice quivered badly.

"You mean, my prison," Liana spoke in a fearful quiet tone. Both of them chuckled oddly, and it seemed to help calm their fears. "What are these strange places that you talk about?" Liana asked. Her body trembled desperately to bolt out of there. Thinking of her children gave her the boldness to go on. She placed her fears on the back burner.

"Well, well, to start off," Melanie stuttered, "inside each portal is a different dimension, and inside every dimension, there are many portals, and once a person enters inside anyone of the dimensions, time changes; meaning, a day inside other dimensions it could be days or weeks or months or even years, however, not only does time change but the seasons as well. And in some dimensions like here. We don't have seasons." She squeezed Liana's hand even tighter not feeling her hand going numb. "The cultures are different here, and the people are different. These portals are hidden and waiting to be discovered by someone or anything. I am not sure what future Bronze stepped into in your time, but inside his mansion, he had always kept his nasty creatures inside the portal within his historic museum, a thousand years."

As the two walked, the rats were not as many it brought somewhat relief. Liana thought back to the first day her car broke down and entered Bronze domain. It was strange. Some days seemed like hours, and some hours seemed like months, and at other times months felt like years. Liana couldn't help but feel the urge to bombard the young girl concerning her people especially where her girls and Roger could be in these unknown places. Her thoughts were put on hold, feeling a powerful draft. "Where did that gush of freezing air come from?" Liana shivered.

"I am not sure, but..." Melanie stopped abruptly, hearing a familiar sound. "Get down and hold your head!" She yanked Liana down with her, all-of-a-sudden, tons of bats swooped past them, making an ear-piercing sound. During this fearful moment, rats begin to crawl over them as if doormats. Liana and Melanie tried not to scream but squirmed around on the moldy floor, attempting to shake them off, scared out of their wits, their hearts beating twenty miles an hour about to burst.

Liana believed the bats were gone after a minute or two, but it felt like an eternity. She helped Melanie to her feet. Both shaking like a leaf. She turned to face Melanie, seeing her dimly with the torch that she had quickly relit and held in her trembling hands.

Liana said with nervous lips, "All I can think to say is that we must continue and run the race, something that I had to learn throughout the years. We must not give in to defeat." Liana grabbed Melanie's hand, and both pressed forward.

Melanie stuttered again, "It, it can't be much longer. This dungeon goes in all kinds of directions, Ajax the butler, which I overheard your kids call Mr. Clean, told me to continue straight, stay on the path, do not look to the right or the left, but to stay the course and eventually, we will see the light coming from the cracks of the portal." Liana suddenly recalled how the butler warned her not to go near Bronze's museum. Now, she knows he was trying to protect her and her children without Bronze catching wind of it.

Melanie, however, started to wonder whether the butler was correct concerning the location of this so-called portal. Fear gripped her firmly, causing her heart to race even more, fearing what would happen if the portal was somehow hidden out of sight. Melanie dreaded what Bronze would do to her. She began hyperventilating, something she'd done since Bronze had taken her captive.

Liana wrapped her arms around her, calming her nerves as they walked. Liana gave the girl words of comfort. "Everything is in God's hands. Good can come out of the bad. How about you tell me more about what is going on. Hopefully, that will help us not think about the Nightmare on Elm Street." Liana kicked another two rats off her feet.

Melanie barely spoke a whisper. Her voice was shaking. "Well, I'll begin where that evil monster ran from King James, and just when he thought he was done for Bronze accidentally fell into a portal. I am sure Bronze felt it would be better in the portal than confronting his enemy. But before he had fallen, I heard that, as he turned around, revolting beasts of different sizes and shapes began to devour most of his men. The captain of the guard, a wolverine—a dreadful-looking beast—witnessed the bold braveness of Bronze. It knew he had wonderful leadership and power to be used for their benefit. Wolf Fang, the strange beast, told Bronze that his clan was searching for a great leader. If Bronze led him and his clan and provided for their needs, they would serve him to death's door. If not, Wolf Fang told Bronze and the rest of his men they would die there on the spot. Wolf Fang was unpredictable and had snarled with the rest of his beasts, who circled Bronze. I was told Bronze was protecting someone but was never told who that was."

"How did you learn this story?" Liana questioned her.

"As before, Miss Liana, I listened to the others when doing Bronze's biddings; well, it didn't take that bloodthirsty man long to make a decision. He fell into an alliance with the beasts as their leader, thinking at least this would give him time to find his way out of there. Bronze led them in many victories. He overthrown many territories of strange, repulsive animals and brought them into his fold, which grew each day and rapidly still growing. But I had forgotten to mention before he had fallen into the portal. I was told that night that the moon was full, and for him to enter within it, the portal door had words engraved asking the question, 'What is the greatest gift of all?' Surprisingly, Bronze knew the answer. He spoke up and shouted, 'Love!'" Melanie's kind eyes flinched.

"Now, how would that monster know of love, his heart unbelievably stained and corrupted? Well, anyway, my lady, his answer caused a door to open, but before he entered, a firm voice spoke, saying, 'You may enter into the future, but you can never return without the three keys of the kingdoms' "And if he did become brave enough to enter, Bronze could only enter through one portal, which was the portal of no return or the hidden pond which I believe your children had entered. And if he lost the battle to the kingdom to come, he would lose his life in that kingdom. Bronze entered a smaller version of King James castle, a mansion that resembles the king's royal palace.

"But after he had fallen into that portal, the many creatures went through the door before it slammed shut. Inside that portal of all those nasty creatures, time stood still for Bronze. A thousand years felt like a day for him and a day a thousand years. As the years passed by, Bronze began to realize that he did not age. This gave him much time to locate another portal of escape. But when he stumbled into the portal of your world, searching diligently for someone, as his outward body continued not to age, he could feel inside he was changing. He experienced a constant battle to keep his sanity, for as time passed, he didn't look like an animal, but within his mind, he felt like he was becoming one of his beasts. He feared his time was drawing near and needed to locate another portal fast before fate set in. He managed to locate another door, a portal that, when opened, his mini castle came alive with the past but also brought him further into the future of your time. I heard Bronze brag often, saying how he overheard King James mentioning to his daughter, Princess Lilly, how he sensed Bronze's presence inside the room where Queen Leah's portrait hangs, almost as if King James sensed Bronze's ghost. I hope …" Her words hung as both began to gag.

"What is that reeking smell?" Liana questioned. Melanie swung the torch to the left and right, both appalled when they spotted dead bodies piled high and thrown on top of each other. They begin to vomit; the smell is extremely foul and putrid. Melanie tried not to pass out, realizing Liana needed her, "We must go on!" Melanie yelled out, scared senseless that if they did not find the portal soon, her dead body would be discarded, added to the rotten-smelling pile of corpses.

Liana and Melanie, terror-stricken, dashed like running a marathon past the corpses, hoping they didn't trip over rats or, worse limbs. They held onto each other while holding their noses until far enough away where they could breathe without throwing up.

After walking a little longer, Melanie's tears poured from her sweet eyes. She was losing hope of ever finding the portal. "Miss Liana, I am chickening out. Do you think we should turn around? I will take you back to your room? It may be our only hope of survival. Maybe Bronze doesn't know you are missing yet."

Liana answered. Her voice was shaken after witnessing the dead bodies, but she had determination. "I feel we are close by."

Melanie asked, troubled. "How can you feel something of that sort?"

Liana, still beside herself, was frightened. It made her blood turn cold. She broke out into a cold sweat but remained brave for Melanie and her children. She answered the best she could. "Well, I guess it's intuition, somewhat like a gut feeling." Liana was cut off guard as something out of the ordinary happened. Her necklace began to glow and pull her forward.

The two saw the light ahead—what a relief, they ran toward it, but with caution, in case there were more dead bodies, soon enough, they stood stressed-out in front of the secret entrance of the portal. Liana looked at the door. She noticed a carving in the shape of her necklace.

Melanie was desperate to escape that dreadful place. She cried out urgently. "Hurry, place the necklace inside the carving and turn it!" Melanie was about to flip out. Liana did exactly what the young girl told her, and the door opened. She went to enter the unknown. She was quickly stopped in her tracks. Melanie cautioned, "Remove your necklace from the door, never let it out of your sight, and never let Sir Bronze get ahold of it, or it shall be the end of everything for all of us."

Chapter Seven

An Escape

THE VISION OF THE QUEST

Bronze returned to Liana's room and found it empty. His subjects searched the entire mansion and came up with nothing. He learned Melanie was missing, finding no trace of either of them. His blood boiled. He pictured Melanie's body sliced and fed to his wild beasts.

"Liana!" Bronze screamed. He clutched his dark hair between his fingers and pulled wildly, banging his head into the bedroom stone wall.

Bronze's butler, his head white as an eggshell, stood in the doorway waiting for his master's wrath to subside, not being his punching bag in the state of mind he was in. Bronze spotted Ajax from the corner of his eye. The butler had no choice but to speak. "We still find no signs of Miss Liana or Miss Melanie. What do you wish for us to do now?"

Bronze exploded. "Keep a look out! Keep searching! Do not stop unless I give the command! Tell the others: if anyone sees them, apprehend them and contact me immediately, now go and do what I asked of you!" the butler departed. Bronze slammed the door shut. He missed the pleasing satisfaction upon the butler's face, planting the seed into Liana's mind to meet Melanie on day one of her arrival. Bronze made his way over to Liana's bed. He fell upon it and wept. In disbelief, his trophy had slipped out of his hands. "Liana!" he screamed.

Bronze, in a fit of rage, returned to his museum. He entered through the mysterious door and entered a gate of time to speak with his comrades through the open doors of their minds. He attempted to contact Sorelle but to no avail. Bronze successfully reached Wolf Fang.

"Yes, master," Wolf Fang answered immediately,

Bronze was a loose cannon. "Liana and Melanie are missing. They must have entered through the portal. Listen closely, no harm is to come to Liana, or it will be your life for hers, and make sure nothing happens to her necklace. I hope you get my message. Wolf Fang, do not fail me as you did with Liana's rodents enough is enough, now, am I understood?"

"Yes, master. I understand, and this time I shall not fail you. I give you my word. But what of Melanie? Do you desire her back in one piece?" Wolf Fang asked.

AN ESCAPE

Bronze, fuming mad, answered. "Do what you want with her but make her suffer terribly!" Drool fell from Wolf Fang's mouth. He grunted pleased, displaying his jagged teeth. "Will do, master Sir Bronze." The winged wolverine eagerly arched his back.

Bronze returned to his threats and came across in a deep, harsh voice that Wolf Fang was familiar with that raised his pitch-dark fur on the back of his hunchback spine. "Wolf Fang, I hope you are obedient to every word I have demanded of you; like I had said, not only your life will be at stake, but the wolverines under your leadership, in a drawn-out death that would leave you screaming, wanting the endless torture to end with a desire to be at death's door quickly." Wolf Fang was quick to reply. "As I had said earlier, I will not fail you."

Bronze was not giving in to a setback. "For now, draw away from finding Liana's three children. Keep your eyes focused on finding Liana. As long as I have the mother, her kids will eventually seek her out and fall into my lap. Liana will be the bait that draws the pains in my neck into my torture chamber," he smirked. "Yes, forget the Quest, being that they're just a speck in my eyes, nothing compared to my large army of the magnitude of power. They're just a little nuisance of dirt underneath my fingernail, now, depart and do what I have commanded, and again do not fail me!"

Bronze left the time warp but remained inside that portal. He checked on his beasts of war, preparing for the upcoming battle against King James. He then entered his museum. It was empty. He spoke to someone, but no one was there. His voice bounced off the cold, stone wall. "Yes, after I crush the First Kingdom of King James in my mighty hands. I will take over other kingdoms and dimensions, kicking their legs out from beneath them. They won't see what was coming, but I must have those keys!" Bronze threw his fist into the cold crisp air. The butler walked by and heard his master scream non-stop behind the thick door. He wondered who he was speaking to, knowing no one else was in his museum. Bronze exclaimed. "Yes, I agree with you. I should have ripped the key off the brat's neck when I had the chance! I must move fast before the Kingdoms might decide to ally themselves with King James, becoming a threat to my scores of beasts and men who

THE VISION OF THE QUEST

had joined my fierce mass of armed forces but then again, who will be so stupid to come up against the likes of me!" Pride was evident in Bronze's loud boomerang voice.

"As you already know. I am all mighty! I have been impossible to destroy throughout the centuries, trapped inside this warped dimension. I've captured numerous slaves as the sand on a seashore sending out my monstrous beasts to do my dirty work. I gave my orders on what to do and how to do it. I did this, and I did that. I am invincible. And hear this too. I will not be satisfied until my work is complete. I've captured righteous men throughout different dimensions throughout the years, forcing them to make weapons for my defense. Soon, I will have these men rise against their good and noble king, not giving them a choice; else, I would slay their wives and children, placing their heads on a block and chopping them off with heavily weighted blades of a vast guillotine."

Bronze's handsome face cringed. "Now you know, even with my army, I still need the keys to becoming completely victorious to conquer all." Bronze proclaimed a thunderous declaration: "And when I do, I shall rule over the kingdoms of old and the kingdoms of now and kingdoms to come!" Bronze, overwhelmed by greed and pride, thirsts for more. He boasted, "With even just the one key in my possession to the Kingdom. And with Liana at my side, not even God Himself could stop me! Who can conquer someone as great as I?"

As Bronze babbled on as if someone was still listening, Wolf Fang and his comrades, journey was tedious as they searched, and as another adventure begin for Liana and Melanie.

Liana was compelled to continue following the path through a wooded area—a tugging in her spirit to remain strong to be reunited with her girls and Roger. After two days and a night with no food or water, the two were faintish. Liana did not know where she was or where she was going.

Liana, weak in her knees, slumped down on a nearby log, and something small fell onto her head. She looked up, thinking she might be hallucinating. She asked Melanie, baffled, "Is it just me, or am I seeing bananas now? But then again, what is there not to believe? Maybe I am dreaming and just need to wake up."

Liana pinched herself, but nothing changed. She now smelled the fragrance of honey. Melanie was resting her head facedown inside her folded arms, lying on a patch of grass. She flipped over, looked up, and witnessed the same thing—big yellow bananas of all sizes hanging off countless trees.

Melanie said with joy. "Miss Liana, I am so hungry. I could eat a whole tree of them."

The bananas hung low enough to reach. The two were lightheaded but stood to their feet and grabbed a bundle of them, eating until their stomachs were full. They decided to sit and relax briefly, breathing in the fresh air.

Melanie perked up. "Miss Liana, I can hear water flowing. I am extremely thirsty. Let's journey there. We can also soak our feet after walking long and hard on foot. I am sure it doesn't get no easier."

Liana responded. "I was going to ask how you hear everything, but then I thought you being locked up with that maniac all those years, your ears must have always been itching hearing Bronze's devious plans."

"Itching?" Melanie questioned. Liana replied. "It's a term where I come from. I will take you up on that offer. I could drink a gallon of water. My tongue is sticking to the roof of my mouth. Lead the way." Liana was quick on her feet and followed the young girl past all the hundreds of banana trees. Finally, they arrived at a crystal clear lake, dehydrated. They gulped down a good amount of water, not paying any mind to the beautiful array of colors dancing upon the lake all around them. Their cotton-dry mouths were quenched, and finally both sat back, enjoying the splendor of the colorful lights radiating over the lake from the rainbow sky. They had slipped off their shoes and soaked their sore feet into the cold lake, desiring to stay for hours, dreading the long journey ahead. Liana and Melanie understood the importance of not stopping for any reason.

But worn out, they agreed to rest their eyes for only five minutes. The two drifted off fast to sleep. Melanie bolted up, awakened by an annoying, loud, humming sound. Liana slept right through it. She shook Liana's shoulder before the young girl had time to speak. Melanie turned her head, and flying apes were everywhere.

Congo, the leader of the Conchidas, remarked, "What is it with you people? Do you think this is a Safeway? Where you can come and just partake of anything you desire? We Conchidas have to eat, too, in order to survive but now that you are here and trespassing, grant me to know, are you friends or foe of the king?" Congo desired answers right away.

Liana sluggishly stood to her feet. "What king?" She asked, half-asleep, rubbing her eyes baffled, not believing a large, purple ape was talking. She questioned. *Am I dreaming? Will I wake up and find my girls and Roger safely tucked in their beds?*

"Come, come now," Congo replied. "You cannot be in this kingdom and not know of King James the Great."

Liana replied with a clear conscience. "The only King I know of is the King of Truth." Melanie brushed her hair out of her lightly freckled face. "My lady, it's King James of Abethar. I had mentioned to you about."

Liana nodded her head toward Melanie. She noticed behind Congo's massive body wings fluttering, which kept him afloat. He came eye-to-eye with Liana. Congo thought she spoke of the same king. He answered. "Yes, our king speaks the truth, reaffirming that you are our allies. With that being said, there were others. There was a little girl who looked like you. She was with a dark-headed girl and a young man. They headed toward the Second Kingdom with others. You must be Miss Liana. They had mentioned your name to me."

Liana was filled with questions as hope rose in her spirit. "Yes, I am Liana. They are my children! Can you help me find them? How long ago were they here? Are they okay?"

Congo shook his head. "Most female species, always full of questions and seeking answers—a puzzle to the mind that is never complete. But I tell you this, your children, the chosen ones, have the protection of the king's knights. I have no doubt of them reaching their destination. But the warriors are being followed by an evil force of wolverines. Some fly as others run swiftly on foot. The only reason you haven't been snatched up yet is the awesome power of the fragrance of bananas and honey. Otherwise, the fierce beasts would already have overtaken both of you."

Liana replied, stupefied. "Maybe I am hearing wrong—warriors, the Quest, and wolverines?" Liana didn't know what to think or feel or even believe the things she was seeing or hearing, but again she would do anything to find her children. She questioned the leader boldly. "Can you take us there?"

The ape shifted his weight as his feet dangled in the air. "I cannot take you there. I must remain to protect my comrades. I will send a few of my Conchida's and allies with you to follow the trail of those of the Quest. Now, enough has been spoken. Therefore, Miss Liana, let me introduce you to the Stingers and my other powerhouse soldiers. You and the young girl standing beside you will be well protected in their presence until you find the remaining Quest."

Liana questioned daringly. "The remaining Quest—are there others missing from this marvelous group you have spoken about?"

Congo answered, "That will be you, Miss Liana. You see, the three children and yourself are the chosen ones concerning a prophecy spoken of long ago."

Liana heard enough. "I want to find my girls and Roger and get them back home safely."

Congo replied, "Well, I will end with these words: the Pathfinders, my warriors, sensed the children's presence many weeks ago. They are gifted in the area of sensing spiritual matters. We have been going throughout these lands sometime now, searching for this great Quest. Instead, the Quest has come to us."

Liana heard a loud humming sound above her head and looked up, amazed. She witnessed giant-like bumblebees with stingers the size of a unicorn's horn. After hearing of Pathfinders having some spiritual knowledge, upset, she stated, "What is there not to believe, flying talking monkeys, giant bumble bees, and keys to secret kingdoms. Have I lost my mind or what? And if this is a nightmare, don't bother waking me up. I want a happy ending of finding my girls and Roger."

THE VISION OF THE QUEST

Congo, seeing the confusion in her eyes, answered. "All things are possible to them that believe."

Liana asked, surprised. "Where did you hear that saying?" Melanie also anticipated the answer since she had heard Miss Liana say it to her more than once.

"All things are possible to them that believe," Congo repeated. "I heard Queen Leah mention it quite a few times before she was destroyed in that awful fire and nowhere to be found. Now, Miss Liana, know this: your mind is fine. You are just in a different dimension at a different time." Liana saw Congo's sprawling shoulders. She noticed his muscular chest, the width of one of her oak chests that she owned. He touched the ground with his feet. His creamy color wings stopped flustering. He leaned forward seven feet tall and searched into Liana's deep blue eyes. She felt like a grasshopper in his sight.

Congo explained the vastness of his realm, speaking to her kindly but boldly, "Concerning the Stingers, each sting but five times, but afterward, they breathe no more. The Stingers will be at your side to defend you at all costs. My two Conchidas, Cain and Abel, will lead the group to find the Quest."

"Lastly, the Pathfinders I am sending with you come from a different dimension through a portal in my land, through a time warp."

"What is amazing about them. They transform from one location to another, only at short distances, with the capabilities of reading the thoughts of others and speaking to the minds of men and beasts."

"Their appearances are of two forms. Their original form is of a panther the size of a tiger with a body as black as night. With a refined look of silk and upon their heads rests unique helmets covering their faces, including outstanding guards for their paws, but as the Pathfinders come from their dimension into ours, somehow they're transformed into blue people." Congo paused. He again searched Liana's face and saw bewilderment. He calmly said to her, "Yeah, Miss Liana, I know what you are thinking. 'Wow, strange blue people, how weird.'"

Liana kindly replied, "It can't be any weirder than standing here and talking with a purple flying ape." Cain and Abel snickered in the background.

AN ESCAPE

Congo cleared his throat. "I will introduce you to them, but you must know, these Pathfinders are not as superb warriors. I do not doubt their strength and bravery. They will be willing to fight for you to death's door. They are strong but do not let their strength fool you; they're used to a higher degree of dealing with the spirit and soul, helping others to make intelligent decisions. They rely on their wise insight more than their strength. Perceive for yourself when the time comes and see that the Pathfinders have fascinating intuition. But then sadly, there are not many of their kind left. Bronze's army came against them time and time again and brought them down. They threaten Bronze, for somehow they penetrate his darkness."

Congo felt it was time to contact the Pathfinders. He closed his eyes and concentrated, then spoke quietly. "I am calling on Quantum, the leader of the Pathfinders. I hope your mind mends with my mind and come to my aid, bringing eleven of your men for a special mission on behalf of King James of Abethar."

Liana tried not to laugh at the big ape's silliness. She remained quiet to show her respect. But soon enough, she stood stunned as twelve tall blue men appeared unexpectedly out of nowhere.

"Odd-looking," Liana nervously whispered into Melanie's ear.

Liana stared wide-eyed at how blue they were, with unique eyes shaped like lizards. On each forehead was the symbolic marking of a path. She noticed their attire was of silk and silver. She gazed at the long strands of strange cloth that hung on the ends of their garments, with beautiful diamonds woven into the strands. She did not realize the jewels were sensors used to feel and touch and sense things in the air to determine how far away someone was, allowing them to read people, be conscious of their emotions, and understand whether they came in peace or strife.

The Pathfinders did not say a thing, but Liana observed their leader Quantum, thinking he resembled Spock on Star Trek. She was sidetracked as Congo faced her. "It is time. I am sending you twelve Stingers, Twelve Pathfinders, and eight Conchidas, and of course, including Cain and Abel, who will lead your group to find the Quest."

With confidence in his soldiers, Congo stated, "These warriors will be a guiding light and help lead you to your children. Now, go in peace, and may you have the king's protection."

Liana barely heard what Congo said. Her thoughts were tossing in all directions. It finally hit her. *I really lost it.* She turned to Melanie and searched the young girl's hazel eyes. "Please explain what is going on. Could the stress of my husband's tragic death possibly cause me to lose my mind, or am I really inside another dimension at a different time?"

Melanie was blunt, "I will explain more to you, but first, we must journey and fly the skies to hurry and find your loved ones."

"Fly, that is a breath of fresh air. Flying is something I am familiar with." Liana bubbled over, "I do not need first class. I'm just grateful we have transportation. But I am super surprised you guys have planes, not that I am complaining; I am thrilled, well, enough talk, take me to your airport that we may board and be on our way!"

The purple ape Cain smiled. "Welp, what are you waiting for. Hop on, lady, it's time to board. Nightfall will come before you know it."

Liana was at a loss for words. It was a jaw-dropper. She looked stunned as she watched Melanie jump onto Abel's back.

Cain waited. Liana did not change her position. "Come on, lady, I can't be that bad. I had a bath two weeks ago, maybe three, but who's counting?" Cain looked at the other purple Conchida. "Are you counting?"

Abel grinned. "No way! I've lost track of the last time I've taken a dip." The two chuckled. The others bent over in laughter, including Melanie. Liana softly rubbed her eyes to wake up possibly, and coming to grip with the big, strange, and purple, whatever they were, she finally spoke. "By the way, my name is Liana. Now, let's clear the airway so we may breathe a little." She winked toward them.

Cain and Abel again looked toward each other, smelling their armpits, and laughed even harder.

Cain shouted. "I think I like her spirit!" Liana climbed onto his back and held on tightly. The Conchida gladly took off into the air. She became lost with the time if seconds felt like minutes or minutes felt like hours. She was tired, hanging on steadily until the warriors needed rest. They landed safely on the ground. Melanie sat down onto thick green blades of grass. Liana sat down beside her. She looked into the young girl's face with many questions in her blue topaz eyes. She asked, "Please, explain more about what is going on?"

"Okay," Melanie sighed. "I had mentioned to you about the rise and fall of the great king and the love that Bronze had for the king's wife. Before Queen Leah became Queen of Abethar, she loved Bronze at one time, but because of the turning of his heart. Her love for him diminished, and because of this, my lady, Bronze, is now jealous and desires you and the king's throne."

"Me? Why me?" Liana asked, disturbed. "I have never known Bronze, only for the few weeks he held me as a prisoner, like a madman, and that's as far as that goes."

Melanie bowed her head in respect. "Because you, Miss Liana, come from the lineage of your great ancestor, queen Leah. I know you are from her lineage because I overheard Bronze mumbling about it while going through a brown leather book in his library that had some kind of seal on it. I believe Bronze knows something that we don't."

Liana was stunned. "That's why he desired to be near me and stare at me for hours. I could feel his eyes boring into me even behind my back." She had many unanswered questions about things she had forgotten and emotions she could not shake. She silently cried. *Why would I wake up and find the man caressing my face? At times I felt like I belonged near him, almost like I knew him. Where are these feelings coming from, now that Melanie shares more with me? I feel odd.* Liana reasoned. *I will keep this to myself.*

"What are you thinking about, Miss Liana? You seem a thousand worlds away." Melanie asked.

Moist tears slid down Liana's flushed cheeks, not understanding herself. "Oh, nothing much," were the only words she could think to express.

Liana listened closely when Cain shouted to the group, "We must go quickly to locate the Quest without delay." Her Protectors headed toward the glaciers of Crystal mountain, remembering the direction the Quest headed to outwit the wolverines. The day Congo's comrades fought hard to slow them down. However, this day was slow for King James. At his palace, he sensed the Quest's heart beating as one, alive and well. He observed the trees next to him, their roots deep, buried in soil with raw minerals, soaking in the dew of the ground, breathing life through the trees' branches. The leaves blew joyfully in the warm breeze, sending a sweet melody to the king's ear, giving him hope that his knights and the chosen ones were alive and giving him faith that his people and land would flourish once more.

Chapter Eight

THE ICE LEGEND

THE VISION OF THE QUEST

Liana and her Protectors traveled for days and entered Crystal Mountain, the Ice King's domain. They crossed over the vast glaciers. It was freezing. Cain and Abel decided to land and find shelter from the gushes of boisterous winds. Liana and Melanie found a few dry sticks and made a small fire behind a large tree to block the strong winds. They sat upon the cold ground and warmed their numb hands before getting frostbite. Liana thought a truck could fit into the unique tree as she wrapped up with Melanie in a fur blanket. Quantum had brought acknowledging these lands are quite cold. The two still felt a chill in their bones. Liana dreamed of sitting beside her warm toasty fireplace. Her thoughts were interrupted as commander David, and his Ice soldiers stood over them.

The sensor of the Pathfinder's leader jingled along his garment. Liana and the others heard a voice in their heads. Quantum said, "These ice people are not a threat. I sense the Quest has been here."

Is that my conscience, or did I hear a blue Spock speaking to me? Liana was startled to hear the voice answer her question.

"Yes, it is Quantum, leader of the Pathfinders. But who is Spock?" Liana turned around and saw him staring. She felt uncomfortable, upset her privacy was invaded and answered out loud but with kindness, realizing he had gone out of his way to help her. "This is not the time for a conversation, especially as cold as it is." Quantum did not push the issue.

Liana brought her attention back to the icemen, standing tall and completely solid ice. All she could do was shake her head in disbelief. She stood up with Melanie sharing the blanket. The commander asked Liana, "What is your purpose here? We have seen each of you on our borders earlier. Furthermore, how is it that you made it past the evil forces that lay between us and where you traveled from?"

Liana still terribly cold, was bringing her thoughts together. Abel jumped in on her behalf, "We have been careful on the lookout. We come under Congo, our leader. We will surely have the blessing and protection of King James of Abethar. We are on a mission, reuniting a mother and her children, the chosen ones carrying the keys to our future and yours. We have come to ask your leader whether he has seen the chosen ones with the king's guards."

Commander David asked boldly. "You are friends of the great King James?"

Liana's lips shivered as she daringly spoke up. "Yes, we have allies with us—the Stingers and Conchidas and Pathfinders, fighting for the same cause in finding my girls and a young man named Roger, please, have you seen them, and then we will be on our way."

Commander David replied. "The Quest has been here seeking help from my father, the Ice King. He has agreed to stand with King James in the battle to come."

Commander David looked at Liana. "I notice you carry a jewel around your neck similar to the ones the blonde and dark-headed girls had."

"Yes, my daughters, but was a young man, Roger, with them?" Liana asked, feeling like an iceberg in the Antarctic.

"Yes, there was a young man named Roger. Also, the dark-headed girl has touched the heart of our leader. You must be proud to have such a brave daughter."

Liana shown forth tears of joy, refreshed in her spirit to hear her girls and Roger were safe. She began to worry about Emily with the coldness concerned about her asthma. But ecstatic they were on the right path. Liana cried out. "But where may we find them?"

Commander David answered. "I will tell you this: we left those of the Quest at the border of our vast land, but the molten men ambushed us. The Quest aided us, and we fought them off, and upon informing our king of the bravery and true grit of those of the Quest, that's when our king gave orders. We have now allied our forces with the forces of King James."

Liana didn't bother questioning concerning about the molten men. She was just happy her kids were guarded. "How many days ago was that? Were they headed toward the Second Kingdom?" Liana asked.

He answered. "It was quite a few days ago when they departed, and yes, they are heading toward the Second Kingdom. If you like, I will send a company of my soldiers that will take you to the borders of our territory and set you on course in the direction of the Quest. But as I had told the Quest, you must be alert and do not delay, especially when you are weary. Be quiet not to alert the molten men, for there are many. We barely made it out of there alive. Is there anything else I can assist you with, my friends?" Commander David asked.

Liana asked as she continued to shiver in the icy winds, "Do you believe in the power of prayer?"

Commander David was thunder bolted. He spoke firmly, "Power? Prayer—what is this you speak of? Do not speak against the king. There is not one in Crystal mountain which will not defend King James for what the Quest has done for us."

Liana spoke boldly, unashamed of her faith. "That is not what I meant, Commander David. I meant prayer to Jehovah God."

"We think highly of King James," the commander replied, bomb shelled, not understanding who she spoke about. "I have already told you; we have allied ourselves with him. Now, go for every second that is lost is a delay in finding those of the Quest, persevere and run the race, and hope to regain your goal."

"Well said," replied Liana, smiling. "We shall go quickly. In peace, lead the way, ice soldiers." Liana felt a sense of authority and denied the feelings inside her, even though she sensed royal blood flowing through her veins.

Commander David and his men led the Quest to the borders of his land, covered with endless, snow-capped mountains. He cast his long arm forth ice formed at his fingertips, making a path of ice that traveled fast a mile ahead. He pointed toward the path of ice. "Go in that direction. That's where the Quest had fled after the battle on Ash mountain. We can go no further again. Stay alert." Commander David saluted Liana's team and with his ice soldiers they departed and slid swiftly to their home on Crystal Mountain. The Stingers, carrying Liana and Melanie on their backs.

After quite some time, Liana's Protector's landed and decided to walk. The Pathfinders disappeared and reappeared, checking out the territory. Liana and her company journeyed through a quiet, lonely place—a ghost town—but in this case of high rocky mountains, Liana and Melanie were glad that the climate was changing, becoming warmer than hotter the farther they traveled. They figured it had to be the place Commander David warned them about.

The Pathfinders' appeared in front of Cain and Abel. Their strands of jewels moved on their garments. Quantum telepathed to everyone's minds. "We are sensing danger right under our noses. We must make no sounds."

Liana again thought of Spock. Quantum looked at her oddly. She was glad Melanie took her mind off him. "This place is unusual and eerie. I don't even hear birds chirping," she remarked.

"Define the word unusual because here everything is unusual to me, concerning birds, this place is a bunch of rocks. Do you blame the poor birds for ..." Liana stopped seeing molten men everywhere, coming out of every part of Ash Mountain, blazing fire of sizzling flames, standing still and staring at their targets. They were holding rocks of hot lava, snickering and waiting patiently for the command to fire and destroy.

"What are they?" Liana demanded. "Are they the molten men? Commander David warned us about them. They are coming out like roaches. A fly swatter isn't going to take care of this. We might be the ones getting smashed by rocks of burning lava. This isn't fair!"

Cain replied with an edge of sarcasm, "Roaches, swat flyers? And you look at me like I am from a weird planet."

The fiery men taunted them with a game that hit them first and won the most points. Liana and her company didn't know what to do or where to go. There were too many. Quantum pointed in the direction of a cave. He spoke to their minds. "If all of you can fly full force and fast enough, their fire rocks might miss you. It's our only option to survive. My Pathfinders will disappear and reappear, and maybe that will keep their focus off all of you, enabling you at least a few minutes to get a head start to escape."

Abel agreed. "He is right. Look at them on that mountain, watching and waiting for the perfect time to devour us. If we stay here, we are roasted meat for sure."

"I agree, like wieners over an open fire." Liana started desiring cold breezes from Crystal mountain.

"Wieners! Fire! Ouch!" Cain said.

She ignored him as her lips curled up nervous as the molten men straightway pulled back their arms to aim, shoot, and fire. "I suggest God speed!" Liana exclaimed.

She, and Melanie, each hopped onto Stingers the closet ones to them. The Stingers and Conchidas in awful haste, flew speedily toward the cave. The Pathfinders disappeared and reappeared, acknowledging which rocks of lava would be thrown next but after five minutes. They found themselves running out of energy and disappeared and reappeared at the entry of the cave, waiting for the others to arrive.

Liana and Melanie grasped tight onto the Stingers' horns to keep from falling off, dodging the fiery rocks. The Conchidas' and Stingers' hearts racing pushing hard to survive. Several of them were not sure if they would make it.

The Pathfinders sensed their negative thoughts and encouraged them. They telepathed within their minds, "You can do it! Do not give up! Do not give in! Fly with all your might!" Hearing the positive words, each of them felt a burst of energy and forged ahead with everything in them, and eventually, all safely landed on the outside of the cave that sat high off the ground.

Cain was baffled why the molten men would not come near the cave. He smirked, shouting out, "Do you want some of this?"

Cain turned to face Liana. "I didn't think they could handle me."

Liana smirked. "Well, Cain, as I said before. Have you ever thought it could be your not so pleasant hygiene, keeping them at bay?"

Cain sniffed around him, making a sweet-smelling expression. "Aye, it's the sign of a hard-working ape." Liana and Melanie snickered.

Cain brought his focus to Abel. "We are surrounded by those hot heads. I believe the cave seems to be our only option to get away, since the molten men seem to be fearful of something inside this place."

"I agree," Abel answered. "From where we are standing the cave seems to be enormous. Going through it may get us around Ash mountain on a different route to find the Quest." The team shook their heads in agreement.

The two discussed it with Liana, "If that's what it takes to find my children, it seems like the wisest decision." Cain and Abel entered the vast mouth of the cave. The others followed, and as they ventured further inside away from the entry, the light from the outside diminished. It became pitch-black. The fiery men turned around and returned to their clan, informing their commander of the events that had taken place.

Cain found a stick. Melanie ripped off a section of her blouse sleeve and handed it to Cain. She then reached into her pocket and brought out the matches that she carried in the mansion to light Bronze's candles. Cain and Abel had the others wait as they searched deeper in the cavern hoping, to find something to make more torches. They went around a small bend. The two didn't have to go far. Torches were already lit hanging on the cave walls. Cain whispered. "This is bizarre." They returned to the others with seven torches and passed them out.

"Where did you find them?" Liana asked.

Cain answered. "Oddly, it was not far from here hanging off the walls, but let's get moving and find another way out. The sooner the better. Who knows what we may find inside this place," Cain and Abel led everyone through the wide tunnels, and the further they walked, they found it filled with statues carved out of solid rock. Liana and Melanie looked closer at the extravagant craftsmanship of the chiseled faces and were impressed. The faces were engraved with the perfection that the eyes appeared real. A chunky Stinger hollowed out. "I saw one of the statues' eyeballs move. This place gives me the willies!" Abel corrected him. "We don't know what's in here, you knucklehead. If you keep screaming, it's enough to wake the dead." They advanced and observed more statues, outstanding pieces of artwork crafted out of solid rock, well, that's what they thought.

Unexpectedly, everyone heard a loud noise: a heavy door slamming shut behind them. "Well, that's great, now, we might as well be buried alive!" the same plump Stinger complained. "I mean, if I am going to die, at least I like to die an honorable death. You know, in battle by

THE VISION OF THE QUEST

a sword, a blade, or even a claw of a wolverine, just something, but not shut up in a dark, damp cave, surrounded by these dang statues. I mean, come on!" He cried out frustrated, "Someone might as well knock me out!"

Abel spoke, annoyed. "I'll put you out of your misery if you don't shut that trap of yours." The plump Stinger ignored him. "I am telling you; the statues are watching my every move. Is everyone too blind to see it?" Abel had enough. He reached back and threw a heavy punch. The Stinger swiftly flew to the left just in time. Cain standing behind him received a hard right punch to his mouth. Cain shouted. "Ouch! I tell you. I am probably the only friend you got, and you're trying to kill me!" Everyone chuckled.

"Sorry, friend." Abel apologized. He turned toward the Stinger. "Chunky, do you have a name?"

"Nope," the Stinger answered quite frank.

"Well, your name for now on is Grumble Bee, now, keep that trap shut or next time I promise I won't miss."

"Grumble Bee, I like that." he smiled.

Liana and the others thought whatever had slammed shut. They were unable to turn back their only option was to press ahead.

The warriors became puzzled moving deeper into the cave. Grumble Bee and a few others were overcome with a great fear of losing their sense of direction. The Pathfinders were perplexed, unable to sense which tunnels lead outside, away from the molten men, and into the fresh air.

Grumble Bee wasn't the only crazy one. Others began to feel the statues' eyes, watching their every move as if the statues were alive.

Melanie tried to keep herself from going off the deep end. She whispered fearfully to Liana, "I do not believe your children have come this way. How are we going to get out of this place? There is such an eerie presence in here. I cannot shake it. I agree with Grumble Bee. Every single move we make is being watched. It's nerve-racking. How about you? How do you feel about it?"

Liana grabbed Melanie's hand then called out to Cain and Abel. "Something in my spirit compels me to keep going forward." She turned toward the frightened girl. "Melanie, I agree the kids did not come this way. I also feel we are being watched. Stay close to me, I will not let anything happen to you." Liana spoke again to Cain and Abel. "What do you know of this place? Do you know of a way out of here?"

Liana listened as Cain and Abel conversed with the Conchidas and the Stingers, with noises of apes and bumblebees. The Pathfinders' sensors moved slightly, unable to dance. Cain and Abel returned to Liana's and Melanie's language. Abel answered her. "We have never seen these caves or traveled through them, but we can smell the fresh air, maybe blowing into a cavity or a large opening which will lead us outside—before weaners smash us."

"That's a fly swatter." Liana gleamed but it was difficult seeing her in the dim light.

"I tell you, it's always a losing battle with a woman. We are doomed." Abel softly snickered.

His torch enabled Liana to see him smile in her direction. She returned his smile, taking the edge off everyone's fears. The Conchidas walked on as the Stingers flew above their heads. Liana continued to follow the compelling of her spirit and said to continue straight. The warriors could feel a brander breath of fresh air coming from somewhere. Abel spoke. "Liana, whatever is compelling you is definitely leading us in the right direction. When I am ready, I would like to know more about this Jehovah God that brings you this peace beyond your own understanding that I sense about you. This presence about you is new to me, but for now we all do feel uneasy about this place. We must stay alert and be aware. I feel danger is near."

Just as the words slipped out of Abel's mouth, the statues slowly walked toward them, barely dragging their feet. The ones chiseled into the rocks too came alive, but only able to move their eyes, expressing an eagerness to be free. Liana felt it was a benefit the statues lacked speed, giving them enough time to find a way out before surrounding them, possibly to the end of their lot.

The monuments were staring at Liana, knowing she held the key, but what key? Was it the key around her neck or the key that opened the door to a different kingdom—a heavenly kingdom, the kingdom of

THE VISION OF THE QUEST

heaven's throne that resided within her heart? The remarkable statues moved forward. Liana and Melanie's mouths dropped, shocked when a stature opened its mouth, boldly speaking. "Retrieve the key, that we may live again, brothers that we may walk the earth alive! Alive!"

Cain and Abel were moving at high speed. "Follow us now, before we are smashed to pieces!" Abel cried out.

Cain gave orders, "Quickly, warriors, circle around the women to protect them, as we find a way out of this place, my warriors, protect them with your lives!"

"Long live King James!" the Protectors yelled bravely, prepared to battle until the end.

Cain and Abel moved fast to find another opening to get away. Right in the nick of time, a young Pathfinder named Orion finally screamed. "Follow me. There is yet hope! I finally sense an opening of some kind up ahead!" They followed him.

The statues gained ground. Cain and Abel and the others promptly managed to flee through an extended archway, hoping for safety, feeling it welcomed them with open arms. Open arms it was for out of the rock wall, long arms of stone reached out to grab them, one hand stretched forth, touching one of the Conchidas turning him into a boulder right before Abel's eyes. After witnessing this, he screamed forcefully, in a boomeranging voice throughout the cave, "Go forth, and do not allow them to touch you or you turn to stone! Stay alert!"

The cave shook with the many statues coming alive. Everyone but Liana felt they were inside an open grave, soon to meet their fate. They came to a fork, which split into three different directions. The Stingers shouted to Cain and Abel, "Which way? Hurry and choose, for there is not much time for escape!" The Pathfinders were again unable to sense the right direction.

Cain and Abel were unsure. The wrong choice and their comrades and friends would possibly come face-to-face with death. Abel looked toward Liana for her guidance.

Melanie, petrified, was happy to hear Liana holler out, "Bear right, it's the safest route to go!"

They listened, seeing the truth in her, and trusted her instincts. Abel called out two of his Conchida's, giving them a firm command. "Rush ahead of us to the end of where this tunnel is leading and check out the surroundings, and report back to me." His Conchida's took off. Immediately everyone pushed forward, and ventured about ten minutes through the long, tunnel that became narrow. The statues slap-bang stopped in their tracks.

Cain and Abel cautiously walked in front, ready to meet anything coming their way head-on. The tunnel dropped into a large cavern. Abel spotted his two Conchidas and saw why they had not reported back to him. Cain and Abel observed how the Conchidas were positioned before they turned to stone. Their fellow apes fought hard to survive. The leaders felt for them but pressed on, regardless, wondering what kind of cave this was.

Liana, and Melanie, with her Protectors within the walls, began hearing voices shouting, "Come join us, be a part of history!" They could not figure out where the voices echoed from. Liana was stunned, surprised to see her famous forefathers. She'd learned about them in her world. She tried to grasp why such marvelous men, who had accomplished such wonderful things, were stone and inside this dimension.

The statures had stopped moving. They ventured deeper into the cavern. It became even larger. Liana was now holding a torch, seeing how towering and roomy this part of the cave was, and watched a few Stingers fly upward, disappearing into the darkness and flying back. They looked upon such tremendous beasts from another time, maybe even another dimension. The Conchidas and Stingers had trouble comprehending, wondering whether these types of creatures ever actually existed. They felt relieved as they seemed still and unmovable or they would have a big problem on their hands.

Liana witnessed doubt in Cain's and Abel's faces in what they were staring at in awe. Liana shared. "The beasts you are admiring are called dinosaurs, yes, from my dimension years ago, and these breeds of dinosaurs are called Tyrannosaurus rex and Velociraptor, and the amazing thing is these dinosaurs are from a much smaller breed. There

THE VISION OF THE QUEST

are ones that are probably more than one hundred feet tall or taller. I guess now is the time for you to asked what dimension do I come from?"

Cain's and Abel's eyes became the size of saucers. Liana smiled. "What is there not to believe, now, boys, flying apes, oversized bumblebees? But in your unbelieving generation, it's too difficult to believe in fly swatters and roasted wieners. I now have a better understanding in what it means to believe in the impossible," Liana snickered.

"Ha, ha, very funny," Cain and Abel made light of it, coming to their defense.

"Hmm, excuse me. I don't feel this is a good time to be horsing around," Melanie interrupted. "I mean, last time I checked. I believe our lives were in danger. I certainly don't look forward to being turned into a rockhead, like some hard heads I know of right now."

Melanie now spoke with much fear in her voice. "I am not trying to come across as rude. I am grateful for everything all of you have done for us, but I have an issue. I had been hiding it very well up until now. I am claustrophobic. I've had all I can take of these tunnels. What I am trying to say politely is …" She took in a deep breath and shouted hysterically, "I want out! I want out now, before I panic!"

All of a sudden, the specular rock dinosaurs moved and came alive. Melanie yelled, upset. "Oh, that's great, now you apes woke up the dead! Ha, ha, now who's funny?" She asked, dreadfully.

The monstrous rock dinosaurs shook the cave walls, the earth under them trembled slowly, edging toward them, speaking in sharp tones, "There is no escape! There is no escape! Why run? We will find you out! Where will you hide?"

Cain wondered where they would hide to find shelter. The tunnels seemed endless as if they could go on for hours or even days or maybe forever.

Cain yelled, "Pick up your pace! Pick up your pace! These beasts are quicker and seem to know the tunnels' ins and outs! Do not grow tired or weary! Fight the fight! Do not give up!" Cain thought to fly

Liana and Melanie on his and Abel's back but worried it would be more dangerous flying right into the arms of the beasts at a fast speed.

"Where will you run? Where will you hide?" the dinosaurs repeatedly screamed, their voices like a knife scratching terribly down a plate, "There is no escape! Where will you hide?"

Melanie clapped her hands over her ears. "I wish we could put corks in their mouths!"

No sooner did Melanie scream than Liana yelled forcefully, "In the clefts of the rock! We shall hide!" The beasts shrank backward and slowly degenerated into sand. Everyone stood silent, staggered at what happened. They wondered what power there was in Liana's words.

Cain and Abel stood speechless, pleased to have Liana on their side. Liana shouted. "Let's go forth in victory!" Cain winked at Liana, admiring her bold strength though wondering how? He finally asked, "Why didn't you shoot out those powerhouse words earlier, the first time we were being attacked on Ash mountain?"

"Yeah, I agree," Abel said while the others listened. "I mean, those molten men were pretty aggressive."

Liana, with the light from the torches, winked at both of them, "I wasn't compelled."

Cain and Abel were stumped, hearing Melanie burst out laughing, "Now, that's funny!" Liana and her Protectors were glad upon watching Melanie taking in a deep breath, enjoying the openness of the place before venturing into another tunnel still fearful of what lay ahead.

Two Protectors holding a torch stumbled into another large room bigger than the first cavern with unlimited width and height, seemingly without end. Liana and the others heard them yelling. "You have to come in here. It's awesome!" Liana heard their excitement and hurried and entered the cavern. She cried out, "This room has life in it! I can almost feel it breathing. I can feel it!" Liana did not understand what she sensed in her spirit, a little nervous what to expect until the history of this unknown territory became more alive to her.

The others entered behind the Pathfinders. Quantum spoke out loud, "Miss Liana, for some reason our sensors work in here. What you sense is a good thing; my Pathfinders and I feel what you are experiencing and it is incredible."

The others started acknowledging what Liana was crying about, feeling their past, alive and breathing, causing their hair to rise on their bodies. Something they had never experienced before.

They became silent as a mouse, leaving them awe-struck. Within a matter of seconds, they had heard history from the beginning of time into the future, listening to the history of their forefathers, speaking one to another. They could hear the battles of wars fought long ago and the voices of great kings who had walked the earth. They were utterly taken back hearing everything they had ever spoken about in the past. They all marveled. It blew their minds, thinking, *how can this be?*

The cave lit up with a glorious, bright light, wonderful though not blinding. What they beheld rendered them speechless; to the right and left, they saw mirrors as numerous as the stars in the sky, reflecting pools of water contained within countless windows surrounded by mirrors. They were seeing the reflection of water going on never-ending, keeping them in wonderment as each of them glimpsed into the very windows of their lives, like vast movie screens displayed before their eyes. Suddenly behind these countless windows, the rocks cried out and began to speak, proclaiming historical and future events. It made Liana think of two phrases of old. *I tell you…if they keep quiet, the stones will cry out. The stones will cry out from the wall…*

The room was larger than a stadium. However, the height seemed timeless. Liana stood dumb-struck as she gazed into the pools of water. She passionately placed her hands over her mouth, catching a glimpse of her childhood, seeing her mother standing and holding her in her arms inside a room of gold, with much elegance around them. She felt a burst of happiness, feeling her mother's immense love and affection, something she had forgotten until this day. She could not understand why she had no pictures of her and barely remembered her until now or even what she looked like. She watched another scene, her mother giving her three necklaces on her death bed. Tears ran down Liana's eyes, not even knowing what she died of. Liana gripped her gold chain with precious jewels, now recalling the same jewelry around her mother's neck. The same necklace she and her girls have grown to cherish, but strangely the one her mother wore was all three of theirs intertwined as one.

Liana ventured farther into the cavern. Scene after scene flashed before her—scenes of her childhood that boggled her mind. She stuffed it inside, keeping it to herself until she understood who she was.

Liana pressed on, advancing, astonished to see a glimpse of Bronze and his evil hordes fighting against what she believed was the army of King James—an event in the future. Silence lingered as each of them continued witnessing glimpses of time from the beginning of creation into the future until the end of days. Their hearts stood in wonder, experiencing something as fantastic and stunning as this.

Liana and Melanie and her brave warriors soaked up the eye-opening things they heard and seen. Each realized there was much more, knowing they could not contain it, too much knowledge to digest all at once. Their journey through the reflections of the pools of water was coming to an end, however, not history. Liana acknowledged before there was time. God became our time. She realized there are still numerous and abundant words and lives to be recorded throughout history.

Abel was behind Liana, about to exit with his comrades. Liana stopped, frozen in her tracks, fixed on a noise that took her by surprise. She dropped to her knees and wept, hearing hammers banging and banging and banging, and a voice she was all too familiar with crying out, "I did this for you!" The long, hard nails driven into her Christ's flesh at his crucifixion, suddenly she heard his voice shouting. "Father, forgive them, for they know not what they do!"

Liana sobbed that she had to leave this extraordinary room. Abel helped her to her feet about to walk out. She stopped unexpectedly hearing a criminal hanging beside the one she loved asking for his forgiveness, hearing her faithful King cry out with overwhelming love and compassion, "This day I tell you: you will be with me in paradise."

Liana slowly exited and realized she was learning the wonders of the world. She reflected on it, pondering what dimension paradise may be in.

She and the rest of them left the room. They paused, still astonished by all of it. Each absorbed it within their hearts, up until the rock statues, surprisingly, came alive again. Liana was disappointed, leaving cherishing forgotten memories of her past and learning the great things of the future. Unfortunately, the wonders she was comprehending had to be put on hold. The cat and mouse chase continued; the chase was on.

Statues—mere replicas of their forefathers, false in every way—were on the move, desiring to touch and turn them into stone, control and force them into one of them. What was not real, and what was reality? Where rocks birthed forth into statues, with energy kept secret through the ages of time, and unknowingly, to Liana, Melanie, and the warriors, the statues formed their images within the spirit of the rocks of these splendid men of old, from what they have recorded throughout history. These false replicas desired to rob Liana of her key, hoping to rule the Kingdoms and force everyone into stone.

Liana could feel Melanie's side press up against hers. The tunnel was becoming tighter and tighter. She felt the young girl trembling with anxiety than with a mother's care. She wrapped her arm around her.

"Thank you," Melanie choked up and tried her best not to hyperventilate. "Miss Liana, while Bronze held me captive, there were times when, in his evil hands, I wouldn't do his sinful biddings. He locked me inside a small metal box. I was cramped there days at a time until finally, I would pass out and wake up again to find I was still in there. He's a, a...."

Liana yelled, furious at what the man had cruelly done to an innocent child, "A complete monster! An awful beast! But you're with me now. I will not allow him to hurt you anymore. He will have to walk over my dead body. Do you trust me?"

"Yes, Miss Liana." Melanie took comfort in her voice, taking in slow, quick breaths. Orion overheard. He couldn't believe someone would be that cruel. But hearing it was Bronze, he puts nothing past that man. Orion witnessed the first-hand devastation Bronze has caused his race.

Cain and Abel led them into another tunnel, hoping to escape the counterfeit monuments. The tunnel was narrower, making it difficult for the annoying statues to fit through. But that didn't stop them. They busted their way through, causing a gush of damp air to blow out two of their torches making it more difficult to see in the darkness. A few of the Conchidas and Stingers tripped over each other.

Melanie ran out of matches. She could no longer stand beside Liana but behind her. She realized the tunnel was growing smaller when her hand hit the wall. She felt the cold, hard rock. The young girl yelled out in absolute fear, "We're going to die in here!" Frightened, she threw her arms around the back of Liana's curvy waist things looked hopeless. Liana had her doubts and wondered whether they would make it out of there. She whispered in fear. "What would become of my children?" Her hopes were beginning to diminish.

Quantum heard in Liana's voice disappointment. He unflinchingly said out loud, "My lady, go with the encouraging Spirit that's deep inside your soul. I discovered the day you entered Congo's land I sensed a power within you that I do not quite understand. I do know this unlimited power you possess can overcome any fear that tries to lay hold of your conscience. Lift it up! Believe in this strength that lives within your being. There is nothing that can stop you, not even fear itself. This is your time! Grasp it and lead us to safety."

She knew the blue Spock had spoken the truth. She soaked it into her heart, mind, and soul. Liana bowed her head and gave thanks to her God…boldly. She lifted her head and screamed out, "Abba, Father! Make a way of escape! Open!"

Liana shouted it only once. Her voice echoed—her words repeating over and over. Louder and louder; even within her mind, she heard her voice repeating the exact words again and again. Her necklace began to glow with a breathtaking illuminating light. The statues stood in place, not moving an inch. Before Liana knew what hit them, a growing power within her necklace demolished the side of the wall. Liana and the others moved to venture through the remaining tunnel. All of them saw sunlight coming from a large opening about one hundred feet away.

THE VISION OF THE QUEST

Abel yelled, "There is hope after all! I never thought of light being so beautiful!"

"We made it!" Liana breathed with delight. The twelve Pathfinders sensors were now able to dance, ringing out a melody of freedom while walking closer to the outside light.

"Liana, your necklace is still glowing," Abel stated still overwhelmed with the things he had witnessed. "Yes, yes, we need to get out of this place! The statures are on the move again!" she replied hastily.

"Move quickly!" Abel shouted. "We still have a small stretch getting outside." They shuffled as fast as they could without falling on each other and edged closer, ultimately reaching the brilliant ray of sunshine. Joy filled their eyes with only a few more feet to go.... a large statue bust through the remainder of the narrow tunnel, squeezing and forcing its way toward Liana. It reached for her necklace.

Abel yelled to everyone, "Hurry!" He quickly grabbed Liana with his broad, solid arms and threw her outside the cave. Liana stood up slowly and brushed off the dirt. She had skinned her knees and elbows but was glad that no bones had broken. She understood it was for her protection. The Stingers and Conchidas followed suit. Liana searched around for Melanie. The Pathfinders were already outside except for the young Pathfinder Orion. He grabbed Melanie into his arms. She was too frozen to move without Liana at her side. "Trust me," he said. Orion disappeared and was transported in front of Liana outside the cave. He said, cheerfully at the girl before letting go of her. "I can get used to this." He then gently let her go. Melanie crossed her arms toward him. "Yeah, and you can keep dreaming too."

The team was thrilled to be free of that crazy place. Melanie quickly cried an ear-piercing scream. Out of nowhere, a titanic rock hand reached for Liana to force her back inside. Still, as the sunlight hit the colossal hand, all marveled and witnessed it crack and wither, falling into a downward spin, turning into a beach full of sand, and settling around their feet. Liana finally had the chance and inhales a deep breath of fresh air, content to see clouds and hear birds singing to feel a warm breeze brush against her face. She threw her arms toward the open sky and praised the one she loved. The others lift their voices, grateful to be out of there and alive.

Abel nudged Liana. "We are a team."

"Yes, a team that sticks together until the end." Liana took Abel's big hairy hand into hers. She spoke sincerely. "Thank you for all that you and your warriors had done for me this day. I will never forget it." Abel bowed his head in high regard. "No, thank you, Miss Liana, it's because of you and your children, being the chosen ones, that Abethar may become strong again." Abel bellowed out. "For the cause!"

"For the cause!" Everyone joined in with a loud shout.

As the shouting simmered down, Liana's Protectors surveyed the area and observed they were nowhere near the molten men noticing layer upon layer of thick green grass in fields far as the eyes could see. They felt the heat of the sun but nothing compared to Ash Mountain. Swiftly all of them traveled to a safer spot to find rest and consult with one another, preparing for any other hardship that came their way in finding the Quest and the battle to come.

Chapter Nine

Faith of a Mustard Seed

THE VISION OF THE QUEST

Congo's soldiers agreed to stay on course. Exhausted, they traveled for hours in the sun and came to a place with the reflection of one huge mirror wrapped around a large body of water. Similar to the reflection, everyone witnessed inside the windows of the cavern, but nothing more spectacular or eye-opening than what they experienced. The Protectors sensed something was wrong. There was no life, but all pressed on and flew through a barrier, a large crack reaching inside the dome. The crack closed once they ventured through. They saw water to the right and the left. Cain and Abel spotted a field and landed the team to rest. The torch of the heat bared down on their backs. One of Cain's and Abel's comrades moved fast and flew toward the sea to cool off. When his feet touched the water, he began to disintegrate rapidly. The Conchida screamed out in horrific pain. "It's acid!" he warned them before ultimately diminishing. Liana and Melanie cried out loudly, witnessing what happened to him.

Abel spoke with authority. "We must move quickly. Be careful with every step we make! The barrier we crossed must had brought us into a place of illusions. We are seeing visions of things that are not what they seem to be. I believe we are on a different path to finding the Quest, be on guard for anything that looks out of the ordinary or anything that looks normal, for that matter."

He seriously looked toward Liana. "Pray to your God for guidance. I will never forget witnessing His power inside the cave but as for now, we shall take to the air. I feel it may be safer. Liana flies with me, and Melanie, you fly with Cain. We shall move slowly, that we don't run into any traps or dangers." Abel turned toward the Pathfinders and spoke strongly. "Quantum, consult me if you have any foresight or knowledge of how to get out of here. Stingers and Conchidas, you surround the women for protection."

The team traveled again for hours, nothing out of the ordinary, except for bodies of acid scattered in different locations of the bizarre land. Out of the blue, the sky resembled a black silk sheet as a bed of thunder and lightning boomed forth wildly. Heavy clouds broke, releasing large amounts of rain.

The tempest was terribly strong. The heavy winds blew forcefully, making it difficult for the warriors to fly. The Pathfinders had trouble transporting from location to location to keep up with the others. Cain worried. He yelled at the top of his voice over the fierce winds. "We have to reach shelter fast, or we all perish! The storm is too overpowering. It will drive us possibly into the body of acid, disintegrating us within seconds!"

Quantum telepathed into Cain's mind. "We sensed the danger of the storm beforehand and found a safe area to shelter us. My Pathfinders had also quickly collected wood for a fire." Cain searched and spotted a large cave with a big opening in the rocks. Quantum standing in front of it waving his arm toward him. Cain shouted. "Up ahead! Follow me! Hurry! Before it's too late!"

"Not another cave!" Melanie cried out, afraid. She gripped tightly around the ape's thick neck and yelled above the winds. "I will rather stay outside in the storm and take my chances!" Her anger surfaced—hate toward Bronze for everyone he has hurt to have power and rulership. She felt the strong winds brush up against her warm face as she rampaged. "There is no way rocks statues inside another cave will chase me! They can forget it! I am not being closed inside any more tight spaces! And that's final!"

Melanie watched Abel land with Liana and the other Protectors venture inside the cave. She nervously hopped off Cain's back. Orion, a few years older than her, appeared. He sensed Melanie's fear and tension. He walked inside the cave touching the walls with his strands of jewels and felt positive energy, and poked his head outside the cave, reassuring her. "If my sensors are correct, this place is safe. You have nothing to worry about."

She stood shaken outside in the cold rain, unsure of the blue guy who remained. Melanie faced him and spoke with slight sarcasm, "Hmm, let me see, now, if that's the case, why didn't you tell me about the other cave not being safe. Or maybe your sensors were wrong about that cave as they're wrong concerning this one. I guess you didn't know about those crazy statues to warn us? Did you?"

THE VISION OF THE QUEST

Orion answered her honestly, "Yes, I knew there was danger before we ventured inside the cave but once inside, I couldn't sense anything."

Melanie felt her hand rise to smack the tall blueberry but refrained, "Why did you not warn us? I was terrified."

Orion thought, at how funny the girl looked, soaked from head to toe, sensing her need to smack him with thinking of him as a giant blueberry.

"Well?" Melanie asked, upset. "I can't wait all day." She tapped her foot with her hand on her small hip.

"Well, what?" Orion asked, now being ornery, and watched the girl curl up her freckled nose. She began to sneeze. He became concerned about getting her out of the rain before getting sick.

He answered, "Well, to tell you the truth, I didn't tell you about the dangers because I didn't want to scare you ..." he paused. "I sense pent-up anger within you like you may use me as your emotional dart board."

Melanie could scream but held back her tidal wave.

He spoke calmly. "Give me time to explain my reasons?" Melanie's arms were now crossed up against her chest. She tapped her foot even more. "This better be good!" she exclaimed.

He answered. "We had no option but to go inside the cave or be burned alive outside of it. We had to take our chances, and we did, and we survived. I didn't have the heart to tell you, because I had sensed your fear as I do now. I felt the need to protect you." Orion decided to speak to her mind. "Come inside. I promise I will protect you with my life."

Melanie reacted bluntly. "Mr. Blue Boy, I am upset that you are in my head. It isn't necessary! I don't see any immediate threat." Orion couldn't get in a word edge-wise. She continued like a broken record. "I don't care for you popping in and out of my mind like I am a used doormat. It would be politer if you just speak to me." Orion had heard enough. "You will be amazed at what this blueberry can do. There will be a time when you will be thanking me for saving your butt. Now come on before I carry you inside."

"You will not touch me! I can walk in on my own two feet. I am not some baby." Orion retaliated. "Then stop acting like one." Melanie's freckles blended in with her hot steaming face. Her fuming madness helped diminish her fears and finally followed Orion inside. She slowly looked around and saw the cave was open and wide enough to shelter everyone but a bit chilly. She looked toward Cain and Abel. Melanie spoke, upset. "This is as far as I am going. I will stay only in the mouth of this ridiculous cave, but I am not going through any more tunnels."

Liana looked up at her and reminded the young girl. "I told you I would keep you safe, my dear. My word has not changed. Come sit next to me by the fire. The Pathfinders had collected wood before it rained. They sensed the storm coming when the skies were clear."

She sat down close to Liana and curled up her legs, throwing her arms around them, shivering, hoping the heat would soon dry her soaked clothes. Orion took a stunning white robe out of his bag. He gently wrapped it around her shoulders.

Meanie embarrassed lifted her head from staring into the fire and spoke to him. "Hey, I'm sorry for giving you a hard time. I don't normally act that way. I realize now you were only trying to help me."

"I understand. By the way, my name is Orion."

She sneezed a few times, "I'm Melanie."

Orion, said softly, "You're forgiven," he sat down beside the leader of the Pathfinders. She thought. *"I wish I could forgive that easily, then maybe I wouldn't feel so weighed down."*

She felt Liana's arm wrapped around her, bringing her comfort. The beautiful white robe helped her not to shiver. Liana hoped someone was comforting her children. She thought of them as she listened to the Protectors share information about where they had come from. Then all eyes fell on Liana and Melanie.

Liana spoke first. "Well, I am the mother of two special girls—Alicia, who has grown into a beautiful young lady, and Emily, my nine-year-old, full of life and spunkiness, definitely keeps me on my toes. I am fortunate that I have Alicia to help me out. She has always been such a blessing."

THE VISION OF THE QUEST

"Now, there is Roger, a sweetheart but a little testy. I guess he's at that age desiring to feel his oats. Though I am happy Roger has become a part of our lives. My husband and I practically raised him." Liana's voice choked. "Excuse me, please," she dried tears from her stargaze eyes. She said, hurt. "My husband, Ken, died in a fatal car accident about two years ago. I miss him so much. How I wish he were with me during this scary time." Liana became quiet in remembrance of him. Abel broke the silence. "I am very sorry for your loss. I can see he meant a lot to you, but I hope you don't mind me asking. You stated a fatal car accident. What is a car?" Liana sat straight up, surprised. She answered quite frankly. "It's a vehicle that a person drives, and depending on the size of the vehicle, eight people could fit into it."

"Gosh, that car must have some powerful wings." Abel marveled at the thought of it. Liana stared with a perplex grin. "No, friend, tires, there are no wings, whatsoever, and the car drives on the ground, on roads through mountains and highways at very fast speeds."

"Does it ever get tired out?" Cain peeped in.

"No." Liana enjoyed the amusement. "It's machinery with a motor."

Cain was curious. "This car must be a giant beast to fit you and your children on top of it." Liana giggled. "No, we drive inside of it. It shields us from the cold and the heat."

"Wow, you drive inside a metal mechanical beast, and this metal keeps you cool or warm during different climates? What a source of great transportation." Cain proclaimed.

Liana answered. "Well, we have four seasons, winter, spring, summer, and fall. It's not like here, a land of glaziers of icebergs and icemen and hot molten men on a scorching volcano mountain, within a short couple of hours. You must understand our seasons last for months at a time." The Protectors looked at her with unbelief. Liana shook her head in amazement.

"Well, let's get back to where I left off." Liana removed a long bang out of her peaches and cream porcelain face.

"Now, after I lost my husband two years ago, I managed to go on, no doubt, it's been difficult, but I have learned to live one day at a time. I try not to worry about what tomorrow holds. However, I worry about my children's whereabouts but feel better now, knowing they are in safe hands."

Liana's facial expression became troubled. She spoke out, upset. "When I was at the mercy of Bronze. He had some type of power over me. He had brought me so many cups of tea that I now wonder if he was slipping drugs into them. Who knows? But what I know is that my car broke down near Bronze's mansion, and, now that I think of it, it might not have been a coincidence. It was almost as if he had been planning it somehow."

All silence fell to hear Liana as she continued. "It's funny; now that I share all this, I am beginning to remember what happened. There was a storm and powerful winds, and my car conked out in the middle of no-man's-land. The strange thing was it was summer, but within a short period, it felt like winter. It was almost like how the weather changes here. I knew I had to get my girls and Roger somewhere safe. I spotted flickering lights, and we decided to head toward them. That's when we discovered Bronze's mansion."

"I think it's more like he discovered you," Melanie interrupted. "Miss Liana, you're right. Bronze had it planned somehow. The night before your arrival, he paced the floor for hours, looking out the windows, searching for something. A servant came into his room. He said his guest had arrived; the only thing Bronze didn't have prepared for you was a long, red carpet."

Liana was unsure how to express what she felt but spoke anyway. "This might sound goofy, but I am starting to believe there is unlimited power in mine and my children's necklaces ..." Liana stopped her sentence, wondering if she had gone overboard. Her Protectors knew her statement had truth to it. They witnessed the power and energy of it, unknowing that her gems, diamonds, sapphire, and rubies represent God's word of life, power, and truth. Her key opens doors to ask, seek and knock, finding everything suitable. The absolute treasurer, her God, has for His people.

Liana's mind pondered on the great mirrors, reflecting pools of water contained within the unlimited windows, witnessing the reflection going on forever. It still rendered her speechless when she saw a glimpse into the windows of her own life. She dwelled on her mother holding her in that most elegant room, wearing fancy clothes and the necklace around her mother's neck—all three necklaces but connected as one. Liana remained quiet.

Melanie saw Liana's eyes hold questions. She shares troubled. "You are already aware that Bronze's mansion is a duplicate version, a copy of the original castle of King James, but much smaller. The only difference between the two is light and darkness. But my Lady, Bronze desires the keys as much as he desires you. He desires to overtake King James castle and his throne and force you to become his queen."

Liana became agitated. Her voice boomed like thunder. "That is absurd! I am appalled by the thought of it. The audacity of that, that, that …."

"The devil himself," Melanie completed.

"Yes! The audacity of that snake, thinking he can do with me what he wants, treating me like I am a piece of ground! All I feel right now is the mother of my children, and I desire to have them back home living in peace and safety." Cain and Abel voiced their concern.

"That is all we desire, too."

"Peace and safety for all." The other Protectors followed suit. Quantum stood up and placed more wood into the fire.

Cain spoke with hope. "Liana, Melanie is correct. The tables have turned. Again, it's been foretold a small company shall come, with keys that will unlock the door to the kingdoms, to retrieve the water of life and leaves from the tree of enlightenment. That will heal the king and kingdoms, and all may flourish, prosper, and live in peace."

Everyone was silent, taking in what Cain shared—a prophecy being fulfilled right before their eyes with Liana sitting before them and part of the key hanging from her neck. The Protectors are willing to risk their lives to see this prophecy pass. Melanie broke the silence. Orion noticed a change on her speckled face. Her cute blunt nose turned slightly upwards. He sensed a heavy burden lifted from her shoulders. Melanie spoke, revived. "I am thrilled the prophecy is finally coming to pass. I see Bronze as an evil adversary. He better prepare for a challenge as he comes up against his opponents." She turned and faced Liana.

"Miss Liana, there is something strong within you. I only hope your girls and Roger carry that same Spirit, wherever they go or whatever they come up against." Orion caught himself staring at Melanie's red candy apple lips. He looked toward the Pathfinders hoping. They couldn't sense what he was feeling for her. Quantum, his father knew. He smiled at his son. The other Pathfinders didn't catch onto it. Orion thought. *They catch everything else. That's weird. I can hide things from the others except for my father. I don't understand it, but I like it.*

Melanie sneezed and glanced around the gloomy cave. She spotted Orion looking at her. She was quick and spoke to his mind. "I don't think so." Orion smiled even more. He sensed her thinking of herself being downright homily. He sees her beautiful as she continued to speak, he focused on the kindness in her lovely eyes. "Quantum's tribe isn't the only ones separated. My people are also in different dimensions, linked through portals and time warps but, as I said before, in the hands of three children and you, Miss Liana. You are one of the keys that hold all of this together, bringing the answers to light."

Liana knew there was some history to what Melanie had said—something about her past—but she was unsure. She was missing something of value, unable to place her finger on it. Quietly, she wondered what secrets lay in her path in finding her girls and Roger, and maybe she could find out who she was.

Melanie broke the silence to share more of her life. Liana listened. "There was a time, not too long ago, I lived in a country with my people who were strong and of great courage and boldness—a proud people of a long generation. We lived in peace with others until the coming of Bronze. He was cunning and deceitful and lusted after power and conquest. He came like a peaceful lamb but was an evil wolf in sheep's clothing. When my people found out how wicked Bronze was, he released his evil hordes upon us. Destroying our country and separating our people, killing innocent men and women and, at times, children when it benefits him, and placing many families in dungeons. He took me, including a few others, to be used for his dirty work to fortify his future kingdom."

THE VISION OF THE QUEST

Melanie looked at Liana, "That's when I discovered you, my lady, that he needed you to be a part of his future domain. I had mentioned this before. Bronze chose you because of your likeness to your great ancestor, Queen Leah. But I didn't tell you why Bronze desires the three keys to the kingdom." Melanie now had Liana's full attention. "Why?" she asked hastily.

Melanie answered, upset. "Because Bronze desires ultimate rulership over every walking, crawly, moving thing; man, woman, child, or beast, not giving a rat's rear end, who he hurts that steps into his path, sometimes, everything he touches turns into a pot of gold. The man irks me!"

Quantum expressed his concern. "Yes, we, too, desire peace. Bronze's beasts have come up against my Pathfinders numerous times. I almost lose count because of this. Many of my Pathfinders live in Congo's time zone due to another force at work not allowing us to transport back. We have families we must return home to and ensure they are safe."

"For my kind to pass from one dimension to another of faraway places, we share a diamond rock the size of a large fist, in the shape of an oval. With the touch of a Pathfinder, it absorbs one's energy and gets powerful enough that we may transport great distances. This rock is the source of energy on our planet."

"It takes seven of us to touch the rock with enough concentration to be transported. Our kingdom, like others, has many unopened portal doors. Some of these unopened doors lead through time warps, which can take you anywhere in the universe, into the past or future, where you can explore the very beginnings of civilizations. Other unopened doors lead you through portals of dimensions where you can venture from one kingdom and into another kingdom."

"Beam me up, Scotty." Liana joked. Quantum looked at her funny. Liana said in a friendly manner. "It was a joke like ha, ha. I know I believe in anything is possible but all this seems unbelievable." Quantum spoke up. "Talking about unbelievable. I have been to your time, and the people are ungrateful, whiners, and truth breakers. A visit was okay, but a place to live was not happening. Your people have disrespect and no integrity, and on top of the list, what got to me the most was selfishness for themselves. I say in your language, it was a piece of cake." Liana snickered. "I think you meant it was no piece of cake." Quantum was frank. "So be it...but what I do know is that your people will be eating each other in no time." Liana was taken back. "And why would you say that?" He replied that he was a black panther in his time warp. "Because majority of your people are obese."

"Where exactly did you meet these unthoughtful obese people?" Liana questioned. Melanie and the others hung onto the edge of their seats but in this case a rock floor, waiting for the answer. "Well, it was in a crowded city; every street corner had a small building lit up with lights on the outside reading, Bar. Why, do you ask?" Liana begins belly laughing. "Oh, later I will explain what goes on inside bars, but concerning obese, it's called beer pop bellies."

"Do you mean pop belly pigs?" Quantum asked.

Liana laughed even harder. "No, no, no beer pop bellies."

Quantum shook his blue head. "Well, I have traveled many places throughout the universe, but your earth is the most confusing." Liana finally managed to catch her breath. Melanie was pleased to see her joyful after what Bronze had placed her through. Liana slowly calmed down. "Please, continue. I should not have deterred you from your subject." Quantum continued. "No problem. Now, there is a gate where no eye has seen or foot had trodden in the spiritual realm of darkness with a portal the wicked enter as they breathe their last breath. It leads into a downward spin of no escape of fire, brimstone, and eternal damnation and swallows up only the departed souls that left their mortal bodies, finding torment and misery. I wish this place on no one, not even Bronze. I finally come to the conclusion we are only specks in this universe."

"Now, please understand, we originally came to Congo's territory because we sensed this evil force of Bronze desiring to take over our dimension. We came here to aid King James in overcoming this dark presence. We had sensed the prophecy unfolding and knew the only chance for our race's survival was joining forces to fight in this war. Still, sadly, again, there are many Pathfinders like myself unable to return to our dimension to check on our wives and children to know they are safe."

Liana felt compassion for his race, forgetting he could read her mind. She thought. *I wonder why Spock doesn't communicate to his wife through his mind to find out if all is well?*

Quantum answered Liana's private inquiry. He spoke up, embarrassing her somewhat. "We cannot communicate from two different time warps. We can only telepath others within the same dimension. By the way, because of enduring trials and tribulations one after the other, I have not properly introduced myself to you and Melanie."

"My name is Quantum. My dimension is not of Star Trek, but concerning my name, you may have the privilege of calling me Spock if it comforts you."

Melanie searched Liana's face saw she was displeased. She was thwarted by how the blue men sometimes cause distress.

Liana took in a deep breath. *Pull it together. Don't say anything you will regret later, but then again, I will not tolerate this kind of behavior. It's rude.*

Liana tried speaking in a pleasant voice, "Yes, it will comfort me, long as you will hold to the integrity of Spock. Stay out of people's heads only when necessary, and keep your nose elsewhere, and that's finding more beneficial things to do." She ended with those words, exhausted. She called it a night and about to lay down.

Quantum clapped his hands softly. He looked at Liana before her back was turned. "Spoken like a queen. But in all honesty, I sense wonderful leadership in you. I am not ashamed to have a woman stand up and put me in my place. I will take it as a learning tool."

Liana slightly smiled, too fatigued to say anything. She lay down on the cold, hard floor. Melanie lay near her, close to the fire and fell fast asleep within minutes.

The others are just as tired. They, too, crashed for the night.

Liana felt her body become stiff in the early hours of the morning. She turned from her right side onto her back. Her eyes shut. She sensed something wasn't right and opened them. Liana's instincts proved correct; hovering over her with a spear in his hand was a Snaken.

She was frightened as what she saw reminded her of when she was a prisoner of Bronze's. She witnessed unsightly things run through his garden, searching for something. She thought it was a nightmare, but now she learned it was reality. She stared face to face with this snake man hissing down her throat. Suddenly, Liana's mind was screaming. *These awful creatures were searching for my children on that dreadful day*! She witnessed terrible spiders arched in a forward position, ready to attack, and wolverines with nasty drool hitting the cave floor, impatient to rip their flesh off their bones. Three Snaken's stood at the entry of the cave for no escape. The Snaken staring face-to-face with Liana. His spear tail came crashing down, frightening her to her very core. He missed purposely knowing, she had to be brought to Bronze unharmed. With a frightful scream, she awakened the others from their deep sleep.

Cain and Abel swiftly jumped to their feet, but before knowing what hit them. Liana watched the hideous spiders shoot steel webs around her faithful comrades, spinning them into thin metal, cutting off their circulation. The Stingers immediately sprang into action, distracting the spiders from their two loyal commanders fighting forcefully to bring the ruthless spiders down. Liana, with courage, maneuvered and dodged the spear a second time. She found herself hard pressed against the cave wall with nowhere else to move.

Grumble Bee looked back. He saw Liana at the mercy of the Snaken, terror written across her face. He boldly bolted like a silver bullet behind the ruthless thing and jammed his large horn into the beast's slivering back. He pierced straight through his body. The Snaken hissed in agony, his body dropping to the ground like a rock falling off a mountain.

The other Stingers attacked forcefully upon the repugnant creatures. Drove their horns repeatedly into their flesh, bringing down as many as possible with five stings before each perished.

Liana stood up. She cried out for Grumble Bee to cut free Cain and Abel as the Stinger managed to save them from the steel web. He heard Liana scream frantically. "Watch out, Grumble Bee!" It was too late; a thrust of a Snaken's tail stabbed mercilessly into his back. Grumble Bee dropped to the ground. The dreadful beast ripped his deadly, poisonous tail out of the Stinger's back, causing him greater pain. Cain and Abel witnessed what happened. The mighty warriors worked together, using their massive strength to pounce upon the Snaken's ugliness. They angrily brought the beast down, beating him to a pulp. He looked like a smashed tomato when the two were through with him. Liana and Melanie ran and stood at the side of their friend, each shedding tears of sadness. Grumble Bee searched up into their faces, his sight becoming blurry. He spoke softly, for the pain was unbearable. "It's a warrior's death for the cause." He closed his eyes and breathed no more.

Cain, Abel, and other warriors attacked the spiders who attempted to spin them into a cocoon and watch them suffer. The strong Conchidas were on top of the spiders quicker than someone could count to one, smashing the nasty creatures like giants stepping on a pile of ants.

Liana's Protectors didn't see they had an audience. Wolf Fang hid in the shadows of rocks and weeds near the cave, watching and observing their every move. He glared beside him at Zoroc, pure white as the driven snow but just as evil, under Wolf Fang. Wolf Fang boasted. "Now that I have learned their weakness. I know how many I will be up against, their disadvantages, vulnerabilities, and strengths." Zoroc gleamed, satisfied. Wolf Fang bragged. "Sir Bronze shall be pleased with me. I shall have the sweet victory a dish served hot and handed to me." Wolf Fang searched Zoroc's black eyes and had his full attention. "The Pathfinders are too busy fighting for their cause. I have something up my dirty paw. Sir Bronze's has rubbed off on me. Quantum will be worried about his son soon enough and never think to search us out. On top of that, we shall bring Sir Bronze Liana. His prize possession and receive all the credit." Wolf Fang snarled. "Let's lay low; our patience will pan out. I have planned this out well." They continued to watch.

As the Pathfinders disappeared and were transported to different spots amid chaos, striking down Bronze's beasts, Liana ran to attend to a wounded Conchida. She cried out for Melanie to follow her. There was loud growling, with abrupt hissing. Liana was unaware that Melanie was not behind her.

Melanie was quickly snatched up by a Snaken taken through a tunnel. Orion, while fighting, heard Melanie's dreadful cries and could not find her. He touched his strands of jewels onto the side of the cave and sensed she was in grave danger. He transported to the area she had been dragged into inside a cavern. Orion, within seconds, appeared face-to-face with the Snaken, which had Melanie by the back roots of her hair. She faced Orion and was shaking uncontrollably.

Orion searched Melanie's face and sensed she hadn't been hurt besides her hair being pulled. But extremely frightened. The Snaken hissed loudly. He circled the Pathfinder, sliding his upright snake bottom across the cavern and dropped Melanie to the floor. He aimed. Threw his arrow-shaped tail toward Orion. Melanie managed to stand to her feet but frozen with panic. Orion swiftly pushed the shaken girl back down to the floor out of harm's way. He disappeared and reappeared on the opposite side of his enemy. The Snaken missed and smashed his sharp arrow into the rock wall. The arrow sliced downward into the hard rock, splitting a fine line across the floor. Melanie stood up again but this time managed to run to the other side of the small cavern near Orion.

The Snaken was furious. He taunted, "I just want some fun with the little lady. I will make sure after I tear her limb to limb that I will put her out of her misery, if she isn't already dead! Would you like her with or without skin? But the way I see it, Blue, three is a crowd and that includes you!" the smug thing slanted its head back in mockery.

He hissed wildly. "I guess you can say I am cocky like one of my leaders. His name Saige that your fat Stinger plunged with his big unpleasant horn." The Snaken eyed his prey up and down. "Both of you will pay dearly!" He purposely threw his arrow tail across the rock surface, creating an ear-splitting sound. He glared at petrified Melanie, again too frightened to move. Her feet felt nailed to the cave floor, with every bone in her body trembling. His threats were deathly. The scaling smooth-talking Snaken brought his focus back to bullying. He looked at the Pathfinder. His bottom half spun around the cold floor and mocked.

"Pathfinder, after I destroy you, tear you, limb from limb. It's a shame you won't be around to hear your little woman scream for her big, blue man. Oh yeah, your fat, Bee, that killed one of my leaders. Did me a favor. It places me up higher in rank second in command." Orion remained quiet, seeing it liked to talk. "By the way, my name is Bork. Too bad you and your little woman won't see me rise to greatness. Little Pathfinder, may I have the honor of your name before I strike you with my deadly poison?" Bork rattled his razor-sharp tail, making a loud, annoying sound. He swung it back and forth in front of him.

Orion did not flinch. He spits across the small cavern and into Bork's face. "My name is of no value to a dead Snaken. For after I am finished with the likes of your disgrace, your leadership can go to someone better than you, maybe your little sister! You don't need to threaten me with your baby rattle. It's a toy to me!" Orion bravely stood his ground and smirked angrily at the beast.

Bork was enraged and aimed for the young Pathfinder. Orion was disappearing and reappearing. Bork tried a few more times, but the same thing happened. He saw a pattern. Orion transported back and forth between two and three different spots. The place was tight, with only a few areas to protect Melanie from being hurt. Bork had a hunch where the blue boy would reappear next. His narrow squinty eyes beamed satisfied and took a foolish swing. He waited patiently. Within two seconds, his patience paid off. Orion appeared right where he thought he would. Bork was ready! He sliced the Pathfinder across his shoulder, leaving a deep cut into his flesh. Bork hissed vehemently, now circling him, taunting him with his victory.

"Leave him be! Let him go! It's me you want!" Melanie cried out for Orion's life to be spared. Her voice quivered with much fear as she sprinted back over to Orion.

"It's me you want! It's me you want!" Bork shouted with a sharp hiss and faced Melanie feeling he was invincible. "Oh, yes, it is you that I want. I desired you the first time I witnessed you in my master Bronze's dwelling!" he boasted. Orion moved fast, gripping one of his long sensors. He powerfully, flanged it directly into Bork's face, blinded him instantly. Awkwardly, the Snaken couldn't see or smell, only lasting for a few minutes. It crawled around blindly, screaming blasphemy, striking his tail repeatedly into the air, hoping to kill him.

Melanie was terror-stricken, holding tightly around Orion's neck. "Keep your arms around me!" he demanded. She cried in his ear. "Someone would have to peel me off of you!"

Orion's heartbeat fluttered pleased. He tried to transport them elsewhere and failed taking a great deal of concentration for something of this magnitude to succeed. Bork still striking blindly, endlessly into all directions. Orion ducked with Melanie still clinging to him. He enjoyed her warmth up against him. He whispered into her ear. "Like I said before I could get used to this." Melanie rolled her eyes. "This is not the time or place to be joking."

"Wow, I like a feisty woman, and who said I was joking?" He ducked again from Bork's dangerous rocket tail. Orion began to feel too weak to fight. The poison venom reached throughout part of his body. He started to panic. He tried again to transport but failed. Orion worried, not for himself but for what the beast may do to Melanie. He concentrated harder, strained with all his might, and after the longest minute, they were finally transported back into their team's presence. The transport was overwhelming for Melanie. She passed out in Orion's arms.

Orion looked weakly around the cave and saw the fight was over. He observed a number of Pathfinders standing with everything in disarray but regretfully spotted a few Conchidas and Stingers on the cave floor, dying. Orion was relived, seeing Liana was not harmed. He watched Bronze's hordes scattered with their tails between their legs, retreating, as the dying Conchidas and Stingers bravely tried not to flinch. It caused additional pain to run throughout their bodies. Cain and Abel grievously realized in a short while their faithful comrades would be dead. Orion took note of their sadness. He laid Melanie gently onto the cave floor. He bent over her, striving not to fall over, for the poison had spread more rapidly throughout him. She awakened and found Orion's eyes looking deeply into hers.

Melanie asked, "Did we make it?" Orion was weak and faintly said. "I told you that one day I would be saving your butt."

Melanie reached up to touch his wound but found none. "Didn't you get hurt?" she asked, concerned. "You do not look well. I am confused. I witnessed Bork strike your shoulder."

"Yes, but we are different from others in many ways," Orion barely whispered. He began to feel the room spinning.

Melanie was baffled by how he was struck with no evidence of a wound or bleeding. She stared into his deathly ill face, worried for him. She asked nervously. "But what do I do? I need to know how to help you." Orion feebly smiled. "Is it because you care for me after all?" his voice cracked softly. Melanie was about to answer when Orion collapsed. She caught him to break his fall and screamed. Liana and a few others came running to his side.

Quantum, outside searching for further danger, suddenly sensed his son needed his help. Wolf Fang's plans had gone into effect. Quantum had drawn away from finding the additional wolverines lurking nearby and transported himself quickly back into the cave and found Orion. Telepathically he called for one of his Pathfinders. He appeared swiftly. Quantum spoke, "Triade, we need your gift of medicine."

Triade, without hesitating, placed drops of a herb that heals Pathfinders from one of his sensors into his mouth it slowly dripped down the back of his throat.

Quantum saw worry and sadness on Melanie's face. "I hope I comfort you in some way. I cannot promise you, but I sense he will be fine."

"He saved my life," Melanie cried. "I am unsure of what is going on. I witnessed Bork slicing Orion's shoulder severely, now the wound is gone, but he lays on the cave floor, almost dead." She sobbed, pouring out her heart. "I am sorry for how I treated him last night." Liana, now beside her, placed her arms around Melanie. She calmed down.

Quantum spoke up. "Pathfinders heal fast on the outside, but internally, he is bleeding, with the poison raging throughout his body. A few of our Pathfinders are gifted with certain healing powers that work only on our Pathfinders to bring healing if we get to them quickly enough."

Quantum rested his sensors on Orion's body. He spoke, relieved. "I am beginning to sense life and wholeness return to him." He happily looked at Melanie, "Don't worry, my son will be fine."

"Your son?" Melanie asked, surprised.

Quantum smiled. "Of course. Can't you see he has my good looks?" he tilts his face upward-moving it left to right. Liana was able to see that the leader of the Pathfinders had a sense of humor.

Orion returned from unconsciousness. He slowly returned to himself and stood up, "Now, father we both know I get my good looks from my mother."

Cain and Abel were nearby, helping the wounded. Orion snickered, hearing Cain whisper to Abel, "Can you imagine what his mother's face looks like? I will hate to see that sight." The ape shook his head, imaging it. Orion communicated to Cain's mind. "With an ugly ape face like yours, my mother's face would be considered an improvement." Cain looked up at Orion nonchalantly as he saw Liana leaving Melanie's side, running over to help the Protectors. She begins cleaning out the wounds of the Conchidas and Stingers that still had breath in them and closing the eyes of the Conchidas and Stingers who heroically died defending the cause.

Melanie, about to help Liana, appreciated that Orion saved her life. She wrapped her arms around him and cried with teary eyes. "You risked your life to save me. How can I ever reward you for such bravery?"

Orion gift- wrapped his arms around her. He again enjoyed her warmth and charm. "I think I am getting more used to this. I must save you more often." Melanie shook free and scolded him, "Are you ever serious?" she asked, with a gleam in her pretty round eyes and thick eyelashes. Orion replied truthfully. "I don't know what to say. I am overjoyed we both made it out alive in one piece." Orion wrapped his arms back around her waist. Melanie did not resist him but again scolded. "But don't expect me to kiss you or anything. That's where I draw the line."

"Oh, my little chatterbox." Melanie again opened her mouth to complain. Orion cut her off as he touched her soft cheek. "I mean, I did

THE VISION OF THE QUEST

save your life and...," his words ended abruptly. He heard Liana crying out for more help. Orion reluctantly removed his hand, and both ran to help. An hour slipped by as they buried their dead, covering them in rocks. Being aware, they must hurry and get out of the illusion of mirrors to find the Quest before another attack occurs.

Abel asked hastily, "Liana, where is the necklace tugging your spirit to go?"

Before boarding Abel, Liana looked up with a broken heart, grief in her eyes, with all their losses. Sadly, she pointed north straight ahead. Melanie gently wrapped her arms around Liana's neck. The young girl found comfort in her strong spirit.

Liana threw her motherly arms around her, giving her a sense of security. She gently stroked Melanie's hair as she would her child while she mourned those who gave their lives that others might live.

Liana whispered in Melanie's ear, "They laid down their lives for a friend, something Jesus did for us." Melanie wasn't sure who this Jesus was, but she enjoyed it when Liana spoke of him. She found comfort in that name.

Abel exclaimed. "North it is! We need to move quickly and find a way out of here, away from the evil hordes desiring Liana and her necklace. It's only time before Bronze's nasty creatures return." Abel looked toward his comrades. "There seems to be dangers lurking around every turn. Don't let Liana out of your sight. Keep Melanie in your reach as well. Bronze would go to any lengths to kill her for helping Liana escape."

"Not in a million years. He will deal with my wrath first!" Liana exclaimed.

"Wow, woman, I would hate to get on your bad side." Cain smiled.

Wolf Fang also gleamed as he moved far enough away that the Pathfinders sensors would not pick up on them. He spoke to Zoroc. "They took many of Bronze's beasts down. Go gather up at least fifty wolverines. We will attack when they least expect us. We will have the advantage three of their Pathfinders are seriously wounded and a few Conchidas and Stingers killed. Now, go!"

Cain and Abel too were on the go and departed with the others. They traveled north, lost track of time, and found themselves at a great fire wall inside the large dome. Spread out like a blanket circling the mirrors that reached high over their heads, unable to fly out. They felt trapped inside.

Cain sent Abram, a Pathfinder, out to transport into many locations within the illusion to check out the surroundings. Abel sent out a Stinger which flew horizontally and vertically, scooping within the dome. Abram finally returned and reported. "There's an opening on the other side of this land toward the south, about an hour from here and there may be more."

The Stinger returned. He remarked. "I saw an opening west from here but further away, but as for the fire, it goes on endlessly inside around the dome."

Cain looked at Abel. "South sounds like the best option. That's the route we should go." Liana hearing them, found and gripped a small rock into her hand. She threw it aimlessly through the burning flames. She watched it disintegrate right before her eyes. Her necklace tugged around her neck, prompting her to venture through the fire. She was on pins and needles, shaking from head to toe.

Suddenly, the Pathfinders sensors shook wildly. Immediately, behind them, the Conchidas, with dynamic hearing, had heard a snarling pack of wolverines. The Stingers, eyes superb, seen them from far off. They wondered where they came from; to make matters worse, it was over fifty of them. "I see Wolf Fang and Zoroc!" a Stinger shouted.

Abel yelled out, "Wolf Fang had outsmarted us. This has been planned!"

Cain called back, "We have no choice but to turn and fight them in order to make it to that opening Abram spoke of." Cain inside sensed defeat along with the Pathfinders.

Abel retaliated. "There are too many wolverines. It will be sure death for us all. We will not make it."

Cain replied. "Then have Abram and another one of our fastest soldiers fly Liana and Melanie to that opening at less they can escape. Keep them safe as we fight off many hordes as we possibly can."

THE VISION OF THE QUEST

Abel disagreed. "They won't make it to the opening, the wolverines will by-pass us and sniff them out." Cain protested. They disputed back and forth. Liana's necklace pulled harder. She took a deep breath. There was no other choice. She prepared her heart to take a step of faith and experienced the saying of shaking in your boots. Closing her eyes, she prayed. "Though I walk through the valley of death, I will fear no evil," with her body trembling. She leaped through the wall of fire and landed on the other side, falling onto her knees. She cried out. "My God, you saved me!"

Liana heard Melanie yelling. "Go through the flames! I heard Miss Liana praying on the other side." Liana watched Melanie and her Protectors venturing through the scorching flames, reminded her of Shadrach, Meshach, and Abednego in the fiery furnace where only their ropes burned off, and a fourth man appeared among them.

Cain blared happily. "Oh, Jiminy Cricket! I think my annoying nose hairs have finally been zapped."

Abel complained. "About time, as much as I've watched your finger up that hairy snout of yours searching for gold. I am surprised you're not rich."

Liana, with the others, were, pleased they made it out of there alive. She did a quick headcount and became alarmed. "Three Pathfinders are missing!"

Quantum spoke up. "Three of my Pathfinders agreed to stay behind to destroy as many hordes as possible, giving us the time to find the Quest. We will honor them. They have committed a courageous act."

"Why?" Liana shouted, upset, thinking of him not being worthy of Spock.

"Please understand, my three Pathfinders would have dropped like flies. Their wounds were serious, deep on the inside since we left the second cave. Unfortunately, our herb was of no effect on their injuries. We must remember, it's upsetting but true, that sometimes the cost of fighting for freedom is great."

Liana felt she was wrong, that maybe Quantum, after all, did deserve the honor of Spock's name. She said, disappointed. "I am dismayed with many losses in one day. I will continue to remain strong for my children and Abethar. Your men will not die in vain but for a noble cause."

"Yes, for the cause. I am relieved nothing happened to you, Miss Liana, but let's not make it a practice ever to come this way again." They all agreed. Straightway, the Pathfinder's sensors went off all at once. "Our enemy is only a couple of feet away." Quantum warned everyone.

Wolf Fang and his hordes stood outside the wall of flames in the exact spot where Liana and her team had stood minutes before. Wolf Fang couldn't comprehend how Liana and her warriors escaped the incinerating flames. He bared his teeth and foolishly sent four of his wolverines leaping through the wall of fire all four fell dead at Liana's feet.

Liana was startled. Melanie gagged at the stink of it.

"We must be on the move, and follow the leading of Liana's necklace to continue north!" Abel shouted.

Wolf Fang smelled burned flesh. He hollered as four of his wolverines was tossed back to him and landed near his paws. "This is the work of those purple apes!"

Quantum's three wounded Pathfinders were further, off fighting and killing off Wolf Fang's beasts. They disappeared and reappeared out of nowhere in front of Wolf Fang, catching him and his remaining gruesome things off guard and fighting hard, bringing down a number of them but growing weary. Death was upon them. They still put up a fight. "For the cause!" each shouted. Two Pathfinders died struck down cold. Wolf Fang became satisfied as he slew the last one, digging the might of his claws deeply into his chest. The Pathfinder went limp and dropped to the earth. Wolf Fang gnashed his teeth, making a high-pitched growling sound. He exploded. "Liana got away! I shall have that woman's life soon. Forget Sir Bronze! Her blood will be spilled!"

"I will have her bones in my jaws, snapping her delicate body in half, like a twig off a tree, devouring her flesh, leaving nothing behind." He shook a large amount of drool from his crooked teeth.

Zoroc came up from behind and quickly reminded him, "Master Bronze said to spare the woman's life or your life for hers. Did you forget that easily? What does Sir Bronze see in you? I can honestly say, Sir Bronze and you are two peas in a pod, both backstabbers."

"Master Bronze is not here, is he? I am first in command! I will take care of this annoying headache!" Wolf Fang exposed his jagged teeth as he glared hatefully toward Zoroc. He felt threatened that Zoroc may attempt to lord over him and take charge. His wolverines circled their two leaders and remained quiet. Wolf Fang growled. "Know your place Zoroc. I can destroy you at any time. And, you traitor, breathe a word to Sir Bronze. Mark my words, you shall die right along with Liana!"

Wolf Fang stared at the other wolverines. He threatened. "Same for all of you. If you know what is best for you! Let's find another way out of here. The necklace must have allowed them through the barrier. Now, they have a good lead!" Wolf Fang took to the air. Zoroc followed him below and leaped faster than an arrow, boiling mad. Zoroc thought of nothing but desiring Wolf Fang dead; his carcass left for the vultures to feast on. He dreamed of a time he would make this happen. The remaining wicked hordes followed the lead of their two terrifying leaders.

Chapter Ten

Hope in Dire Times

Cain and the others were happy to finally be out of the mirrors but felt a sad heaviness for the ones who had been lost. They picked up their pace, putting a good distance between themselves and Bronze's cohorts. Liana and Melanie flew on the backs of Cain and Abel for half of the day. The Pathfinders were teleporting from one location to another to keep up. Liana's Protectors decided to land and walk to find berries and odd things to eat, enough to give them strength to go on.

"May we sit for a few minutes?" Melanie asked. "My feet are killing me. The soles of my shoes are worn out. I feel like I'm walking barefoot."

"It won't be your feet killing you," Cain reminded her, "but Wolf Fang, if we do not proceed. We do not have enough soldiers to keep you and Liana safe. Our only hope is putting distance between them and us until we find the Quest."

Abel heard a rustle inside bushes behind them. "I think we are being watched," he whispered.

In hushed tones, Cain answered, "I believe you are right. Well, Melanie, you get your request. Hop on my back, take a load off those tired feet, and we take to the skies once more. Liana, you on Abel's back, and hurry."

The Conchida's and Stinger's wings fluttered and prepared for departure. They were interrupted. Chip burst forth, leaping out of a bush, screaming, "Wait! Wait! Please don't leave without me! I have already been left once! Please!"

Abel turned around and looked down. "Who is this little one whose voice we can barely hear, yet he asks us not to depart?"

He blurted out all in one breath. "My name is Chip. I was sent on a quest by Princess Lilly to protect three special ones." Liana gripped her hand over her heart, possibly being her children. "We were on our way to the Second Kingdom but were attacked by a deadly dragon. We have slain it in battle, dropping it to the bottom of the sea. I came to the water's surface to reach the land but passed out on a rock under the cliff where they couldn't see me, so my comrades had departed without me, likely thinking I was dead, but here I am, alive as can be."

Liana's hand was still over her heart. "Who are the three children you are referring to?" Liana asked, enlivened as she looked at the chipmunk's adorable smile, which took up half his face. It reminded her of Charlie's fish in the tuna commercials.

Chip wondered who the pretty lady was and answered, "Their names are Alicia, Roger, and Emily. They're under the protection of the king's guards, but I must ask you: who are you? What is your interest in them?"

Liana wiped joyful tears from her eyes, learning her girls and Roger were safe still under the king's guards. "I am their mother. I have been worried sick about them. I long for the day I can again hold them in my arms." She began to bombard him with many questions. "Chip, this Second Kingdom you mentioned. Do you know the location? Do you know how to get there? All we know is to head north."

"Oh, how do I. Graven had bored me more than once with how to get there. I have been all ears." Liana was startled as Chip's little body transformed into a giant ear, returning to himself. The Protectors laughed. The Pathfinders sensors jingled in harmony. Melanie then giggled. She caught herself glancing at Orion. She quickly turned her head as Orion noticed her. He had a smile just as big as Chips. She was pleased.

"Will you join us?" Liana asked, now laughing.

Chip beamed. "With pleasure. I will like to be a help. It gets lonely out here by myself. But I hate to be the one to break up all the laughter. Let's go! Without delay to find the Quest."

They all agreed and left in a hurry. The Protectors with Liana and Melanie traveled a good measure of time without knowing the Quest was still actively locating the Second Kingdom. As Graven tumbled into a new dimension, flying full force toward the sun. He warned. "Quest, keep your eyes shut so as not to lose sight, not opening them for any reason. This is an order!" In a short time. Graven no longer felt the pressure of the sun's light beaming down on him and felt cool breezes blow over him. He opened his eyes and shared. "We are out of danger for the most part." The others opened their eyes, still flying. The girls and Roger were falling over in what they beheld below.

THE VISION OF THE QUEST

"Wow, where are we?" Alicia cried out with strong emotions. Roger exclaimed. "All I can think to say is good googa mooga! How are we surrounded by water when we headed toward the sun only seconds ago? This place is not of this world or dimension?"

The Quest landed and stood directly over the top of a sky-scraping waterfall in extraordinary knee-deep water, making them feel vibrant and strong. Roger talked loud over the loud falls. "This is mind-boggling 3-D images coming right at us. Look, everything seems to be in front of our faces yet far away." Alicia bellowed out. "I agree. It's cool. Look at the thousands of drops of water coming right at us in slow motion, then dropping back down. I have never seen anything like this before."

Graven, and White lightning, both at the same time, asked. "Don't you have waterfalls where you come from?"

Emily had remained quiet long enough. "Not like this!" She yelled, bopping her head up and down, flabbergasted. She stretched out her arm to hundreds of doves, and butterflies seemed inches away from her nose. She tried touching one and withdrew her hand, disappointed. She blurted out. "Everything is 3-D, just like Shrek."

"Yeah, this is better than my Oculus VR headset." Roger was ecstatic.

Graven peculiarly glanced at Roger and Emily. "Shrek and Oculus or whatever you speak of?"

"It's a gear I wear on my head and play for fun. I will explain more about it later!" Roger shouted over all the noise.

The kids listened as the rapid falls became louder, carrying a beautiful melody, yet piercing to the ears. Graven scoped out the area for any dangers that might be in their midst. His voice heightened. "It's too loud! We need to find our way below and enter behind these vast falls! I believe it's a shortcut, and our only option at this point is to reach the door to the Second Kingdom!"

"What! That's crazy!" Alicia shouted. "They are too powerful and will overtake all of us! It's bad enough now. If it gets any louder, we might lose our hearing!"

"We have no other choice unless ..." Graven's words ended. The waters rose and circled them, becoming a tall, towering wall, standing elevated, stationary, and unmovable. Emily complained on her cheetah's back, "Spot, the water is getting us soaked. Calm down, water!" she protested.

The Quest heard a strong voice that showed no form. "Who is this with such a little voice to speak that way to someone as powerful as I?" The voice boomed.

"Show yourself!" Graven valorously demanded, instantly, the water took the shape of people circling about them.

Alicia complained. "What is it with all this? First the Icemen, now, these whatever they are."

Emily, terrified, buried her face in Spot. "I want out of here!"

The queen of the waters showed compassion and whispered to calm Emily's fears. "Now, there is no need to be afraid. The king is a big teddy bear." She shot him a sharp look for frightening a child. The queen no longer particles of water had suddenly shapeshifted into a lovely mermaid. "Is that better sugar?" she sweetly asked. Emily slowly brought her buried face up off of Spot. "Are you a shapeshifter?" she asked surprised. Alicia and Roger also wondered. The queen smiled. "Yes, we have extraordinary powers." King Hydro fast interrupted. He spoke firmly.

"I am King Hydro of the Oceans and Seas, leader of the Neroean people. Who is your leader?" he boldly asked the Quest.

"I am!" Graven spoke unafraid, his griffin body, on all four talons, tall and strong, appearing physically robust. "We need to enter the door to the Second Kingdom. We mean no harm and will be on our way."

Alicia gave King Hydro no time for another question. She shouted, "King Hydro, can you assist us? You are mightily powerful and can hold back your waters for us to enter under the falls!"

King Hydro's face took on the appearance of delight. "Are you the ancestor of Queen Leah? I notice the necklace around your neck." He then brought his gaze to Roger and Emily. "Are you the few mentioned years ago who would eventually come and give aid to King James of Abethar?"

THE VISION OF THE QUEST

Alicia reached down and gripped her necklace. "Yes, we are the chosen ones."

King Hydro abruptly moved powerfully and circled his waters about them with the wave of his trident. His long beard hidden by the pressure of the cyclone. The Quest began to tumble and spin in circles.

Emily beamed, no longer frightened. "This is better than a carnival ride!"

Alicia starts feeling dizzy. "No, Emily, more like inside mother's washing machine."

Roger blared. "No, more like inside a tornado, only we are not drowning." Roger combed his fingers through his hair, removing unwanted dirt. "The way I look at it, I wanted a clean shower. I guess this will have to do." Graven thought, *a carnival ride, a washer machine? I'm not even going to ask.*

It wasn't long—before the Quest was dropped safely behind the falls. They shook off dizziness and regained their footing.

Alicia complained, "I have a headache. I'm drenched. Whatever happened to the rinse cycle?" she twisted the water from her hair. The queen pointed north. "Go that way. The portal is close by."

King Hydro spoke in the voice of many great falls, a voice that echo's from here to eternity. He looked at Alicia. "Be careful, for danger lies ahead," he handed her a clear, round glass globe filled with the purest water. "Before you depart, know this, our kingdom is of the oceans and the seas, and when you, young lady, look into this glass, it will show you the strength of our kingdom. The Neroean people—only because of the power your necklace holds…when you are in trouble in desperate need of our help, then, and only then, will you remember us. Call upon us by calling into the globe. We will hear your voice and will come to your aid. Now, depart quickly, for many dangers lie ahead."

Alicia carefully placed the round globe into her leather pouch inside her bookbag, and although the globe was full of water, it was as light as a toothpick. She swung her bag over her shoulder. She graciously bowed her head and brought her head back up. The Neroeans people blended in with the massive falls and were gone.

Chapter Eleven

Are You Worthy?

THE VISION OF THE QUEST

The Quest had found a portal in the direction the hydro queen had pointed, but as the Quest ventured inside, they soon found out it was not the door to the second kingdom, though it was leading them in the right direction.

Long, hot, weary days, they traveled, finally reaching what they had searched diligently for and were satisfied with anticipation as they stood before a beat-up rugged door at the entrance of the Second Kingdom. Guarding the door was a fierce centaur, a guardian of the gate.

"Are you worthy?" the centaur asked boldly, without moving one muscle in his enormous body.

Graven, not intimated, replied firmly, "We have the two keys for the door!" Graven realized the third key was needed when they reached the third kingdom, but he put the thought aside.

The centaur asked again, not paying any mind to Graven's words. "Are you worthy?"

Graven became impatient. "We did not come all this way and fight off enemies of our king for nothing. We are here this day through prayer, not to be asked whether we are worthy. I say step aside and let us pass!"

The centaur's upper body of a man and lower body of a horse carried a massive sword with an armor of thick iron. His every inch of muscle filled this heavy piece of armor. He spoke fearlessly to Graven. "I cannot and will not stand aside! I am the Protector of the entrance to this kingdom. Now, choose who is worthy amongst you to meet me in battle. If you defeat me, you shall be deemed worthy and shall enter with your keys. If you are defeated, you must leave in disgrace. But I know on this day that you shall face your fate and death of shame as I erase you from this place."

Graven pressed his chest forward and fiercely answered, "I accept your challenge!" The mighty knight of King James stepped forward with confidence in Christ. Being his shield and his guiding light with knowing that he displayed no fear.

The centaur's heart was proud. He spoke strongly. "I have been victorious against all who had raised a standard against me to force their way into the Second Kingdom without being worthy to enter."

He glared in arrogance at Graven's powerhouse body of a lion and the face of a mighty eagle. He demanded rudely of the great griffin, "Tell your comrades to step back. This is our battleground, where we stand!" The Quest heard the centaur's sharp command. Graven nodded his head toward his faithful comrades. All stood back in respect of their valiant leader.

The powerful knight, knowing time was essential for the needs of King James, came face-to-face with the strong beast. Graven, within a flash and precise aim, dug his razor-sharp claws into the centaur's chest without mercy, ripping the beast's iron armor off him. Graven flung it to the ground like a sheet of paper, leaving the centaur's chest wide open for attack. But not without Graven paying the price of a slice across his back by the powerful creature.

The big one-eyed beast, with ease, gripped Graven's thick neck and aimed his sword toward his heart to finish him off with one decisive blow. Alicia, Roger, and Emily cried out in his defense.

Graven's sharp eyes saw the shiny sword coming, like an arrow that hits its bullseye. His beam blasted the heavy weapon out of the centaur's hand. Swiftly, Graven was caught off guard as the guardian of the gate maneuvered behind him. He managed to grip tightly around the griffin's throat strangling him.

The knight could not break loose. He took to the air soaring at a terrible speed heading toward the sun with the vile thing hanging from his neck. Graven, exhausted and bleeding from his wounds, moved with greater full force, compelled further toward the sun. He heard the screams of the centaur. The damage was done. The sun blinded his opponent's eye. Immediately, Graven shook it off, like shaking dirt from his fur. He turned and, with his eyes, blasted him like dynamite. The centaur, barely alive, felt the cold, crisp air blowing hard against his flesh. His warm blood splashed into his face, a wound caused by Graven's light beam. The centaur spins rapidly through the air. Before long, gravity threw him hard to the ground. He reached his final destiny inside a cold grave.

In an instant, the illusion in front of the rugged door vanished that stood before the Quest. The hidden entrance to the second kingdom

THE VISION OF THE QUEST

appeared out of nowhere, a remarkable gold door shining with bright letters formed into the shape of Alicia and Emily's necklaces, spelling out the word WORTHY!

Alicia and Emily ran up and threw their arms around Graven. Emily cried out, "I saw that thing hurt your back? Are you okay?"

He winced due to the soreness. "I am a big boy, but if someone is so kind, rub my lower back. I might live."

Emily waved her arms up and down. "I will! I will!" Graven arched his back. "Well, I guess you're the one for the job." He looked toward the Quest. "By the way, I think I pulled a muscle in my upper back, too."

Roger said, "Don't get any ideas about me doing your back because it's not happening." He kicked dirt up with his shoe and joked. "Not bad fighting that Centaur, but I could have done better."

Graven firmly looked past him. "Great! This is your chance. His better half is right behind you."

Roger quickly turned around and found out he had been tricked. He rejoiced with everyone else in high spirits in Graven's victory.

"Well, I hate to be the Grinch that stole Christmas," Granite smiled at Emily, who shared the story, "but we have a mission to complete." He looked at Graven. "I am pleased you took care of the likes of that arrogant centaur." Granite came up behind the girls and, without warning, lifted Alicia and Emily like feathers into the air. Emily squealed with delight. Alicia placed her necklace into the carvings and helped Emily with hers.

Illuminating light burst forth in splendid colors, outlining the clear, blue sky with the word "Worthy." Instantly, the gold door opened slowly, revealing a quiet village and green fields with farms in the background. A colorful horizon outlines the sky.

The Quest was weary, and they delayed before entering, wondering what this adventure into the Second Kingdom would be like. What they might have to come up against.

Graven's voice interrupted their thoughts: "It's time to enter. We are pressed to find what we require for the king!"

They prepared to go inside until Emily shouted, "Wait, we need to get the necklaces!"

ARE YOU WORTHY?

Granite lifted Emily back up onto his rock shoulders. She attempted to receive it, but the jewelry would not budge. Emily giggled as Granite threw her up high into the air and caught her before setting her back on the ground.

"Again, again!" Emily squealed.

"We will play later, little squirt, but first, we have a mission to complete." Granite watched her run over to Spot, as he heard Alicia asked, Graven concerned. "That's odd. The keys didn't budge. Do you think it will be safe to leave them?"

"Yes, in this kingdom, I guess we must wait until we leave here because the three of you"—he looked at Alicia, Roger, and Emily—"are the children of prophecy. With that said, only the three of you will be able to contain these keys, besides your mother. If anyone tries to remove them, the power of the keys may kill the unfortunate one."

Acorn and Spot led the way, and, upon entering the land, everyone saw the village was torn up with a nasty smell that lingered in the air. But worse, something felt bizarre; though the horizon was beautiful, there was a feeling of heaviness, a darkness that could not be seen but sensed, deep oppression that lingered all around them. Oddly, this darkness could not overtake the Quest amid this shadowy bleakness. Wherever the warriors walked, they saw men and women's faces looked drawn out and bags under their eyes—as though they hadn't slept in weeks or months, and queerly, there was no laughter of children playing, no crying or complaining—no children whatsoever in the camp.

The Quest noticed how the villagers stared at Emily. Spot was on guard to protect his little friend. He spoke quickly. "Roger put Emily onto my back for precaution."

"Hey, I want to walk," Emily protested.

Alicia immediately corrected her. "First, we have to make sure you are safe. This village might not like children. Now, you must listen."

Emily searched the people's faces. She studied their expressions and became nervous. She agreed with Alicia. Without fighting, she allowed Roger to lift her onto Spot.

Unexpectedly, a handsome man with ruffled dirty blonde hair approached. His deep monastic eyes showed kindness. He looked no older than thirty-five. The man introduced himself. "I am King Triune, the leader of my village, and beside me is Croc, a commander, who stands at my side. What do we owe this visit today? Who are you? And where do you come from?" He asked boldly, standing tall and solid as an oak tree.

Graven spoke promptly, "We have come from a far-off land under the protection of our king of Abethar to locate gifts he requires."

"You will find no gifts here but only misery. A terrible curse has been placed upon us." King Triune spoke bluntly.

Graven was quiet, for Alicia had spoken up. "Where are all the children? I notice there are none here at all. How your people look at my little sister makes me feel uncomfortable."

Emily perked up, clinging onto Spot's neck. "Yeah, I wouldn't mind having someone to talk to that's my age. I get bored easily. I've already counted the dots on Spot's back. He has at least one hundred and three, but I may have missed some…."

Graven watched Roger tap Emily softly on her shoulder. "Okay, short fry, come up for air."

"But Roger I…" she became quiet as King Triune spoke words that tormented his heart. "Sadly, all of our children have been taken from us, taken captive by Malock, an evil beast who rules with a terrible strict hand over his tribe called the Enox's, part-men-and-part- beast, are extremely strong and terrifying. Malock and his tribe's lower bodies are in the form of a man with legs like myself but bulkier. Their upper back is ached and hairy. With dull grey faces of men mixed with the form of fierce-looking wolves." Emily now, fearfully, wrapped her arms tightly around Spot.

King Triune looked into the eyes of each Quest. He continued to speak. "Now, we are of the Arcaining tribe, but during the night, we are not a pleasant sight to behold due to the curse that's been placed upon us. We transform into hideous creatures of the night with the thirst for blood, werewolves with deformed hunchbacks, covered in

ARE YOU WORTHY?

thick hair and awful sharp claws. We are dreadfully dangerous to be near. We destroy everything that we build during the day."

"Sadly, sometimes we destroy each other. We lose our minds, unable even to think. We lose all sense of direction and destiny, unlike Malock and his tribe, who can think and communicate with one another. It's hard for us to concentrate, being more beast than man." King Triune had the Quest's attention. "Unfortunately, because of this, none of you can be here at nightfall, then you will not be considered an ally. We will destroy you and think nothing of it. Though during the day, like now, we have our minds and understanding and are in good spirits. But by your face, I know what you are thinking. Why have we not tried to save our children? The answer is we have tried and lost many men and women fighting against Malock. His tribe is determined as a bull and as powerful as an ox. They can leap high as if they have wings, making it harder for us to win any battle against them. The second time we attempted to save our young ones, we again failed, but this time in retaliation, the evil Enox's slew many of our children and paraded their corpses around our village, bringing much grief to my people. Therefore, we do not attack them anymore. It has been two years, and yes, we are in peril. We no longer know what to do other than survive and care for our women."

The Quest sensed discouragement in King Triune's voice. He had spoken from a despairing heart. Spot, Acorn, and White Lightening remained silent. Granite scratched his rock head. Alicia and Roger also remained quiet, not knowing what to say. Graven spoke to give King Triune hope.

"There was once a wonderful queen that shared with me the things of God. She used to tell me to have faith because all things are possible, and circumstances can change with the help of friends. King Triune, ally yourselves with us, and we will devise a plan to deliver your children. You will be free, have joy back in your lives, and know what it is to love again. Do you believe in this?" Graven asked boldly.

King Triune spoke openly but quietly that his people could not hear. "It sounds like a prayer answered, but there is beyond despair here. My people have been overthrown numerous times. Their hearts

THE VISION OF THE QUEST

had been ripped out of them losing their children. I fear if we fail, my people shall cease to live but do speak on, for you have aroused my curiosity."

Graven asked. "Is there a place we can go to converse alone, not amongst your people? With the looks upon their faces, they are alarmed enough."

King Triune answered. "Yes, all of you are welcome to come inside my tent and speak of this great hope. Please follow me." As he led the Quest toward his tent, the village women admired Emily, desiring terribly to have their children back. Emily felt her leg cramp. She jumped off Spot and walked snuggled up against him. She kicked her feet nervously on the dirt road, feeling awkward with all the eyes staring at her.

Roger kidded with Alicia as they walked. "Well, this is the first time I've seen the half-pint withdrawn and bashful. I think I am enjoying this."

Alicia elbowed him softly and whispered, "This is ..." she was interrupted.

Roger brushed his hair behind his ears. "I know, I know this is not the time or place to be joking. You sound like Miss. Liana." He thought that the things Alicia used to do irritated him to the core but now appealed to him. His heart fluttered.

The Quest entered King Triune's large leather tent. King Triune spoke. "Please sit down and make yourself comfortable." Granite spurted out. "Thank goodness. My body aches all over." Emily giggled. "There's always something wrong with you. I agree. When Chip was here, he said the same thing about you. I miss Chip." Granite lightly touched Emily's cheek. "I do too." He plopped into a wooden chair matching a dark mahogany table and crashed loudly to the floor. The chair was scattered in all directions. Emily shook her head at him. King Triune overlooked Granite and observed the Quest looked worn-out. He had directed his servants to bring food and hot apple cider five minutes earlier. King Triune spoke wisely.

ARE YOU WORTHY?

"I sense you are weak from your long journey and need strength. Please partake of what I have offered and eat until you are full. We shall talk afterward."

The Quest looked at the food on top of a long wooden table and was grateful and ate heartily, feeling strength returning to their bodies. They remained at the table and devised plans to deliver the children out of the hands of the Enoxs.

Croc became restless and wiped the sweat from his long face at forty-nine. His skin, due to stress, looked like a worn-out leather wallet. Listening to what the Quest had to say about coming up against his King's enemies. He could no longer remain quiet. He was irritated. His inch of brown hair mixed with a hint of grey displaying his large blunt forehead. He yelled out livid, "What makes you think your small group can save the children!" The man, upset, got up from the table and left the tent.

King Triune motioned in a subdued manner. "Please, I apologize for my commander. I informed you earlier of the wickedness of Malock, how the beast had paraded ten of our children through our village, dead, hanging from ropes inside a large cage. Sadly, Croc's only two children were among the ten. I, too, still hear the father's sorrowful wails and terrible groans of lamentation—something I will never forget. Malock struck deeply into the heart of Croc on that dreadful day. However, now I feel stirred up within. I feel good in my spirit concerning the Quest, eliminating our enemy, though I don't see how. However, I understand how Croc feels... being against many, but something inside me is giving me peace that I sense it can be done. Your Quest has given me a small hope which brings a flicker of light into my soul. Now, my friends, night comes fast, and the sun is slipping away from us. Please understand that the sun setting is relaxation for others, enjoying one another's company, but for us, it's a curse of death. We will talk tomorrow morning."

He and a company of his soldiers led the Quest to a fortified tower to be hidden and tucked away securely for the night. King Triune spoke with sincerity. "Not one of you must leave this tower for whatever reason, or your life will be in grave danger."

THE VISION OF THE QUEST

"What you say shall be honored," Graven replied. King Triune turned toward his men. "Lock all entrances on the outside until the rising of tomorrow's sun, hurry, do not delay. Darkness is almost upon us." The soldiers bolted the large doors. King Triune moved hastily. He slipped the key under the door, giving it to Graven to hold onto for safekeeping until he returned at first dawn in the morning.

Chapter Twelve

DELIVERANCE

THE VISION OF THE QUEST

Inside the tower, Graven and the others locked up the entrances from within, taking no chances. The Quest went to the balcony and skimmed over the village, beautiful and peaceful to behold until the sun went down, then all hell broke loose. They saw beasts like creatures in a confused state of mind, clawing and biting at one another, fighting over a piece of meat, and destroying parts of the village. Alicia held her hands over Emily's eyes.

Graven said, "Get Emily into the tower. This evil is too much for her."

Slowly, the Quest settled down for the night, resting from the horror and the screams from outside. Emily, afraid, curled up beside her big sister. She pressed her hands against her ears, shutting out the terrifying noises. Everyone was relieved when Emily finally closed her eyes and fell asleep. They hoped she was out for the night. Spot laid close to her in case anything was to happen.

Everyone tried hard to shut out the chilling screams. They managed to fall asleep but were awakened by Emily's terrifying cries. Alicia realized she had a bad dream. She held her little sister in her arms, singing her a lullaby her mother used to sing to her when she was much younger and afraid.

"I had a nightmare the villagers were eating all of us." Emily tried not to cry, not wanting to sound like a baby, but tears ran from her big eyes. Alicia caressed her back and kept singing. Emily complained, "Alicia, I am nine years old. I'm too old for lullabies." She ignored her and began to hum instead. "But they were hurting our friends, ripping them apart!" Emily exclaimed.

Alicia held her tighter and caressed her face, smoothing her thick, blonde curls behind her ear, "You are safe. Nothing will be able to hurt any of us."

"Why did Chip have to die?" Emily sniveled and slowly began to calm down. The Quest remained quiet hearing the mention of Chip.

"I know, I miss him too," Alicia replied. She continued humming for a good length of time. Emily eventually drifted back to sleep. But the night was slow as the king's knights took turns staying awake. Graven was the first to keep watch. Acorn came on duty nearing morning. It was still black outside, but the scary noises were non-stop. Time slipped by slowly, and as the hours passed, the sun began to shine its morning rays. King Triune was banging on the two big double doors, yelling loudly, "Is everyone okay? We need the key!"

Graven awakened hearing Acorn calling from his guard post, "The night's been good! Hopefully, the day shows us favor!" The others had awakened. They observed Graven and Acorn trying to unlock the bolts but unable to with their hoofs and talons. They yelled, "We could use some help with these bolts!"

Granite jumped up to the rescue, and pulled the heavy doors off their hinges. He stood there, holding both doors in his big, rock hands, bolts and all. "Oops! Did I do that?"

Graven shook his head. "Sometimes, I wonder how much rock is inside that thick noggin of yours or whether you have a brain at all."

King Triune stood outside. He looked at Granite, blown away at his strength. "Well, I guess I don't have to worry about asking for the key," he said, pleased Granite was on his side. "Don't worry about the doors. I will send a crew out here to fix them." He entered, glad to see everyone unharmed. "We will eat and then begin to plan."

"So be it." Graven agreed in a firm tone.

The Quest followed the Arcaining people's leader back down the mountain to the dining area of his king-size tent to eat. They talked back and forth amongst each other until King Triune spoke up. The others became quiet. "I would like to share with you about my kingdom, for in the days of old, there was one great king who ruled all the kingdoms. There was peace in all the lands, but as time passed, the kingdoms were divided, and my father Anthor became king over the Arcaining people. He ruled with justice and honor, but because of the evil deceitfulness of the Enox's, he was betrayed. His village was raided by the Enox's under Malock's leadership, and my father was taken prisoner, along with one of his close servants—a little boy named Thor. The lad had always brought joy to the king; in return, my father held him in high esteem. Strangely, I feel Thor is of royal blood, possibly flesh of my flesh, but that is a mystery in itself... rumor has it that the Enox's killed both of them, along with many others. I was made king in his stead."

King Triune noticed everyone had finished their breakfast. "It's time to plan the escape of the children." King Triune and his advisors shared crucial information on the easiest ways to get inside the camp.

Graven spoke up, knowledgeable about battles. "It will be wise to have some sort of diversion, a good strategic plan."

King Triune put his hands to his face inhaled and exhaled stress. He was glad to have the backbone of the knights of King James's courts but nervous knowing the children and villagers' fate and what they would face if things go sour. He believed in the importance of their freedom. He warned. "Be aware as we try to save our children if all else fails. It is every man and woman for themselves. The Enox's will show no mercy and hold no captives besides children or royalty. Choose who will divert the enemy out of the camp as others enter and get the young ones out." He humbly remarked toward the Quest. "I am King Triune, son of King Anthor. This is our last hope. We shall free every one of those children or die trying. Now, hear me, my faithful comrades. I have ten sticks in my hand. Whoever chooses the two smallest sticks will distract the beasts. They will chase you far off, but whoever holds the remaining sticks will fight their hardest to free the children. The rest of the men shall encamp around the territory. Whatever tries to enter or flee shall utterly be destroyed. Now, let's choose." The warriors formed a circle. King Triune staged the sticks for Emily's sake. He allowed each one to choose one. Everyone held out their stick. King Triune saw that the two small sticks had fallen to Graven and Emily as planned.

King Triune remarked, "Hope and faith are with us may the blessings of God fall upon us all, for sure who is faster or swifter than Graven? Malock desires to have Emily for being a child. The two will stray far from his camp and find refuge. It will allow us to save the children with the assurance that Emily will remain safe, guarded in the hands of Graven."

King Triune noticed hours passed discussing their plans to destroy the Enox's. There was a restlessness upon his warriors. The stress of what might happen the next day, not knowing whether they would be able to cause utter damnation to Malock and his wicked hordes, preventing Malock from destroying the ones that meant the most to them—their women and children. It caused a grave fear in their hearts.

King Triune spoke with the boldness of new hope, but inside his heart too broke, thinking if his village were defeated, the people would lose all hope and wither and die slowly, seeking death and an early grave. Regardless, he spoke courageously, "Men, may we all have valor and wisdom tomorrow morning. When the sun rises, we go. Now, my friends of the Quest, we will meet for lunch and dinner. But afterward, you must be locked again in the tower for the night. Hopefully, you will find rest, for the morning will be upon us in no time." He turned and faced Granite. "My friend, in the morning, maybe someone else should unlock the doors," the young king advised him as he walked away.

The nightfall came upon them. Inside the tower was horrible humidity and hot, with not even a slight breeze. The noises heard from the outside were unspeakable. The Quest grew restless, yearning for the noise to stop and morning to come quickly and be outside the tower feeling the wind on their backs instead of experiencing another wild night, not knowing what dreadful things might happen.

Slowly, the hot night faded away. However, they couldn't fall asleep. Finally, an hour before daybreak, things begin to get quieter. Weariness had overtaken them, drifting into a deep sleep; morning soon came. King Triune and his soldiers knocked on the doors of the tower repeatedly. Graven eventually had awakened hearing the banging and awoken everyone. He had Granite help him unbolt the doors. Granite was more careful. Graven glanced at the hard rock-head. "I guess there's hope for you, my friend."

King Triune rushed inside. "What have you been doing? We have been knocking for the longest time. We are getting a late start. There cannot be any additional setbacks."

Graven answered. "You must understand we are constantly awakened by all the noises outside. This was the second night we barely slept. We finally drifted off to sleep."

THE VISION OF THE QUEST

King Triune was nervous for his people but ready for battle. He nodded his head. "I understand, but we must depart, for our journey is long."

The King watched Emily run to the door to pester Granite. Granite teased at her. "How is it that we overslept? I slept like a rock." He enjoyed getting Emily started.

"You are a rock. How many times have I told you that?" she giggled. Roger, too liked seeing Emily's face light up. He rolled up one of his dirty socks and threw it at her head as he slipped into the armor a servant had given him. Immediately, King Triune's soldiers brought in a harness and placed it on Graven's back, big enough to fit two small children.

"What is this foreign object?" Graven asked.

"I had my blacksmith make it for you to hold Emily in place since you will be flying at immense speed. Plus, there is additional room for the second child, as we planned."

The Quest departed with King Triune and his soldiers. They stayed hidden, walking through an uncharted wooded area that's never been traveled on. Their eyes were alert, especially as they reached Malock's territory.

They remained hidden and looked over their surroundings, and waited patiently for the right time for their plan to succeed. The mighty warriors see children working in gardens with selected large mixed breeds. The Enox's whipping and yelling, demanding them to work. The cries of the children and the beast's screams kept them from being heard. Alicia felt sorry for them, seeing they were about to drop from exhaustion, noticing how ugly and scary the Enoxs looked. She observed a lookout mix breed remaining calm, constantly scoping all his borders for threats. She figured it to be Malock. The seven-foot hairy beast stood firm as a bull with a head full of silver hair, which swayed side to side down his lower back. His body covered in old wounds being sliced from previous battles. Different places on his flesh that once had hair were concealed with burn scars.

Alicia overheard King Triune whisper to Graven. "The quiet one you look upon is Malock, be cautious of him. Some say he can easily snap the neck of any man or beast. Also, I do not doubt that Emily will be kept safe. I couldn't leave her in the tower alone and frightened. We did the right thing when we planned those small sticks." Alicia was pleased with their decision.

King Triune waited for Malock to look north, and as he did, the king spoke. "It is time."

The plan was set in motion. Emily securely on Graven's back with momentum speed, he swooped down into the garden and snatched up one of the children. He took off again into the air, soaring toward the sky, and paced himself for the Enoxs to follow him. The petrified boy screamed, soaring in midair in Graven's talons until he could place him upon his back into the harness.

Malock yelled, "Chase after that griffin at once! He has to land at some point! Bring him to me that I may kill him myself!" A multitude of vast armies, two different breeds, of hybrid of half wolf and half man and half wolf and half beast. Many with pitch-black hair flowing down their backside stood straight up as a man and ran with powerhouse speed, as the others ran like the wind on all four paws, their arched backs covered with brown and matted coarse hair. Both breeds united on foot in the direction of Graven. The Quest's plan was working. Graven led them far from camp. He fast landed and dropped the screaming boy to climb onto his back, but he was too terrified, not knowing who to trust. Emily shouted. "Graven is my friend! We are taking you to your mom's. Hurry, climb up before they catch up to us!" The frightened boy stopped shaking and moved as fast as possible but was weak. He climbed onto a boulder, jumped onto Graven's back, and slipped into the harness. As for the other children, Malock screamed at several of his hybrids. "Stay behind! Place the children back into the dungeon that none might escape!" Malock, too, took off furious on his jet-black horse with another part of his army riding horses behind him in pursuit of the remarkable warrior.

King Triune has seen Malock had left with them, taking at least three-quarters of his clans with him. The king was relieved at last the numbers looked even. He and his men with shields dashed forth and wielded their swords skillfully, fighting off the remaining Enoxs on the outside, bringing them to their knees in disgrace. King Triune, with his soldiers and the Quest, entered the first wide gate, then the second considerable size steel gate. They fought long and hard when they finally reached the temple. Underneath the floor, they could hear the children crying while being held in a dungeon. King Triune's soldiers came in contact with additional large, disgusting clans. They slew many of them but also lost a few comrades.

King Triune and a small squad of his men, with Granite and Alicia, ran boldly, finding a trap door to the dungeon, and entered. Alicia was appalled to find many children in cages buried in the earth. Granite broke thick cast iron bars off over the top of them. King Triune's men fast reached down and released the children from the cold, damp holes. The children were frightened, screaming, and crying, not knowing what was happening. Alicia spoke firmly but with compassion. "We are here to help you, but you must remain calm and listen to your king." King Triune called out toward them, "You will follow Alicia and Granite, who is standing to my right. They will take you to a place where it is safe. The place you once called your home. Now go swiftly. Our time is limited. Make haste, children!" They slowly begin to follow Alicia and Granite through the trap door and enter the temple.

Malock's hybrids felt struck hard that they could not conquer King Triune's warriors. With cunningness, rock walls emerged by pushing a secret panel, separating King Triune and his soldiers from Alicia and Granite and a few of his men with the frightened children.

Alicia yelled out, but it was too late. The barrier separated them and trapped them like bait on a mousetrap until Malock's returned. King Triune looked for ways of escape. A few of his soldiers did manage to get through hidden cracks within the walls leading through different passageways. They slew beasts without mercy that stood in their way.

Alicia knew if they didn't find a way out, the innocent children would be in grave danger and would be tortured, leaving many standing in the balance of life and death. She, in that instant, felt the glass globe within her leather pouch vibrate and remembered King Hydro. She removed it from safekeeping and witnessed a dim light shining, and as she walked, the light became brighter, leading the way until it brought her to a dead-end of three different paths. She knew to stretch forth the glass globe. It became much brighter toward the center door. She felt for sure it was the right direction. The children continued clanging desperately to Alicia, Granite, and the few soldiers who had saved them from the Enoxs.

Alicia comprehended. *There are too many children. It will take a miracle to get them all out of here to safety with the hours we had been trapped in this place. The sun will tuck away soon and subside into the night, activating the curse on King Triune's people, including his soldiers. They would change into killers.*

Regardless, Alicia followed the globe's brightness. She walked through the center door through an eerie, dark, rat-ridden path. The globe became hot to the touch, and after a few more twists and turns, she found a path leading them outside. The shaken children were not out of danger. King Triune and his soldiers were still trapped inside the temple. But being a wise king, he had planned strategically. He had a number of his men with Roger, Acorn, White Lightening, and Spot stationed outside, watching and staying alert in case of an attack surrounding the temple.

Roger and the others helped Alicia and Granite get the children outside the second gate. It was difficult to think with the screams and terrified cries of the kids. At least a hundred of them, each child praying that Malock did not return. They knew that their punishment might be torture or death. Alicia followed the plans of King Triune; to get them to the tower at all costs and remain inside until morning. Without delay, Alicia hurried and coached them to rush in that direction. "I know all of you are frightened and have been hurt deeply but remain brave and strong. We must move fast, for nightfall will be upon us before we know it." The children here and there sniveled quietly as they followed Alicia and Roger. Granite remained in the back to protect them from behind. Acorn, White Lightening, and Spot were scattered amongst the children.

King Triune and his men still searched for ways to escape the dungeon. They finally managed to get back to the main entrance. By then, it was too late. Daylight faded like a petal that falls off a flower.

King Triune beat his chest and grievously cried out. He realized he and his men were turning into werewolves.

Malock, following Graven for many hours. He was full of fury and taunted by the griffin, unable to contain him. The night settled upon the savage barbarian like a dark blanket. He returned with his army and entered the large gates leading up to his sanctuary. Malock's scarred face recoiled even more in rage. He could not believe the damage he beheld, opening the doors to the main entrance of his temple. King Triune and his soldiers now, wild beasts exiting from behind his temple walls, including those who surrounded the camp, came forth attacking, ripping, and tearing upon his mixed breeds, slaughtering Malock's army.

Malock was inflamed, watching his army being slaughtered. The battle had turned against him. He fled on horseback. Hearing the cries of his subjects, he did not bother to turn back, fleeing to his safety. His intentions were evil, with no compassion toward his beast but satisfying his evil ways.

King Triune and his soldiers had won the night, but their minds were far from victory, thinking not as men but as wild animals smelling the children causing them to go more insane as they pursued them on foot.

The children were hungry and weak and gave out, having to walk fast. Granite and Acorn carried on their backs, ones too young to keep up with the others. Spot and White Lightning carried the sick children with no more strength from working in the fields and left them to die in the dungeon.

The moon shined, lighting their path. Roger watched a six-year-old boy collapse. A boy, a few years younger than Roger, attempted to carry the child but was too weak. Roger immediately picked up the young boy and threw him over his shoulder.

-"What is your name?" the boy asked as he brushed long and matted dirty blonde hair out of his eyes. The boy was skin and bones. His clothes were held on by a few threads torn and ragged like all the other children's clothes. Roger noticed most were barefooted, making it more difficult to walk, having cuts and blisters on the bottom of their sore feet working day in and day out in the fields. He sadly could see where the boy had been whipped repeatedly.

"Roger Davis," he answered.

The boy showed gratitude, "I will remind the lad of what you have done for him because, on your back, you carry the future king of King Triune's people. He is King Anthor's son. You see, King Anthor was our king and a good one. Sadly, he died in the dungeon after being tortured for the longest time, but before his death, he asked me to look after the child to protect his name from being revealed or Malock may kill him." The boy became quiet as he walked and remembered that day. He continued. "The king was weak. He must have known death was knocking at his door when Malock caught him whispering to me. The raging bull struck him down in cold blood, but not without our king putting up a fight. The small boy witnessed his father's brutal death. Since then, I have fought hard to keep him alive. Locked inside the dungeon, I gave him the little food I had to survive. Now you have come to bring hope to us all." The boy looked seriously at Roger, "Remember this, I solemnly promise that I will not forget your name or any of the Quest's names because of what you have done for us this night." He weakly extended his hand. "By the way, my name is Joel Knight, and I shall be a future knight for my king."

Alicia glanced over and caught herself admiring Roger helping to carry the young boy on his broad shoulders. She turned toward the children with a reassuring smile, hiding that she wasn't certain what would happen before morning. Fear gripped Alicia's heart. She recalled King Triune's people's monstrous noises when they were locked inside the tower. Now they were right in the midst of it. Alicia is concerned for the children, wondering how the curse could be lifted. She thought of them hiding inside the tower, hearing the screams of their loved ones night after night. She was worried. But she reasoned it would be better for them to be in the arms of their loved ones during the day than to be tortured and killed by whips and starvation at the hands of the Enoxs.

She smiled again for the children's sake. "You are almost home, and soon you will be in your parents' arms, but as I said, we must go to the tower until morning until things are safe." Her words helped them carry on a little longer, but as they neared the tower, King Triune and his men were upon them, running swiftly to slaughter their own flesh and blood.

Graven returned from the chase. He heard the children's terrified screams, weary though he pushed forth. He found the Quest and the young ones preyed upon, ready to tear them apart. Like a bolt of lightning, Graven dropped Emily and the small boy off his back next to Alicia. Spreading out his outstanding wings, stabilizing himself in midair, he shot beams of laser separating them. He did not desire any of them to be harmed. Graven understood a number of them were the children's loved ones. He did not need them returning home to empty arms. He continued to shoot his lasers as long as he could. His strength was wearing out. The line of fire was thinning until it diminished. Graven was able to create another line of separation. However, the flames fizzled out within minutes, leaving them vulnerable to attacks.

Screaming in terror, the children could feel something awful was about to occur.

"Run, children, run!" Alicia and Roger screamed. The children froze in fear, too frightened and horrified to run. They barely felt themselves breathing. Graven, mustering up every last bit of power, shot his powerful beams—this time by creating a higher wall of flames, hoping to keep them at bay. King Triune's men grew wilder and fierce by the minute. Fear now gripped the Quest, watching a few that became brave enough to leap over the fire.

King Triune's remaining soldiers leaped out of the woods as men and women rushed from their village, running on all fours, grunting, and growling with thick piles of drool, and headed toward them. They, too, jumped over the fire walking around the petrified children with lips rolled up, glaring sharp pointy teeth. The eerie sounds and distorted faces of the wild animals caused some children to wet themselves.

The Quest was well aware. There were too many of them. Possibly hundreds.

Instantly, far off, Alicia's necklace glowed brightly inside the door called Worthy. Alicia heard a strong word repeating inside her mind, which gave her strength and courage not to lose heart. She sensed a boldness and a divine power and screamed out with the confidence of a bold warrior, "Yahweh!" Alicia's one spoken word caused an incredible light to appear, shining from the door that held her and Emily's necklaces. The illuminating light blinded the villagers and King Triune and his men, wandering in complete darkness, bumping into one another, fighting, and tearing into each other with their jagged teeth.

Full of madness and blurred vision, one of them had sniffed a child out. Her scent was familiar to him. He grabbed the little girl by her leg and hung her mercilessly in the air. The Quest moved to help her with all the other children they could protect until morning arrived. Sadly, they knew many young, innocent lives would be lost. The child screamed, petrified, yelling for someone to save her. The little girl's hope of survival fleeted. She cried out her final words, "Daddy," The beast looked into her eyes. Something inside him transformed like a hot iron ran up and down his heart. He was startled and confused and didn't understand. He saw a birthmark on the opened palm of the little girl's hand, in the shape of a perfect star, a sign of Orion, representing opening eyes for others to see. The girl's love and forgiving heart had caused dark scales to fall from his eyes. He sensed the burning sensation of his heart getting hotter and hotter until the dark curse burned off him.

Falling to his knees, he sobbed and slowly changed back into a man and lamented, grabbing the little girl into his arms. He now realized it was his daughter. The love had broken the spell and the touch of a small child, blessed with a power, removed the curse from his people. The curse was no more as they changed back into the men and women of the village. The people wept bitterly because Jordan, the father of Roseshanah, his little girl, had the blood of a Pathfinder running through her veins, through the lineage of her grandmother, causing freedom to ring loudly this night. The villagers knew the story of how Jordan's mother married a man from King Anthor's kingdom but sadly, because of his mother's powers being a Pathfinder, certain men within the village were jealous. Being ruthless, the men killed both his parents only a few days after giving birth to him.

THE VISION OF THE QUEST

Jordan remained hidden at the house of an aunt and uncle who raised him as their son and watched him grow into a decent man. He had no outward appearance of a Pathfinder. However, his daughter Roseshanah was born with great capabilities. She was young and unaware of them. Her father realized one day, she would blossom into a young lady, and so will her powers. Jordan cherished Roseshanah and kept her safe from men who might desire to possess her strength to use her for their glory. Jordan kept her from the truth of who she is, and now this night, the villagers shouted their liberty and freedom heard throughout the mountain tops. Alicia was captivated to see everything unfolding before her eyes, knowing the children were safe, and the villagers were no longer werewolves but freed from the evil curse caused by the Enoxs. She grabbed Emily and Roger.

Roger beamed. "Okay, I guess this is one of your hallmark moments. Bring it on." Roger loved the feeling of her arms wrapped around him.

Alicia, full of joy, held both of them close. She looked toward the heavens and whispered. "My Father, you have never forsaken us. Thank you for the healing taking place tonight." Alicia searched the faces of the villagers mourning for the children who didn't survive in the hands of the Enoxs. She knew they would continue to hold them close and dear to their hearts. But all hope was not lost as Alicia saw men and women crying joyfully for the children that had made it. King Triune spoke with tears: "Jehovah granted all of us victory this night. We shall never forget this moment, this night of deliverance! We shall always be grateful that he had granted us favor for this wonderful freedom and blessed us with friends- the Quest!"

Chapter Thirteen

The Sound of Wisdom

THE VISION OF THE QUEST

The villagers and the Quest returned to King Triune's land for a special celebration. Graven saw how his people were back in good spirits, with the stress of the dark curse removed—arched tall on his four talons. He spoke. "King Triune, I stand on behalf of the chosen ones. We humbly ask for your guidance to the water of life and the tree of enlightenment I know the third kingdom's whereabouts but am not sure what door to take. Do you know what I speak of?" Graven hoped this wonderful leader would know something.

King Triune looked surprised. He questioned. "Why didn't you tell me in the beginning that the kids were the chosen ones?"

"For in the circumstances, you and your villagers were in with Malock. I could not afford Malock getting wind of it. I thought it was wise to wait. You had enough on your plate at that time." Graven answered.

King Triune, standing, rested his hand on the top handle of his sword that dangled at his side. "My friend, that was wise of you, but I am sorry. I do not know what you seek. I have heard of it, but I am unaware of its whereabouts. However, don't lose hope. The wise elder of Eldon, who lives in the Valley of Willow Trees, has much wisdom. I am almost certain he will know what you seek. I will lead you to him to help keep the chosen ones safe as you had brought our children to safety, but my men will travel on foot, for the Enox's had taken most of our horses. After seeing the elder, I can only lead the Quest outside the second kingdom. I would be crazy to leave my people for too long in case the Enox's decide to war again. I will bring enough of my men with me but leave many men of war behind to protect my village."

Graven bowed his head in respect. "In the short time, I have come to know you. I have seen you are a man of outstanding principles and leadership and will carry out your word. I know of the elder of Eldon of the Willow trees, for we go back many years ago. We are eternally grateful for your help."

King Triune bowed his head in turn. "It is I who am eternally grateful. If it wasn't for King James's quest, our children would still be missing and our people under a curse. Now tell me, Graven, do Roger and Alicia know how to handle a sword?"

Graven was pleased to answer. "Yes, in our spare time, we have taught them how to defend themselves and to fight as mighty warriors. Alicia is gifted at her bow and arrow. Her aim is precise. I overheard Roger tease her and call her Robinhood. I have never heard of a Robinhood but it sounded like a good thing. She has no fear but does lack confidence of her own potential. Now, concerning Roger, he is strong for his age and handles the weight of his sword as any man. He can wield it precisely, even cutting the wings off a fly. His balance is excellent. I am stunned by how he throws spears, daggers, and knives. Roger does need a great deal of assistance in keeping focused and alert. I will have to admit both youths lack survival skills to survive alone in a desert or forest if need be."

King Triune spoke with confidence. "This is but a small task for me; they are already gifted in these qualities. However, both shall learn more by my hand beginning tomorrow. My men will wake them up early in the morning and work with them for their success. Alicia and Roger will learn to have confidence in themselves and stay focused and alert. When completed, we will head to the elder of Eldon."

Graven left for the tower to share the good news with Alicia and Roger. He found both sound asleep on their cots thrown together that night for all beds were destroyed when the villagers had turned into wild beasts. Graven decided not to wake them, but morning came all too soon. The two sleepy heads were unaware of what was taking place as two soldiers went into the tower and deliberately dragged them out of their warm comfort zone.

Roger cried out. "Hey, the sun's not even up!" He heard Alicia complaining clearly on the other side of the tower and slowly got up out of bed. *She is quite a bold thing*, Roger finding himself amused.

"What is the meaning of this?" Alicia questioned, jumping back onto her cot. She placed her pillow over her head, only to be pulled out of bed again. She broke loose. "This is my first night in months sleeping a full night on something comfortable and not on a hard, rock floor or the cold, wet ground. Where are your manners, being rude as to drag me out of bed. I am making a complaint to King Triune. He will not be pleased with how you are treating me." Alicia swung back her long black hair.

"Have you ever heard about a lady needs her beauty sleep? Now, please, leave me alone." Her cocoa eyes glared, upset. She again headed toward her cot. Roger walked across the tower length and stood in front of her. He enjoyed the show.

Roger yawned and rubbed his tired eyes as one of the soldiers spoke up. "King Triune is well aware of our treatment of you. We are here and obeying his orders through his command."

She protested. "Then I need to see King Triune. Period. End of story. Because this is way too early, the sun is barely up. If it's even up at all."

"Have it your way," the soldier replied. "But you will not get far."

"Alicia, give it up." Roger jumped in. "We are being trained and prepared for battle. Do not fight the soldiers for more sleep. It's time to learn."

Annoyed, she asked, "Oh, since when did you become so mature?" Alicia slumped into a sitting position onto the floor, losing hope of curling back onto her cozy cot.

Roger ignored her words as he observed Alicia's fine lips and was pleased at the beauty of her dark complected skin. His heart fluttered. "As I had said before I will go to any extent to become a successful warrior to protect the ones I love."

She looked up at him, surprised, noticing a change since he became a part of the Quest. Alicia stood up and found herself again touched by his charisma. "Well, then, what are we waiting for? Let's get started." She replied half-heartedly.

The two followed the soldiers outside. Both began their monotonous training, thinking it would never end. They were too exhausted even to speak by the end of the day. Alicia, with heavy feet, dragged them, walking into the tower. She crashed onto her cot. Roger made his way inside and flopped onto his. Their heads hit their pillow, and both were knocked out for the night, only to be awakened before the rooster crowed.

Without complaining of sore muscles, the two teenagers followed the men outside to tackle another tiresome training. Alicia and Roger were set up with a surprise attack as five soldiers came at them with a spear and sword. They worked together on how to overcome them as a team. Alicia high-fived Roger. "Hey, we didn't do too bad. We took down three of the men." As soon as the words came out of her mouth, a big husky soldier pointed to a path. Alicia and Roger begin to run through it and run for miles testing their endurance. Alicia finished five minutes after Roger. She dropped at the soldiers' feet. "Are we finished yet?" She wiped the sweat off her face. Roger with rapid breathing answered. "Nope, they said we are hunting game next and cooking it while scoping out the territory."

"Well, that seems easy enough. I worked myself up an appetite." Alicia responded glad and soon found out hunting the game took longer than she had thought. However, hungry both enjoyed eating it. Afterward, they were relieved on finding out they only had two more events left to tackle. Alicia and Roger went underwater, moving a stack of rocks from one location to the next without releasing air. Alicia popped up first and Roger thirty seconds later. "This is hard!" Alicia complained while catching her breath. "I second that!" Roger fully agreed.

"Five more times back and forth." the husky soldier said. Alicia and Roger looked at one another but did not desire to quit. Each did what they were told.

"The last test is capability." The same big man informed them. "Thank God!" Alicia exclaimed. His five soldiers stood thirty feet away, throwing short spears with false tips. Alicia and Roger dodged the spears climbing up over a small rock wall, attempting to avoid getting stuck and definitely not falling. They were pleased when the training finally ended for the day. Pressed for time, they endured one more day of strenuous and crucial exercises, and not giving up until fully prepared for anything that might come their way. The soldiers felt it was time and had informed their king.

King Triune was pleased with the report. He said to Graven. "It is time my friend. We shall depart tomorrow morning and speak with the wise man of the Willow Trees. I hope he will be a help to the Quest."

Graven stood upright and steadfast. "We shall be ready. I will inform the others. I appreciate your assistance in helping Alicia and Roger become better warriors, fully developing gifts lying dormant inside them. Their gifts have been stirred up, creating a fire within them, now the two warriors have the faith not only to move one mountain but to move the mountain behind that mountain. They have the confidence to believe in a greater power that already lives within them."

"No, my friend. The Quest had done so much more for my people. I have a debt I cannot pay. Please accept my gratitude for all you have done, for we live in peace and harmony once again."

Graven replied humbly, "There is no debt that needs to be paid. Alicia is but a teenager, but she has taught me it is better to give than to receive. My friend tomorrow we shall speak to the elder of the Willow Trees." The leaders bowed their heads in reverence, one toward another. They departed to prepare their comrades for the next day.

Nightfall came and went. The sunlight shone through the windows of the tower. Alicia and Roger did not need to be dragged out of bed. They were ready and prepared. The journey has begun. Alicia and Emily removed their necklaces from the door of the second kingdom. Hours slipped by as King Triune and his soldiers walked. Spot flew the long journey with Emily on his back, surveying their surroundings, ensuring no danger lurked ahead. Acorn did the same, with Alicia on his back. Roger stayed on the ground near White Lightning. Graven and Granite remained on the ground as well for any onslaught attacks. The day's heat was more tolerable, as clouds covered the sun. Hours had faded away into midafternoon all were satisfied to reach the weeping willow trees. Acorn and Spot landed and walked with the others. Everywhere they turned were willow trees. They walked a stretch hopefully to find the hidden gate, but a powerful, strong wind stirred up, making it difficult even to stand none could go on—not even Granite, as solid as he was.

"Who is entering my domain? Show yourself and speak up that I may hear!" a demanding voice boomed.

King Triune spoke over the strong winds. He could not tell where the voice had come from, "I am King Triune, leader of my people of the Arcaining's tribe. We have a question to ask the elder of Eldon, the wise man of the weeping willow trees. We have come a long way on foot may we proceed forth? Our journey has been hard." King Triune stood unyielding, digging the heels of his combat boots into the hard dirt. Granite did the same and spread his arms around the chosen ones to keep them safe on the ground.

King Triune was at ease as the forceful whirlwinds calmed down, and a light breeze circled them, and then, right away, the winds became strong once more, blasting a straight path through the willow trees. Their branches parted, making the path visible to a white, enormous gate, which swung open.

The voice in the wind echoed, "Venture through!"

King Triune with his men and the Quest cautiously followed the straight passageway as more excellent trees up ahead parted and proceeded to lead them down a long, narrow path. They arrived at a small cottage high up in the treetops in the middle of nowhere.

King Triune, still not seeing the man, boldly repeated. "I am King Triune, leader of my people, the Arcaining tribe. Graven, the griffin standing beside me, is my faithful ally. The Quest needs the assistance of the elder of Eldon, the wise man of the weeping willow trees."

King Triune, at last, eyed an elderly man slowly proceeding down a rope ramp. His long, snow-white hair blowing in the wind, with a long beard as long as his hair. He observed the wise man's face, seeing time had taken a toll on him. There wasn't a place on the man's face a wrinkle had failed to materialize.

King Triune waited for the elder's reply. However, Emily saw the old man's long white beard blowing in the wind. She shouted excitedly, "Hey, is, is, is …" She was tongue-tied.

She had gotten the curiosity of the old man. He assisted her. "Go on, child, spit it out."

THE VISION OF THE QUEST

Emily exclaimed all in one breath. "You're the wizard in the Wizard of Oz! Oh, gosh, where are Dorothy and Toto? I mean, why not? There's a griffin here and everything else."

King Triune was about to speak when Roger laughed. "Emily, I think you mean Gandalf of the Lord of the Rings."

"Who's he?" Emily squealed. She was upset at Roger for deflating her dream of tapping her shoes and landing her back into her mother's arms.

King Triune noticed Graven's sharp eyes lit up with curiosity, but the elder this time desired to know what particular words the chosen ones spoke of. The long-bearded man looked at Roger, "Who is this Gandalf, and what of this Toto?"

Roger answered simply. "Gandalf is an old man, and Toto's a dog. But I had asked someone before of how do your people live without watching television? But I respect the majority of the ones who live here fight for what is noble and right."

The wise man asked, stunned. "Is she calling me a dog? I've been called many things in my life, but never a dog, but to set the record straight I am not a wizard. But you can say I have wisdom with the coming of age. I am the elder of Eldon, and not the Shaggy D.A." Roger's and Emily's eyes widened—the size of quarters—how he would know about the Shaggy D.A. dog. The elder smiled, giving the two something to think about. He brought his focus to Graven, "Now, how may I help you? What can possibly be so important to bring you all this way, step closer that I may see you. My eyes are dim in my stage of life."

Graven stepped forward and observed how much the elder of Eldon had aged since he had last seen him. He held his peace, now was not the time to speak of the past. "We are searching for the water of life and the tree of enlightenment for King James's sake. We are on a quest. May you help us?"

Graven ventured closer, the elder was happy to see him, but he, too, showed no emotions for the same reason. The old man's bright, blue eyes shined at the mere mention of King James's name. "Yes, yes, by all means, please, come inside, and we will talk." The old man observed White Lightning and Acorn, who now were hovering in the air, skimming the ground. He saw the remaining Quest and King Triune's men, being many. He spoke wisely to Graven, "But please, just your leaders may come in, for, as you can see, I cannot fit this magnitude into my small cottage that's only made of bark and timber I found deep within the forest."

King Triune assured him. "My soldiers will remain outside and be on guard," Graven nodded at the Quest to do the same.

The man was pleased with Graven, who he could trust to seek out his advice. The elder was well known throughout the lands. Men and women searched for him and even came from other kingdoms to partake of his wisdom, though the people came and went. Therefore, because of lack of fellowship, the elder of Eldon spoke much to the winds and willow trees, and grew a special bond. The winds and trees protected him from any dangers that might arise. Countless times evil men, envious of his gift, wished to do him harm.

Graven followed the elder and King Triune up the long ramp of thick rope. King Triune entered into his small cottage. But as Graven squeezed through the doorway. His bulky body became wedged in it. He tried to wiggle himself free. Graven heard the Quest and soldiers outside enjoying his free circus show, and with one last attempt, he pushed through and landed inside the cottage. He stuck his head outside the open door and looked down at everyone, laughing hysterically.

Graven heard Roger shout, "That's a side of you I have never seen before and, frankly, a side I wish not to see again." Alicia stepped in, giggling. "Roger, that joke is lame. Sorry, Graven, where we come from, it's not every day we see a griffin's backend wedged into a doorway. This is a special event for us. Something we will never forget."

Emily came to his defense. - "Don't worry, if the hole was any smaller, it could had taken you all day to get out!"

Graven smiled at her. He shut the door blocking out the noise below, and he chuckled. He stood on all four talons, almost afraid to move, hoping not to fall through the floor something else to add to his circus show. Graven and King Triune expressed their concerns to the elder concerning King James's needs and the chosen ones necklaces.

"But the girls only have the two keys and not the third one." King Triune said. The elder replied. "What you seek will be no easy task. The path is hard for many who desire the three keys to control all the kingdoms. There are only a few whom you can trust. Many are deceitful. For that reason, you must choose your allies cautiously. These words I speak must not be taken lightly. This advice is essential to get the chosen ones headed in the right direction."

The bearded man shifted his eyes back and forth between Graven and King Triune. "Listen to what I am about to say, out of the hands of babes and the lineage of a queen and with the help of a young ally will arise two keys that, when added to the queen's key, shall open the door to the third kingdom, and peace will be established in the king's reign with the help of a faithful Quest, and know this, it is the blood of their ancestor that runs through their veins. Now, it's important to guard those keys with your life so we may live in peace and harmony again. But understand this: to enter the Third Kingdom, you must have all three keys. Without the third necklace, it is impossible to enter." The elder spoke wisely.

"How can we obtain this third key?" King Triune asked, remembering the heartache he experienced with his people desiring peace for his kingdom.

Graven interrupted. "I have my suspicion where the third key may be, but for now, it is best it remains with me in case it slips out of this room and reaches the wrong person. I cannot chance that happening. It's something I must remain silent about."

The elder listened as King Triune asked boldly. "Graven, this third key, is it possible to find before King James runs out of time?"

Graven opened his mouth to speak when the old man leaned forward toward King Triune. "Excuse me, sir. I should have asked this before. I know Graven, but earlier I did not catch your name. You were standing too far away, and my hearing is not up to par."

The leader extended his right hand out. "I am King Triune of the Arcaining tribe."

The elder looked dumbfounded. He bowed his head with reverence. "The son of the wonderful King Anthor…yes, I remember you now, as a little boy. I would kneel in respect for you but my knees are feeble. I may not be able to get back up again." The elder stepped closer to his king. "Sometimes the hardest things to seek in life can be right before us, right under our noses, and we must reach out and quickly receive it."

King Triune looked toward the elder, puzzled by what he had said. "You speak in riddles. What do you mean, 'receive it quickly'?"

The wise man answered strongly. "What I have said. I have spoken. Now, you must leave quickly. There is nothing else I can do for you. With every precious moment wasted is subtracted from our peace, freedom, and liberty. Be cautioned, my friends. People from the second kingdom, even Malock, may know of the necklaces. God speed unto you all!"

Chapter Fourteen

REUNITED

THE VISION OF THE QUEST

Graven and King Triune left the elder's tree cottage in haste. The second Graven crossed the draw rope. He shared firsthand with Alicia and Roger. "The elder feels besides Bronze that there are likely others aware of your necklaces that desire this power to find the water of life and the tree of enlightenment. We must stay alert at all times. After the king receives his healing, we are prepared to advance to fight a great battle. Then finally, this hardship will be over with."

Alicia cried out firmly. "Do not forget my mother's safety that Princess Lilly promised me."

"Yes," Graven replied. "The king is true to what he speaks. Now, we must journey to the second kingdom and make haste. Enough time has been wasted. Everyone gear up. It's time to go."

The warriors desired rest, enjoying the little time under the weeping willow trees, shading them from the sun, as soft, cool breezes had soothed their warm skin, but they all knew it was a must to continue and push on.

They begin the long journey, speedily leading the Quest outside the second kingdom.

Alicia was not sure what they might come up against. She wondered why Bronze's creatures had not found their trail or whether they were even searching for them. She thought of the danger that would lie ahead. After a couple of hours of traveling, Alicia looked at Emily, full of mischief. Granite tossed her playfully high up into the air.

"Again, again!" she laughed. In the blink of an eye her joy turned into fearful screams. She clanged onto Granite, hiding her face under his rock arm. Wolf Fang and Zoroc and other fierce beasts circled them.

Granite observed they were ambushed everywhere he turned. He was relieved to see Spot run over to Emily. Granite peeled her frightened body off him and threw her up onto Spot's back.

"Keep my little live wire safe." He yelled out to Spot. "They are too many to defeat! We are outnumbered by many!" Granite's face shown he was ready to do some real damage to keep the chosen ones out of harm's way. He realized that winning this battle would require a miracle. Spot took off away from the place. Emily spotted her big sister. "Be careful, Alicia! Be careful!" Emily yelled out before disappearing out of sight. The Quest obeyed and ran in the direction as King Triune yelled boisterously, pointing his sword forward. "Follow me!" He had spotted an opening.

The black wolverines that flew soared down at exhilarating speed and thrust their razor-sharp claws into a few of King Triune soldiers' flesh. They jerked them up into the air like bait on a hook. King Triune and his men with the Quest managed to reach a haven, a clear spot in a field where the sun would be to their advantage. He prepared his soldiers for battle. His men stood brave with their swords drawn as other men shot hundreds of arrows up into the atmosphere, taking down several of the reeking fur bags. The sky was still covered with their nastiness. The once-blue firmament looked like enormous, dark shadows. The white wolverines on the ground were just as fierce, including Snakens, Spiders, and other dangerous creatures. The Shanks desiring a bite of the action, attacked, shooting their poison scorpion pins into their prey, and more good men fell.

Graven flew at high speed, beaming his laser eyes and hitting his targets. Granite ran full force, smashing anything in his way, but they kept coming. King Triune searched around, and things looked hopeless. He felt reproach was soon to come, and all would be lost when suddenly the enemy became distracted. They saw out of nowhere an awful gargoyle that appeared humongous in stature, reaching a height of twenty-five feet or more, that attacked their enemies.

King Triune was encouraged to see they had an ally of that magnitude as he sliced his sword through hellish odd-looking creatures coming at Alicia, who was taking down many with her bow and arrow. She was elated that this wonderful gargoyle had come to their rescue. But she knew the gargoyle could only hold off the darkness for so long. She suddenly recalled the words of Hydro, the Water King: "Only in dire need will you remember me." Alicia removed her water globe from her leather pouch. She gripped it into her hands, speaking directly into it. "Hear my voice, King Hydro. We are in desperate need of your help. I call upon your strength in a time of peril!"

THE VISION OF THE QUEST

The globe shook in her hands with such force she could not contain it any longer. She dropped the globe onto the ground. Surprisingly, the glass did not break. Alicia stood back in amazement and watched an astronomic arm of water sweep across the sky, wiping out over half the wicked forces, dismantling their bodies with an inspiring of power. The water coiled back into the glass globe. Alicia, still quite stunned, carefully bent down to pick it up, burning her fingers. She used her arrow and pushed it back into her pouch, hoping it didn't burn a hole through her leather bag.

She didn't waste a second and picked up her bow and directed her arrows again, picking off the enemy with precise aim. She saw the giant gargoyle still killing the deathly things as King Trine's soldiers continued shooting the wolverines from the sky. And Granite continued having a field day, unaffected by the scorpions' poison, rolling them into a ball and throwing them into the Snaken's. This caused their pointy pins to squirt deadly poison into their comrades' flesh, killing them. Graven was still shooting his laser beams but growing weary, it sapped him of his strength, but he faints not.

Wolf Fang did not like what he saw. He called to his dark cohorts, "Retreat! There are other forces at work here! Retreat, or we will all perish!" Enraged, Wolf Fang left to speak with Sir Bronze about his failure.

But as for the Quest and King Triune and his men, shouts of victory rang forcefully through the open field as they watched their enemies flee. Spot heard the shouts of triumph and returned with Emily still on his back. Alicia and Roger focused on the tremendous gargoyle that walked toward the Quest. They felt a slight shake of the earth below their feet and marveled at the gargoyle's size. The gargoyle asked Graven, "Are you in need of my services any longer?"

Graven and Granite grinned at one another, surprised, they questioned. "Can it be?"

Alicia and Emily didn't recognize who it was in disguise, for as Chip moved aside stood their mother with Melanie and Liana's Protectors. Liana dashed for her children, crying out their names. She longed so long to hold them in her arms. Tears of joy saturated her eyes like a downpour of heavy rain.

"Mom, Mom!" Emily jumped off Spot, running as fast as her legs could carry her. Liana dropped to her knees. Emily flung her arms around her. Liana hugged her daughter tightly, not desiring to let go. Alicia remained frozen in the same spot. Her mouth opened, too stunned to move, wondering if it was an illusion, thinking could it be possible. Emily must have read her mind. She cried out, "Mom's real, Alicia! She's real!"

Alicia, still unsure, her mother called out, "Anything is possible to those that have faith to believe!" She dropped her bow and arrow and tearfully ran to her, soon engulfed in her presence. Roger ran swiftly toward her, enraptured that she was out of the hands of that murderous Bronze. He stood in front of Miss Liana and saw she looked unharmed. He beamed, "Group hug." Alicia threw her arms around her friend.

Graven and Granite and White Lightening, Acorn, and Spot had their reunion, just as exhilarated to be speaking with Chip.

"We thought you were surely dead! Where were you, and how did you live?" Graven asked.

Chip transformed back into a chipmunk. Granite placed him upon his shoulder to hear him. Chip was happy to see everyone. He explained. "I was able to fight my way to the surface of the water, but I had passed out, and by the time I had opened my eyes and had reached the top, you knuckleheads had left. I was on my own until I ran into Miss Liana, Melanie, and her Protectors."

"But what is miraculous," Chip exclaimed, "We were led here by the power of Miss Liana's necklace, or we would never have found you. It's quite hilarious when I think about it. Bronze sent out enough of his military force to overpower such a small number as us. His forces were heavy onto us, sniffing us out. We hid amongst the berry bushes and honeysuckles. The fragrance around us was strong, and the enemy could not detect us, but if they had, they would have killed us."

Chip with his Frito Beano grin. "It stunned me that the trick worked. However, I give recognition to Miss Liana. It was her idea. She had total confidence it would succeed, though. She doesn't remember where her knowledge came from concerning the berries or the honeysuckles. All I know, these fragrances had camouflaged our scent. Bronze's army bypassed us and ran into all of you."

Graven remarked. "Upon seeing us, they must have thought they hit the jackpot."

Chip replied, "Jackpot? I guess a new word you learned from Roger after I was left for dead. You bean heads just sat back learning new vocabularies—if you knew what we went through to get here."

King Triune overheard their conversation and asked boldly. "Graven, is this your little Chip? I had heard a lot about speaking such big words if he only knew what we had gone through."

Chip transformed back into the twenty-five-foot gargoyle.

"Okay!" King Triune snickered. "Go ahead, tell us of all your troubles."

He transformed back into a chipmunk and climbed back onto Granite's shoulder. "I thought you would see it my way," Chip said, with a wide grin. King Triune kidded. "I certainly don't desire to mess with you my friend."

Alicia and Emily looked over and recognized Chip. They were still being held tightly in their mother's embrace. Happy to have their mother back and realize Chip was alive.

Graven looked at the chosen ones, pleased they had been reunited with their mother. But knew they had to leave that place at once. He informed them, "We must travel. Our enemies will be on our trail once more, most likely with a substantial amount of Bronze's army."

Liana heard what Graven said. She succumbed to her fears. "I must take my girls and Roger back home with me! I witnessed enough heartache and had seen too many crazy things."

Alicia cried, "Oh, Mom, we cannot go home now. We have traveled so far. We must find the Third Kingdom and seek out what the king needs."

Liana's thoughts ran rabid. She placed her face in her hands and quietly prayed for guidance. It was all she knew to do. *I taught my children to fight for what is right and remain unmovable, unshakable, and trustworthy until the end. In all that is true, if I walked out now, I would defeat everything I had ever taught them. What am I to do?* She looked toward Melanie and remembered she had promised to protect her.

The two Conchida leaders had never left Liana's side. Cain placed his hand on her right shoulder. Abel touched her other shoulder for support. "We are with you all the way. No matter what, life or death, we are with you to the end."

Liana was grateful. "The two of you are very special to me. Your loyalty and dedication had been beyond measure. I am sure Melanie feels the same way."

Melanie glanced over at them. "We would not have made it this far without the two of you and the others." She then brought her focus to Liana. "Miss Liana, remember it will take all three necklaces to open the door to the third kingdom. This cannot be done without you or your children, and in the process, this will help me locate my family."

"You are right, dear, as you had kept your word and helped me find my children. I am also a person of my word. I will help you locate your family as soon as we find the gifts for the king. I can't be separated from my girls and Roger ever again."

Melanie wrapped her arms around Liana, drawing strength from her. Liana asked. "Well, let's go. What are we waiting for? I am sure we have a long journey ahead of us." The young girl wiped happy tears out of her eyes. Liana let go of Melanie and found herself laughing at the man with the enormous rock head.

"To infinity and beyond!" Granite shouted. He beamed at Emily, knowing she had a friend back home named Buzz Light Year.

Chapter Fifteen

With Hope There Is a Way

THE VISION OF THE QUEST

Wolf Fang and Zoroc, followed by Sorrelle and Bork, returned to the open gates to speak to their master Sir Bronze. Wolf Fang screamed words of defeat. "We found Liana with the Quest. Liana and her children are nearing the Third Kingdom and becoming stronger in power! We were forced to retreat!"

Bronze was furious. "I should have known if I want something done right, I must do it myself. My spying bats seconds ago informed me they are near the door of the portal of no return. So be it if I must lose the present to gain my future. It is time for me to enter the fray and lead you duds to victory, stand back while I enter the portal of no return. Thanks to you idiots. I could have been ruler here, as well as there! I have enough power to do this a couple of times. It is time I use it wisely to get what I want!" Bronze rushed through an open door that just appeared. He knew he could make no mistakes. Within seconds he stood before his riffraff's.

His eyes shone with fury. "You had failed me again! I am enraged at how far the Quest had taken the brats with the keys to my freedom. I will have them crawling for mercy! I will no longer underestimate King James' knights involved in aiding Liana's little terrors and now aiding Liana with her Protectors. Those little insufficient specks! What are they to me but a nuisance, trying to gain my goal and you fools!" Bronze glared at Wolf Fang and Zoroc, then eyed up Sorrelle and Bork. "Whenever I try to get my hands on those necklaces or when the Quest's backs are in the corner, you let them escape! I am tired of your whining!"

Wolf Fang nervously asked, "What is your wish, master?"

Bronze shouted, "Victory, of course! Send out your quickest, most cautious spy. I want every movement the Quest makes and numbers, yes! This time I want correct numbers in my hands. Every time I turn around, it seems like the Quest is growing. I desire to know the powers each is equipped with, but due to a lack of information, you provided me. I know nothing! I must know the names of those who are leading them. Now go while I plan for my total success!"

Wolf Fang walked backward from his master's presence and remembered a different encounter. In His Wrath, he mercilessly struck him with hard blows across his hunched back with his heavy spiked stick. He still carried the wounds. The black wolverine slipped out of Bronze sight and snarled at full volume. He screamed out his master's commands to a Shank. "Report back to me at once with results and no excuses! Just results!" The Shank gave the command to his group of scorpions. They left to take up the task of doing Bronze's will, too, desiring their master's approval.

After witnessing Bronze trickery with what the Quest was up against, King Triune decided to assist his allies in finding the entrance to the third kingdom. Graven was pleased with his decision, for Bronze mastering his scheming plans to reach the hidden door made it more difficult. After hours of strenuous traveling, they entered an unknown portal inside the second kingdom in the land of no return, not knowing where they were. Graven inside the portal pressed hard to find the door to the third kingdom. He recognized King James need to return to his people. He understood the fears they had of the Enoxs and the evil Malock. His men needed the support and confidence a king gives his people.

Graven's mind was far from the beauty Alicia was breathing in. No matter where she walked or looked, in all directions, it was peaceful. Liana and Melanie marveled with her, listening to the breathtaking music created by the soft breezes brushing in harmony against tall, full trees, marvelous in splendor. There was a delightful feeling with nothing to fear—they enjoyed the overwhelming fulfillment of the waters and forests and mountains. They were losing themselves in peace and contentment, such calmness, forgetting to be on the lookout for the enemy, when unknowingly all beheld the coming of the Twiddles, foot-tall resembled little elves and flew, similar to fairies. The warriors were fascinated by the little creatures'.

One Twiddle asked, "How may we be of service to such a great host?"

King Triune spoke in a stern voice. "We seek the Third Kingdom." The Twiddles began to jabber amongst themselves in a language foreign to all of them. Emily giggled. "Mom, they're so ugly it makes them look cute. May I have one? It will be kinda like the cat I never got. Please!"

THE VISION OF THE QUEST

Granite couldn't let this one pass by. "Well, Emily. Don't you still want Acorn for your pet? All he needs is a tight leash."

Acorn retaliated, "I'll give you Granite's pile of rocks to take home after I break that hard skull of his."

King Triune paid no mind as the Twiddles chatter became louder. Graven wondered what the little things were saying when he overheard Roger. "Alicia, these munchkins sound like the UFO aliens that we watched on my iPod not long ago. Remember how cool it was?" Graven had heard enough crazy things. "I don't know who sounds more foreign—these twinkle toes beneath my feet or you kids, with the strange words you speak, but I would like to know more of this eye-pot your kingdom has. It sounds interesting."

"No, no," Roger laughed. "It's an iPod. Pot is a whole other story and bad for you, too, if it's not used properly for medicine."

Graven shook his head in confusion. "How is a flower pot bad for you? What kingdom are you from?"

"Surely, not a kingdom that has talking animals and peculiar-looking ones, too," Roger said, smiling.

"Who are you calling peculiar-looking ..." Graven words were left hanging, as the first Twiddle at last spoke up. "I had words amongst my kind. We know of this Third Kingdom that concerns you. We can lead you there in peace if this is your desire."

King Triune nodded toward Graven in agreement to follow the Twiddles, but first, he consulted with Quantum. "Do you have any vibes concerning the little creatures?" Quantum answered. "I cannot read their minds in this place, but it's funny. My Pathfinders and I can commute with all of you."

King Triune thought, what harm can they do. He looked down at his feet and spoke. "Yes, lead on." The Twiddles led the hosts with laughter, again speaking in their foreign language. Graven, after a while, sensed something was seriously wrong, yet the little things looked innocent. King Triune sensed it too, again he wondered, *what could these little things do?*

He heard White Lightning converse with Roger. "Why is it I feel uneasy as if we are sheep being led to the slaughter."

"Well, the little things do seem to know where they're going; besides, would not our leaders know what is best for us?" Roger replied.

White Lightning still felt a tug of uncertainty, and listened as Alicia shared quietly. "It's hard to believe they can lead us to the final kingdom this easily." White Lightning agreed with her. They became hypnotized in the sounds they heard, while the Twiddles paraded around them happily. King Triune, unsure again, questioned. "Quantum, do you or your Pathfinders yet sense anything out of the ordinary?"

"Again, oddly, our sensors have not been working in places of these sorts. I don't understand why, but they do look innocent."

"I guess you are right." King Triune answered while the Twiddles chitter-chattered pleased to have gained their trust.

As for Bronze, he was not a man to be trusted as he finished fiercely scheming. He had Wolf Fang return to his presence. Wolf Fang slanted his head slightly, humbling himself before his master. Wolf Fang hid his hatred from him that Bronze had become as much a beast as he. Grinding his teeth, he asked, "What is your next strategic move, master?"

Bronze answered sharply. "I am furious; Liana slipped out of my hands. When we find them, I no longer want Melanie dead. I want her to regret what she has stolen from me. She will seek death, but I will not allow it. She will die slowly with anguish and suffering—there is an entrance from the point of no return. We will arrive there and wait patiently for our spoil, but not a scratch is to be made on Liana. Do I make myself clear?"

"Master, what in the world are we standing here for?" Wolf Fang asked. "This portal is everlasting, without end, a kingdom only one way in and one way out. We should have already been out of here?" Bronze angrily smashed the wolverine with an extreme force across his head. The strong blow caused his knuckles to bleed.

Wolf Fang tried everything within him not to snarl. The first taste of Bronze's blood upon his tongue, he would crush his bones inside his strapping jaws. He knew this was not the day to bring him to his knees in shame, still in need of Sir Bronze's assistance. Wolf Fang raged inside. *"When this war is ended. I will turn on that jerk and kill him."*

Bronze firmly gripped his sword in the hand of his bloody knuckles. "My strategic plan is no concern of yours. At less, I bring it up to you! Now, let's go! I need to regain all that was lost. Time is essential."

The uncaring man and his beasts moved hastily. As for the Quest and the others, days and nights had passed. The beauty of the eternal portal no longer intoxicates them. King Triune's men grew more impatient, desiring to get home to their wives and children to ensure no harm came to them. "When are we ever going to arrive?" Croc asked the leader of the Twiddles.

"You must trust me. We are getting closer, and upon our arrival, none will have to risk their lives again. It will be a safe place. It will be like living in heaven."

The twinkle glanced over at the kids. Alicia, and Roger, Emily, and Melanie, because of their youthfulness, were trapped in some kind of time frame, unaware of the true reality of time not realizing hours were days of traveling; unlike King Triune and his men, and the others who shook themselves free from this lie.

Though, Alicia became annoyed with the little creatures. She wondered, *what do these rodents know of heaven?* The Twiddle's squeaking voices became exasperating to Alicia and everyone. Alicia pulled her hair back into a ponytail, thinking to herself. *They sound like rats looking for food, but I wonder who's on their food chain list? But then again, what am I thinking? The things are aggravating but cute and seemingly harmless. They probably eat berries.*

She watched the Twiddles speak joyfully in their unknown tongue and wondered if they understood her thoughts. They came closer to the hidden door to bring them out of the endless land, but another was added to their fold, unbeknownst to the Twiddles. Chip became one of them. He listened to their jibber-jabber as they spoke of their master, waiting on the other side of the door to conquer his prey, a door that was a complete lie to the Quest.

The leader of the Twiddles spoke: "Out of your hands, Master, and into the pit of our stomachs. We will hand over your Liana, as promised; yours for pure pleasure, and Melanie, to be tortured to death, as she deserves, stealing your pride and joy from you, but the griffin, the unicorn, the cheetah, and all the rest belong to us. But Master, the rock man will be no use to us. I need you to do away with him!"

Chip could not see Bronze but could hear his voice. "Granite will be no problem. He is not to be feared! I will blast him out of this place and into the next kingdom!" Bronze gleamed at the thought of it.

The Twiddle's leader sneered hysterically with the other Twiddles. "We shall be rewarded greatly by our master, delivering these irreverent, disdainful beings into his hands. Our bellies will be satisfied, feasting upon the Quest, King Triune, and his men. We will not need a meal for a long while."

Full of eagerness, it was too much stimulation for the Twiddle's leader to talk about. He and his forces were starving beyond words. His pointy devilish teeth showed. The twiddle turned his back to his victims, which were only a stone throw away and clamped shut his mouth, stretched out like a big, round balloon, hoping he wasn't seen.

Chip was no longer blindsided. He heard enough. Secretly he transformed into himself and, within a short period, reached Graven climbing up into his fur. He couldn't get his words out fast enough as he spoke into his ear. "We are nearing a false exit, but it's a death trap. The only way out is to turn around quickly—go back to where we first entered this place."

Graven asked, surprised, "Why? We have traveled so far. What is it that you had found out?"

Chip responded, "Bronze is on the other side! The Twiddles are evil. We have to go back!"

King Triune was with his men walking upfront. Graven swooped in his direction and flew rocket speed to him. "You must stop your people and refrain from this spot and return to the entrance of the door of no return, or all is lost!"

King Triune heard Graven's urgency and went into action. He yelled a loud command. "We must stop and return!" The Twiddles heard. They all, in unison, shouted, "No!" changing from sweet little Twiddles into the form of hideous demons preparing to attack, showing forth their bladed teeth, with nauseating globs of green pus oozing down their fat lips. Liana attended to Emily. The rank smell was exceedingly potent. It didn't settle with the child's stomach. Emily threw up, gagging.

Graven shot powerful beams hitting the Twiddles in one powerful blast, disintegrating them into ashes. Granite watched the Twiddles dust blow away with his humorous grin. He declared. "You could have saved some fun for me. You always have to be the hero."

"Always a comic, aren't you?" Graven answered. "We have lost days from reaching our destiny. For King James's sake, I hope all is not lost!"

But two remaining Twiddles, unknowing to them, had miraculously escaped. The two secretly opened a concealed door—a secret passage unknown to the Quest—to seek their master, that their plan had failed. The two reached Bronze's ear as he still waited impatiently outside the false entrance for the Quest to fall into his lap.

Upon hearing the report, Bronze became inflamed with hatred, numb with boiling rage. An abhorrent beam of fire came out of the pits of his inner being and out of his hellish eyes. He consumed the last of the Twiddles.

His body became rigid, "I am so tired of failures! I am so tired of excuses! I demand results!" Bronze led his hordes inside the portal of no return to pursue the chosen ones to destroy them.

The Quest with the others backtracked their steps and moved speedily to break free out of that place. The warriors had been on the go for days, hungry and exhausted and needing rest. Chip transformed into a falcon and checked out what was ahead of them. He returned but was being chased. Everyone heard in a far distance loud, hissing noises. Chip proclaimed, as he landed and transformed back into himself. "Bronze is within this portal and his hordes are close on our tails." Chip swung into action with a diversion before anyone could share their thoughts.

He spoke hastily. "I have a plan if you would like to try it."

King Triune's adrenaline was running. "Speak on if only it will buy us more time."

"We know Bronze is rapidly closing in on us. I need everyone to remain completely still, with no movement whatsoever. Similar to how Miss Liana had us camouflaged with berry and honey smells, but in this case, I can become a vast rock wall and camouflage around all of you. I hope it fools Bronze and his hordes and perhaps give us enough time to escape through the entry we had first entered. Are you with us on this?" Chip nodded for King Triune's approval.

"Make it so," He responded and commanded the others. "Comrades, be silent. Do not move an inch. If you have to sneeze, hold your breath. If this plan fails, lives will be at stake." He looked at Emily. "Do you understand, how important it is to remain quiet?" Emily, seeing the Twiddles turn beyond ugly and reeking of strong odor, nervously nodded yes.

Granite picked up Emily and lightly tossed her up into the air. "I tell you what. Suppose you don't make a peep. I will toss you so high that it will make your mom scream."

She beamed and quietly whispered, "Three tosses, and it's a done deal."

He sat her back down. "What, little girl? You drive a hard bargain. I don't know if my back will kill me first or your mother."

Chip heard the sounds getting closer. "Okay, rock head, it's time to be quiet." He moved into action formed himself into a substantial rock wall surrounding everyone. No sooner was his mission complete than Bronze arrived with his hordes. Orion saw Melanie was shaking. He quietly wrapped his arm around her shoulder. Bronze slowed down near the immense camouflage wall. He thought looked out of place. He searched everywhere and sensed something was wrong but saw nothing. Wolf Fang and Zoroc sniffed around. They sensed a trace but they too saw no one. Bronze head hit the roof, not finding Liana, her children, and their necklaces. He pressed on a little longer, and was slammed dunk that they slipped through his fingers. He clanged his hands into a tight fist. His nails made his hands bleed. Bronze left the area and begin searching elsewhere but in the wrong direction for the Quest.

King Triune and Graven traveled once more toward the door of no return. Roger noticed Emily's restlessness and spoke calmly to her. "Don't worry. We will be there soon."

THE VISION OF THE QUEST

Liana overheard and said to Roger, "As long as we are together, we have hope, and as long as we have hope, I know we can make it."

Liana was glad King Triune had everyone make camp. She watched Graven take to the skies to search the area for any danger. While, White Lightning and Spot stood guard. Watching Granite as he honored his word.

He threw Emily high into the air. Emily felt she could touch the clouds. Excited, Emily spotted a garden close by. "Food!" she shouted happily and pointed in that direction. Liana and everyone beyond hungry didn't think of the consequences and rushed to the garden. Soon afterward, the food caused them to fall into a deep sleep, not yet, figuring out the place was a portal of no return. They were fighting to shake themselves awake, lost in horrifying dreams and visions, taking over their senses and controlling how they think, feel, and believe. The portal was a trick of the enemy, giving them a false sense of peace, where lies appeared real, a place where the strong eventually feel the effects of having disturbing dreams and visions of the future—terribly twisted with a bad outcome.

They all tossed and turned screaming out their love ones names. "No, no, no!" Liana cried out, dreaming, feeling her children ripped out of her arms by a wild beast bleeding and crying out for her help. She couldn't shake herself free. She panicked until she heard a still, quiet voice, remind her. "I have never left you or forsaken you." She screamed. "The God of the heavens and the earth wake me from this terrible lie!" the power of her God shook the ground, and the earth trembled under her. Liana awakened, with Granite and Orion, and the others. Melanie was the only one still dreaming. Orion nudged her, but she did not budge. She tossed and turned violently, screaming as if being tortured by something brutal and vicious.

Only Melanie knew the depths of terror she was experiencing in her brutal nightmare, which seemed real with what Bronze's wickedness was capable of doing unfolding before her eyes. Her heartbeat was hard against her chest. Melanie covered in sweat as her body convulsed, jerking all around. Orion placed his arms around her to calm her fears, but it made it worse. She thought it was Bronze. He let go of her.

Liana came to Melanie's aid tried her best to awaken her. It seemed impossible. She wasn't shaking free. Liana cried out for the young girl who had saved her life, "This is Bronze's doing! That wicked man!" She exclaimed as she sat on the ground and rocked Melanie in her arms, the only thing she could think to do.

Melanie suffering endless torture endured the agony of watching Bronze cutting down her loved ones with no mercy and getting satisfaction from it, taunting the terrified girl, "Look what you have caused your family, death and an early grave. I get the fulfillment that you are next. Who can save you, now, wench?" Bronze jerked his dark head back with mockery. Melanie watched her mother drop to the bloody floor with the slaying of her father and then her little sister and twin brothers, crying out for her help. Her whole family now lay before her, dead. Bronze ridiculed sternly. Stared harshly into Melanie's face. "Come, Melanie! What you witnessed of your family is minor compared to what you will feel under my blade. They died quietly. It's your turn to seek death and not find it! I think I am going to have a grand time."

Melanie saw a torture chamber. Instantly, she felt a sword penetrate the back of her neck, sensing the touch of the cold, sharp blade. She screamed, knowing this was the end of her life, a corpse to be thrown out with her parents and siblings, most likely thrown inside the dark dungeon on top of the other dead, rotting bodies. She felt rats nibbling on her flesh, even though she wasn't dead yet. Melanie began to gasp for air. Liana saw the girl's face go pale. Life was being sapped from her. Liana immediately cried out to her source of power, reaching the heavens. She fell to her face and prayed.

Melanie screamed one last time, feeling her last breath being taken from her, but as she heard Liana praying, she began to shake free from her hellish nightmare by a brilliant, beautiful light. Granite was beside Liana and leaned over Melanie to see if she was okay.

She finally opened her eyes. Granite's face, at first, was a big blur. Melanie screamed louder. "Help, help!" Immediately Liana with Orion calmed her down. She finally realized where she was. She touched the back of her neck to confirm Bronze's cold sword didn't cut her. Her vision cleared. She slowly became herself again. Melanie looked up at

Granite and desperately pleaded, "Granite, next time, please do not be standing over me when I wake up."

Granite reasoned with her, "Come, come, now, is the sight of me that displeasing to you?"

"Well, you're not someone I would drag home to show my Mama."

"Oh, we have a new comedian, but I do see your point," Granite clowned around. Melanie seeing Liana thought it was funny and relaxed a little more.

She couldn't relax much. King Triune knew not to slack and had everyone on the move again, traveling a day's journey until they finally located the original door they first entered. They were glad to exit the portal, overcome with great relief.

The Pathfinders experienced relief as well. Their sensors could finally sense life. The Quest, including the others, were inspired, knowing it was about time they were on their way to finding the Third Kingdom. Though they were bone-weary, this knowledge generated enough strength to keep them motivated to run the race and stay the course.

Chapter Sixteen

Many Faces of Stone

THE VISION OF THE QUEST

Bronze traveled to the main door of the portal of no return and found no sight of the Quest. Aggravated after failing his search Bronze returned to his mansion and entered his museum. He created a portal through his wickedness, a strength that came from his conquering and overpowering different kingdoms, giving him access into spiritual realms of domains, of many devilish portals, places filled with evil, where light has no dominion and in this dreary bottomless pit of death are souls chained to rock walls and tables and inside pits of fire, tortured for eternity, feeling a continued emptiness of complete loneliness. Unfortunately, a realm that once a soul enters, there is no escape. They are trapped in this awful place full of ghastly, frightening, evil spirits on the move to bring more souls to their fold. Bronze loved the thought of higher power; these cunning spirits deceived him in return for his soul, giving him the power to create an illusion of lies with the breath of a word for ruin to hurt others, therefore gaining more control over all the kingdoms. These strengths, however, were extremely limited. He was aware of each failure. His power became more exhausted and grew weaker. Bronze's warped mind used his evil to form a clear barrier, a wall of deception, that would cause the Quest to walk into his concealed trap, leading them into his illusion of fears.

The Quest and the others continued their long journey searching for the Third Kingdom, still fatigued and running low on their supplies. The Pathfinders sensed darkness but didn't know where it was coming from. Bronze's up to his malicious mischief again. They walked right into the devious man's trap of uncertainties. They would face their worst nightmares, except this time, they would not be dreaming.

"Weird," they all thought. The sun disappeared, becoming pitch-black. Many cried out as others complained. "What manner of force is this that we are dealing with?"

Graven wondered himself, as Alicia helped Roger light a few torches, he had taken off his back. Immediately, Chip became a pole of light.

Allowing, Graven to see somewhat as he spoke sensibly to the king. "How much more can they endure until we come to our destination? We may not get there at all if we don't get there soon. But as we push on, my friend, it will be wise to command Cain and Abel to go to the rear for any onslaughts from behind. I will fly ahead to keep watch for sudden attacks."

"So be it," King Triune replied.

Graven moved with haste within the darkness. Everyone heard a threatening storm. Their hearing was correct. It was a matter of minutes before hail the size of golf balls fell to the ground. Everyone ran for cover toward the mountains spotted a short distance ahead. The ones with wings flew across, not certain what they may crash into. King Triune's men ran and tripped over each other but made it into several caves. A number of them ran under a substantial overhang of rocks that protruded from off the mountains. The hail and wind blew out their torches. They could only see through Chip's lamppost, which wasn't easy. Chip complained. "Granite, I hear your heavy breathing. You better not step your big foot on me."

"That's one way of putting out your light." Granite made fun of.

Chip ignored him as the bizarre storm continued for about an hour. Finally, the dark skies cleared, and the danger of the hail lifted. Everyone was put at ease, but not for long. Above their heads was one huge, unusual steady cloud.

"Something is not right!" Graven shouted. "This storm cloud is abnormal. How is it only a few feet above our heads?" As soon as Graven expressed his concern, the dark cloud not only burst forth spiders immediately. Brown and black hairy spiders emerged from the ground and every crack and corner within and around the mountain and under the cliff.

Emily and the girls panicked, petrified the spiders would go into their mouths as they screamed. Roger ran over to Alicia, knocking countless spiders off her back. Liana and Spot quickly sheltered Emily. Melanie ran in circles with shaking hands and knocked off what she could. Orion appeared behind her and brushed them out of her hair. The others ran uneasily in different directions while crushing many of them with their hands.

King Triune yelled out, "Everyone to me!" He saw his men's different routes and knew he had to bring order. His men, with difficulty, attempted to listen.

Ironically, that fast another shocker occurred. The climate went from warm and became ice cold. It began to snow. The spiders dropped dead. King Triune's men and the Quest would have frozen to death, but they worked together and collected wood to burn campfires. It was becoming a team effort to stay alive. The leaders spoke among themselves. King Triune questioned. "What place is this no matter where we go? It's as if our worst fears are coming upon us." Quantum spoke up. "You are correct. I sense nothing but darkness here."

King Triune looked toward Graven as he shared, "I agree. Somehow we have entered into an unknown territory not familiar to us. We must be caught in a dimension of our terrors. There has to be a way out of here." Cain and Abel shook their heads in agreement.

As the leaders continued speaking. Liana was glad the snow slowly stopped, and the chilly winds calmed down. The group picked up their belongings and moved on only to enter another illusion trapped inside where mirrors were far and wide and fear had spread like cancerous cells, tearing away at their insides piece by piece, slowly removing boldness, courage, and strength from them.

Liana asked. "What is it with mirrors in your dimension?"

Everyone could see their reflection but didn't know where to move. The many mirrors reminded Liana of a fun house, only one could take them the correct way. They surely didn't want to select the wrong one, not knowing if they would make it out of there alive.

"Follow me! I know the way out!" Melanie shouted at the top of her voice. She remembered the many hallways in Bronze's mansion. She had become familiar with the twist and turns and saw how the mirrors had a similar pattern. "This again is the hands of Bronze! Does that man ever give up?" Melanie questioned disturbed. Everyone was quick to follow her. She traveled through the maze of glass mirrors when finally, she came to an abrupt stop and searched and fumbled for a door but found none. "It's weird. It should be here." Melanie said. Liana perked up. She knew without a shadow of a doubt within the long weeks held captive inside Bronze's mansion. This was the spot that always led her back to her bedroom prison. She would not give up and searched up and down the mirror. Liana was stunned as she looked into the mirror. She beheld an image of herself, staring back into her face, yet, seeing herself dressed as royalty, her hair pinned back in an old-fashioned style. "Who am I?" she gasped and placed her hand over her mouth, seeing the image looking back at her, beckoning her to come forth. Liana, as before, knew it was the right choice.

Liana grabbed Melanie's and Emily's hand, as all three walked right through the glass in the blink of an eye. The three were out of everyone's sight. Spot quickly followed to protect Emily. Cain and Abel moved fast for the safety of Liana. White Lightning stayed near Roger and Acorn beside Alicia, vanishing through the mirror and the others followed.

Graven was the last to enter. It brought them all out to an open sky. Graven flew upward, searched the area, and returned to the Quest, "I don't know how, but we are still in the portal of fear. We must push forth and travel on foot with no hesitation." He looked toward Liana. "Pray to your God that we are going in the right direction." He was unsure how after receiving the gifts. Would they get the gifts back to King James without confronting all their enemies.

Liana perceived his worry and pressed a rewind button back to Graven. "The Spirit has been with us, and I pray he continues to be with us until the end."

As the words slipped from her mouth, she listened to Roger respond with a troubled tone having doubts. "Will the Spirit continue to be with us? What of King Triune and his people? The evil forces will try to rid them from the face of the earth by assisting us, and will our allies support us when we need them the most?"

Liana became quiet, speculating on the outcome. *What of the allies?* She wondered herself. *Will they be true to their words?* Liana put the thought aside, as she and the others walked far, following her intuition. Her directions again proved right, lessening the burden of finding and exiting the illusions of fears. Worn out and drained, they continued to push forward to the mark of their calling.

With Graven and King Triune's help after traveling for days, they finally neared the Third Kingdom, a hop, skip, and jump about a mile away. King Triune decided to have his men set camp. He set plans in

THE VISION OF THE QUEST

motion for the Quest and Liana's Protectors to follow him to the third Kingdom's door. He would bring enough soldiers with him but leave most of his men with Granite inside the camp, noticing his men were tired. He assured Liana. "I am well aware only the chosen ones who embraced the keys—You, Alicia, and Emily—could enter to receive what is needed, as well as Roger. Once we reach the outside of the portal, I will guard it and give my life to keep all of you safe. I will also have a few of my selected men with me standing guard outside the entry until you return. But my forces were the ones I left behind at camp. I believe they would assist with any adversary that comes their way."

King Triune looks toward Graven, Liana, and her kids. He spoke as a courageous true warrior. "With saying that, with Graven's guidance, I will lead you to the entrance of the third Kingdom not far from here. Now, we must move like the wind. Bronze brings death and death is on the move."

King Triune was correct. Bronze freely released his power to a bold, harrowing conspirator named Medusa, standing for many faces of stone. The trickster with great influence over this ghastly woman. His orders were firm and direct. Bronze communicated to her mind: "Slay them all, place Melanie in chains but keep Liana safe and retrieve the keys for me!" Medusa was pleased with such a mission. She waited unwaveringly and stayed hidden near the portal door of the Third Kingdom until the Quest arrived.

During this time, Bronze received word from his two spying bats that rushed into his presence. The tallest bat screeched in a high-pitched tone that annoyed Bronze. "Master! The Quest is nearing the portal of the third kingdom. Liana and her kids are tired, resting on top Graven."

The shorter hideous bat's wings were damaged from his previous battle. He sensed a need to receive glory. The bat shrieked loudly, "Master! Would this be a good time to attack, seeing how tired the chosen ones are? King Triune's men sit about a mile from the third door. His soldiers seemed fatigued and stayed back inside their camp along with Granite. Granite will be a hard one to bring down. Should we attack King Triune's camp of his mighty men now that we have the advantage?"

Bronze was pleased with the report. "When the cats are away, the mouse plays." He contacted his army of repulsive creatures, giving orders to capture his enemies and take them to his ancient domain bound in chains. He was ecstatic, lifted his arms toward heaven, he screamed with pride, "Nothing can stop me now, not even God!"

King Triune arrived at the front entrance of the gate. The Third Kingdom's portal was only a few feet away; none of them could believe their eyes, their hearts overzealous, the Quest shouting with joy and feeling the exhilaration of a successful triumph.

Until, Quantum spoke up. "Something is not right. I sense danger lurking close to us, but I cannot pinpoint its location."

No sooner than he finished speaking, an arrow skimmed King Triune's side, slightly wounding him.

The Quest followed the arrow and beheld Medusa. This treacherous creature had slipped out behind a mass of rocks, standing elevated and superior in front of the portal, preventing the chosen ones from entering.

She was grotesque to look upon. Her waist down shaped like a horse's front legs, and layers upon layers of dreadful snakes, hissing and slithering, circling her skull. A repulsive odor emerged when she opened her mouth of destruction with spiky, jagged teeth. The Quest noted how the woman's scarlet eyes shone with gross evilness. A warrior's heart could faint.

The Quest moved with caution closer to the portal door. Medusa wore a determined expression, appearing unshakeable. She began attacking them with her beguiling eyes.

Graven yelled out. "Look away from her eyes! Or turn into stone!"

"Not this again!" Melanie exclaimed, troubled. The Quest wasn't sure what the young girl meant, but Liana and the Protectors understood fully. White Lightning realized in that instant; that it was crucial. He observed Roger becoming enchanted, staring into her windows of death. Fast, he knocked the young man to the ground. He covered his eyes with his long paw being not only his guardian but had become a trustworthy friend.

Graven observed Spot in action, sheltering Emily, while Cain and Abel sheltered Liana and Melanie from harm. Acorn didn't have to say a word. From the corner of his eye, he looked at Alicia's position for battle without coming into contact with Medusa's rebellious deadly stare.

Graven admired that she had the same strength as her mother, Liana. Alicia reminded him of Queen Leah for a moment. She looked nothing like her with her dark hair and tanned skin. It was how she positioned herself, held her ground, and gave that look of the strength of mind and willpower. She sensed Graven staring at her, Alicia glanced over at him. Graven nodded his head of approval. Friendship had developed with a spirit of unity amongst them.

Bronze overlooked Alicia and clung his fist toward his trophy as he stood proud and arrogant, watching from his oval mirror, which enabled him to access others with a simple hand gesture. The mirror craftsmanship was eye appealing, with gold designs circling the edges and bold letters carved into the wood with the prophecy of old.

Bronze stared non-stop into it. His eyes didn't flinch. "Liana shall be mine!" he breathed. He became outraged as the mirror stopped working. He kicked over a small nearby table, disturbed that he needed three stones from ages-old linked like a puzzle within the frame to have its full power and potential. It disturbed him to the core only catches slight pieces before the images fade away, and stirred to no end that when he eventually finds all three treasured stones of emerald, ruby, and sapphire, Bronze will see the history of the past, the presence, and the now, anything his corrupt heart desires for a certain length of time.

He again stared into it and noticed it was working once more. Full of discord, he missed hearing Graven voice forcefully. "This creature is the crookedness of Bronze!" Graven eyed the malice defiant challenger. "Stand aside! This does not concern the likes of you!"

Medusa held her head high as if the griffin was a joke as the many snakes danced upon her head. Bronze gave her a boastful spirit to combat all who opposed her. She spoke dauntlessly. "I am Medusa.

What hope do you have to slay one that cannot be slain? What chance do you have to get past me to your destination? You never met one like me. I am your hell on wheels. Come and meet your end!"

Graven took a bold step forward. Alicia bravely stepped in front of him. She spoke with the courage to conquer. "We come against you with the hope of our salvation and the faith that moves mountains! You are but one mountain that shall be removed!" Roger stepped forward to defend Alicia.

With a forked tongue and decayed lips, Medusa looked at her adversary and expressed no alarm. She was a beast of mythology and strong stature, bound and determined to have total control. She swung her decompose green, six wiry arms of flesh, taunting the Quest and their company. In each hand, she held a sword, waving them relentlessly to strike down her first victim. She edged closer to attack Alicia and Roger. Graven blasted his rays countless times toward her. With the power of her swords, Medusa shields off Graven's hot beams of light. He only pierced one of her arms. She threw back her head, mocking them all.

King Triune secretly crept up. He jumped onto her back, and, with a powerful blow, he ran his dagger down into her spine. She shrugged him off like a strand of unwanted hair and flung him high with Chip's quick thinking becoming a soft pile of sand. He landed safely on his back and jumped back up. King Triune again stood his ground, running toward Medusa with his two-edged sword, but there was no fight. She was too powerful. Instead, her sword sliced into his arm. He stepped back to regain his bearing. Melanie witnessed the deep slash it left him. She moved swiftly, with a needle and thread in her apron, hoping to sew the gash. He would not allow it. He was determined to help the others fight this cruel insult. Melanie did manage to tie a cloth tightly around his wound to help stop the blood flow.

Medusa strikes again. Alicia daringly aimed her bow and shot an arrow right into her chest. Roger moved fearlessly and threw his spear with precise aim, striking into her stubborn heart. Two of Congo's stingers flew full force, ripping their horns into her repeatedly, but to no avail; both Stingers hollered out. "For the cause!" and they had taken their last breath. Sadly, out of twelve, only two Stingers were left.

Roger was frustrated that two lives ended because of that ruthless thing. "What kind of flesh is this—airplane material?" He questioned impatiently. Graven was upset as well. But glanced at Roger with interest of what is an airplane and stored the word in the back of his mind. With a simple twist of her wrist, Medusa snapped off Alicia's arrow. She jerked Roger's spear out of her chest, looking at the two youth with a luminous sneer. The snakes went wild. Despite Bronze's warning, she edged toward Liana, preparing to strike a violent blow of death.

Medusa had plans of her own. She desired Bronze for herself with a determined, jealous heart. She craved Liana's death and pictured her six snakes firmly gripping the woman's throat, squeezing the very life out of her, choking off her dreams. Liana was not even aware of it yet, preventing them from being fulfilled.

Medusa aimed her arms toward the gorgeous Liana as her many snakes danced with eagerness, slithering back and forth and hissing, waiting to strike their lethal poison into their victims, desiring a taste of warm, fresh blood which to feed Medusa and render her even more powerful.

Medusa's arms flew toward her. Emily screamed out, "Mom!" Spot held back the frightened little Goldilocks.

Alicia and Roger ran full force in an attempt to overtake the abomination after witnessing Medusa's magnitude of strength. Liana shouted with all her might until her lungs could burst. "No, Alicia and Roger!"

Medusa mocked. "Oh, what a shame your children are ready to die so soon!" Her appalling disfigurement moved to strike a blow of hatred upon her seed. She was amused as she watched the horror in Liana's eyes close to striking down her children cold-bloodedly, just for the fun of it. Medusa relished with content, sensing that having the upper hand was only moments away.

"No!" Liana screamed, again, panic-stricken. Her legs gave way. She fell to the ground and wept with loud lamentations, unable to watch who meant the most to her being brutally murdered mercilessly right before her.

Medusa chuckled even more, enjoying Liana's anguish. Both young warriors shouted a battle cry and felt the air from Medusa's swords swinging in all directions. They ducked her fatal blows, and, as Alicia and Roger jumped back onto their feet, they smelled her foul odor.

Graven saw it was a losing battle and nodded at Cain and Abel. The two Conchida's flew quickly and picked up Alicia and Roger, dropping them safely away from her. "My mother is in grave danger!" Alicia hollered as she and Roger again took off running, focusing their attention on the creature without looking into her eyes.

Liana could barely lift her head as she witnessed the two racing back to the destructive back stabber. In a rush with everything in Liana. She jumped to her feet sharp-witted and yelled, "Take me and not my babies. It is I that you seek! Please, I beg of you!" Desperate tears flooded her eyes. Liana surrendered her arms in the air and walked toward the heartless creature. "My life for theirs!"

Medusa, unaware that Bronze, stood inside his museum of old in the private quarters of his sanctuary, gripping his mirror in the palm of his hand. He heard Liana scream again, "My life for theirs!" He experienced fear for the first time in a long time. Bronze could not bear the thought of losing her. He opened his mouth wide and screamed extremely loud that his chest had tightened, "Nooooooooooooooo!"

Tears slipped from his dark eyes, realizing he would be fighting for the kingdoms in vain without Liana the one he fought for so long to have standing beside him. He again cried out as he did the day Queen Leah slipped from his hands. "Nooooooooooooooo!"

Liana thought she heard the echoing of a familiar voice. Within a millisecond, she was caught up in another time and place, gazing into Bronze's eyes, saying her final goodbye, touching the depths of his heart, and crushing his dreams by her decisions.

Liana again questioned, "Who am I?" She was brought back to reality by the screams of her children.

"Mother, run!" Alicia cried out in dismay. Terror filled the air as all stood alarmed, expecting the horror that was about to take place.

THE VISION OF THE QUEST

Liana moved closer. She smelled Medusa's hot, putrid breath inside her nostrils. Medusa raised her swords to slice Liana up piece by piece. Her abhorrent snakes stretched forth to join the fun but were stopped. Chip dashed, jumped into Liana's arms, and transformed into a silver shield.

Medusa swung all six arms and struck this shield with such a massive force the earth trembled, and the others fell to the ground. Liana landed hard on her back and had the wind knocked out of her as she lay lifeless. Medusa thought, her for dead. Her snakes slithered as she edged closer. She glared down into the silver shield and witnessed her reflection. Startled, she shrank backward and gave an ear-piercing shriek. She saw into the depths of her wicked self and turned her into stone. Liana in a turtle pace began to move with her back still on the ground. She slowly searched around with a big headache and was overwhelmed with happiness to see her children were alive. She looked at Medusa, pleased she was a lifeless statue. Bronze was just as pleased. He nearly dropped his mirror, seeing Liana unharmed.

Alicia and Roger sat up with their heads spinning. Graven gained his footing, brushing off much dirt. Graven observed Chip transformed back into himself and shot up off the ground. Chip exclaimed, "That was the ugliest thing I have ever looked upon in my life! Even uglier than Granite, and that says a lot."

"Have you ever heard sticks and stones may break my bones but....," Granite was cut short. "You big rock head! You are made of stones. Graven and I had been right about that airless brain of yours." Chip then looked over and couldn't believe Medusa was now a boulder, motionless and not going anywhere.

Chip turned toward Graven, "Well, this looks funny. Her snakes turned to stone, hissing in all directions, a bad hair day. Wouldn't you say?"

"I agree." Graven answered with a merry heart, seeing Liana moving around and alive, "Come on, my little friend, there's a great deal more work that needs to be done."

Alicia and Roger were finally able to stand to their feet. They ran to Liana, including Emily. Alicia exclaimed, "Thank God you are alive!

We thought with a blow like that. You would have been gone! And Chip too!"

Liana said softly. Her strength drained. "My breath was knocked out of me. I could not move after quite some time. I, too, thought it was over, kids."

King Triune motioned for the chosen ones to come near the entrance of the final kingdom. He held onto his hurt arm, the deep slice needed tending to, but first, not until he ensured they were safe behind the portal door.

"Place your necklaces inside the carvings that you may enter. As I mentioned, I will remain here safeguarding the entrance until your return." Liana spoke. "King Triune, you have been good to all of us. I wish somehow, I could bless you."

"Your kids had already done enough when they had saved my people's children out of Malock's claws. This is just a little thing I have done. I wish I could do more."

Liana brought her focus toward Melanie. Hoping she would be fine when she disappeared behind the door. Melanie saw her worried expression. "Miss Liana. I will be okay and waiting for you when you return. How I see it, Orion's constantly keeping a watchful eye over me. He's not going to let me out of his sight. I will mend King Triune's wounds and ensure he receives the proper care." However, deep inside Melanie hid her fears. Liana was content, seeing Melanie was becoming braver. She turned and placed all three necklaces inside the grooves of an impressive gold door, the portal opened, and the chosen ones entered. The door slammed shut and could not open until their return.

Chapter Seventeen

FRIENDS OF THE KINGDOM

THE VISION OF THE QUEST

Bronze, fed up of his past screw-ups, suffered too many drawbacks by underestimating the Quest. The liar is prepared to reap the benefits of a greater surprise attack. He craftily planned his revenge, thinking up a brilliant stratagem to end the vision of the Quest.

His plans were coming into effect. King Triune, with Graven, White Lightning, and the others, remained guarded near the portal door, waiting faithfully, hoping all was well, a few days with no sign of Liana and her kids. King Triune, in a refreshing cool breeze, not surprised heard the Pathfinder's sensors jingle. Quantum was alarmed for what he sensed. He informed the King. "Something of a vast multitude is coming this way." The king boldly gave orders. "Quantum, go with your son and warn my soldiers within the camp to come to our assistance promptly. God speed." Quantum quickly left his side to find Orion as the king stood puzzled. Cain and Abel not far off heard the king speaking to himself. "I had commanded my men yesterday to meet me at the door of the Third Kingdom. Quantum would not have to seek them out if my order had been obeyed. What could have happened?" Cain and Abel remained quite unsure themselves.

The humidity was bad outside. King Triune's hand pressed up against the top of his sword. The young king wiped back strands of thick blonde hair matted to the sides of his face when he spotted a tall alarming bat. Bronze's spy realized he was found out. King Triune swiftly took out an arrow and placed it into his bow. Rapidly the bat turned to flee. The king, skilled not to miss his target, shot the unsightly thing through its hunchback, it ripped out his chest. The spy fell to the ground with a hard thump. Cain and Abel flew over, checking if he was dead.

Quantum was also on the move, following his orders, telepathically briefly explained the situation to his son. Orion was about to answer his father when he eyed Melanie about ten feet away, sitting silently near where the portal door had disappeared. He noticed how fearful she looked, worrying about Liana sitting there for hours. There were moments she cried softly, afraid of what might have happened. Liana was gone for days. Melanie, when Bronze's slave, had hurt her emotionally. Orion longed to hold her and comfort her. He questioned himself. *It's impossible; what will she see in me? Her nature is different than my kind.* Regardless, he transported in front of her. "My little chatterbox. I am not used to seeing you quiet. Believe it or not, I am missing that side of you." He gently placed his hand under her chin and lifted her face; their eyes met. "Please don't be so downcast. I hate to see you this way. Liana will be fine. I have to leave with my father, make sure you stay near King Triune. He will keep you safe at all cause until I return." She forced a slight smile hoping he was correct.

The young Pathfinder heard his father telepath his name a second time. "I will be back. Stay safe." He quickly disappeared and stood in front of his father, and both were transported to speak with Croc, the commander left in charge. However, though time, Croc's heart became stone-hard, holding a deep grudge over King Triune for Malock's killing his two children a deep root of resentment festered inside him, choking out the good within him. Croc craved to take over his king's rulership and often thought of betraying him. However, King Triune was unaware of how the heart of Croc, was turning dark against him.

Quantum boldly appeared before Croc, "Your king is in peril. He needs his men right away, for danger lurks in the air. I sense Bronze's hordes drawing near. It will only be a matter of time before something dreadful takes place."

"Why would I believe you and trust you, and why are you here without our beloved king?" Croc rudely questioned. "You are not of our people. We will stay and wait!"

Quantum, after several failed attempts, exclaimed, "Enough!" He transported back to King Triune and firmly spoke. "Your commander did not believe me. He dared to say that we serve Bronze and are raising a standard against you."

King Triune turned to Graven. "This has to be addressed expeditiously—Croc's putting everyone's lives into danger—even his own. I will need you to fly me there that I may take care of this matter," he then turned toward Quantum. "Know this Croc will be reprimanded."

Quantum asked. "Would it be wise for the rest of us to come with you? If Bronze comes here first and finds we are not at this location. He will search us out and maybe draw him away from the portal of the Third Kingdom and away from the chosen ones."

"I agree. It would be wiser, but unfortunately, we cannot take the chance of them exiting the portal with no one to fight for their defense. They would be left on their own to accomplish an impossible mission without the help of the remaining Quest. I had promised I would defend them at all cost. Quantum, how far is this darkness from us?"

Quantum calmly answered, "What I sense is a little more than an hour. I hope the soldiers will make it back in time to aid us."

King Triune climbed up and sat onto Graven's back. "God willing, we will return shortly." Graven spoke up. "God speed!" He took off hastily. His mighty wings propelled with such momentum. They made it to the camp within ten minutes.

Graven landed and stood erect beside King Triune. The king came in contact with Croc. "What is the meaning of not trusting the captain of the Pathfinders and disobeying my orders? We have been in their presence these past few weeks, and there has been no reason you should have distrust!"

Croc was cocky. "You were not here. I made the decision. It was in the best interests of my men, now stand aside, King Triune, that I may finish my job!" he demanded disrespectfully.

King Triune angry at his outburst spoke with authority. "Know this, Croc. I make the calls. Step down! You're no longer commander!"

Croc's face turned flaming red. He angrily drew his sword. King Triune's soldiers quickly circled and protected their king with weapons drawn.

Croc placed his sword back onto his side, dwelling on a day he would remove this hindrance from the face of the earth. He surrendered, lowered his head, throwing himself at his mercy, and manipulated. "My honorable King. I am truly sorry. I don't know what got into me. Many crazy things have happened in these last few weeks since we have helped the Quest, and with all that, we have been through with Malock. I wasn't sure that I could trust Quantum."

Under pressure, King Triune had to make a choice fast with lives at stake. He felt compassion for his commander as he recalled the day of Croc's significant loss of losing his two children. He strongly established. "I will spare your life. However, this is the last time this will happen. Step down from being commander. I will allow you to fight with the soldiers, and deal with you latter." Croc found grace in his eyes for the time being and bowed his head even more. "I shall ensure this does not happen again." Croc walked away tall and satisfied, rehearsing plans to kill his king.

King Triune yelled, in a high-pitched voice, toward his men. "We must travel fast and must not stop until we reach the portal of the third kingdom! Prepare for battle and stay alert; our adversary is as a roaring lion, seeking whom he can devour be in your full armor, with your breastplate, and your double-edged sword, your special shoes to ground your feet, and your shield to fight off the fiery darts of the wicked one!"

Their ruler raised his sword into the air. "Take courage, men! Victory shall be in our hands! We shall not be a defeated foe!" King Triune moved at a fast pace. His soldiers marched in rhythm.

No sooner had he and his soldiers reached where the portal door had disappeared. The sky became covered in complete darkness with an earsplitting sound, drawing closer to them, becoming louder and louder, nothing like they had heard before. Cain and Abel and others looked up, hearing a sound like that of many locusts. They thought wolverines, but as the darkness neared, appearing as thick, black smoke, King Triune became aware of many of Bronze's beasts—huge gargoyles shooting arrows aimed at his men.

King Triune shouted with full force, causing his throat to burn—"Shields!"

Orion speedily transported to Melanie's side and grabbed her in his arms, keeping safe the one he was falling in love with. He felt her body trembling and tried to transport her elsewhere but could not with the loud noises, and fear rampant.

Chip formed into a mighty shield to protect the Quest and the Protectors. Granite arched and covered Melanie and Orion. The two curled up tightly, keeping all parts of their bodies underneath his massive rock.

Soldiers' placed their shields above their heads in the nick of time, with arrows shooting at them in all directions. A few men fell wounded as the sharp-pointed steel penetrated between their shields; others dropped dead to the ground, hit from the side.

In an instant, out of nowhere, a big blast shook the earth. Not knowing where it came from, the Pathfinders were caught in the middle of transporting, but, as a result, they were protected from the gargoyles' sharp arrows. They only could be trapped while transporting for a short amount of time, or the mere force of energy would destroy them.

Unexpectedly, the aftershock of the vast explosion knocked them into different locations, separating them. The Pathfinders knew what to do and headed toward Abethar, to seek King James's help for the others. Transporting a short distance within a certain amount of time, much of their journey would be on foot, making it longer to reach Abethar. Quantum telepathed Orion. He worried and received no answer.

Graven was worried himself, for he shot his lasers toward his enemies with extreme force. His beams were only red sparks in the dangerous skies compared to the numerous gargoyles they were up against.

King Triune and his men, with the Quest and Protectors, formed into a tighter circle with their shields above their heads. Bronze witnessed it through his crow since he had locked his mirror away for safekeeping. He sneered with delight. "The trap has been set and soon to be sprung, bunched up into my overpowering straight jacket unable to move or escape, no matter how strong Granite is…., not even Graven's beams of immense heat would destroy it! Let him try!" The arrogant man mocked haughtily. "I moved as a shrewd, devious cobra, cunning, and crafty, to bring my enemies into my dark domain to torture and pry information from." He acted as if someone was in the empty room listening to his nonsense. "Yes, I will kill—the thorns in my side—with the swiftness of my blade, my perfect moment finally arrived." He held his head high with pride as the dark webs of his mind took control. The cobra had struck.

King Triune felt the sting of Bronze's bite as all of them was quickly circled by a mighty host of gargoyles. Bronze sent out another tremendous blast the ground trembled once more. The soldiers fell on top of each other. Chip remained in the form of a shield. The blast flung him like a frisbee far into the woods. He transformed back into a chipmunk before hitting a tree and enduring a hard impact; he passed out.

King Triune yelled as he tried to stand to his feet, "Be brave, men! Hold on!" But it was too late; Bronze's evil hordes charged. Before they could do anything, his men with the Quest and the Protectors were trapped and tied into a huge net of strong material snatched up by many gargoyles, hanging in midair, unable to move. Abel's nose was forced up under Cain's armpit. "Oh, this is great. I am being tortured before even falling into Bronze's cruel methods of pain!" Cain stayed quiet, realizing it may be their end.

Graven too, had his doubts as Melanie held onto Orion like glue. She cried into his ear. "I can't go back to Bronze! I would rather die!" She continued crying. Orion caressed her arm. "I won't let that happen to you; my little chatterbox, try to remain calm. I will try and transport us." He failed. Melanie sniffled quietly. Orion blocked at all noises and concentrated and tried harder. He was losing hope when he heard Melanie cry out. "I believe in you!" Her words sparked something inside him. He concentrated believing and at last managed to transport both of them. Melanie's head hurt slightly from the transport. She slowly slipped from Orion's arms. She searched around. It was dark outside as they stood in front of a broken-down car. "What is that big piece of metal? I never seen nothing like it before." Orion replied. "It's a vehicle. I have been here with my father to places like this." He opened the car door and searched the glove department, and brought something out. They squinted their eyes, and with the help of the moon's light each looked baffled down into a photograph. Melanie stuttered. "This, this, is Miss Liana's car where they had broken down. Or why else would this artwork be in this car of her and her kids?"

"It's called a picture," Orion corrected.

"Please, tell me we are not where I think we are?" Melanie asked nervously. Orion pointed toward hundreds of candles inside many windows. Her eyes followed the direction of his arm. She whispered. "Bronze's large mansion—a mini copy of King James castle. I know it like the back of my hand."

"We will get through this together." Orion said. He attempted to transport them numerous times out of there, but there was some type of barrier making it impossible. Melanie rested her head nervously on his chest as he thought of what to do next.

Bronze's heart pounded within his chest with the explosion's impact and caused a few of King Triune's men to be flung away from the net. The warriors tried to gain their barren when heavy, rusted chains were placed around their ankles and wrists and were ruthlessly dragged along a gravel road linked together with a long chain.

Bronze was exhilarated about his accomplishment, allowing his gargoyles to carry King Triune and his soldiers, with Graven and Granite and White Lightening and the others tangled up within his large web, back to his old kingdom, nowhere near his replica mansion of King James castle. His nearly fallen-down castle was covered with darkness and dust.

Unfortunately, two soldiers walking in chains had been wounded by arrows, slowing down the pace. The gargoyles grew restless and unleashed them to be slain. Their leader screamed out, "Don't waste your time! Let the two suffer and die slowly. The crows will be nibbling at them soon enough!"

King Triune's remaining soldiers felt the chains dig into their flesh. While approaching Bronze's kingdom, they felt a dark gloominess overshadow them; one of them whispered to a comrade, "This land is not a place flowing with milk and honey." He was banged hard over the head and knocked out cold.

"Get rid of this one! He doesn't even deserve the crows to pick at his corpse!" Pleased, a gargoyle slew him with a sword through his heart. Bronze gloated, still observing through his crow, and smirked. "Correct, he is. It's not a land flowing with milk and honey but torture

FRIENDS OF THE KINGDOM

chambers and the heaviness of death; a depressing domain, a shadowy realm of a slaughterhouse. Ha! It was land at one time covered with King James's enemies—a people who despised him and his righteousness because he stood for what was good and noble. What a Fool!"

Bronze consulted himself even more. "My purpose and existence are to dominate the weak, conquer and kill, and destroy without mercy all who gets in my way. I am destined to reign and have complete control! My patience has finally panned out; three years I waited and managed little by little to triumph over this domain and overpower it. I conquered King James's enemies with a firm hand, killing off their men and making their women and children my slaves. This land of torture and death is now my Kingdom of Old, my dark domain."

His accomplishment elevated Bronze's ego. "I trapped King Triune and his men with the Quest. Now, all I need to find is—Liana and her annoying rodents. But where is that wrench, Melanie! How did she slip out of my grasp!" With the back of his hand, Bronze ruthlessly slapped his crow out of sight. With the help of the power of the underworld, he stood at the third portal door without the keys, where Liana would be exiting with her kids. He placed his hands on the ground, and the portal door appeared out of thin air.

Bronze swelled with pride. Using the gesture of his hands, the dashing man daringly exclaimed three bold words, "It is finished!"

Suddenly, a magnificent thunderous voice with the splendid of much rushing waters boomed from the heavens. "It is only finished through my blood." Saith the Lord.

The power of God's voice alone caused vigorous bolts of lightning to strike the door. It vanished once more, and in a split second, without warning, a bolt of lightning struck Bronze powerfully, knocking him to the ground. He lay silent on the earth, not flinching, knocked out cold. His comrades close by knew he needed serious attention. They picked him up and carried him to his safe haven—His gloomy Kingdom of Sorrows within his evil domain.

Bronze laid upon his back, feeling close to death, and as he was slowly healing, the chosen ones still gazed around inside the portal, amazed at what they heard, saw, and smelled. What was more striking, they could taste something delicious without entering their mouths. They had been there for a few days, thinking only a few hours.

Alicia marveled at the place's splendor; wherever she walked, she was staggered, struck with awe by it all. "The portal of no return cannot be compared to this kingdom in a million years," Alicia said.

Liana answered, "Yes, dear, I agree, but it's too bad Melanie could not come. She would have loved to see this place. Though I am happy knowing the others are protecting her. I need to look after her until she finds her family, wherever Bronze had them locked away."

"Mom, I too have no doubt that Cain and Abel are watching over her with a close eye, especially Orion. I have seen how he is drawn to her like a magnet." Alicia reassured her.

Roger interrupted. "I am grateful for what Melanie had done, bringing us back together as a family. We could never repay her for her bravery." Emily's thick curls bounced, nodding her head, agreeing.

They each continued to walk through the spectacular dimension, still unable to comprehend the beauty of what they saw or heard or felt inside the glorious place, which was exquisite and pleasing to the mind, with the superb fragrances of flowers as far as their eyes could see.

Emily marveled at millions of butterflies that flew all around them, small to great sizes. She perked up. "Mom, these butterflies are nothing like King Hydro. These have new colors I had never seen before, and mom, these waterfalls seem even more alive!" Liana remained quiet, not knowing what to say, smelling lovely fragrances all around her and noticing the stunning doves resting on limbs of breathtaking trees, singing enchantingly, one to the other as the vast falls of water created a mist that surrounded their senses, giving life to everything that lived, making time appear to stand still.

Liana could not explain the peace and refreshing love she felt within herself. She prayed in her spirit to find the location of the water of life and the tree of enlightenment. She and her kids walked, following the sound of the waters, searching diligently for the gifts for the king.

Still, after traveling, what seemed like minutes were hours, and hours were days, and not finding the gifts, their days could become years. They didn't waver in their faith nor lose hope, and at last, they ran into the Farlings, tall spiritual beings with striking, long ears wearing gold bands around their foreheads arrayed in sparkling white gowns. The Farlings were peaceful; they confronted Liana asking in unity, "Why are you here, and what do you seek?"

Liana answered. "We are friends of the King James. We seek the water of life and the tree of healing, and please understand that the king is weak and weary and is in desperate need of these important gifts. May you lead us to what we seek?"

The tallest of the Farlings glowed. "My name is Gabriel. You have asked, and now you shall receive. I will lead you to this place, but you must leave without delay after acquiring what is needed. I, too, have already sensed in my spirit that the king's time is short." The other Farlings shook their heads in agreement.

Liana replied earnestly, "As you have spoken. It shall be done."

They were still taken back by the overwhelming peace. The last thing on their minds was leaving this paradise. Gabriel asked. "Form into a circle and join hands and close your eyes." The chosen ones listened and did just that.

Gabriel spoke one word: "Behold!"

They opened their eyes and found themselves standing steadfast, planted not far from the water of life and the tree of healing. Gabriel was nowhere in sight. Alicia spotted a canister on the ground where Gabriel once stood and picked it up.

She walked about ten feet away from everyone and stood near a unique body of water she had never seen before. She edged closer to it and was perplexed. She gazed up into the tall trees that flourished with luxurious green leaves of healing but lost her focus, staring past the trees and up into the unfathomable, deep, clear sky. Her thoughts grew disoriented as the sky became her spotlight. Alicia's head began to spin as dizziness set in, feeling like she was lost at sea. The sky seemed to go on forever. She dropped to her knees and knelt before the streams of living waters, and as her head completely cleared, she regained her composure and brought her attention back to the gifts.

She heard Emily giggling, "Mom, Alicia's on her knees. Our family has been praying more often."

THE VISION OF THE QUEST

Alicia took the canister and leaned over the pure and alive miraculous waters. She immediately thought of the scripture. *Whoever believes in me, as scripture has said, rivers of living water will flow from within them.* She marveled at her reflection, experiencing a change within herself. She saw a mighty warrior.

She noticed it, flowing mightily yet very still, with abundant tranquility and peacefulness beyond measure, absolutely full of life and energy.

Alicia carefully lay the canister in the spotless water. It touched her skin. She felt life radiating throughout her body and became conscious and alert, discerning somehow the waters knew her and wondered how. Straight away, Alicia became sensitive to an inspiring presence sensing the gift of knowledge, discerning things that before she could not understand, and as she scooped it up into the canister, it again touched her skin. She then felt healing throughout her whole being, becoming refreshed not only in her spirit and in her flesh.

She discerned if she stayed there too long, she might become a part of it. She quickened her pace. With a sound mind, Alicia withdrew from its power and focused on the healing tree, wondering what she might experience from the grand tree that she gazed upon. What fulfillment she might receive from the leaves, as she had with the outstanding waters of life.

Alicia carefully, with steady hands, touched and marveled at a luminous leaf, ran her finger down it, and drew her hand away; the leaf felt smooth like flesh. Startled, she reasoned it was a leaf and not actual skin.

Alicia reached forth and gently placed her hand upon the tree's thick bark. She was fascinated hearing the thumping's of a heartbeat becoming one with the tree, overwhelmed, sensing nothing in the world could touch her and that everything would be alright, with an all-loving peace. She removed a long dark bang from her eyes, savoring the moment, resting in everlasting comfort.

Alicia inhaled a deep breath; instantly, she was caught up in the Spirit and transported, finding herself standing before a translucent open gate called beautiful.

She stood in awe and marveled at the breathtaking glory displayed before her eyes and dwelled on the memory of the eye-opening first and second kingdom, concluding that the beauty of the kingdoms put together could not dare come close to what she beheld now. She took in another deep breath, attempting to comprehend the place was extraordinary which words could do no justice.

She inhaled and loved the smell of a wonderful, sweet fragrance pleasing to her nostrils. Her taste buds tasted the sweetness, like homemade butter on a hot bun. Her senses were extremely fortified and energized, breathing out powerful words through her full of life. "His loving kindness is better than life. His breath of life is substantial."

Liana and Roger watched Alicia closely, her body stiff as a board. They saw a glow about her and could tell she was experiencing something astounding, not sure what, but knew it was a good thing.

Alicia's five senses were still on mega steroids, then amazingly, something warm rubbed softly up against her feet. She looked down to find she was barefooted with vibrant, multicolored flowers cuddling up against her flesh like hush puppies, singing melody songs, making her heart burst in happiness. She laughed as she heard the flowers giggle in pure delight.

Without warning, her father appeared before the open gate, full of joy and glory, smiling, exceedingly delighted to see her.

Alicia stood, utterly ecstatic in noticing how young and vibrant he looked. She desired to run into his arms to embrace him, a powerful force contained her that prevented her from doing so.

She saw her father had a beam of radiating light emanating from his glorified spirit, making it almost unbearable for her to look upon him, and even though he was in a car accident, his spirit was made perfect—without spot or blemish. Ken spoke in a tone of love inside a dimension of the Third Kingdom that she was given access to. "My daughter. I am so pleased with you; know that you have always been a blessing."

Alicia became shaken because, as he spoke, she heard hundreds of different languages speaking. She wondered to herself, *how is it possible that I understand all these different languages at one time?*

She was blown away, aware her father had read her thoughts. She still found it difficult to see him but was taken back from witnessing him in her mind. She sensed his warmth and joy and was swept off her feet, loving every moment.

He spoke out loud, answering her thoughts. "My daughter, because of where you are today, know this: all things are possible."

Alicia was astonished, standing immobile, wondering if she was alive, if breath remained in her. "Is my heart still pumping blood? Has my heart stopped beating?" she asked. Her father smiled. "All is well."

Finally, she managed to speak, "Father!"

She listened as he enriched her. "Alicia, you are favored of God. Continue on your quest and look toward the hope of your calling. Look not to the right or the left and run the race with persistence. Keep your eyes on what is important, and let not your heart fail. Rejoice my daughter in righteousness, and be prepared for what is to come."

She somehow, knew their conversation was coming to an end and dreaded the thought of it. Her voice echoed, "I love you, Father!"

She was speechless hearing him speak to her mind knowing he somehow searched her piercing eyes full of questions. "I know, my daughter. I know," and within a flash, he was gone. She faded back to reality and found herself standing before the tree of healing. Alicia gathered her thoughts together, seeing her father and all that she sensed, smelled, or touched; everything was alive and full of life. She was blown away by everything.

Emily startled her with a loud outburst. "Come on, Alicia! You've been dreaming by that tree for hours. Mom made me stay quiet the whole time. I could just burst right now!"

"Hours?" Alicia shook free and looked at Roger for confirmation. She was surprised when he nodded yes.

"Wow, it felt like only minutes," she answered, baffled.

"We can chat later," Roger said in a hurry. "Let's finish what we have come here for."

Her head was still in the clouds. She quickly placed leaves of healing carefully into her bag and turned around and beheld Gabriel standing before them, shining in bright light. He spoke with a grand boldness.

"It's time for you to go and make haste to the king, remain focused, and stay the course, and in due season you will reap your reward."

"What is this about staying the course?" Alicia asked. "It's enough that I hear my mother saying it. I heard my father saying it not too long ago."

Liana wondered why Alicia talked about her husband like he was alive but thought she would open up to her in her timing. With Gabriel, they formed into a circle and held hands. The Farling gazed into each of their eyes. He spoke one word: "Return!"

Alicia opened her eyes. She stood about twenty-feet inside away from the portal door in a daze. She did not desire to forget the joy she felt seeing her father but suspected this was not the end, for one day, she would meet him again at the gate called beautiful.

Roger looked back and caught Alicia in bewilderment, her silky black hair flowing down her thin back. He came quietly beside her and slipped his hand into hers, relishing her soft touch. It was a special moment, a feeling of love and compassion. She walked with him toward the open portal, happy. Gradually, their hands slipped apart inch by inch, reaching her mother and Emily.

Liana was the last departing through the portal door. Once outside, she turned to retrieve the necklaces and stood thunder bolted, seeing them take shape into one exquisite grandeur piece of jewelry, no longer three but intertwined as one.

All at once the jewels radiated with spectacular colors of all sorts—a glorious display of celebration. Still short-lived, the lovely colors faded, and the third door of the kingdom disappeared. The only thing they found standing was the statue of Medusa.

Straight away, it fell to the ground. Liana was drawn to the necklace and reached down with careful hands. She felt it was not hot to the touch and placed it around her neck; instantaneously, she remembered her mother vividly as she had seen her in the cave of many mirrors. Her memories came in waves seeing her a second time, lying feebly on her death bed but still looking like royalty. She saw the necklace intertwined as one around her thin neck. The same piece she had just placed around hers. Sadness overcame Liana again as she witnessed the glorious firework display fill the room as her mother drew her last breath. In her memory, she watched the necklace break apart into three different pieces. And as Liana recalled crying upon her mother's silent breasts, she looked up for comfort and spotted Graven in the corner of the room. She whispered. "What? How can that be?" Liana shook herself free with too much to take in. She again safely tucked her memories away and hid them in the back of her mind.

She searched around. *Everyone is gone, but where?* she wondered. Liana remembered the way back to King Triune's camp, but they found it empty. She worried about what might have happened to her Protectors, especially Melanie. Alicia and Roger figured something horrible had taken place, and thinking where the others could be was unthinkable.

They continued heading north, not knowing what else to do; however, after some time. They heard something in the woods and moved with caution until they felt safe. It was getting late, and nightfall was imminent. Alicia helped Roger to make camp for the night and gathered sticks to make a fire. She prepared food stored inside her bookbag, and listened to Emily, as usual, who was dying of starvation. She was glad her mother made her little sister pitch in and help cleared spots on the ground to sit and eat.

Liana said grace, and as she prayed Alicia was quiet, thinking about what she experienced inside the portal of the third kingdom. Her head spun in circles as she tried to digest the unspeakable joy and was full of glory. It was late at night. Alicia finished eating, felt fatigued, and lay on a cleared patch of grass. The others did as well, and they fell fast asleep within a matter of minutes.

There was a slight noise; however, no one blinked an eye and slept through it. Roger turned at one point and searched, thinking it to be a small animal but saw nothing and fell back to sleep.

Chip was alert, checking for enemies that may have followed his trail. He sneaked easily into the camp and rested beside Emily.

Soon enough, the morning sun begins to shine. Emily had awakened. "My nose tickles," she said softly and opened her eyes. Chip was curled up close to Emily's face, sound asleep. The spunky child became carried away at the sight of him. She yelled with an earsplitting scream, "Chip, hey Chip!" Her screams woke everyone.

Chip jumped into the air, shocked, and landed on his feet, holding his chest, "Chipmunks can have heart attacks, you know! I do believe I just had one!" he exclaimed, happy to see them.

They, too, were glad to see their little buddy and quickly began throwing questions at him. Chip fast filled them in with everything that had happened. He searched Liana's worried face, "You have been gone for three weeks."

Liana was thrown off, "For three weeks? I believe maybe three days. And you do know; you have a habit of popping out of bushes."

Chip smiled, "Yeah, I have been showing up in odd places lately, but about the three days for you, it was three weeks for us. Melanie may had shared this with you already, but in some places time is a lot longer, and in other dimensions, time stands still. During your absence, a lot happened. I have been searching for the others to Bronze's old domain, but he has some force field around it. I cannot get in, and no one can come out of it. I heard a lot of screams for help. I felt useless." Chip anxiously reached down, picked up a long blade of grass, and nibbled on it, attempting to take his mind off what they could be going through. "I came back here and waited for your return. I was nearby when you exited the portal to the Third Kingdom. I followed you at a distance making sure you were not being stalked. I entered your camp late at night. I slept peacefully until Emily scared me out of my wits. I left a wet puddle in the grass. Who needs a bush?"

"Oh, do I need to potty train you after all." Emily paraded with a smile.

Liana blocked out Emily, fearful of what Melanie may have endured. She thought how she promised to keep her safe. She thought of Cain and Abel and all the others. "Chip, we need the help of King James to free them." Her voice firm though quivered.

"You are very right, my lady, that's a wise choice; you have the wisdom of your ancestor. I agree King James will be their best hope."

Chip observed Roger was quiet up until this point but became quick on his feet and exclaimed like a grown man, "Chip, let's not delay, let's go to the king!" He didn't wait for a reply and hastily gathered their belongings. Alicia threw rocks on the fire and covered their tracks with branches. Chip watched and took note of their strength and boldness, seeing the excellent warriors each of them had become.

They traveled for a few hours; the climate changed, becoming hotter and hotter, their surroundings looked more like a desert. Alicia felt her shoulders sizzling from the scorching sun and blistering heat. She remained quiet, not to worry her mother, for Emily did enough complaining. She listened to her little sister's cries. "Mom, my shoulders feel on fire look, see the little bubbly bumps?"

Liana observed Emily's skin and saw what the sun was doing to her. "Oh, my goodness." she cried, then faced Roger. Roger spoke worriedly. "Our water supply ran out. We need to find shade and rest then continue during the latter part of the day when it is much cooler."

"Well spoken." Chip said. "I will search for a shaded area." Chip was quick about it. He transformed into an eagle and speedily took flight and, within minutes, returned. He informed Liana, "I had spotted trees up ahead." Chip saw Emily's light skin was becoming worse, including Liana's. He transformed into an umbrella sheltering the two, leading them toward shelter. The heat begins taking a toll on him as well. Finally, they had never been so happy to see an abundance of trees.

Once inside the woods, everyone practically fell down dead tired, appreciating the shade and soft breezes pleasing to their skin though Emily was quick to complain again. "Mom, I am thirsty. It hurts to swallow."

Alicia spoke before her mother got a word out. "What are we going to do with no water?" She turned the bottle upside down not a drop fell out. Liana worried for her children's sake. She looked toward Chip. "They cannot live without water. It's essential to survive, especially out in this scorching climate. Where will we search …" Liana's sentence dropped as Congo flew out from among the trees, landing in front of them.

Liana jumped up and wrapped her arms around him. "Oh, Congo! You are a happy sight to see!" Emily peeped in. "Mom, doesn't the big purple ape look like Barney I used to watch?"

FRIENDS OF THE KINGDOM

Liana saw slight traits but held her tongue and was polite about it. He motioned them deeper into the woods where a few of his Conchida's had made camp. Congo pointed to his food supply and water. "Help yourself, but don't go bananas over it." Congo smiled.

Roger could hear his stomach growling. "Bananas and honey, my kind of meal." He scanned the area then sat down next to Alicia. They all sat in a circle listening to Chip inform Congo of what happened to his soldiers and with the others.

Alicia spoke up. "I realized you had already helped us outwit the wolverines and looked after my mother with your Protectors. I am internally grateful, but I need to know if we can count on your support for the battle to come. We need all the allies we can find; sadly, time is not on our side. Will you still stand with us on behalf of King James?"

Congo had a twinkle in his eyes, "I daresay you have the strength of your mother. We are at your service; we have allied ourselves with the king." Congo leaned toward Emily and winked. "This Barney gets around."

Alicia was pleased.

Chip, with the chosen ones, sensed it was time to leave. Congo supplied them with water, bananas, honey, and a salve to put onto their blistering skin. He pointed them on a quicker route to find King James. The climate would be much cooler, in fact, quite cold.

After traveling a few days and entering the outskirts of Crystal Mountain, where it wasn't as cold, they met with the Ice King and his son Commander David—the Icemen still true to their word. They could be counted on in time of battle.

Liana sensed relief, with only a couple of days, of reaching King James. Their hearts filled with hope, with eagerness to get to this sovereign ruler in time—not only to give him his gifts but request aid in helping the knights of his court and the others trapped within Bronze's hellish domain. They walked another day's journey. She just hoped they will get there in time.

While time passed slowly, the climate became much warmer as the cool night slid in softly. They decided to set up camp. The moon radiated its light. Chip sensed something out of place, locating shining, red eyes watching their every move. He transformed into a snake and slithered slyly toward the blood-red eyes, locating three enormous seven-foot bats. Bronze's ruthless spies.

Chip slid back undetected into camp and transformed back into himself, and found the girls missing. He questioned Liana. "Where are Alicia and Emily at this time of night?"

"Alicia has taken Emily not far off to relieve her bladder," Liana saw the worry on Chip's face. "Is something wrong?" she asked.

Chip didn't need Liana to panic. He spotted Alicia standing near a tree and figured, waiting for Emily. They stood about fifteen feet away from the cruel bats. He waited anxiously for the girls to return and would attack when the time was right.

Liana asked again, concerned, "Is everything okay?" Chip didn't answer, watching the three large bats crouching and lurking behind tall bushes. His heart skipped a beat. Their scarlet eyes moved and fixed solidly onto the girls. He realized he must move fast without jeopardizing them. He casually whispered into Liana's ear, eyeing the gut-wrenching spies from the corner of his eyes. "Don't show no panic in your voice whatsoever, but call Alicia and Emily back." Liana quickly opened her mouth. "Alicia and…" It was too late; the large bats took off, moving toward their target.

Chip transformed into a thriving eagle swooping down with immense speed toward the repulsive things. He mercilessly crushed one of the spies' heads in his strong talons, squeezing it like soft dough; blood spurted everywhere.

Emily seen it and screamed, horrified. Liana ran toward her girls. Alicia grabbed Emily's hand, both running fast toward her. Emily jumped into her mother's arms, petrified. Roger moved wisely and snatched up his spear, and ran to help Chip.

Chip swooped fast toward the other two spies. He crushed a bat's lower body and kept it alive for questioning but could not stop the third loathsome bat. It took off through the air and disappeared out of sight.

"Well, it looks like you didn't need my help after all," Roger said with his spear in his hands, prepared for a good fight.

Chip had transformed back into a chipmunk. He glanced up at Roger as he found long, strong vines to wrap around his enemy. "You can help me tie this repulsive thing up. We have some questioning to do."

Alicia hurried over and helped Roger bind up the screaming spy enduring the dreadful mammal's high-pitched shrieks ringing close to their ears. It felt the pain of the ropes strapped tightly around his broken sliced-up body.

"You haven't felt anything yet; we have just begun!" Chip shouted at him.

Not too far away, Liana ran over to Alicia and Roger, finding out they were safe and seeing Emily had followed her. "Stay back, dear. This will scare you even more." Emily saw the bat was bound and jerked her head back, displaying her bravery. "I'm not afraid, Mom, as long as Chip is here. He will protect us, right, Chip?" she beamed.

"I would listen to your mother." Chip warned. He transformed back into a large bat and began to interrogate him.

Liana rushed Emily back to the camp as its screams became louder and louder. The spy fast spilled his guts, for the torture was too much. Chip received what he longed for as the vile thing took one last breath and died.

He moved rapidly and transformed back into himself to warn Liana. "We must get to the king as soon as possible; time is against us. Bronze is planning an attack on King James. I had figured the bat that got away was Bronze's spy. I have no doubt he's informing him we are alive and have obtained the gifts for the king."

Chip with Liana and the kids left without delay, traveling throughout the night. Speaking of the night, the bat that escaped had finally reached his destination. He yelled. "Master, your two spies had been slaughtered by one of the king's knights. The chosen ones had got away!" Bronze stood only a foot shorter than the bat. He was beside himself mad hearing the report. Three weeks had passed since he regained his strength after being struck by the bolt of lightning. He raised his sword in the brisk air to strike off the bat's head.

His spy retaliated, "I have important insight, Master!" Bronze slowly lowered his sword and listened impatiently. "I was lucky before being pegged out by a chipmunk, the king's knight. I stayed low and overheard the chosen ones discussing plans. They are in the process of seeking the help of King James to raise a standard against you."

Bronze became even more heated, the bat smirked with delight, supposing he found favor; with a flip of Bronze's wrist, his sword separated the bat's head from his body. Sorrelle and Bork stood close by and watched. They were never too sure of Bronze's actions.

His eyebrow arched upward angrily; feeling threatened, he blurted out to his two Snakens. "I will die before I let King James hold my remarkable gifts in his hands! He will not get ahold of its powers and become strong as he was in his youth. He can count on me to stop him!" Bronze a walking time bomb. "It's mine and mine alone!" He searched Sorrelle and Bork's faces and saw fear in their eyes. Bronze, out of habit, smoothed his hands down the front of his black button-down shirt. He glared toward his two Snakens. "This all started when those brats entered the pond hidden for generations. But now, because of that, nothing can contain me! I was prohibited from reentering without the keys. It may be a risk a task in itself but will be worthwhile. For I will enter the portal of no return a second time, but if I lose the battle of the kingdom to come. I will lose everything!"

Bronze demanded. "Get moving! Gather together a substantial force to stop Liana and her pesty insects from reaching their goal. Do not allow them to reach King James, or your head will be on a platter on my wall. Am I understood?" The Snaken's fast nodded their heads, yes. But before they departed, Bronze declared bald-face amongst his two evil cohorts. "I will fight to the bitter end and claim the healing powers of life stolen from me! Now, find Liana and bring her back to me! If I have to place a nook around her fine neck to force her to rule at my side, then so be it, go, make this so!"

Minutes, after the Snakens left. Bronze yelled in a blind rage, blinded by something he couldn't pinpoint, unable to find Liana in his mirror or through his crow, for the place she traveled was vast and kept him unsure of her exact location. Liana and Alicia continued at a fast pace. Roger walked quickly behind them, carrying Emily on his back as Emily was wheezing lightly. He thought it was funny, how Chip rested on Liana's shoulders with his feet kicked back, without a care in the world until the ground yielded its strength and opened up. They screamed, falling into a downward spiral spin, whirling through darkness smelling dirt and clay, as a cold, damp breeze surrounded them. Emily gasped at Roger's throat, choking him, as everyone else desperately tried to grasp onto something, only finding loose dirt falling through their empty hands as the earth swallowed them up—or so they thought. Chip turned into a haystack to break everyone's fall.

"Ouch!" Roger yelled. "Who's on my head? Please get off."

"With a head as hard as yours, I can't imagine that little bump hurt you." Alicia countered back.

They sat up and shook the dirt off. Their eyes adjusted to the darkness, with a small amount of sunlight from above. They searched around dimly and noticed the extraordinary space around them. "What large thing lives in here?" Alicia whispered.

Roger joked, breaking the ease of the unknown territory. "Whatever lives in here. It's not something Emily could potty train, that's for sure."

"I would hate to see the size of their droppings. I wonder what we are up against. I am figuring the earth opened up and swallowed us for a purpose, I certainly don't want us to be a meal." Alicia murmured.

She was startled by a strange grunting sound and quickly grabbed an arrow, placing it into her bow. She softly spoke, "Roger, tell me that's your stomach growling. I pray this is one of those moments."

"I wish it were my stomach; that noise sounds robotic and, ..." Alicia cut him off. "Big! No doubt about it."

"Nope," Chip chimed in. "Believe it or not, it's something small, for I heard by the digging it could be no other than a mole." He transformed into one.

Roger thumbed through his pocket for a match and lit a torch from off his back. He faced the light in the direction of the noise, finding out the hole was bigger than he imagined. Chip started believing maybe the kids had a point as the digging noises became much louder. Something large entered the expansive opening from where they stood. Chip found himself leaning backward and looking up, staring into the face of a humongous mole the size of an elephant. He didn't know what to think.

He sensed he wasn't a threat but now understood why the mole couldn't hear him. He transformed into its size and rapidly conversed back and forth, finding out his name was Moses. Chip told him of the gifts King James was desperately in need of. Liana and the kids listened; however, they couldn't understand a word they were saying.

Moses replied. "My family and I will help you. It will be an honor to assist our king, that we may have peace in our land again, and my little ones and their little ones will live in harmony. Now you are only a day's journey if traveling underground to the king's castle; however, traveling aboveground will take two or three days; this is the quickest way."

Roger and Alicia, still not understanding their dialogue, knew it had to be terrific news. Chip was waving the back of his tail non-stop.

"Hey, Roger!" Emily exclaimed with spunk. "Stand me on your shoulders. I can reach Chip's tail and swing off it. Come on; it will be fun, hurry!"

Chip chuckled, hearing Emily as he transformed back into a chipmunk and informed Liana. "Moses and his family will lead us to the first kingdom underground. It will only take a day and keep us out of Bronze's sight." Chip became quiet as everyone heard what sounded like a stampede for Moses had left and returned with a few members of his family.

"Wow! Their supercalifragilisticexpialidocious." Emily clapped her hands.

"Let me take a wild guess; it's a name of one of your potty-trained pets. Isn't it?" Chip asked. "No, silly, it's off Mary Poppin's, it's a…" Alicia cut in before Emily had time to explain. "Well, this has always been your wish Emily---to ride something of this size." She then spoke to Roger. "Roger, maybe we are in a dimension where dreams do come true or what we desire, think, or speak comes to pass. I would never have imagined this in my wildest dreams!"

Roger slipped his hand into Alicia's. His heart was captured by her sweet spirit.

She found warmth in Roger's strong hand, feeling secure, having him standing alongside her. She became sidetracked as Chip again began speaking with Moses.

"We understand the danger we may be placing you and your family into with that ungodly Bronze if he were ever to find out you had aided us in helping King James, he would try and eliminate you and your family; for what you had stood for."

Moses and his family understood the sacrifice they were making for freedom and rallied around them, lowering their bodies onto the dirt floor. Chip and the others climbed up onto each of their backs.

Moses firmly warned, "Hold on tightly; we travel with incredible speed." And took off like a jet.

"Boy, they weren't kidding!" Roger yelled out. It was hard for them to believe the immense power each mole displayed, running through the tunnels, with its many curves and bends and the rapid pace they traveled. It was nothing they had experienced before. Emily shouted. "I told you it was Supercalifragilisticexpialidocious!" Alicia and Roger agreed with her as they traveled many long hours throughout the night beneath the underground world, holding on for dear life, it caused their knuckles to become stiff and sore. Moses and his family finally stopped to give them a break. They dismounted, stretching their legs and getting the kinks out of their fingers, when Chip hollered, "Get back onto the moles! We are under attack! Flying wolverines!"

Before Chip and the others could mount back up, Moses shouted to his family, "You know what to do!" In a split second, the vast moles ran in different directions. The sound of snarling and grinding of teeth was heard not too far away. The fluttering of their black wings made a loud noise within the wide-open space of the tunnels. The moles didn't mess around and located the wolverines and rapidly caved in substantial piles of dirt, burying the malice tormentors alive.

The moles as quickly as they could open up the earth, were just as fast, filling in the huge holes. Chip transformed back into a chipmunk after helping them. He yelled while spitting out dirt. "Is everyone okay?"

THE VISION OF THE QUEST

"Yeah, after we get the dirt out of our eyes and ears," Liana answered. Chip fast crashed onto the dirt floor, exhausted. His small chest heaved up and down. "How did they know we were under the earth? I hope it was just by chance because..." His words suspended as Emily complained of her growling stomach. He began to think the girl had a bottomless pit.

Moses moved in haste and found them plenty of vegetables. The kids never thought cucumbers, carrots, and tomatoes would taste so delicious on an empty stomach. After they had finished eating, each of them rested for a peaceful ten minutes, talking with the excitement of only being a half day's journey closer to King James. Chip stretched his arms back and yawned, ready for a good nap but knew they had to press forth in case Bronze was onto them. They hurried and boarded the moles again. Moses and his family took off powerfully, the impact of their speed and weight shook dirt off the walls. Liana was glad she managed to tie a thin cloth over Emily's mouth until the dirt settled.

Chapter Eighteen

KNOW THE SCRIPTURE OR PERISH

THE VISION OF THE QUEST

Chip and the chosen ones were unaware the moon had tucked away as the morning sun arrived, as they traveled non-stop, long intense hours under the earth. With excitement, they finally reached the secret underground entrance of King James' castle and dismounted, expressing gratitude to the moles. Moses and his family bowed their heads in reverence to the ones who held the keys of the kingdoms, and within a quick space of time, Moses and his family were gone. The Quest could hear the sound of their heavy, rapid feet and feel the vibration of the ground running through the twisted tunnels and out of sight.

Chip beheld a huge door with unique carvings of Hebrew writings in pure gold. The beautiful letters were unfamiliar to Liana and the kids.

Chip read the writings. Fear overcame his face. He asked Liana, "Maybe there's another way that will lead us inside the castle. This does not look good, and I do not have the answer."

Alicia spoke up before Liana could answer. "We did not come this far to depart and go another way. Time is running out for everyone involved if we waste another minute. Chip, many may die. Please let's get on with this."

Liana searched Chip's face for answers.

His voice cracked, "Please understand there is but one key that will open this door, and we have that key, but the problem is there is a riddle. If we answer wrong, we all perish." Chip's concern for everyone's safety made him feel helpless. He couldn't transform into any shape or form to get Liana and the kids out of this one. He felt a heaviness around his neck, sapping his very breath from him.

"What is the riddle?" Liana asked, seeing the worry deepen on Chip's face.

Chip despairingly read the Hebrew writings slowly out loud. "Whosoever is worthy and holds the key, turn the lock and fall on your knees. What shall you ask? What shall you seek? Who is it that knocks? What scripture do I seek?"

Chip finished reading the riddle and looked at Liana, troubled. "This one I cannot help you with. I am sorry, My lady."

Liana, with confidence, boldly stepped forward. She smiled at Chip. "You have done so much for us already, my friend." She took off her necklace and placed it within the groves of the door. She watched the gems somehow form into the shape of a large key and radiate many unique colors. Chip closed his eyes for the first time and silently prayed. Liana fell to her knees and with her head toward heaven. She yelled, "The scripture you seek is Matthew chapter seven, verse seven!"

Fast the chosen ones stood appalled, hearing a significant voice echo, "You may enter, for you are wise." Liana reached for her key, seeing the door had opened. It was cool to the touch. She thought without a shadow of a doubt. *The true key to my heart is my creator.*

Chip opened his eyes and was floored everyone was still alive, "Hallelujah!" He yelled out with great relief. He quickly shouted, "Group hug!" Liana stared at him. "Hey, I've been hanging around your kids too long, and they're rubbing off on me."

Alicia and Roger embraced, over the moon to be standing at the secret entrance of the King's castle.

Chip let go and jumped up onto Emily's shoulder. The child exclaimed. "Well, what are we waiting for? The door is open. Let's go inside and eat some grub. I am starving!"

Liana placed her hands firmly on her hips. "Young lady, where did you learn that from? I hope it was not Roger."

"Wrong person," Roger spoke up, pleased it wasn't him.

Emily blurted out Chip's name, pointing toward him. "He's a chipmunk, not a person!"

Chip swallowed and threw up his arms. "Hey, teach me manners later. It's time to celebrate!" Chip began to break-dance, something Roger had taught him. Liana couldn't help but smile.

She walked through the door and came upon a much bigger door. The others followed close behind her. She opened it and poked her head inside, and glanced around. It was her first time in Abethar. She spotted Mr. Clean near a man with a long ponytail posted at the door taking shifts and waited patiently for their return. She wondered why Mr. Clean was in Abethar, not inside Bronze's mansion, but too tired to care. She dropped the thought until a later time. They followed the two servants into the huge grand hall with Roman columns and high cathedral ceilings. It reminded Liana of Bronze's grand hall. The only difference this room was much larger. Liana looked at the servant with the long brown ponytail. She questioned him. "I have seen you before."

The man replied. "It depends in what dimension." He displayed his handsome dimples. She noticed his kind eyes but also observed he was someone not to be messed with. "Caleb?" Liana asked him baffled, unsure how she knew his name. Everything was a mystery as she stood in the grand room. "Caleb, it is My lady." He winked at her. Alicia was listening and glanced over at him. He was faded far from her mind like chalk erased off a board. Caleb answered Liana. "This is where the important guests wait for the King besides when he has a grand ball, please. I am needed elsewhere." As Liana watched Caleb walk off. She observed guards stationed on each corner from where she stood in the massive room.

The chosen ones waited ten minutes when Princess Lilly kindly came and spoke with authority. "It is time. Please follow me." She gracefully took them from the grand hall into the King's court. A lovely room with walls covered in white marble and a throne of gold.

King James remained hidden behind his lattice glass stretching from his grand hall to his court. He watched the chosen ones enter and marveled at Liana. Though she looked tired and her clothes filthy, there was a sense of royalty about her.

He could not imagine how she had gotten through the underground entrance. He surprisingly found himself captivated by her beauty and presence. She held wisdom standing like a queen with power and love and grace. She would stun any mortal being. She struck his heart hard. He hadn't even thought of another woman since he had lost his wife. There was something about Liana, that he could not put his finger on. Whatever it was, it was drawing him to her.

King James, behind his hidden glass, looked at the others. He commanded his servant to relay his message. "Knights of the court. My great warriors. My servants had brought warm water up within large basins full of fresh-scented herbs for bathing and placed them into each of your rooms. I had prepared for you. My servants will provide you with clean clothes, then strengthen yourself with food and drink afterward. I know you are weary and need your rest."

Without hesitation, they accepted his offer. Emily was beside herself and blared out. "We smell worse than Cain's armpits. That's pretty bad if you ask me." Liana shot her a sharp look. Princess Lilly laughed silently, but King James recalled when Queen Leah would give him that same stern and loving stare when in a serious disagreement. It made him quietly wonder. *She has inherited many of Leah's traits and characteristics. If she was alive today, they could almost pass for twins.* He then watched the chosen ones with Chip follow Mr. Clean to their rooms. The kids have never been happier taking a bath and wearing clean clothes. Alicia and Roger met out in the hallway. They checked out each other's apparel. They didn't feel in a fashion but quite bizarre. However, they felt they were cool looking like in movies from the dark ages, and even though the clothes were weird, they began oddly feeling at home. Caleb escorted them to the dining hall. They sat down at a large, elegant table. Mr. Clean had a red clay pitcher in his hands, prepared to pour their drinks when their mother walked in with Emily at her heels, wearing a gorgeous colorful white and silver dress. She looked like royalty. The kids dropped their utensils and marveled at her. They found themselves standing up. Liana smiled. "Please, sit down. I am no Queen." Though inside, her heart tells her differently.

She sat down with her kids and ate a good hearty meal. They felt their strength return and were led to the grand hall to present the King with his gifts.

The Quest waited patiently, sitting on a stylish sofa. Liana observed it was made of beautiful hand-carved wood covered with areas of thick rawhide that was smooth to the touch while covered in soft fur. Liana thought. *I didn't notice the sofa the first time I stood in here. Its the fur of an animal.* Emily must have read her thoughts. She perked up. "Oh, Mom, who killed these sweet little animals?"

"Well, dear...," Liana's words trailed off as Chip teased, "Don't worry, most likely it's the fur of those big nasty wolverines. I'll rest my tush on them any day. Now that they're dead, they can go to hel...." Chip's words came to a halt, hearing Liana clear her throat.

THE VISION OF THE QUEST

Liana looked up, watching Princess Lilly walk into their presence, and motioned them to follow her. She walked into the King's court and sat down with authority to judge and proclaim the law upon her father's throne. Everyone bowed their knees in reverence.

"Oh no, not this again. These people pray a lot too." Emily complained restlessly.

Liana gave her a look to remain quiet. Chip whispered to Emily. "Well, I guess I'm not the only one who misbehaved today."

Princess Lilly spoke as guards stood on both sides of her. "Arise! Knights of the court!" Everyone rose. "What tidings do you bring this day?" she asked.

The King marveled behind his lattice glass once more at Liana's presence.

The kids looked toward their mother. Chip nodded toward Liana to speak on everyone's behalf. Liana stepped forward. "We have acquired the water of life and the leaves of the tree of healing—gifts for the King, as he has requested. We also have crucial information that does require his presence." Liana spoke bravely, not wavering in her spirit.

Princess Lilly stood up. She approached the Quest, and Liana handed her the gifts. "I speak on behalf of the King. He is pleased with everyone's successful mission, showing determination, dedication, and unwavering faith. I am also grateful. My father's healing is only moments away from being whole again—complete, revived, and healthy." She remained strong though she spoke with tears. "But I am sorry, you cannot see him. I will, however, inform the King that..." Princess Lily was taken aback, stunned. The majestic King James left his comfort zone, appeared behind his daughter, and stepped forward.

She didn't know what to say, startled, and not knowing, deep within the King's heart, he was drawn to Liana's spirit with a strange desire to be close to her. Quickly all in reverence knelt before him. Emily went down on her knees and kept her complaints to herself but was soon on her feet as the King asked everyone to rise.

King James searched through his black iron mask holes, covering the deep scars upon his face. He looked, puzzled, into Liana's eyes wearing black leather gloves, hiding his disfigured hands. He motioned to Liana to come closer and gestured for her to speak.

Liana did not hesitate. "King, we have obtained the gifts you desired and placed them into the hands of Princess Lilly. We also have important tidings that need to be addressed promptly. Bronze has abducted friends of ours and the remainder of the Quest. There have been quite a few that gave their lives to protect ours. We must at all costs free them before Bronze's sinful hands destroy them." Liana felt his eyes boring through his mask. He noticed that her deep blue eyes were the same color as his deceased wife. She spoke more boldly. "Who knows what that wicked man may do to those who fought hard for your deliverance? We ask that you will help them immediately? Your time was short, but now you have the gifts you require, and your life will be prolonged. Therefore, it will be the right thing to do to help our friends because now their time is short." Liana respectfully dropped to her knees, bowed her head, and waited for the King's reply.

King James admired her spirit of devotion, but most of all, her likeness to his lost love. She made him forget how he looked underneath his iron mask or his mangled body completely covered within his royal robe. He began to feel strength and purpose in his life.

The King spoke boldly. "Please arise that I may see you."

He stepped closer and stretched forth his hand, gently helping her back up. As Liana stood, her mind went blank, remembering something of this sort happening before. Again, she shook it off.

King James hesitated, letting go of the mysterious woman's hand. Nevertheless, he slowly slipped his hand from hers, feeling his heart race, face-to-face with this woman he barely knew, but inside, his heart told him something else.

Liana was bold. "Your majesty, I sense within the loyal King that you are, and you will somehow find a way to free your loyal servants and friends."

The King found himself hepatized by her beauty. He slowly shared. "I must make you aware. I was already informed of Bronze's treacheries a few days ago. Quantum, captain of the Pathfinders, appeared out of thin air with a few other Pathfinders not long after him. He informed me of these things, and as fast as the Pathfinders appeared within Abethar, quickly they disappeared and returned to the land of the Conchidas, to Congo for their leader to gather his soldiers for battle but before he had vanished from my sight. Quantum mentioned his concern about the whereabouts of his son. He sent a few of his Pathfinders to look for him. Quantum had hoped you would make your way to my kingdom. He said it's important that you know he had last seen Orion with Melanie. He does not feel Melanie is in the hands of Bronze."

Liana softly cried, hearing the good news. She remained strong and replied, "Yes, the Pathfinders have risked their lives, remaining faithful to the cause. I pray that Orion and Melanie are found safe and sound, but now that I know she is not with Bronze, I can breathe a little better."

The King, with this, called in his loyal knights and friends. He spoke with compassion. "This night, I have received virtue, wisdom, and great strength, without even partaking the gifts, where many have given and risked their lives that I may be healed. Now, we shall risk our lives to save theirs to win back the kingdom and have peace." He looked at the general of his army. "Prepare your men to rescue the remaining knights and allies who fought for my life, and soon enough, the rest of us will meet Bronze face-to-face in battle, which only one shall leave in victory. It will be us!"

Liana couldn't see behind the mask as the King smiled at her he asked his daughter for the gifts. Princess Lilly had transferred the living water into a gold vessel and gladly handed it to her father. He carefully held it in his gloved hands, gratefully drank from the water of life, and waited patiently, and slowly, he felt strength return to his body.

He opened the leather pouch, held the healing leaves and partook in its bright colors, and stood still, feeling heat throughout his entire body. He knew something was happening. He ripped off his leather gloves, observing his hands thoroughly. Then, he lifted off his iron mask and, with steady hands, rapidly ran his fingers down his smooth face, requesting Caleb to bring him a mirror.

Caleb approached him, handing it to him. The King looked upon his handsome face. His ivory skin glowed, revealing the color of his deep blue eyes. His blonde hair at the age of forty-one didn't have a hint of grey. Alicia and Roger looked at one another, surprised, and immediately thought he resembled the actor Chris Hemsworth. It was hard for the King to believe he was healed, no longer carrying the deep scars from that dreadful day. He sensed freedom of deliverance rise up within him and lifted his head toward the heavens to praise God.

Princess Lilly cried with gladness as the knights yelled out, repeating, "Long live King James! Long live the King!" Happiness grew inside the castle. Hope arose within the hearts of Abethar. The King commanded his knights and soldiers to mount up for the first time in a long time.

"All who believe in justice and truth ride with me into battle to overthrow the rotten-hearted Bronze for good. We must travel long and hard to reach our destination." King James turned toward Chip. "Prepare yourself to rescue the warriors from Bronze, his old domain, and meet us on the battlefield but take ten of my men with you. God speed!" There was rejoicing and shouting throughout the castle. The King's soldiers left to prepare their armor and horses for a tremendous battle. They waited so long for this day like fire shut up in their bones. Now finally, it arrived. As they shared this excitement, Chip anticipated freeing those trapped inside Bronze's cruel kingdom, hoping they were still alive. Chip claimed deliverance was right around the corner. However waited for Alicia and Roger to seek Liana's permission to battle against the enemies of King James.

Alicia and Roger about to say something as Liana turned to leave but heard King James call out her name. She turned and faced him when instantly, she saw herself wearing a beautiful ball dress and dancing. Her hands are in the King's hands. Her head tilted back, laughing. Her long blonde hair swung behind her. She watched the vibrant younger King smiling compassionately toward her. In those split seconds, she had no care in the world. She immediately shook free hearing the King's voice. "I fear you may be tempted to leave the castle with the battle going on to check on Alicia and Roger's safety. I will watch after them as if they were my own." Liana's face dropped. She couldn't imagine sending them off into a battle. "However, I will feel better knowing you and Emily are safe here in my castle until our return."

Alicia and Roger witnessed her place her hand on her hip. They knew what that meant. She wasn't giving in an inch. Liana declared. "Alicia and Roger will remain here with me. I don't desire them out of sight, traveling to a place as dangerous as Bronze's old domain. I heard stories of it, and the horrors Bronze could subject them to if caught. And concerning the battle, it's out of the question. There's no way under the sun the two of them will fight in a blood bath. Roger and Alicia are not going. I cannot bear the thought of it."

Alicia bit her tongue long enough. "Mother. They need us, and Chip will keep us safe. Look how far we have already come. God is with us! Please reconsider!"

Roger stepped in. "Miss Liana, you always taught us to fight for what is right and to believe the impossible. That's what I am trying to do. Please give Alicia and me this opportunity. Chip will not let anything happen to us. Please, believe in us." He pleaded with an urgency in his voice.

She looked at Alicia and Roger. She saw how much Roger had grown into a fine young man and Alicia into a high-spirit young lady. She realized they were not little anymore, and even though it hurt, she spoke with a changed heart. "I lost both of you once because of Bronze. I cannot lose you again, but as difficult as this will be for me, I understand that you must go, for our friends are in vast need of deliverance. I have witnessed the two of you battling against fierce creatures. I have no doubt you will be a big help to our friends. But you must be careful. Stay under the protection of the King's knights. That way, I have hope both of you will return to me."

She embraced them both tightly in her arms. As Liana let them go, she looked at Chip with worry on her face. "Keep them safe, my friend. I desire to see all of you out of harm's way, safe and sound, back in the King's court, or my heart will stop beating and break to no end." Liana took out a handkerchief and dried her eyes. "My life will be shattered into little pieces. I fear I may break down and be unable to go on." She softly cried but knew she was doing the correct thing.

Alicia kissed her mother's cheek. "I reassure you everything is in God's hands. Roger and I will return unharmed." Roger stood tall. He faced Liana with a look of hope. His once short brown hair is now flowing down the back of his neck. "We will return. I will let nothing happen to Alicia, and I give you my word."

She again wrapped her arms around both of them, this time not desiring to let them go. Finally, she loosened her grip and stepped backward. She searched Chip's face for confirmation. Chip jumped up onto Roger's shoulder and looked square into Liana's eyes. "I promise. You have my word. I will give my life to keep them safe." Sincerity was found in his voice.

Liana cleared her throat and straightened her back. "I do not doubt that, Chip. You are honorable and trustworthy. I appreciate that you had sacrificed so much. I can never repay you for all you have done." King James remained quiet as he observed Liana wipe her tear-filled eyes with her small handkerchief, which looked all too familiar.

Chip, too, noticed but remained quiet, for again, he saw the special light in Liana's eyes. He could not explain it, yet he was drawn to it. He felt himself beginning to believe in the faith of Liana's God, with the covering of his presence upon her. Chip asked, "May we also have the same favor upon you, for I ask that you keep us all in your prayers. I know the Spirit hears you." Liana answered. "Yes, you better believe I will storm the throne room of heaven on all of your behalfs." Chip replied. "My lady, I do not doubt it." And as the three turned to leave, Liana shouted, "Chip, please find Melanie!" he nodded in agreement and departed in haste, preparing the king's soldiers for their long journey to save those who could still be saved. Chip wondered how he would get through Bronze's force field and thought one thing he learned from Liana was her faith. He prayed quietly within himself for wisdom.

Liana returned to her bedroom that servants by the king's order had prepared for her and Emily. She shut the door behind her and began praying for Alicia, Roger's safety, and all the others. Emily, in the bedroom with her, fell fast asleep on a thick goose-feathered mattress.

Liana heard a faint knock on her door, and she opened it surprised to find the King standing before her.

She bowed her head. "Your Majesty, please, how may I be of service to you?"

She lifted her head back up. The King saw the worry for her children in Liana's eyes. He felt for her when hearing the uncertainty in her voice and spoke with kindness. "Yes, I have a few questions to ask of you. If you feel they are too personal, you need not answer. My lady, please sit and rest yourself." he remained in the doorway.

Liana sat down in a red velvet chair facing him, wondering what personal questions the King could have for her.

The King proceeded. "When you were in my court earlier, I noticed you with a handkerchief and the same one you hold in your hand right now. Sorry for my intrusion, but where did you get it from?"

She answered baffled, "You know, I can't remember, but I know it's mine. It's beautiful and gives me comfort. Why do you ask?" Liana questioned.

The handsome king replied, unsure. "It has a gold design that I remember from long ago, but that would be impossible. May I please hold it in my hands?" Liana seemed puzzled. She got up and handed it to him. He examined it thoroughly and to his amazement. He was correct, and it had the emblem of his ring upon it. He required answers. "Please, tell me: how did you come upon this handkerchief? Did someone give it to you? Did you inherit it? It looks identical to my late wife's handkerchief."

"Your many questions, Your Majesty, all I can tell you is that I feel it has always been with me."

The King's heartbeat intensely. His mind lost focus on everything else, only to discover who Liana indeed was, but fate would not have it. A messenger stood outside Liana's opened door and bowed his head in reverence. "Your Majesty, your enemies are on the move."

King James realized seeking answers would have to be put on hold and gently handed it back. "Please, we will complete this conversation later." She reached for it; their hands touched. Liana's mouth dropped open. Strong emotions stirred up within her toward a man she had never met until this day.

The King, too, sensed a familiar bond, as if their hands had touched before, but each second was essential, with no time to spare. He dreaded to leave her but had the battle to be won. He kissed her hand with respect.

Liana did not shrill but accepted it, causing another wave of emotions to rise within her. It was a pivotal moment as if, at one time, she had known the King in a personal way.

King James thought again how much she looked like his Leah but knew it was impossible. She came from a different time. He dreaded leaving her behind if anything was to go wrong. Liana could do nothing but stare in amazement at him. She too with no desire to let him go, afraid this might be the last she saw him. Liana's heart pounded. Her mind became filled with warm memories she couldn't understand.

He slipped out of her doorway and was gone, but she pictured him still standing there, with average height built solidly with stunning, charming features. She thought of his exquisite blue eyes and attractive waves of brownish blonde hair. She took in a deep breath. Liana softly talked to herself. "I had not felt this way toward another man since my husband had died." She cried lightly in complete confusion. "Why do I oddly sense a bond of flesh and bones? And how? This can't be! Where is this sense of attachment coming from? I have never been physical with the dashing ruler, but somehow I felt connected as one body. Why?"

Liana still remained baffled, as if her better half had walked out the door and might never return, leaving her puzzled about who she was and why she felt this way. She wasn't the only one wondering. King James, too, pondered. *"She has to be an ancestor of my sweet Leah as the old prophecy had declared. I can't fathom how Liana looks so much like her, but where are these emotions arriving from? The first moment in her presence, it's like I have known her a lifetime."*

For the first time in years since Leah's death, the King was content as he thought of Liana. He walked outside the large doors of his castle and located Chip, still quickly preparing his men, loading into wagons

THE VISION OF THE QUEST

what was needed. The King pulled him aside. "My faithful knight. You have been faithful to your King and our kingdom. I am honored to have you as a knight of the King's court. Still, now I will ask of you a great favor: to protect Alicia and Roger that no harm comes to them, protect them at all costs, even if it means your life for theirs."

Chip answered. "I already pledged my allegiance to Liana that I would do just that, for I once heard her mention to the Quest that the greatest love is laying down one's life for a friend."

His Majesty replied. "She is a wise woman, but I am curious. I know she has royal blood flowing through her veins, but I cannot get over how much she resembles Leah. I have heard that you could look alike through one's generation. Now, I believe it."

Chip bowed his head, knowing his love for Leah went deep, and answered him carefully. "When I traveled with Miss Liana, she would tell me her heavenly Father's blood flowed through her veins that she sat with him in his kingdoms, with her Father declaring his righteousness and glory to all for those who believe." Chip wiped the sweat from his fury brow. "I used to snicker, but now I wonder who is this King of kings and Lord of lords she speaks of knowing as if he's right there with her, and though he's unseen, he's real," Chip shook his head. "I cannot explain it, but then again, who can explain all the wonders of such a mighty God Liana had shared with me. Now, besides that, she too reminds me of Queen Leah. She is compassionate, loving, and brave, as was her great ancestor."

"My Majesty, do you know what I find peculiar? Through her hardships in our lands, she has established that the three keys she holds, which mysteriously had become one necklace, were passed down from her mother, which she cannot remember? She has some mental blocks and does not understand who she is. I saw her in one of the mirrors we adventured into on our Quest. I was taken aback as Miss Liana searched into the mirror. I witnessed Queen Leah stare back into her face. It gave me goosebumps." Chip had seen King James with many questions in his eyes. Chip said honestly. "That's all I know, my King."

The King was quiet concerning the mirrors. "I know of the keys, but I don't believe I have not seen them myself. Maybe when the battle is over, Miss Liana will kindly show me the necklace. But for now, I release you, my friend, take care of Alicia, Roger, and remain safe. Go speedily, God speed!"

Chip reaffirmed. "God speed it is." King James found Caleb. He spoke with compassion. "It had been quite some time which you had humbled yourself to be a servant unto me within the walls of my castle. However, I would like to once again reinstate you as my commander over my soldiers, this day and at this time for the battle we are about to fight." Caleb bows his head in reverence. "At your service my King, I leave your presence now, to help prepare the soldiers for Bronze's defeat." Caleb quickly left his side and helped his men fill up the wagons with food, water, swords, spears, and bows, among other essential weapons for the vast battle.

Chip was ready, as well transformed into a large, fiery dragon. He wouldn't chance it before with the possibility of scaring Emily and flying them right into an ambush of an unknown trap, possibly getting them killed. But with the help of Congo, he shared a safe route. With that in mind, he had no fear of Alicia and Roger on his back to make haste to Bronze's dark domain, to free the remaining Quest and others, including the men and any women or children, before the battle began.

Chapter Nineteen
Dark Shadows

Alicia and Roger were helped onto Chip's large back. They thought of Pete's Dragon and gripped strongly onto a tight rope wrapped around its thick neck. The two placed their feet into a manmade halter. Chip took off and blended in like a chameleon with the different colors of a rainbow. Alicia and Roger were thrilled and frightened at the same time as they flew at an extraordinary speed. Within only a couple hours, the three landed a few miles away from Bronze's torture chambers.

Chip transformed back into himself. The three walked quietly the rest of the way, arriving at the force field of Bronze's bleak domain. They waited patiently from a far distance, outside the broken-down gates. Chip tried to figure out the force field but was unable to. Hours had passed when King James' ten men finally arrived on horseback and tied their horses inside the woods. Chip informed the men. "We will watch and wait for Bronze and his army to leave the premises to head toward the battleground to war against King James. That's the only thing I can think of when he lets down his force field. We will sneak inside to rescue the others. Let's hope they are still alive."

Chip waited what seemed like an eternity. Finally, the huge rusted gates opened, and the force field around the dominion was lifted.

Chip and his crew remained hidden behind big boulders, witnessing Bronze's monstrous army on the move. They remained still as a deer, hoping the wolverines couldn't sniff them out, hearing them grunting and snarling, thick piles of drool hitting the dirt. His Snaken's slithered across the ground, while his creepy scorpions and gruesome porcupines totted behind them. His multitude of bats lagged further behind with their twisted legs. Their wings drooped downward toward the ground, not daring to fly until Bronze gives the command. Chip couldn't see Bronze eyeing his large spiders and his other deadly creatures, sitting on his black stallion. His men followed on horses as the rest of them marched on foot in the back, keeping the hideous creatures in line. Chip tried waiting until his army disappeared out of sight, but the dome began to slowly close. He knew it was now or never. With the others, he quickly ran and quietly slipped inside. They made their way toward his shabby, province cautiously unseen and undetected by the enemy.

Bronze's force field reactivated and wrapped itself completely over his depressing, shadowy, slaughterhouse. Chip realized they were trapped inside, but with the help of the others, he hoped, to figure out a plan when leaving.

Chip located tunnels and entered them which had the smell of death. The place gave everyone a sense of hell and dropped them into what they thought was a gloomy dungeon with everything pitch-dark. He knew not to transform into a beam of light, or the enemies would detect them in a heartbeat. They all fumbled around like blind mice, not seeing a thing until their eyes became adjusted to the blackness. Far off, they caught a glimpse of a light flickering and came closer, observing the area. They realized the tunnels had led them into the castle.

Odd, everyone thought, for there appeared to be a small campfire inside the run-down place. They heard groans—the sounds of ones in severe pain.

Silently edging near the campfire, they were horrified to see about half a dozen gargoyles torturing a few of King Triune's men. Their bodies lay helplessly on top of blocks of wood, hands, and ankles chained tightly together, cutting into their flesh. The gargoyles carried on each time they placed a torch of fire under their feet. They bravely did not scream though did groan in agony. Their moans echoed and bounced off the bloody dirty walls.

The deformed, bent-over gargoyles screamed. "The master needs more information! Our master desires to be your friend! Give us information, and the suffering will end!"

Their crooked wings shook with pleasure, mocking them, making a sport of mutilating the soldiers—with anguish, suffering, and torment. The gargoyles continued with their games and became angry that the men were not giving in to their methods of abuse, knowing these stubborn warriors would rather die than talk.

Chip noticed King Triune and Graven including White Lightning, Spot, and Acorn were not among them. They spotted Granite hanging upside down in midair with thick heavy, rubber straps around his rock legs and straps upon his arms. How they had him hanging made it difficult for him to break free, for no matter how hard he tried to pull

THE VISION OF THE QUEST

or stretch, it was of no use. Granite screamed, listening to the men's groans, enraged he could not help them.

"Hey, get your fat ugliness over here. Pick on someone your size! I'll set the record straight! I'll rearrange your little chicken nuggets like there is no tomorrow. Come on, make me happy!"

Chip saw many of King Triune's warriors locked away inside what looked like extremely tall bird cages. Each man appeared terribly weak. The warriors acted brave and ready to die for the cause.

He noticed to the left of the soldiers held captive were many bodies and remains of King Triune's soldiers piled onto each other and watched a gargoyle set them on fire. Chip now knew what the foul odor was. He had to think fast that no more lives were lost and searched around. There wasn't much resistance, knowing that Bronze's and his barbaric cohorts had gone off to battle.

"We can wait no long ..." Chip whispered. Before he finished, Roger leaped out, slicing into two gargoyles flesh. The gargoyles angrily tried to stop Roger but met Alicia's two bows through the chest.

Chip swiftly transformed into a giant gargoyle and flew toward the high ceiling, he cut into the thick heavy rope that hung Granite in mid-air. He released Granite in no time flat, though he was still wrapped tight with other straps, but as he hit the floor, Granite snapped them like rubber bands. The powerful rock man shot up, looking upon his enemies. He shouted boldly, "It's clobbering time! Make my day!"

Chip witnessed Granite snapping the gargoyles' bodies in half as if snapping a stick. "Hey, rock head, don't let that empty head of yours mistake me for a gargoyle! I want to keep my body attached!"

Granite was enjoying his freedom, "What took you so long!" he shouted.

Chip demolished another foul creature, "Long story! I'll love to chat and shoot the breeze, but I have hairy rumps to kick." He picked up two gargoyles and smashed their heads together while as promised keeping a good eye on Alicia and Roger, releasing King Triune's men out of their cages. "Where is Graven and King Triune?" Chip asked, concerned.

Granite rolled his hand into a large fist and knocked out a gargoyle cold. "One down and three to go!" He yelled over all the noise: "They're in the top of the tower, but it will take all of us to free them!"

Chip smashed up another scrumbag. "We need to bring Alicia and Roger with us!"

Granite agreed as he laid out the last gargoyle.

The fighting was short-lived with coming up against the Quest—the smelly gargoyles lay dead at their feet. Chip yelled out orders to the ten men left under him. "Free the rest of King Triune's men and get them safely to the gate!" Roger observed a few of the soldiers, released from their cages, were too weak to walk. He exclaimed. "King Triune's men who have strength left in them help the wounded to the exit near the dome and wait…and know this no man gets left behind, if there's an ounce of breath in their lungs, even if you have to carry them on your backs make it so! We are in this together! Where there is unity, there is strength!" He spoke with wisdom and authority. Fear was not present in his voice. Though Roger was young, the soldiers obeyed.

"Spoken like a true warrior." Chip beamed proudly at him.

"I have learned from the best," Roger glowed, no longer seeing himself as a young teenage boy. But recalled, when gazing into the fountain of reflections into the pond before entering Abethar, he now saw the mirror image of the mighty warrior he had become.

The soldiers threw the faint men onto their backs. The others who were able to walk made their way to the front gate and treated their wounds and received food and water to regain their strength.

The Quest headed toward a tower behind the deteriorating place when out of nowhere six Snaken's encircled them. Chip still a giant gargoyle got ahold of the slime buckets and did serious damage. The remaining Snaken's fled, seeing they could not demolish him.

"Way to go, little Chippy!" Granite laughed. "You gave me time to rest my big fanny, but just watching made me work up a sweat. I do say, it's the most fun I had in weeks."

Don't be a stick in the mud get moving, we still have others to find." The Quest began their search once more, and reached a heavy set of gigantic gates the size of a two-story building that most likely held their friends on the other side. They wondered the best way to get in. Granite bragged. "Stand back, little ones, and watch me at work."

He curled his hands into solid fists. With great force, he struck the well-built heavy gate three times and pulled it off, hurtling it behind him, opening the entry into the other side of the dark, unknown castle, where the tower stood erect.

"Way to go!" Roger yelled. "I thought I only liked to show off my superb muscles."

"More like little twigs." Granite lightly punched Roger's arm, knocking him to the ground, he felt fantastic having them back.

The four warriors walked in and out of unusual areas in the backside of the tower, noticing the rooms were unique, each was bewildered at how high the ceilings expanded fifty feet or greater in height.

"What lives here, giants?" Chip whispered. "I sense something eerie, that something horrible may happen."

"This is no Alice in Wonderland," Roger returned the whisper ever so softly.

Alicia broke the silence yelling an ear-piercing scream, "Graven, where are you! Can you hear us!"

"What are you trying to do, just set off a stick of dynamite." Roger said, upset.

"Well, we are not going to find them by tiptoeing and being quiet as mice. Are we? Do you have any suggestions?"

"You may have a point." Roger, too, yelled out their names, and again there was no reply. They searched diligently, making their way around a wide corner inside another room, all froze encountering an overwhelming shadow. They waited bravely for what they were up against. Alicia's heart throbbed inside her chest, ready to fight whatever came her way, but the anticipation was terrible. Her heart about dropped to the ground as a giant stepped out to confront them.

They scattered to take cover, seeing it stood over thirty feet high, with long, wiry arms reaching right above his knees. Alicia almost nagged with the sewage smell it carried, as thick piles of drool smacked hard against the concrete floor and spattered everywhere. Her alert eyes peeled on its enormous razor blood-stained teeth, but became overwhelmed as she noticed its fingernails were more like claws of a horrific bear, standing erect with titanic goat like hooves, able to crush any mortal man or beast within a spit second. Alicia recognized the beasts revolting face covered in numerous scars, eyes like the size of a moon bared down at them as if ants. Alicia couldn't stand the giants presence any longer and found herself looking away to catch her breath, only to look back, as its long arm swung upward and hit a large hole into the high ceiling. His voice boomeranged off the sides of the walls showing no fear of the Quest. "I suggest you run before I smooch you under my foot like bugs! Leave this place now, go while you still can!"

The Quest dauntlessly came out, standing on the solid firm foundation, determined they were not leaving without Graven and King Triune and the others. They heavily attacked the giant, but to no avail. The repulsive thing seemed indestructible. The Quest became discouraged and irritated. Granite pounded with mighty strength at the legs of the creature of the realm. He hoped for it to fall. Chip saw it was hopeless and transformed into a small bat and past him to search for Graven, realizing they needed Graven's help, acknowledging they would all perish if he didn't act quickly.

Chip closed to his exit. The giant repeatedly swatted at Chip's bat form and missed smashing his huge fist into the side of the wall, creating another immense hole, and stirring him up even more. He went berserk.

"Thanks, Chip!" Granite cried out. "That was mighty chippy of you. Shake him up, a spoiled child throwing a fit, and leave us to do the spanking!"

"I'll owe you one!" Chip squeaked. He speedily flew room to room which were empty, covered in thick mold and dust. He was losing hope of finding them when about to give up. He passed a large room and caught a glimpse of King Triune, bolted down with strong chains. Chip again, transformed into a lofty gargoyle, carefully ripping off the chains that tightly bound him. They had cut into his flesh and stained his clothes with blood.

"I guess you're ready for the battlefield with all those bloodstains. I am glad to see you have no missing fingers or toes." Chip said.

"I am sure pleased to see you, my friend." King Triune slowly sat up for his head spun in circles and then managed to stand up as his dizziness subsided. "But I have one question for you. What took you so long?"

Chip answered. "Granite asked me the same thing. But I can assure you I wasn't on no hot date even though the thought of it sounds blissful. But we are not out of danger, and we need to hurry to get out of here alive. We must find Graven and the others. I hope they are still in one piece."

King Triune rubbed his sore wrist and arms. "Well, what are we waiting for? Graven's in the room across the hall. But I haven't seen White Lightning, Acorn, nor Spot, or anyone else."

King Triune moved slower than usual, fatigued with hunger and thirst. He eventually made it to Graven's cell door and stood beside Chip, resting his hand against the wall for support.

Chip powerfully swung his gargoyle arm and broke the door down with ease. The two of them hurried inside, finding Graven on a table wrapped tighter than a cocoon cutting off his circulation, looking at Graven. Chip warned, "Prepare yourself, my friend. Things are going to become very hot." Graven winced in pain. "It can't be any worse than what I am feeling right now, wrapped in this compacted straight jacket." Chip transformed into a small fiery dragon, blowing flames onto whatever was wrapped around him, burning it away slowly, whatever material it was dropped to the rock floor. Graven was loosed from his captivity but bound so long, not realizing he was free. He remained on the table.

Chip joked. "Are you going to get up, you dumb Bird, or lie there! I mean, we do have the battle to win!"

Graven slowly stretched forth his stiff wings and took high to the ceiling, feeling every bone aching. The more he flew, and his muscles became more yielding with each movement. Graven flew back toward Chip, "Captivity—what a horrible thing. Is this how we all feel at one time or another? What a desolate place to be in our lives! I am pleased to be unbound, feeling such freedom, that I could go sky-high through the roof, except I am weak with hunger and in need of water.

I am indebted to you, Chip, for freeing me, or it would have been a slow, painful death."

"No problem, I couldn't have done it without the others, but we must help them now. I'll explain everything later. Does anybody have a conclusion on how to bring down an abomination?" King Triune and Graven too tired to reply saved their strength for the giant. Chip transformed back into a gargoyle and took off, flying down the spacious hallways. Graven followed behind him with King Triune on his back and flew swiftly, and in the nick of time, they entered the towering room, seeing Granite pinned to the wall like a rag doll. The giant slayer had his hand wrapped around Granite's big throat.

Graven's anger kindled. He shouted one of Granite's favorite lines, "This foul thing is going down!" He flew directly into the colossal tower with King Triune still on his back, shooting scorching beams hitting his shoulder. His arm dropped along with Granite in a downward spin. Chip quickly transformed into a pterodactyl. He found Roger drawing a picture of one in the dirt not long ago and was amazed by it. He caught Granite from smashing up against the concrete floor. King Triune looked down from Graven's back, watching the huge arm drop. Roger dove and grabbed Alicia into his arms, and jumped to the side. It barely missed her. She found herself nose to nose with Roger. His breath in her face. Slowly their lips touched for the first time they kissed. The two blocked out everything as if in their own little world, but not desiring too, they quickly pulled apart, hearing the butcher yelling insanely.

It was outraged, screaming in pain and anguish, gnashing his teeth infuriated, toward Graven, "Bird! You shall surely die today, and bird stew sounds like a winner!"

The giant stretched forth his good arm, swinging it to and fro, Graven dodged left to right and finally it snatched Graven out of midair about to gnawed him, like chewing a piece of gum. Chip grabbed King Triune off Graven's back and threw him into the giant's despicable face. The king used his double-edged swords and sliced through both his eyes. The swords slipped down his face ripping through his flesh pealed like an apple. King Triune went tumbling in midair.

THE VISION OF THE QUEST

The thirty-foot giant of old wheeled in pain, dropping Graven, covered his bloody eyes with his hand, swaying back and forth. Chip fast caught King Triune. Granite from below had swooped low and lunged, attacking again the lofty beast's leg this time toppling him backward. Alicia and Roger again dashed out of the way as the mountain crashed onto the hard floor. The place trembled with the solid impact. The giant lay there, rigid, without his eyes. The creature felt awkward and lost.

Granite shouted, "I am beginning to love this! It's pounding time!"

They watched Granite beat the creature's face into the floor beyond recognition. Graven gave a sigh of relief, and it moved no longer and lay silent, with no breath in him, dead.

"Quest, rally to me!" Graven shouted. "We must quickly find the others that we can reach Bronze and combat him, to help the king attain victory!"

"God speed!" King Triune proclaimed.

Without a moment to waste, they speedily exited the tower and after searching a certain distance, Chip heard familiar voices about twenty feet away and followed the sound to a huge concrete manmade hole in the earth, finding the Protectors trapped inside with a gate of thick metal on top. Granite ripped it off like feta cheese. Cain and Abel, and the Stingers, flew out from their captivity. Abel was the first to storm out and complain. "What took you guys so long? Cain's armpits about killed me. But besides that, I can honestly say it's a relief to see all your ugly faces." Granite grinned. "There's no different from where I am standing." The reunion was brief for Chip cut in and quickly gave orders. "Cain and Abel, get your soldiers to the front gate. We must search for the king's knights. King Triune's men are there and will give you food and water. Get rest until we return." As for King Triune and Graven. Roger gave them a container of water from his bag and what little food he had. Roger then walked beside Alicia, following Chip and Graven and with the help of King Triune and Granite, were attentive and observed their surroundings, searching for White Lightning, Spot, and Acorn, after tedious searching and battling gargoyles bringing them into the jaws of death, finally located a well-hidden, bottomless pit found inside the cruddy fortress through a trap door.

Graven with Chip on his shoulder, flew down many spiral steps to reach the bottom of the abyss, finding Acorn and Spot strapped down guarded by a nineteen-foot dominating threatening three-headed serpent, preparing Acorn and Spot for their meal. Their appetite had grown, and they last ate four days ago, one of Bronze's slaves that had become feeble and no longer a use to the man. Alicia could hear Granite's loud mouth below as she ran down the steps. She tried to remain calm witnessing thousands upon thousands of small spiders. *No, not this again.* She reasoned as many crawled on her as she reached Roger and King Triune at the bottom of the steps. They reached a cold, sunless place. Roger and Alicia had never seen anything like it before except in their video games. Rocks hung in midair everywhere and underneath was nothing but blackness except another large hole that was on the other side of the immense flat rocks.

The three-headed serpent daring to sink their violent fangs, sharp edged knifes into their prey, going against Bronze's strict orders, demanding them to use their hypnotized powers against his enemies to betray their king, King James. White Lightning was already far gone, hypnotized pinned up against a rock wall. The spiring, spineless creature seen Bronze had departed for battle hatefully moved its torpedo-shaped heads in all directions to devour them, confident their master would win the battle crippling the king of Abethar. There would be no need for the king's loyal knights.

The serpents displayed their fangs, hissing loudly, and slithered toward his victims to strike. White Lightning stared in space, not having a clue what was happening. Graven bolted and flew toward the threat, shooting his laser beams, cutting one of its heads from its body, listening as the head spun downward into the bottomless black pit.

King Triune, Alicia, and Roger observed what was happening. Roger moved swiftly and accurately, threw his spear, and stuck the throat of another one, and it dropped limp. The last deadly serpent went on a rampage to destroy all of them. Acorn and Spot watched everything as they remained strapped to a large rock erected over the never-ending pit. The serpent with a powerful thrust of his huge lower half, knocked Acorn and Spot off the cold hard platform, breaking their straps. However, their wings were still bound. It's red hot pepper's eyes became satisfied looking upon Graven's face as his friends vanished from his sight, dropping into a downward spin to their last breath.

The serpent hissing sharply, anxious to hear their heads bang against the sides of the jagged rock wall. He became appalled as Chip leaped over rocks in midair and jumped into the dark hole, transforming into a substantial web, and breaking their fall.

Granite ran, hopping from rock to rock, toward Acorn and Spot, snug inside Chip's netting. He came face to face with the creature to protect them from any other hard blows. Alicia and Roger carefully jumped the big rocks. They came up beside Granite on top of a floating boulder.

"Stand back, kids. This serpent is too powerful!" Granite lifted his arms to hammer it when it stared into the windows of his eyes, easily gaining control over him, luring him into his deadly trap of havoc without a fight or a struggle, falling deeper into his snare without any difficulty.

His web of deception, Granite walking toward the edge to take his plunge. His soon-to-be death of falling into the hole of hopelessness hit the sidewalls, to be scattered into piles of pebbles, gone, and lost forever in that damp, dark place.

The lofty serpent threw back his obese, twisted head and viciously hissed wildly, spitting out his venom. Granite stepped his right foot off the floating rock. After several failed attempts, Alicia pulled back her bow, striking one of the creature's eyes, breaking the control he had over Granite.

Granite shook his rock head, gradually coming to his senses. The serpent prepared to use his curvy, smooth body with enough force to strike him into the bleak shadows of the abyss. Roger quickly threw a spear, slicing the serpent's other eye. Granite remembered his surroundings and what had taken place. He yelled loudly, "Oh! You have made a big mistake! It's clobbering time!" He jumped onto the serpent, took his fist, and repeatedly beat the vile, slimy thing to a pulp. Upon finishing, he noticed all eyes on him in a significant way.

Granite said, "The creature had it coming." White Lightening with the death of the serpent snapped out of his trance. "What? Did I miss all the fun? Hey, don't stand there and gawk. I need some help come untie me? We have the battle to fight and win." Roger ran over, cutting White Lightning loose with the point of his spear.

King Triune looked past White Lightening and chuckled at Granite. "Who were you calling kids and telling to stand back? I will say, if it weren't for Alicia's precise aim and Roger's spear, it would have been more than your knees getting scraped, remember, buddy, who trained them. I will say the two of them ran circles around you."

Granite playfully slapped the king's back. "Alicia and Roger will do fine in anything they put their mind to, but for now, as I recall, we have an appointment with King James on the battlefield. I suggest we hurry."

"Hey, you goofy jughead!" Chip yelled. "Did you forget about us? We are tangled up down here and can use a hand."

Granite called out. "For a little chipmunk you certainly have a big mouth!" Granite reached down and lifted them out one by one. Roger cut off the ropes that bound them, and with momentum speed, each of them carefully hopped boulders and rocks of all sizes, reaching the spiral steps, leaving the hellhole, hastily making their way to the gate near the force field. The Quest strengthened themselves with light food and water to be strong for the battlefield.

"Has anyone seen Melanie?" Chip asked. He found everyone's response was no.

"We have searched this whole place." Chip continued. "Quantum doesn't feel Melanie is here, and I hope she is in no terrible danger."

King Triune with the wisdom of a noble king stated. "It will be wise that I leave a few of my men to continue the search." Chip agreed as four of King Triune's soldiers left hastily, hoping to find Melanie and possibly others.

The Quest had another situation, and they needed a solution to break through Bronze's force field to get out.

Chip stated. "I did notice the shield around this place lost some power when Bronze left. Somehow his presence inside here keeps the force field strong but loosens its hold when the man is out of sight."

Graven was on full alert. "Well, if that's the case, I should be able to bring it down." Without warning, he shot his laser beams. Everyone screamed, ducking, and hit the ground. The lights ricocheted off the clear dome and soared above their heads, hitting a few small trees behind them, snapping them in half.

Granite jumped back up. "At the rate you're going, and we will all be dead. Stand back and let the powerhouse show you how it's done, and they say I am the one without the brain!" Granite flexed his rock arms.

Graven remarked. "Be my guest big boy, but don't get hurt. I would hate picking up your little red pebbles without first finding your brain."

Granite drew back his fist. "Yep, as I said, stand back. This is the way big boys do it. The ones that have a brain." Using every ounce of his might, he punched his fist into the dome and was stunned, being knocked backward ten feet, and landed hard onto the ground.

"Which way did it go, George?" Roger laughed.

"Who's George?" Granite questioned, jumping back up.

Graven asked, "Any more bright ideas, muscle man?"

"You haven't seen anything yet!" Granite dug his feet into the earth and smashed his wide fists repeatedly into it.

He banged and banged. Chip mentioned to Graven. "I have a better solution of digging under the dome. I can at least give it a try. Anything's better than what that airhead is doing." Chip transformed into a terrific mole-like Moses and dug into the earth underneath the force field.

He dug rapidly kicking large piles of dirt into a number of the soldiers' faces. He hoped Granite kept pounding away, for with each whack hit against it, he felt the force field weakening, becoming easier for him to dig. His job was completed and he was up and out of his dugout on the other side and transformed back into a chipmunk, watching Granite tiringly banging.

"Over here, you knuckle head!" he shouted. Granite blocked him out.

The others began walking through it. Granite banged a few more times, giving his all, he had finally, leaned up against the force field exhausted. He looked bewildered, seeing Chip on the other side waving at him.

He yelled out, frustrated. "You're a real smarty! How did something as small as you get through this dome? It's not possible."

"Big brains come in little packages!" Chip exclaimed, puffing out his small chest. "My friend, as I had said before your backside probably has more intelligence than that birdbrain of yours!"

"Yeah, and sometimes a little package can be a real pain in my ..." Granite stopped short as Chip waved his finger, "Ah ah ah! We won't go there."

Granite exited the tunnel. Chip and him went back and forth. Graven ignored them both and had soldiers conceal their secret passage for future use, covering both entrances with heavy brush.

King Triune commanded two of his soldiers to lie hidden, out of sight under the thick brush, on the lookout for the soldiers looking for Melanie and others, to show them the way out.

The rest of them pressed on with the urgency to assist King James in battle. They traveled for hours drawing close to the battlefield. A few complained they had heard shouts of Bronze's men and creatures from miles away.

Chapter Twenty

Light in the Darkness

King James, with his army, began crossing over the Yale river. His messenger hastily ran his horse toward him, warning that evil was nearby.

"My King! Bronze is about two miles away and ready to engage."

"How many do we have to demolish this day?" he bravely asked.

"Oh, great King, as far as the eye can see like dark locusts advancing our way, coming scattered from all directions, not a piece of ground can be seen."

"Who has sided with the betrayer?" King James asked, displeased.

Caleb's hair no longer pulled back in a ponytail but loose over his shoulders, he answered. "His wolverines and gargoyles still stand at his side, including his Snakens, bats, giants, and other creatures great and small, and some unknown to me."

King James looked into the eyes of his faithful servant and stated without flinching, "Good then, we're even!" He sat tall upon his horse, firm and unshakable.

Caleb stared in bewilderment at him and spoke boldly. "Surely you must have the faith of a mustard seed, for the battle seems an impossible task. Bronze's army will cause strong men to faint. I see the faith, my King, that you display, and that's an honor." Caleb bowed his head slightly toward his noble leader.

"Caleb my friend. Faith is having full and free access into the heavenly's. Now, how has he set his battle against us?" King James asked.

Caleb quickly replied, seeing their time was drawing short. "They are scattered all over the land with no form or strategy. Bronze believes he will overcome us by numbers, and in my perception, he sees us as a joke."

The king was not moved by numbers. "Bronze is a shrewd man, and I calculate his pride to be his downfall. I shall signal my men to move forward. We will meet them on high ground!"

Caleb had watched King James throw his arm high above his head and then lowered it, signaling his men it was time. His army was on the move. King James reached the area where Bronze attempted to form his troops in rank. His rebellious creatures made it difficult and showed Bronze no honor.

King James put his men in military ranks and set his battle in array against the forces of evil.

In a matter of time, Bronze sent his three messengers. Pilate, on his horse, is a leader wearing a mask of gold, with an armor of gold over the top of his muscular frame, and approached the King. He jumped off like he was cock of the walk, swaying to the left and the right, wearing a majestic purple robe with a hint of burgundy and looking like royalty, but wore no crown. Bronze had taken it from him.

Ramsey, Bronze's second messenger, stayed on his horse. He observed their surroundings wearing a silver mask, built bulkier than the others, his robe a bright silver. He, too, wore no crown, also Bronze doing.

Herod, Bronze's third messenger, stood a head taller than the rest, covered with a mask and armor of iron, wearing a glittering robe of shiny silk over his well-built frame. He sat direct upon his horse and firm. He, too, was without a crown because of Bronze.

King James looked upon Bronze's three peculiar men who seemed confident and strong. He realized most likely, at one time, they were noble and true to a good cause, victorious in many things. But, Bronze had conquered them and taken their crowns by force, he felt their minds became warped, over months or even years, brainwashed them to look toward him as their incredible master. Bronze rendered them willing to go to any extent to do his bidding, with the promise of receiving a higher crown and sitting to his left and right when he attempted to overcome the kingdoms.

Pilate stood zealous with Herod and Ramsey beside him on their ferocious horses, kicking up dirt with their hoofs.

Pilate demanded. "King James, my message from my master is that you leave this field here today! Bronze will allow you to keep your castle and the lands to the river. He will gain full control of your people and all the waterways within your kingdom, and the kingdom will no longer be yours, and that's to do with as he pleases! Last, if you know of the whereabouts of Liana, you must give my master all the information concerning this woman."

King James replied with authority. "I have but one word: 'Retreat!'"

Ramsey and Herod on their horses smirked haughtily but remained quiet. Pilate cackled loudly and looked the king straight in his eyes as the king still sat upon his horse. Pilate taunted. "I am surprised at such a bold and powerful statement, for your adversaries are great in numbers like the sands ashore. You should be the one to retreat! This day my master will place a dagger into your heart, and your pretty little Princess Lilly shall be sharing my bed." King James clenched his sword. He exclaimed. "A stumble comes before a fall, but it's better to know that you don't have to fall. I say retreat!"

Pilate ignored him. He spoke with arrogance. "I am Pilate known as the Slayer, the leader of higher authority, and at one time the master of the third realm, these two beside me and not that you need to know this, they had controlled the first and second realms, and soon enough you will be brought to your knees! It will be against all odds for your petty army to defeat us, for we are from diverse realms, containing distinctive levels inside different dimensions. Now that I got that off my chest. We are the messengers of Bronze, the conqueror of the realms; for that reason, we claim these lands for whom we serve. All these lands will rightfully belong to Bronze! I ask you: Who do you think you are to come against such a powerful force? You are well aware that defeat is ahead. It will be in your best interest to leave this ground, for you will bring a tragic fate to your people and shall be utterly destroyed!"

The King stepped off his horse, standing eye-to-eye with Slayer, not intimated by his threats, and spoke boldly. "I am King James, the ruler of my people! And know this! I shall not yield these lands or this kingdom to the adversary. Since I am the first royal birth of my father, I inherited his blood running through my very veins.

For this reason, I declare this: I rule this kingdom as far as the eye can see. I will not hand my people over to a ruthless murderer! Death follows Bronze everywhere he goes. Pilate, mark my words, this day shall be your end! Leave this ground before the breath you breathe shall be gone!"

Pilate spits in front of the King. He stood unmoved.

Caleb no longer could remain silent, appalled with his action. He shouted thunderously, "You stool pigeons! Hearken to my King's voice and return to your battlefield where your blood will be shed this day! Ensure you inform the traitor that this is the day he draws his last breath! Depart now and meet your ruin. Inform Bronze of our King's final message!"

Pilate angrily settled back onto his horse rearing it up on its hind legs and departed with Ramsey and Herod. King's James words reached their master's ears, and furious Bronze dashed his sword through one of his creatures, cringing his face. He hollered. "So be it! It shall be an easy victory and his kingdom shall be mine. What a fool! The audacity of thinking he can conquer an army as vast as we are!"

Bronze's good-looking face became twisted and ugly. The corrupt leader turned toward his spokespeople. "Slayer, be in the front lines for attack! Herod and Ramsey! Both of you will follow Slayer with a second and third assault. The gargoyles and the wolverines shall take to the skies, bringing the fourth assault to bring the King down to his catastrophe in this hour. I will have his head on a stick and feed his body to the wild boars. I have spoken! Now get this message to Gork, the leader of the gargoyles, and Wolf Fang and Sorrelle the leader of the Snakens. I will ride with my army behind you! We will take the fields and make them into a blood bath! This will be a day his people will never forget when their King's blood is upon my hands. Furthermore, what is his will be mine! Mark my words!"

Bronze prepared his force for the strategic battle. His army was thunderous with earsplitting sounds. Only the six ranks of troops respected their master's wishes. They listened to his voice, which carried strongly in the wind, feeling it would be nothing for him to overtake King James' crown after the bloody onslaught.

The others acted vicious and savage out of control, anticipating this battle and becoming anxious with each passing moment raring to spill the blood of King James's upright men who had taken a stand against

Bronze's sinfulness. King James's warriors trusted the faithfulness of their true King, even though things looked hopeless. They were willing to lay down their lives for their freedom, family, and friends. The honorable men realized standing behind their King. Many would enter a premature grave.

The forces prepared to engage. King James looked around and saw no allies to the left or the right. The fields were darkened with Bronze's wicked hordes. He looked toward the sky, and all he could see was Bronze's forces in the air. He turned to his men, speaking courageously. "May God give us the wisdom and strength to send all those who attack us today to their final resting places! Do not become overwhelmed by their numbers, but lift your great swords and strike back the enemies from whence they came! Today we fight for the honor and respect for all of our people, even those far off who enjoy the freedom of liberty!" King James galloped his horse on high ground and waited calmly for the first attack from Bronze.

Bronze patience had worn off and commanded Slayer to attack first: "The time is now!" Slayer raised his sword in midair to his forces: "Attack!"

King James, sitting on his horse, watched his men rush into battle, fighting hard, bringing down two to three men at a time. His soldiers' skillful warriors, clever and tactical in how they fought, knew how to fling their weapons and dodge their enemy but were struck by the creatures of the air. A ferocious wolverine swooped down and latched a soldier in his strong jaw, crushing his bones. He dangled painfully. The beast released him and dropped him to his death.

The Wolverines weren't the only ones that loved to play the game well. The spiders and scorpions fast skipped from soldier to soldier, shooting their deadly poison into their flesh. Death lurked around the corner as each soldier brought down many of Bronze's creatures and men they possibly could before drawing their last breath.

The Quest and King Triune and his soldiers with the Protectors drew close and heard the loud shouts of the battle. They broke forth and arrived to aid the King.

King Triune witnessed the mass darkness. He bravely raised his sword upward and shouted, "Victory is King James's today and those that enjoy triumph! We fight!" King Triune and his men rushed into battle.

Graven, Acorn, White Lightning, and Spot, with Granite, took off into the sky to engage with the wolverines and gargoyles and bring them to their end. Chip stayed in eye view of Alicia and Roger.

Alicia gripped her bow tightly in her hand, and shouted, "Bring me many arrows, now!" She exclaimed, taking ones behind her back four arrows at a time, shooting precisely into the heavens, watching creatures dropping like flies as a soldier ran to her two additional large quivers full of arrows. Roger moved just as daringly, wielding his sword left and right, slicing into his enemies.

King James prepared for this tactic and had placed skilled rows of men shooting down these ungodly creatures, but nowhere skilled as Alicia. She was like a talented musician with an instrument in her hands but, in this case, arrows. They were continuedly rushed to her. She continued hitting her targets precisely, alongside the men for a time. Bronze noticed his winged creatures were dropping in large numbers. He sent Pilate to spy on what was happening and immediately bring back a report.

Pilate looked for the skilled sniper battling his way to the threat. He pressed his horse through the battlefield nearly one hour had passed, and still, a third of Bronze's creatures were falling out, severely wounded or dead. Pilate was surprised to find the threat. Alicia and the remaining Quest bringing down as many as they could, but still, King James's men were outnumbered, and growing faint. The King had many of his soldiers fall back from the front lines.

King James raised a large horn to his mouth and blew full force, summoning his men lying low and out of sight. His men rushed out of caves and trees, hidden by the wisdom of their King. These pumped-up soldiers waited for this moment, restless with energy and endurance to combat strongly, a need to bring many of Bronze's dark cohorts to their grave.

THE VISION OF THE QUEST

Bronze finally received word from Pilate. Pilate was still stunned as he spoke. "I had passed the enemy's line to find Alicia causing much damage to your fierce wolverines and gargoyles." As the words still slipped from his mouth...

Bronze burst into flames, an atom bomb, and he exploded, learning the brat was the cause of his dilemma. In his fury, he sent out his two-headed Org to meet Alicia on the battlefield.

"Crush every bone in her body!" Bronze hollered forcefully.

The Org enjoyed the thought of it. The thirty-two-foot beast took off, heading in Alicia's direction. The ground trembled with his tons of weight, and the smell of him was disgusting. He demolished the King's soldiers, smashing whoever got in his way and came face-to-face with Alicia. She displayed no fear of meeting the challenge.

She yelled boldly. "We have taken down a vulgar massacrer like you, it carried that same nauseating smell! And with the help of my friends, we will do it again! I wonder if the beast we killed was close to your heart because by now it has the stink of rotten flesh!" She wondered where Chip was but remained brave. "Show me what you got. Let's get this over with that the wolverines can eat your nasty flesh if they can hack it!" She circled him, watching for any sudden moves of any kind.

Alicia took note as it acted wild and out of control. She glanced around but still saw no sign of the Quest. She saw many soldiers and Roger attempting to get to the Org to defend her. Bronze's beasts prevented them from getting through. Alicia realized she was in severe trouble without the Quest but stood her ground regardless.

Alicia added flames to the fire, buying time for Chip to come to her rescue. She screamed, "It's too bad for your friend that you weren't there. It cried out for help before it fell to its death!"

Alicia still saw no sign of Chip or the others but continued steadfast and didn't blink an eyelash, even though she could not hold the beast off any longer. With swift hands, she placed arrows into her bow.

The angry maniac wildly swung his huge metal club, and it missed her scalp by inches. Fearlessly, Alicia shot arrows toward the unsightly, hairy two-headed Org, and the grotesque thing turned his back to her. Her weapon split into three arrows, hitting his fat, unpleasant neck.

Utter anger aroused it, and it drove him insane. He again raised his walloping metal club as he whirled another club and mocked her, "Your fate awaits you!" He struck with full force. Alicia jumped to the side. His club smashed onto the earth. The area trembled like a violent earthquake. Alicia was knocked flat onto her back with the sheer shock of it.

She struggled to stand up and was lightheaded, taking a hard blow to the ground, wondering if her head hit a rock. She suddenly feared being buried alive under the Org's boat size foot. The giant ground his crooked teeth. He raised his club once again and came down for a final blow. He found himself off guard when something behind him with a disturbing force pushed him forward. He fell headfirst toward the earth. Alicia managed to jump up and ran between its legs to keep from tumbling over her.

The Org's towering body swiped wing creatures from the muggy air, erased and buried in the earth. He stood up, regaining his balance, and blinked his eyes. Though he was looking into a mirror, confused, he remained standing, staring into the face of Chip transformed into the exact image of him.

Chip swung at the beast, striking his target and destroying one of his heads. The head lay limp upon the beast's chest, blood-smeared in his stringy horse-like hair. The Org went berserk and spotted a spear sticking out of the dirt, snatching it. He strongly threw it, barely skimming Chip's arm. Chip had no choice but to transform into his chipmunk form with only a small cut.

The Org, closing in for the final kill, looked toward Alicia with hatred. He threw his clubs down, curled his hands into two gigantic fists, and screamed. "This time, I will not miss! I will beat you like a stake into the ground!" Within seconds, two terrific beams of light came out of nowhere, striking his back, emerging through the front of his chest, and penetrating his heart. The wounded Org watched Graven soar past him as he fell heavily to his death, killing others as his body slammed to the earth. The ground shook powerfully.

Bronze was livid as he sat upon his horse one mile away and witnessed his Org to become a forgotten corpse. He released hell upon

King James, with four different forces attacking against his soldiers. The King's ranks broke. Bronze felt confident of victory and that the battle was almost complete. The Quest and King James soldiers felt pebbles shake close to their feet with the extraordinary screams of Bronze's defiled hordes.

Bronze's lines of offense, unfortunately still many compared to King James. His creatures of the covenant, soldiers, and enslaved people came at King James' forces like many swarms of bees. King James's battle lines dwindled even more, taking awful hard blows and being violently cut back.

King James commanded his soldiers to get back into the formation. Still, he was hit hard again by another of Bronze's onslaughts. He lost many soldiers from this devastating strike. Still, he managed to reform his lines, allowing another line of formation to encounter the next assault.

Bronze stationed tall upon his jet-black horse, pleased with the outcome, and struck harder. His voice thundered, "Destroy! Attain more ground! This is their ending and our beginning!"

The proud man led his beast over to Herod and Ramsey. The black stallion massive to the eyes. Bronze commanded them. "Attack their lines with full force! Show no weakness! Bring me back the King alive so I can make a show of him! No one will ever again have the audacity to raise a standard against me!"

There was such a disastrous hit upon King James's line. Brave warriors fell taken their last breath, knocking the line vigorously back into the King's next line of soldiers. Numerous men tripped and toppled over top bloody dead men which carried a foul odor from the heat of the fight, and a few men vomited.

King James was thrown off his horse with the weight of the impact. He landed on a sharp object piercing his side. Blood gushed out everywhere.

Two faithful knights lifted him, placing him upon his beautiful white thoroughbred, lovely in all aspects. The King ripped a good-sized piece of cloth from his shirt sleeve and stuffed it inside his wound, slowing the bleeding. King James shouted, giving his men hope to go on and achieve victory—even when all looked grim!

"Hold the lines! Hold them back! Move forward!" he commanded again and again. "Move forward!"

The men listened to his voice, fighting aggressively, not allowing the fear of being outnumbered to overcome them but pushing forward to overcome all odds to be victorious.

Ironically, the weather changed. A hot day dramatically turned cold. Cold winds touched the burning flesh of the soldiers, and all too quickly, it changed from cold to freezing. King James looked to the south, full of gratitude at what he saw. The Ice King raised his scepter into the air. His ice men beside him and behind him formed into ranks, prepared with firm faces, to attack against Bronze's sinister forces.

The Ice King permitted this one-time event with the changing seasons to join King James on the battlefield, but it was a matter of time before the weather changed back. They could only fight for so long before returning to their cold environment.

The Ice King stood elevated on his path of ice high above the battlefield. With her bow and arrow and her long, jet-black hair, he spotted Alicia shooting down many enemies. Her bold spirit still had an impact on the Ice King's life. He admired her stance and her belief in her God, it was one of the reasons moving him to come to the aid of the King. The fearless Ice King shouted with a loud victory cry, "God save King James! God save the King!"

He lowered his scepter and led his ice men into the battle. They delivered a mighty hit with a devastating onslaught on Herod's and Ramsey's forces and nearly destroyed their deadly spiders, scorpions, possums, and porcupines, for their strong fist fought hard and long against them. As many loud grunts and shouts of gargoyles darkened the sky. Commander David and his ice soldiers encircled hundreds of the gargoyles and barricaded them in walls of solid ice from head to toe. They gasped for air as they froze to death.

King James's hope raised seeing his allies as his men came under another bombardment, an onslaught, a heavy attack of more wolverines, appearing out of the cracks and crevices from a nearby mountain, hidden, heading their way.

Unfortunately, the Ice King noticed the change in the weather as it began to warm again. He shouted to Commander David. "We must leave before it gets too hot!" The Ice King and his son rushed and rallied his soldiers together into the atmosphere departing hastily, sliding through broad sheets of smooth ice, still taking down as many as possible. All shouted boldly, "Long live King James! Long live the King!" The Ice King and his warriors had fought with a victorious spirit. They were no longer in sight.

In the thick air of war was the smell of death. All at once, the earth shook, and a great noise proceeded over the horizon. Many placed their hands over their ears to stop the immense humming that pierced their eardrums. Amid everything was heard a loud, booming shout. "Destroy the wolverines! Make haste and bring them down! We have the battle to win!" It was a familiar voice to Graven.

Congo and his forces had come to their defense. King James was moved with his allies' willingness to come to his aid as his body became weaker by the hour.

He watched the Conchidas fast at work, using the strength of their strapping bodies and fast thinking, overpowering many wolverines, spinning them through the thick clouds of dirty air to their final destiny, many falling to the ground like ashes from a campfire.

They continued fighting as Pathfinders suddenly appeared before the noble King. King James managed to grin, holding pressure against his deep wound. "I guess my allies make it a habit of dropping in unexpectedly. I am pleased to see you this day!"

The Pathfinders spoke as one voice telepathically within the King's mind. "We will fight with you until our deaths. May we shed light upon this darkness that is before us." King James nodded his approval. The Pathfinders disappeared and were transported into the midst of the bloody battle.

The blood continued to flow from the King's gash. He removed the old soaked cloth, stuffed another piece of fabric into his wound, and was suddenly taken aback. As if time stood still, he became lost in a memory of being anointed by the high priest to be King, he was called to protect the weak and give aid to the unfortunate by bringing peace to the lands.

The clock rolled back further as the King remembered standing beside his father as Graven crashed through their enormous stained-glass window. At that time, his father was King, and with a split second, he screamed out, "Save my son!"

As a boy, he felt his father's strong arms tossing him in the griffin's direction, right before a sword was plunged into the boy's path, missing him, for Graven snatched him up, flying him toward the heights of the skies.

He remembered looking back and seeing the joy on his father's face, relieved his son was alive. As he looked one last time and cried out in horror, witnessing his father's enemies strike him with deadly blows, laughing and spitting into his face, afterward, was grieved and made a promise in his heart there would be a day when his father's blood will be avenged.

Twelve years old. He was indebted that Graven had taken him to a place deep in the mountains and watched over him so that no harm would befall him. However, in time, Graven took him to Enoch of the Weeping Willow Trees, and the young Prince received knowledge and wisdom. A few years later, he took him to the land of King Triune, the time when King Anthor ruled as King.

King Anthor hid the lad and taught him to fight acceptably well. He learned about the war attacks, all done in secrecy, and no one but King Anthor and Graven knew about his training.

Graven and the king had become loyal friends throughout his youth. By then, he was no longer a boy but a young man about Roger's age. Graven had taken him to Congo's tribe to learn a king's humility, honorable, and courageous attributes.

He remembered the day he became of age and raised a standard against his father's murderers and took back his crown.

King James's sat on his horse. His mind went deeper, blocking out the loud commotions of the fierce battle, touching areas of his heart that had grown numb through time. Sadly he recalled the hurt and desperation of not finding his beautiful queen after the fire ceased.

As if in a trance, he found himself dwelling on Liana. His thoughts raced, trying to discern the unknown, questioning Liana's resemblance to Leah and the mystery behind the blue hankie marked with his emblem.

He was jolted back to the reality of war, aware of his surroundings, amidst the blood of battle, hearing the screams of his people fighting. He sat sturdy upon his great white stallion, overlooking the bloody fields from a distance and observing his enemy's intense struggle, feeling his end was drawing near. He prayed his heart would not stop beating until he saw Liana's face and touched her hand one last time.

Chapter Twenty-One
PERFECT SACRIFICE

THE VISION OF THE QUEST

With their terrifying sting of death, the Stingers, along with Congo and his fighters, continued yelling out battle cries, as they heroically fought on behalf of King James. Without mercy, many Stingers ran their horns through the bodies of wolverines and gargoyles, sacrificing their lives in pursuit of freedom.

Slowly, the evil forces began to withdraw, suffering many casualties hit hard also by the Conchidas. They pursued them, tearing and ripping them out of the sky like a condor ripping apart its prey.

Bronze watched as his deliverance was ripped away from him, victory slipping out of his hands, knowing his only hope was to destroy the king's army and scatter them; like sheep without a shepherd. There was barely enough space to stand except upon the littered corpses and the flowing blood. At that dreadful moment, soldiers close by witnessed. Bronze's twisted heart could be seen through the darkness of his eyes. Bronze felt stifled. He called on the aid of his four-headed dragon to destroy the king.

He blew mightily into a horn hanging loosely around his neck, waiting for the beast to heed his call. This surpassing immense eye sore was released from the sea to come to the aid of Bronze and battle the king, a terrifying dragon appeared, spewing out fire and brimstone. Its name was Sacriledge covered with multiple horns representing its authority. One large crown rested upon its head, was given a position of power after conquering four dimensions. With each victory of overcoming much, it gained stronger power. Bronze gleamed satisfied. He had control over this mythical creature.

King James marveled at the size and power the beast displayed. He bowed his head despondently, realizing this day would be the end of many of his men and allies. Once over, many homes would wound up with empty seats at their tables. Children would miss wrapping their arms upon their fathers' legs. Suddenly, a loud voice blared, startling him. The voice echoed, "Sire, we have come to aid you to fight against this adversary, worry not, for we will slay this foul catastrophe in its tracks."

King James looked and beheld the person who spoke in such a piercing voice, only to be astonished to see a three-man pterocentaur, a half-man, and a half- pegasus, riding gallantly toward him. With their lower torso attached upon one great chestnut-colored horse, sporting remarkable golden wings. The fearless men wore shining golden armor, each holding a double-edged jagged sword. Their eyes lack no semblance of fear.

The horse stopped in front of King James. The man in front with the piercing voice was bold, "My name is Ashor, the man behind me is Trod, and the man on the end is Merramac. We are called Tripod. We are at your command, Sire, and will attempt to eliminate this monstrosity!"

King James was honored by their bravery and commanded them, "So be it according to your word."

The Tripod with no time wasted fast thrust off the ground with overwhelmingly strength, lifting into the air, their wings caused the winds around them to blow massively. They neared their adversary in a flash.

The dragon mocked. "Look, the king sent a little horse for me to play with. Unfortunately for you, I don't play nice!"

One of the shocking heads in the shape of a fierce lion shot thick flames toward the Tripod. The men maneuvered their way out of the path of ruin. Their bones cracked like an old man, the swift flapping of the dragon's wings pushing hard against them. Swiftly, the Tripod gained their bearing and flew bravely towards the dragon.

The beast belied its towering body of thick hard scales as it moved swiftly and struck as fast, digging into Ashor's armor, its deadly claws slicing part of his armor in two. Ashor's flesh was left vulnerable to his attack. The Tripod was beginning to again be pushed back. The three lifted their swords and raced quickly, ducking side to side to escape the dragon's fiery breath. They saw an opening and soared toward it. With Ashor's help, Trod robustly stabbed one of the dragon's heads, slaying it but in the process was burned like toast. The pain was unbearable. Trod's breath filled with smoke made it difficult to breathe. The Tripod fought intensely hard to defeat the seemingly overpowering threat.

Merramac was not reluctant to give up and kept pursuing his target and with intense force struck and sliced the throat of the second head.

THE VISION OF THE QUEST

The enraged dragon threw out his abrasive whiplash tail, tearing through Merramac's back, penetrating through the front of his body. Blood gushed out of his mouth, he was barely alive. Tripod was soon down to their last struggles, realizing death was near. Seeing the impossibility of snapping the winged serpent's neck in half, they hastily jumped onto the beast' back and squeezed its neck with substantial pressure using all their might, hoping to take its breath away. The dragon screamed, causing many to stop fighting due to its ear-shattering wails. Being nearest to the dragon proved to be the Tripod's downfall, as the sheer noise of the dragon's screams left them slipping off from its back.

They began falling. Merramac's deep wound was bleeding profusely. Trod close to death with Ashor's assistance plunged their swords into the dragon's thick chest, sliding down along with their blades, leaving two deep gaping wounds. They then slammed violently onto the hard earth but not before they managed to slice into its rigid layers of profuse scales one last time. The Tripod laid dead.

King James was moved by the courage and sacrifice which the three Goliath men had displayed.

The fiery serpent lifted its two remaining heads toward the king. It flew a short distance with the labored flapping of its wings, its lifeless heads dangling downward. The dragon eyed his prey and blew a breath of hot brimstone. King James, a good distance away, was not torched. Sadly, his faithful men who stood guard in front of him could not escape the torturous flames.

The tide of the battle once again turned against King James and his allies. Bronze glared at the king a quarter of a mile away.

Bronze yelled angrily toward him. "Your reckoning has come! It is time for me to claim what is rightfully mine, including Liana! These lands and everything in and out of it is mine! Today, victory is mine, and you shall draw your last breath!" King James, almost falling into unconsciousness, still drew his sword against Bronze. He will not go down without a fight. He had to make sure Liana was kept safe from someone immoral as him. He had to fight to ensure his daughter, Princess Lilly, would rule the throne in his absence and be kept unharmed out of the path of Bronze.

PERFECT SACRIFICE

Bronze commanded the rest of his army to commence their assault. Even when things seemed hopeless and defeat seemed inevitable. King James still stood his ground, fighting for the freedom and liberty of his people until the end. Finally, the Quest was able to get through Bronze's irritating cohorts and joined together seeking to slay Sacriledge.

The Quest moved with aggressive speed to bring the blasphemy dragon to its knees.

Graven, with such momentum and accuracy, shot his laser beams, slaying one of the heads. The gargoyles quickly engaged the griffin on all sides to destroy him. Graven moved like the wind and dug his claws into each of them, sending them plunging downwards. Graven spotted an opening, aiming his laser beams, striking the beast in the chest and wounding it severely. The dragon let loose an ear-piercing cry, sending a cold chill even through the king's body.

Chip looked upon the colourless Tripod and transformed into the image of it, reaching down he grabbed a sword and shield from the honorable warriors that gave their lives fighting for the cause.

Chip forcefully ran toward Bronze's soldiers who was zealously circling around the wounded dragon which hoovered not far off the ground in hopes of protecting it. Chip cut up his enemy left and right until he reached the mega destroyer. Chip lifted into the air and showed it no mercy, maneuvering around it as he sliced through its awful thick flesh. The beast fought hard but was too wounded, its groans of pain echoing throughout the stuffy surroundings. Its foul mouth shouted profanity toward Chip. Chip was not shaken as he repeatedly sliced into it. The dragon slowly dropped to the earth. With Graven's added laser beams and each additional powerful strike of Chip's sharp, two-edged sword, it became weaker. Finally, the dragon met his match, laying slain at Chip's feet, the mangled dragon's multiple heads face down in its thick pile of blood.

Bronze watched in shock, yet full of rage. He yelled at the top of his lungs, "Who is this that comes against me! You must be mad! Tripod, you will pay for interfering!"

His screams were heard within the dark realms of hell as the spirits came viciously to give Bronze power, bringing all the forces of calamity from the bottomless pits, the realm of brimstone and torturing. The skies filled with shadows which King James' men felt strongly, but no one could see this darkness dreary spirits hovered over the bloody fields, together and uniting; only now would Bronze have this greater power to do such mighty things. Bronze raised his hands into the stuffy air unleashing a compelling force upon Chip. A sharp, powerful bolt of light struck him with repulsive force and knocked him to the bloody ground. The battlefield became to him a big blur. Chip tried not to slip into a state of unconsciousness. Chip shook his head to remain focused, but it caused him to feel dizzier. He looked ahead through distorted eyes; he vaguely saw Granite leaping through the thick, humid atmosphere striving to reach his friend in time.

After the solid blow to Chip's Tripod body, the strikingly handsome Bronze, now covered with dirt and bloodstains of an intense battle, leaned over Chip and aimed to run a dagger through his heart. Granite violently leaped onto the loser's back for a brief encounter with death. Chip endeavored to move, fearing whatever darkness lingered about Bronze would destroy Granite. Desperate, he repeatedly attempted to stand up. He found his body was glued to the ground by an unseen force. Bronze could not annihilate Granite on his own accord. His face gleamed. "Take him down!" he screamed. His words released an unbelievable ability upon Granite from the dark realm. Granite was astounded as his body was peeled like an orange, ripped rigidly off Bronze's back with unseen hands, and tossed through the air like a light feather. Granite crashed down into a pile of dead bodies. The strong force jerked him up and held him between the heavens and the earth. He felt being squeezed. "You will have your day!" Granite hollered. Bronze cocky released his powers once more upon Granite, and with dynamite energy, he waved his hand and blasted him into the dust of the earth.

Granite surprised to be in one piece jumped up with his rock fist in midair, running full force toward the jerk. He shouted, "What final will do you have written out?" Graven and the others tried desperately to get to Granite but was held back by many hordes of wolverines.

PERFECT SACRIFICE

Granite, with pleasure, looked forward to adding Bronze to the pile of bloody bodies. Bronze paid him no mine. He again called upon the dark powers, and, with his hand uplifting, Granite was tossed into the air, like a weightless boulder and again held between the heavens and the earth. Chip, still unable to budge, cried out for his friend. With another sudden wave of his hand, Bronze struck Granite with an alarming blow. He didn't see it coming. Granite heard a super loud blast sadly before his rock-solid body shattered into tiny pieces in all directions. The only thing left of him was little red pebbles lying all around. Chip cried out for the loss of his friend. "Noooooooooo!"

Bronze with mockery spit in Chip's face. He jerked his head back in laughter toward Chip, marveling at his triumph. "Now, he's just a pebble under my feet! Chip, you have been a complete headache to me! I will spare you to give me the satisfaction of killing your noble king right before your eyes, and then your life is mine!" He jerked his head back once more, turned around, and fastened his eyes on the king. Roger and Alicia screamed out seeing Granite broke up into little pieces. The chosen ones with Acorn and Spot slew as many evil forces as possible to get to the king to protect him. White Lightning beat them to it and flew swiftly toward his majesty to pull the plug on Bronze, waves of energy building up within him. White Lightning knew this was one of those times. He aimed his deep, grey eyes toward his enemy and let loose. Everyone heard the sounds ricochet from miles away, like a booming bolt of lightning when hitting a tree, creating a big bang. Bronze was challenging to strike, still shielded with an invisible force. After a few brief periods, the shield dropped. White Lightning shot numerous times. Bronze had finally become vulnerable to a direct hit after a tense stretch of repeated misses. White Lightning long last thought he struck gold. His walloping glow of energy skimmed across Bronze's chest and wounded him. The king watched on as he became weaker.

White Lightening observed Bronze was in distress seeing his blood pressed through his black shirt and watched him manage to wave his hands in the air. White Lightning circled Bronze's devastating darkness to strike again. The man opened his mouth, declaring brazen words, and pointed toward White Lightning, he took great gratification gloating at the power he beheld in his hands. Within a flash, White Lightning, the faithful knight of the king's court, with an unseen force was hung frozen in midair. His mighty white wings crushed under the constraint of it. Bronze smirked. "This is what happened to that stupid boulder friend of yours. What a shame you are about to join him in the same heap pile of dead bodies!"

White Lightning tried desperately for the king's sake to aim into the bitter roots of Bronze's heart, it was impossible to hit his target. White Lightning was held in an awkward position; his body stiff, unable to move an inch or even flinch. Bronze searched the ground and noticed a spear pierced into one of his dead wolverines. He commanded the spear to be removed. An unseen force ripped it out of the mangled beast and into his hand. He glared at White Lightning, that no one could save him. He taunted with a sly look with no compassion as he shoved the keen object mercilessly through his heart. Bronze sensed something strange enter him. He became stimulated and let go of his thunderous hold, allowing the fearless warrior to fall to his death. White Lightning tumbled to the earth, and another body was added to the graveyard. Roger felt helpless as he cried out for the life of his faithful friend.

The devil's advocate moved ever closer to the king, within striking distance but halted, doubled over in pain. A long, thick gash bleeding from his chest to his navel, exactly where White Lightning had wounded him. But that did not stop him. Bronze turned his attention back to the king, slowly moving a few steps closer, craving passionately for the king's blood upon his hands and raising his arm into the air. He yelled out foolish words that made no sense. Immediately, the king was jerked off his horse by the same dark presence tangling in midair. The king was at Bronze's disposal, suspended in the musty atmosphere in a still position. Bronze's waved his hand more forcefully, full of himself, forgetting his boundaries. He stepped closer—close enough for King James to lift his hands upward, praising God. And as he did, the evilness turned on Bronze, lifting him off his feet. Neither one could move. The strong sinister darkness attempted to suffocate the king, cutting off his air. Bronze, enjoyed seeing, King James' face turned blood red when he was about to pass out. He heard a loud shout from

Quantum. "You have the strength, O King!" With everything in him, the king yelled out vigorously—a loud, drawn-out holler. "I declare the royal blood of the lamb to raise a standard against you, with the power and authority of the one true King's name above all names to break this stronghold!" The two men one of light and one of darkness fell to the ground, drained. Two strong knights moved fast and placed their king upon his white stallion. The king was in ear range and shouted out his commands. "Do not give up! Do not give in! We shall fight to the bitter end! Do not be moved in what you see but be moved in what you do not see! And that's the power of something greater within you!" The knights then led him to higher ground. Bronze gradually stood up, holding his chest. His men and hordes encircled and protected him. Bronze was delirious, for he knew somehow it was Quantum giving the king hope of standing against his dark powers and glared at him. He mocked under his heated breath. "Blue man's day will come when I will terminate his race as I first planned long ago, ending their existence!"

Bronze, felt too weak to come against King James, still holding onto his chest, which pounded with pain. In the distance, Bronze heard an eerie sound pleasing to his ears. The immoral man stood erect and beamed, aware that more soldiers and beasts were coming to his aid. He screamed, "It is finished, King! Stand down that I may have the honor of taking your crown!" Alicia and Roger felt faint-hearted, grieving the loss of Granite and White Lightning. Things looked bleak. Roger was unsure of what might happen to King James and who would keep Liana and Emily safe.

Roger gasped as he focused on the earsplitting noise which was drawing closer. He beheld the vast force of Bronze's army multiplying like ants out of a hole coming their way. "Where are they all coming from?" he complained, clenching his teeth. The Quest were even losing hope. But in that dark moment, Roger allowed utter fear to grasp hold of him. Roger contemplated. *"I fear death is at my doorstep, I will not be able to protect Alicia. If Bronze gets a hold of her and her necklace, there would be no telling what he might do to her!"*

Roger whispered to a God unknown to the young warrior, though Liana spoke of Him quite often. Now he found himself praying out

THE VISION OF THE QUEST

loud with all his heart and soul for the first time, "Lord, I am weak, and I have heard that you give strength to the weak. I pray, make me strong this moment to save the king; to keep Alicia safe from harm!"

Roger immediately perceived a vital force going throughout his body, and, as the enemy was at his feet, he wielded his sword against them, and for a split second, he gazed into the heavens for his newfound faith. As he fought, he brought his attention to Alicia and stared at her beauty, walking faithfully with her true all powerful King. He admired her strength and determination. Though her face was covered with dirt and blood, she still radiated with a glow. Roger continued fighting vigorously with a renewed mind regenerating a divine presence within him, giving him hands down strength to prevail. He shouted joyfully, "One day, I will marry her and make her my wife!" Alicia standing nearby, with all the noise, could not hear him, though his voice was as a sounding gong going forth into the heavens, repeatedly ringing before the throne room of God Almighty. Roger not knowing but his faith in believing in the impossible would enable his words to be brought into existence.

But as for Alicia, without warning, she experienced an attack within an open door of her mind, spiritual arrows from the dark side. Lies assaulted her, as she feared if she would live to see her mother and the pain it would cause her. She felt weighed down with the sudden pang of despair and additional strength was zapped out of her as she brought down quite a few beasts with her bow. Quietly, she prayed for the hope of victory and was startled hearing King Hydro of the waters speak within her mind. "Remember, in times of darkness, whenever you need our help, just call. Ask, and you shall receive; for help is near."

She remembered the globe inside her brown leather pouch, pulled it out immediately, and called upon the power of King Hydro to aid them in this tense, brutal battle; without his help, more innocent blood would be spilled. Sadly, the crows had already started nibbling on their dead before a proper burial.

The globe broke free from Alicia's hands, rolling onto the ghastly battleground, causing the earth to tremble and shake. Alicia thought for sure it was an earthquake. It surprisingly became so quiet that others could hear their own breathing. All at once, a tidal wave arm raised out of the globe, with ease, swiped over a third of Bronze's forces that were in the sky, snuffing them out as if nothing, and effortlessly King Hydro of the many waters witnessed the damage that had been done, and withdrew back into the globe. Alicia used a thick cloth to pick it up, placing it back into her leather pouch, amazed at what had taken place—killing off many deadly creatures. Bronze's army, no longer like the sand of the sea shore, was diminished. Things now were even in numbers. The battle waxed even hotter; fire was everywhere, arrows were coming and going, swords were clashing non-stop, and yells and screams could be heard no matter where anyone turned.

Despite the help of King Hydro's powers, a continued wave of dread perforated the battlefield; shadows of despair and gloom hung heavy over the heads of King James's men; an unseen evil continued to attack the minds of the upright and respectable men.

Regardless, they pressed on as the air reeked terribly of blood and sweat. Both sides would not budge nor turn back. The lies of darkness and the truth of righteousness; fought hard for the ultimate victory with weariness on all their faces. The battle still was drawn-out and seemed endless. Nevertheless, King James' men and the Quest pressed on to keep the faith, not allowing the absence of light to give into darkness but remain triumphant. Unexpectedly, the earth gave way and caved in underneath. Bronze's forces didn't know why the earth was collapsing. The king's soldiers had enough knowledge to know to run, while the beasts were slow to figure out what was happening until it was too late. They fell into the earth and were swallowed up into a deep, black hole. Nearly a thousand of Bronze's beasts and men scrabbled over each other, attempting to find a way out. Moses poked his head up from out of the ground, "Hey, we're stuck with the leftovers!" He cackled, going back under the earth to destroy more with the help of his family.

The moles, with their incredible claws, tore into their flesh, destroying them by the hundreds. Bronze's hordes began falling into the additional holes they created. A number of white wolverines aboveground unable to fly, began to retreat, seeing defeat coming, as the remainder of Bronze's army continued to push forward. King

James mustered strength and shouted to his knights and soldiers, "Rally forward! Rally forward! No turning back! It's now or never!" His men pushed forward. The King sat up unstable upon his horse, continually losing blood. Gargoyles tried reaching him. His two mighty men of valor moved with whirlwind speed and with an impressive display with their swords, neither one unyielding in protecting their ruler.

The battle raged loudly around the two warriors, but something moved fast and unnoticed. A gargoyle skillfully threw his spear towards King James. One of the warriors fast brought the winged creature down, and missed the king's heart, instead penetrating deep into his left leg. King James fell slowly off his horse and landed on his knees, agony upon his weary face, but not once did he cry out.

A number of gargoyles gained up and attacked strongly, the two warriors fought courageously killing off twelve gargoyles before being struck down a fast gargoyle reached his target and slashed twice into the king's back. Two other indestructible knights tried desperately to reach their king but were held at bay by Snakens. King James put his pain aside; he stood valorous and wielded his sword with full force, slicing the grotesque things in half.

Everything happened fast Bronze, standing near Chip, still pinned to the ground. Bronze saw this as the perfect opportunity to slay the king for the final strike of his grand slam, and even though his chest throbbed wildly with pain, he managed a slight smirk, as he drew closer and stood before the king and stared into the king's face. He lifted his sword, swinging down for the ultimate kill. Unforeseen, an arrow found its way through Bronze's back. He turned to see what fool would dare to do this and spotted Alicia reaching for another arrow. He quickened his steps and took off angrily, forgetting about the pain in his chest. His long legs dashed toward her, rage in his eyes, his sword drawn back. Alicia spotted the king only seconds away from being struck down by a gargoyle. She shot her arrow into the creature, leaving her wide open to the insane man. Roger ran explosively like a raging bull, toward Bronze. Zoroc turned and demanded his beast to stand down, enabling Roger to make it to Alicia in time. For a small piece of Zoroc's corrupt heart began to soften, seeing the girl was willing to lay down her life for a king she barely knew. Alicia placed a third arrow in her bow with Bronze still running madly coming her way. Time was against her. As she drew back her hand, Bronze stood in front of the young warrior, his silver sword covered in warm blood, aimed to plunge it into the pit of her stomach. Roger, out of breath, stopped an arm's length behind the murderer. Bronze had no clue, for his rage went deep against Alicia. With heavy arms exhausted from battle, Roger found the strength to wield his sword with accuracy. His blade came crashing down. Bronze didn't know what had hit him. His head plunged onto the ground seconds before his knees touched the earth. The army saw their master lying dead and were shocked. Fearfully, many took off flying toward the mountains, and while others ran, many stood in place, not believing what they had just witnessed. Zoroc, was relieved to see the downfall of Bronze, and started a revolt against Wolf Fang, shouting, "Stand down, my brothers, my friends, my clan, stand down, Bronze is dead! Have no fear. He can no longer torture us or destroy our families. Our true king is King James!"

"What are you doing, fool!" Wolf Fang shrieked. Zoroc ignored him as he ran and knelt on all fours before the king. "Sire, will you forgive me all of my trespasses against you and your kingdom? I've seen a greater power at work here this day. It was the power of love. Please have mercy upon us all." Zoroc, with a changed heart, began feeling something stirring up inside him as he searched the king's face. The king was feeling tremendous pain. He looked eye-to-eye with the pure white wolverine now covered in caked blood. He replied, "You have committed great treachery and deceived and killed many, but if your heart is pure and wishes only to serve and protect my kingdom and its people, never to rebel against me again, I shall forgive you. You and those who share your sentiments may enter my flock."

Zoroc responded, "Sire. I will never forget this for as long as I have the breath of life within my body."

Zoroc, with his large hunchback, turned and faced his comrades. He commanded with a loud direct tone, "Wolf Fang and all our followers. Those of you who hold true to King James, kneel and ask for forgiveness that you may serve in the army of His Majesty! Those of you who have no desire to serve the king, then you may leave but know this if we meet again, you shall be considered an enemy of him, and you shall be utterly destroyed!" Wolf Fang paced back and forth, listening to Zoroc with a sourer than lemon bitterness. Beholden, a quarter of men and creatures from Bronze's army knelt. Swearing their allegiance to King James, yelling with strong voices, ringing like loud trumpets, "Long live the King! Long live the King!"

Wolf Fang heard enough, infuriated that Zoroc was wrestling control away from him. He howled loudly, "Traitor!" Though, he was pleased with Bronze's death within the depths of his gut. At long last, the tables had turned. His craving had been fulfilled. With Bronze meeting his ruin, he had gained power and authority over the wolverines and creatures. Drool poured from his mouth as he circled Zoroc, glaring at him. He spotted King James's men, swords drawn and realized Zoroc would meet his match another time. Wolf Fang departed inflamed, with many of his clan following behind him. He screamed out as he took to the skies. "Today, you have victory, but tomorrow is a new beginning. In the future, we will see who shall rule the kingdoms!" His voice lingered in the thick heat of the day. The soldiers could finally flock to their wounded king which he asked to be placed back onto his horse. The men asked, "Majesty, what is your command?"

He answered, "Destroy all the demonic forces that had not sided with us and attack and destroy Bronze's castle of old, then report back to me. But first, I have something to say that needs to be spoken!" King James attempted to sit straight up on his horse. He feebly raised his voice as his lungs allowed him. "Men of valor! We lost many on this day, but we fought the fight and stayed the course. I am proud and honored to be king of such mighty warriors who did not give in to defeat when all looked hopeless but remained...." His voice faded. He passed out and fell forward on his horse. Graven flew rapidly over to the king. "We got this." Graven informed the soldiers. The soldiers, seeing the king was in the Quest's protection, shouted, "Long live the king! Long live King James!" They honored the kings request and rallied to Bronze's dark domain to destroy the others who were setting themselves against their ruler.

Chip transformed back into a chipmunk and could finally stand and move around. Each bone in his little body ached from the impact of the blast. His head thumped with pain but not as much as his heart with the loss of his friends, especially Granite, but relieved the king was alive but only by a thread, and Alicia and Roger were unharmed. The Quest moved hastily, preparing King James for the ride back to his castle. King James knew his time was short and acknowledged he would die in peace and honor, satisfied his people would live in liberty and freedom. He was bleeding heavily; though his wounds were wrapped, blood kept pouring through. Some were baffled how that their king was still alive but unaware of his heart's desire to see Liana and his precious daughter one last time. Graven, flying to the castle, could feel the heat of King James's blood upon the fur of his back. He flew with haste while Chip, Alicia, and Roger found a ride with Spot, and Acorn. Graven arrived at the castle and took the king to his bedroom. The servants gently slipped him from the griffin's back and placed him softly onto his bed. Graven saw, with sadness, that he was dying. Two servants removed his old blood-soaked clothes and placed clean ones over his wounds, wrapping, and rewrapping as the blood continued to seep through the bandages. The king awakened, his thick blonde hair matted with blood. He sensed death was near and asked for his daughter and Miss Liana to be brought to his bedside. As the two entered his bedroom doorway, Princess Lilly ran tearfully to her father's side and wrapped her arms around him; crying sorrowfully. He reaffirmed his undying love for her and looked into her sensitive face. He softly touched her cheek, "My Lilly, I am so proud of you. You have been a precious jewel in my life and kept me going since I had lost your mother, but now, I must depart and journey to a much Higher Kingdom, and when I am gone, you must lead your people." His hand weakly dropped from her face, and onto the bed. "Be strong. Be vigilant. Stay focused, always without fail, call upon the name of God for wisdom and foresight make sure no one is judged out of anger or revenge. Be kind to all and remain generous."

Princess Lilly wept much. She replied, "As you asked, Father," she leaned over and sadly kissed him.

The king, in a fragile voice, called for Liana. As he watched her approach his bedside, his adrenaline thrived. Princess Lilly noticed they needed privacy and left the room. Liana stood a few feet from his bed, nervous, sad, and crushed, all at once. She could not bear to see the shape he was in, still feeling she had known him for a lifetime, it caused her heart to break. "Please come closer," he whispered, not sure if it will be his last breath.

Liana, overcome with emotions, walked gracefully closer to his bedside, crying softly. He reached gently for her shaken hand. He searched up into Liana's eyes and spoke tenderly. "The day I heard your voice and saw your face, I marveled at your wisdom and grace, how you walk and speak like a true queen, and I cannot deny in my heart the likeness of your face compared to my deceased wife, Queen Leah, even your voice is familiar. I sense the strong Spirit that compels you to do good." Liana could see he weakened by the minute as she continued to listen.

"I admire your dedication to all I requested of you and your children. I do not know if you can believe this, but my heart is engraved in your hands wherever you go. May you prosper in everything your hand touches, that God may grant you favor in all things." The king began to spit up blood. Liana fell upon his chest and softly spoke into his ear, "You have my heart, Sire. I don't understand it. Somehow I feel a part of you, as though you are the missing piece in my life that had baffled my mind for so long. I never comprehended the emptiness I carried until now, and at this instant, I still don't know why and how I feel familiar with your presence. And now ironically, I realize I found the missing puzzle piece, only to have you slip from my hands." Liana, still lying on his chest, began to grieve for a stranger she felt she had once loved passionately. The king placed his feeble hand in her thick, blonde waves; he, too, cried. Alicia and Roger arrived in the king's room, waiting their turn in the back. Liana realized they, too, needed words with him. Tearfully and slowly, she pulled away from his chest. She gazed sorrowfully into his eyes and surprised herself as she spoke out the words, "I love you." The king's hand slipped through her hair once more. He hated seeing her leave his presence and as she slipped out the door. He requested to be alone with Roger and Alicia. "Roger, please come near," his voice strained. Roger made his way to his bedside.

"Roger, you fought better than any knight out in that field today. I am proud of you, young man. I will ask that you remain to protect my kingdom if you so desire, but first with the permission of Miss Liana, but I understand if you hope to return home." Roger was honored by the king's request, but seeing that at any moment he might leave this life thinking of Alicia, she, too, desired a moment with the king. "I cannot answer now, but I thank you for everything. It was an honor to fight at your side. I would have had it no other way. I take my leave that you may speak with Alicia." The king smiled even amid his discomfort. "So be it."

Roger bowed his head in reverence. He exited his room and walked through hallways and around corners and finally entered into the great hall. He, too, was saddened, seeing the king was an honorable man. True to his word, his life was being snuffed out of him. Roger observed Liana in the grand hall and saw the hurt on her face. It was too much for him to bear, understanding she sacrificed her life to raise him. He held onto the closest thing to a mother he ever had. He admired her love, strength, and compassion. Roger wrapped his arms around her neck, and as she grieved in his arms, he was confused. He could not grasp as he reasoned to himself. *"Where did the spark come from that's in Miss Liana's eyes whenever she was near the king? It's impossible. She acts as if she had known the king but still carries the hurt of losing her husband. It's painful to see her regain her happiness, only to see that glow in her eyes about to be snatched from her suddenly for a second time."* As Roger consoled Liana, the king looked toward Alicia as she stood near the back of the room. Fragilely, he spoke. "Alicia, you may approach." He managed to grin faintly with a pleased expression toward such a brave girl who had fought courageously as any man on the battlefield. Being bold, daring, and fearless, but as Alicia looked upon the King on his deathbed, she felt afraid and powerless.

She edged closer, seeing the suffering in his eyes, and could not bear it. Her legs wanted to give way, but she knew she must stand and be strong. The king's face was ghost pale. He said: "Had it not been for your remarkable deeds and the precise aim of your arrow penetrating my enemy's back, Roger was able to behead Bronze. It was because of you. I thank you deeply for placing my enemy under my feet."

Alicia wept at his words and spoke with a broken heart. "Majesty, you remind me of my father's goodness with his wonderful qualities. For this reason, it makes it difficult to accept your death. However, I am glad I had the opportunity to be acquainted with you, but it saddens me I would've loved the chance to know you better. I sense our spirits are close-knitted in a peculiar way I cannot explain, but I have a request of you, King James."

"Continue," he spoke lower than a whisper. Alicia wiped the blood from his parched lips, hearing his faint breath. She removed a small piece of the tree of enlightenment from her pouch, and in a small canteen canvas, she held the water of life, wondering if it could possibly help even in the time of death.

Alicia replied. "Under the circumstances, I took a little more than you requested and saved it for a time like this. I guess my mother would call it a woman's intuition." She handed the king a small leaf. He was too weak to lift his head. Alicia gently brought it to his mouth. "Partake, King James, receive this gift of healing. Please try to eat this."

He managed to eat the leaf. However, his face lost more color. Alicia spoke hastily. Every second was essential. "Now receive the water of life," she held his head slightly forward and tilted the canteen to his dehydrated lips. He managed to swallow two small drops. She gently placed the king's head softly back upon his pillow.

"Thank you, Majesty," Alicia's voice edged with hopefulness, but all too soon, she began to grieve as he closed his eyes and spoke his last words.

"I go to see my Father. Who is proud of his son? I …" He breathed no more.

Alicia wept bitterly before returning to her friends and family in the hall, waiting their turn. She spoke sadly with a mixture of boldness. "The king is at peace. He's with his Father in heaven."

All felt a piercing of the heart, with a terrible emptiness. It was hard to believe the wonderful king was gone. After a time of grieving, the princess, with loneliness, sat down upon her throne. The Quest listened as she managed to speak bravely for her people. "My first order of business is that we honor the king. He was a remarkable one, someone special who gave us hope and freedom that we will never forget." Princess Lilly's voice cracked. She became withdrawn and allowed the others to talk quietly as she gathered her thoughts together on this sad day. Graven turned around and saw the hurt and confusion on Liana's face. He asked her respectfully. "What will you do now?"

She replied, broken, "Oddly, I don't understand it, but I feel a part of me is now gone, and strangely, that part of me feels empty. I will have to return home, but I don't understand these emotions. I feel I am leaving something special behind." As Liana wiped a fountain of tears from her eyes, the huge double doors swung open. King James majestically walked out with a radiating liveliness. His wounds were completely healed, and his strength had returned.

He smiled at his beautiful daughter. "My princess, don't you think you should check with the king before giving orders?" Princess Lilly was overjoyed, and ran to him bubbling over with laughter. She was ecstatic and yelled, "Father!" King James hugged his daughter, turned toward Liana, and beamed joyfully. "Is it not right to ask your king for permission first to see if you have his blessing to leave?" Liana stood ten feet away, facing him. Hot tears ran down her ivory face as she too ran into his arms with no delay. There was an abundant joy and cheerful yelling in the great hall as they all shouted, "Long live the king! Long live King James!"

Graven, and Chip, Acorn, and Spot, couldn't believe Granite and White Lightning were not there to witness this grand moment but beamed, pleased the King was alive. With all eyes fastened on him, King James proclaimed, "Whether through life or through death, for me, to live is Christ, and to die is gain."

Liana was happy for him but downcast for those who had not made it. She glanced around the room and realized one soul was not present. She cried out, "Melanie! Where could she be at this time? She should have been here!"